Beloved Stranger

Also by Clare Boylan

Novels

HOME RULE
HOLY PICTURES
LAST RESORTS
BLACK BABY
ROOM FOR A SINGLE LADY

Short Stories

A NAIL ON THE HEAD
CONCERNING VIRGINS
THAT BAD WOMAN

Non-fiction

THE AGONY AND THE EGO (*edited*)
THE LITERARY COMPANION TO CATS (*edited*)

Beloved Stranger

CLARE BOYLAN

LITTLE, BROWN AND COMPANY

A *Little, Brown* Book

First published in Great Britain by Little, Brown in 1999

Copyright © Clare Boylan 1999

The moral right of the author has been asserted.

A CIP catalogue record for this book
is available from the British Library

ISBN 0 316 84807 7

Typeset in Bembo by M Rules
Printed and bound in Great Britain by
Clays Ltd, St Ives plc

Little, Brown and Company (UK)
Brettenham House
Lancaster Place
London WC2E 7EN

For my mum and for all those
who hang on for dear life

Acknowledgements

My thanks to the Hawthornden Foundation and Hawthornden Castle, Midlothian, Scotland, where this novel was begun and to the Tyrone Guthrie Centre at Annaghmakerrig, Co. Monaghan.

I am indebted to the many people who offered advice and assistance during the writing of this work, including Professor Ivor Browne, Dhomhnall Casey, clinical psychologist Professor Anthony Clare, Dr Pat Melia, Alan Wilkes, Victoria Glendinning, Michael Holroyd, Noeleen Dowling, June Levine, Anne Dalton, Patricia Ryan. I am deeply grateful to those who shared their experiences of manic depression and to Kay Redfield Jamison's luminous memoir, *An Unquiet Mind*. As always, particular thanks to my editor, Richard Beswick.

The author and the publishers also wish to give thanks for permission to use extracts from the following copyright material. *Sex and Destiny* by Germaine Greer, copyright © 1984 Germaine Greer, reprinted with the permission of Gillon Aitken Associates Ltd. *The Golden Notebook* by Doris Lessing, copyright © 1971 Doris Lessing, reprinted by kind permission of Jonathan Clowes Ltd., London on behalf of Doris Lessing. *The Second Sex*, by Simone de Beauvoir, reprinted by kind permission of Jonathan Cape, UK and Alfred A. Knopf, US. All efforts have been made to contact any other copyright holders.

A lost thing could I never find,
Nor a broken thing mend:
And I fear I shall be all alone
When I get towards the end.
Who will there be to comfort me
Or who will be my friend?

Hilaire Belloc,
The South Country

1

In September, Mr and Mrs Butler discovered broccoli. Lily already had carrots in her bag. She hated carrots but they went with everything.

'What's that?' Dick peered at the green sprigs which had been arranged upright in a wooden box. The stout stems seemed full of sap, the mossy heads chaste and secretive. He thought it resembled a virgin forest.

'It's broccoli.' Lily had seen pictures of it in magazines. 'It's supposed to be good for you.'

'Would we try some?' He eased out a sprig. 'One piece each or two? Maybe it will be disappointing. Just the two?'

They asked the girl at the counter how you cooked broccoli but she had never eaten it. She didn't like vegetables. On the way out Dick noticed that Lily was limping slightly.

'All right, love? Feet at you?'

'It's that toenail.'

'Take my arm.'

'Ruth's coming tomorrow.' She slipped her hand into his tweeded elbow. 'She'll know how to cook broccoli. We'll have the carrots today.'

'Ruth will make your head spin with ways to cook broccoli.'

'You know, Dick, it's an awful thing to say but I sometimes wish Ruth didn't know so much. I can never surprise her.'

'You should have had two daughters.' He shifted the shopping bag containing chops, carrots and broccoli to his other arm and pulled his wife closer. 'A smart one you could ring when you wanted to know something and a comfortable one with whom you could discuss what you had learnt.'

'Yes, that would be ideal,' Lily nodded solemnly. But then nothing in life was ideal. That was what poor Ruthie could never accept.

They fell silent, concentrating on the pavement which was polished with rain. The shopping streets, two miles north of the city, had moved from village to suburban to outer city shabby and now one or two of them were on the way up again. Every so often they threw up set changes to mark the decades. Sweeney's Sweets and Argosy Library was now Meteor Video, and Bertolli's chips and ice-cream had become a health food store. Years out of fashion had left the neighbourhood as sleepy as a rural village, but a fawn haze of urban pollution buffered their horizon, its smell of stout and of the River Liffey as familiar as the smell of a sleeping partner. All in all it was a good address, as Dick liked to say, although a shop which sold nothing but potatoes had always been a thorn in his side.

When they were first married they had been oppressed by the seriousness of their surroundings, the utility shops and red-bricked houses. Sometimes after they had completed an ordinary transaction like buying milk or a newspaper, they would stand on the pavement afterwards, helpless with laughter. They never had any sensible clothes in those days, not even umbrellas. Once, it had rained so hard they had to shelter in an entrance. Lily wondered if Dick remembered the warm rain making a curtain in the doorway, its pulpy percussion on the street. Her thin dress was slicked to her body, her hair painted to her forehead like wet autumn leaves. Freckles and rain drops glistened on her nose. He had begun to push her hair back from her face and then to kiss her. He pressed against her and she felt that part of him that could only be named in comic terms back then. He said he had to make love to her. Had to, had to. 'Stop, Dick,' she said. 'We'll soon be home,' but the rain poured down and the streets emptied. 'No, Dick!' She tried to push him away. 'It's not possible.' She had never said no convincingly and nothing was impossible until tights came in. He was normally a reserved man, but he was occasionally given to rash romantic gestures and was intoxicated by his new marriage. She could still remember the startling pain and heat as he pushed into her, her shocked eyes keeping watch over his shoulder. She had to steady him when someone passed. The man had glanced curiously into the doorway and she had met his eye, and even though he passed by quickly, she knew he knew. She didn't even feel ashamed and as the moment passed she was drawn under by a current of excitement. The rain sluiced over her, on to her eyelids, into her mouth. The harsh friction became an answer to her soft cries. That was the only time she been swept away in the way she read about in novels. She had not told Dick for they did not talk about it. She was soon to discover that he had a prudish side which emerged almost as a reaction to his emotional extravagances. The dress, a pattern of red flowers on white, had been ruined by the rain, as if made of paper.

When she became pregnant she had a craving for the curious flour-and-water taste of Bertolli's ice-cream and had sent Dick at four in the morning to bang on the door of the Italian. 'My wife is expecting a baby,' he explained. 'She has cravings.' The man's wife called down to know what he was doing and he shouted up: 'I getta some ice cream for this lady. She having a baby. She half crazy.'

They came to their street, its sombre brick softened by lines of old trees, and to their tall, narrow house with the black railings gripped so close to its front that it seemed to exist behind a cage. They had lived on the same street, in the same house, for almost fifty years, and were such a familiar sight that people scarcely noticed them. The older residents, mostly living on their own, were aware of Dick and Lily, for they were good neighbours, not because they were sociable, but because they belonged to a time when neighbours looked out for one another. The younger ones laughed at Dick's ancient car rolling slow as a beetle down the street, and some of them had decided that the house wasn't worth ripping off. Otherwise no one bothered with them. Welfare workers observed with relief that they were mobile and independent and that each was in the care of the other. It was only these peripherals that would have caught their attention. That the old folks had any kind of existence within their outsized house would not have occurred to them at all.

2

⚮

As soon as Ruth arrived Dick went off to play the piano. He wasn't making much noise but the notes kept creeping up on Lily like someone walking on tiptoe, and she wanted to talk to her daughter. 'Keep it down there, Pa,' she called to him. The music stopped and he crouched above the keys, drawing on his pipe intensely as if to banish himself within the man-smelling fog.

Lily couldn't understand Ruth. She had been very good-looking when she was a girl, could have had the world at her feet. But she lived alone. She had let grey come into her hair although she was scarcely over forty. 'I'm worried about your pa.' She had to whisper because of the silence.

'Why are we whispering?' Ruth said. 'Why don't we go to the kitchen?'

'There's a leak,' Lily confessed. 'We're waiting for the plumber.'

Ruth sighed, thinking of her parents' kitchen. 'Is he sick?'

'No, he's in great form.' She allowed herself a pause before the discomfort of disloyalty. 'He's been spending money.'

'Ha!' Ruth hooted. 'He really must be sick.'

'Be quiet!' Lily ordered in a whisper that startled Dick. With his pipe clenched in his mouth Ruth thought he had the forlornly innocent, deeply cunning look of a dog caught making off with a lamb chop.

'Quite large sums of money.'

'On what? Women?' Ruth topped up her cup from the whiskey bottle that was on the table. It was the convention, when she came to visit, for Pa to give himself a glass of whiskey and Ma to make two cups of coffee, which both women topped up from the spirit bottle.

'Your pa opened a joint account,' Lily explained. 'He did it for me. He wanted me to understand how to handle a cheque book in case anything happened to him. I saw the stubs.'

'How much?'

'A hundred pounds, two, five hundred.'

Ruth looked at the old man sharply and he sucked miserably on his pipe, knowing he was being talked about.

'I think I forgot to turn off the water, Dick, would you take a look?' Lily shouted out of pity, and he bounded nimbly up the stairs for he hated any unnecessary use of the immersion heater.

'You're a perfect comic team,' Ruth smiled at her mother. She could never relax when Pa was around.

Lily lit a cigarette with curious delicacy. She was seventy-five but still had the pensiveness of a child touching things for the first time. 'It's love,' she said.

Ruth made an affronted move in her chair, a protesting twist of her rump. Her mother looked at her with infuriating under-standing, a bottomless look.

'Your pa and I, we love each other. You have to get to my age to appreciate these things. We weren't married when we were young. We were put together to marry. I think—' she paused to take a sip of the cigarette with lips that seemed girlish and untouched, maybe wondering how much Ruth could take '—a woman is given a mate in order to look after his salvation. You're given a spoilt son and you turn him into a human being. You can't do it by confrontation. That way a marriage breaks up. You have to do it by example. Sooner or later he gets affected by goodness. It's a matter of habit.'

'Ma, you're talking about virgin sacrifices, appeasing the anger of the gods, purification by fire.'

'A little sacrifice never killed anybody,' Lily said.

'Except the victim.'

'We're happy,' Lily said. 'We really are.'

Ruth went to say something but then looked ashamed. Lily thought it was the word 'happy' that made her ashamed, not whatever she had been going to say.

'We need each other. We're halves of the same part. It's nothing you could write a book about. We're old pals, Ruth.'

She patted Ruth guiltily on the knee. She and her daughter, so passionately linked when the girl was a baby, would never be old pals. She looked forward to her visits because she loved her and depended on her, but she always felt relief when she was gone. Ruth never let her get away with anything. She and Pa protected one another. Of course it meant they could never challenge each other. She opened her handbag quickly and took out a cheque book. 'Quick! Before he gets back.'

'He won't come back — not while I'm here, not when he knows he's being talked about.' She began to examine the stubs in a maddeningly deliberate, leisurely way. 'Jesus! A thousand pounds!'

Lily crushed out her half-smoked cigarette and lit another. Like Pa, she looked abashed. 'What did he do with it?'

'God knows. It doesn't say. I suppose it doesn't matter in a way. He has plenty, you know. No, you don't know, do you? That's what makes me so mad. Look at this place.'

Lily looked around, but only for reassurance. She scarcely noticed her surroundings.

'He wouldn't even get in central heating. You'll freeze to death.

But it doesn't cost him a thought to throw away a thousand pounds.'

'We don't know . . .'

'Have you tried asking him?'

'It's probably something complicated. I don't always understand about money.'

'Of course you do. That's just your role.' Underneath the childish exterior her mother was as smart as paint. She was shrewd at assessing other people and had a breadth of vision that was far beyond Pa's. It wasn't just irritation that made Ruth lose her temper; it was fear that she might inherit the same reluctance to face things. She had a big muscular brain that understood all about politics and finance but she still felt a prickle of fear when faced with a time switch or a word processor. 'Would you like me to talk to him, Ma?'

'Oh, no. If there's enough money, then it doesn't really matter. After all, it's his money.'

'Ask him, Ma,' she said more gently. She took out her own cheque book, scribbled quickly and put a cheque for three hundred pounds in her mother's hands. 'That's for you. You're not to say anything to Pa about it. Buy something for yourself or else cash it and keep the money in a drawer and then you'll have some whenever you need it.' She kissed her mother on the cheek and got a fierce hug in exchange. Pa crept down as she got to the hall door. 'Bye love.' He put out his mouth to the air. 'Take care.' She emerged from the arctic hall into a surprisingly warm day. The quiet street, with its trees and railings, its old residents, a few tatty, colourful houses fallen into flats, seemed to her now like a toytown. The impression of her mother's hug was still on her breasts. It made her feel bleak, as if she was being consoled for some bad news she had not yet heard.

3

Dick put out a basin of warm water. He shook in some Radox and swirled it around with his hand, then added more hot water from the kettle.

'Give them a soak first,' he instructed Lily, who sat on a chair to peel off her tights. She was amazed that her toes had grown these casings of true antiquity which occasionally tried to prise the soft flesh from them. Even if she could have coped with this hoofed extension of herself she would have been squeamish about it, but Dick hummed as he fetched a couple of dry towels, a pair of scissors, talcum powder.

He sat before her on a low stool, laid a folded towel over his knee, then lifted one of her feet from the water. Lily was reminded of Jesus washing the feet of the disciples. Even after all the years of marriage, she felt shy about having him perform such a service. He used big scissors with long blackened blades, giving a slight grunt of satisfaction each time he removed a piece of nail. Just once the scissors slipped and she let out a small cry as blood covered her toe. 'Sorry, love.' He sighed and then put the foot back in the basin to rinse the blood away. 'Old eyesight's not the best.' All the same, when she put on her shoes and tights again, the relief was enormous. 'Now, what would you like, Dick?' she said.

'I could face a bite of lunch.'

They had the broccoli with fish. Dick was disappointed by how the green had dimmed.

'Oh, Ruth said to rinse it under the cold tap to keep the colour,' Lily remembered. 'She said you can have it raw too, in a salad with nuts and tomatoes, but that would play havoc with the digestion. Anyway, it's nice, isn't it?'

'Yes, it's very nice.'

For dessert they had tinned semolina with a spoonful of straw-berry jam. The semolina made Lily feel slightly sick. She didn't like sweet things but Dick did and she had learnt over half a cen-tury of marriage that men fed best on the principle of 'A spoonful for you, a spoonful for me.'

They talked about the girl in the vegetable shop, how strange it was to spend your life working with food in which you had no interest. Then Dick watched the news on television and Lily read the *Sun*. It always filled her with grief, reading about battered wives and abused children, pensioners raped by drug addicts. The world seemed a terrible place now. Ruth said the world wasn't much different and that it was Lily's fault for reading a rag like the *Sun*. She would read about different sorts of people if she bought a respectable paper. You didn't argue with Ruth, but Lily thought this was ridiculous. How could a different newspaper alter the state of the world? She read the *Sun* because she liked the shape of it; you could read it without having to rattle the pages to keep them in shape, which would disturb Dick. She remembered how, when she was a young woman and restless, she would often strap Ruth into the go-car quite late at night then walk for miles. Nobody would do that now. It made her feel guilty about the peace and safety of her own home. It wasn't a smart house, nor even particularly comfortable, but it was draped about with good feelings, the way other people hung brightly coloured curtains.

She thought those feelings came mainly from gratitude, gratitude that Ruth was safely reared and the gratitude of herself and Dick for their acceptance and friendship, for all that the other had had to put up with. Breaking in took a very long time. That was mostly what life was about.

She cleared the dishes away and made a cup of tea. Dick put a splash of whiskey in each of their cups and she lit a cigarette. When the drink hit Lily's brain she became quite animated. She told Dick about a case she had read in the paper and which had upset her. It was a young woman whose boyfriend burned her with cigarettes every time they had sex. 'Why is there such hatred of women in the world?' she said. 'If only girls realised that man is the natural enemy of woman, they wouldn't go sleeping around the way they do.'

Dick nodded and watched her with a sweet, remote smile. She remembered then that he hated her talking about feminism, and that he wasn't actually agreeing with her but detaching himself. Years ago that would have irritated her to death but now she knew that he couldn't understand feminism any more than he could understand Sanskrit and was frightened when she talked about it, but he forgave her. And she loved him for it.

4

≈

'Pa has been spending money,' Ruth wrote in her diary.

She had been keeping a diary since the age of nine. She supposed the habit came from having no brothers or sisters, no one she could talk to. From the time she was small, she remembered her mother's anxious whisper, 'Don't say anything to your pa. He'll go mad.' About what? Neither of them seemed to know. At first she assumed it was about money. And Ma agreed to that. But what about the time she had her hair cut when she was fifteen? It was her hair and her money. You would have thought she had spent it on heroin. She came to believe that what drove him mad was any independent action which forced him to think about her or her mother. There was the time she decided to go to university. 'Don't say anything to your father,' Ma had begged. 'I'll deal with him.' And she had watched her mother step into the blaze like a Christian martyr. An almighty dust-up ensued when she announced that she wanted to leave home. Ruth decided then that no matter what they did, he would go mad anyway.

When she was a child the diary entries covered pages. The earliest notes concerned ways to get around her father. She had taken from her mother the feeling that he was a sacred presence in whom anger was a flame that had to be tended. A volcano god. Yet there was another side to him. As a little girl she had been intrigued by the music that leaked beneath the drawing-room door, beautiful notes that suggested streams and mountains, and she thought there must be a different world behind those walls. But he kept this world for himself. Ma wasn't interested and Ruth wasn't welcome. Sometimes she would sneak in to watch him playing the piano or listening to an opera recording. Or he might be bent silently over a jigsaw puzzle. He collected Victorian jigsaws, some of them made of wood. They were as pretty as paintings and probably as expensive, but he liked to recreate the idyll of an English rural landscape beneath his fingers. Ruth tried to make herself invisible and he pretended that she was not there. Once she had crept in while the room was empty and decided to please him by completing a puzzle, but the patterned scraps seemed to fit nowhere and she had had to bend them into place. After that she was banished from the room. Later, when she read de Beauvoir on men and marriage in *The Second Sex*, she realised that he was like most people's fathers at the time, a crusty old blighter, dictatorial and a bit tight-fisted, but that was the role that was allowed to men who gave their protection to women and children, and most women put up with it and most children accepted it. There was something almost comic in de Beauvoir's suggestion that 'marriage incites man to a capricious imperialism', and Ruth always laughed when she came to her description of the power-crazed husband exerting his authority over his wife, so that 'the slightest sign of independence on her part seems to him a rebellion; he would fain stop her breathing without his permission.'

Her pa was an old man now, mild as milk. Rather a sweet old man. She ought to be glad that her parents had each other. They were happier than most old couples she knew – and young couples. A curdling thought came as she nibbled a piece of Gubeen cheese. Maybe she was jealous. Jealous of what? Of two old people's happiness? Or the notion that sometimes vaguely niggled, that she had been the source of contention, that her presence had disturbed the secret pact that lay between them? When she left home it had upset her to leave her mother behind in the rubble of discord. Ma wouldn't blame anybody, not Ruth, not Pa. 'You don't understand him. He's upset because he loves you and he's losing you. He doesn't know any other way to show it.' And seeing Ruth's jaws begin to grind with ire she had pushed a bit of her daughter's wayward hair back from her face and murmured, 'You'll understand when you're married.'

She had never married. She couldn't see marriage as anything but a cage, and a husband as someone to rattle the bars. Besides, she couldn't forsake her mother. All the time, in some distant part of her head, she found that she was listening for her ma in the way a mother listens for the cry of a sick or fretful child. It was foolish because she could tell that Ma was content, almost smug, even if martyrdom was what made her happy. And Ruth knew she wasn't really any use to her as a daughter. Her ma wanted a co-conspirator, a rosy girl who would play the same games and laugh in mock desperation over the hopelessness of men.

She took a bottle of *Pouilly Fumée* from the fridge and perched in a window seat to gaze out at the sea. She had designed these flats and then bought the best one just before the property boom, and now had her own sublime perch in Killiney, only nine miles from the city. She had been hoping to impress her parents when she took them to see it. Neither seemed to notice the way the big windows drew in the spectacular views, or the line of trees planted in a slope in the garden so that the sea light would be filtered by leaves like a Mediterranean landscape. Ma just folded her arms over her chest and gazed abjectly at the view. 'All that wet grey water around you. I don't know how you can stand it.' Ma was the true intellectual, a woman who scarcely noticed her surroundings, had no real interest in food, beauty or the pleasures of the flesh, who only ever wanted a husband in the first place so that she could opt out of life and get on with her real vocation which was the life of the mind.

When she had finished the wine she went and looked at herself in a mirror; greying hair, that forbidding look women get when they think too much. She didn't lack confidence. She had a successful career, she had lovers and knew she could get a husband if she put her mind to it, but years of looking at Ma had led her to believe that pretty women were like a rabbit in a trap. Men just hunted them down and carried them off. She had 'let her appearance go' as Ma would have said. She liked this phrase, as if she had voluntarily given the most delicate and precious part of herself the ultimate gift, its freedom.

When she got into bed she wanted someone to hold. That was the one drawback to lovers, you never really got to the point of consolation. She wondered if her parents held on to each other in bed. She couldn't picture Pa bending enough for an embrace.

Pa spending money.

The thing that caused her so much annoyance was that Pa had never been short of money. He had always had a steady job. Money was power. It was important to him to leave them dangling while he fussed and fumed so that they would realise they were utterly dependent on him. And it meant that by the time they got anything all the good had gone out of it and they always ended up wishing they hadn't asked. That was what made her mad; he wasn't really angry at all, just wielding his domination.

What was he up to now? Maybe he was giving money to charity, buying favours to shorten his sentence on judgement day. Lots of old people did that, and Pa *was* old, after all. She felt sad and mean then, thinking of her pa old and scared of dying. It must follow that a person who had made himself a bogey to the people he loved would see God in the same light. She gave a sudden snort of humour then as a fresh thought occurred to her. Maybe he had a fancy woman. Maybe he was having a last fling. Ma had occasionally whispered to her – half in protest, half in pride – how voracious her father's sexual appetite had been when he was young. She had a sudden image of a plump, middle-aged blonde spreadeagled on pink satin sheets and Pa launching himself on her, pipe clenched in his teeth. Afterwards she would tuck the cheque into her garter. Much as she liked this image she had to dismiss it from her mind. The day Pa spent good money on a woman, he really would have lost his marbles.

5

In the middle of the night Lily woke with a start. It happened because she had turned over in her sleep. Normally she couldn't turn over because of the way Dick held on to her. She patted the empty space beside her. 'Dick?'

Dick wasn't a comfortable man to lie against. Early on, she had tried to claim her own space in the bed, but the mattress sagged and they both rolled into the middle. When Ruth came it was a relief to escape in the night to change and feed her. She thought that as long as she lived she would never get a decent sleep in her husband's clutches, but humans are adaptable. Eskimos live in igloos and saints lie bound in chains. She was so used to Dick now that the moment he released his grip, sleep deserted her.

'Dick?' She was about to go to the bathroom to look for him when she saw his pyjama'd bottom poking out from under the bed.

'Hush!' he snapped.

'What is it?' Cautiously, she slid down on to the cold floor.

'There's an intruder under the bed. I've got him in my sights.'

She snapped on the light and crouched beside him, lifting the blankets.

'You were dreaming. There's no one there.'

He backed out on all fours. Last of all came a shotgun. 'Bugger got away when you created a diversion.'

6

⚭

The local cinema where they had seen *Brief Encounter* and walked out of *Night of the Living Dead* had become a pine barn. Their excursions to the pictures now took them to a multiplex in the centre of the city. The startling level of sound and vision that was hurled at them seemed no more than a considerate adjustment to their sight and hearing. As they watched a pleasant comedy called *Moonstruck* they were occasionally disturbed by a rattle of machine-gun fire or a sudden sweep of violent music from the cinema next door. When they came out into the night they were shocked, as always, by the starkness of the city; traffic and neon lights, police and ambulance sirens, sharp-faced youths wrapped in blankets. In their day it was stray dogs that shivered in the streets, now it was stray children. A cauldron of greasy smells hit them from the fast-food restaurants. It made Dick hungry and they stopped to buy chips.

When they got home he poured her a glass of whiskey to go with their supper and they watched *The Late Late Show*. 'That girl looks a bit like Ruth,' Lily said when Mary Robinson came on the screen. The left-wing lawyer was being groomed as a surprise presidential candidate.

'Ruth?' Dick squinted at the screen. 'Is that Ruth?'

'It's Mary Robinson, Dick. She's had a what-do-you-call-it – a makeover! Doesn't she look nice? Do you think she'd ever stand a chance as President?'

'A woman in the Park!' he laughed. 'There'll be a woman pope before that day comes.'

'I suppose you're right,' Lily yawned. 'Dick, do you think you should have your eyes checked?'

He reached out and patted her hair fondly. 'Lily, the Worrier Queen! Stay away from the medics. If there's nothing the matter they'll find something. Remember, that's how they make their living.'

Suddenly she felt worn out. She filled a hot water bottle and went up to bed. As she took her night dress from under her pillow she found two coconut biscuits. Dick had taken a liking to sweet things and had developed a habit of stowing them away in peculiar places. He was growing absent-minded in more worrying ways too. Neither of them had mentioned the episode of the intruder under the bed. Where on earth had he got the shotgun? She didn't fall asleep immediately but lay under the blankets thinking. Downstairs, Dick played the piano softly, so as not to disturb her. 'I'm seventy-five,' she thought. 'How did I get to seventy-five?' The people she had been were all still inside her, very neatly packaged. She used to imagine that old age must be awful, the death of everything. But it wasn't so. Nothing died. The child and the young girl and the mother and the middle-aged woman full of rage and grief and dawning wisdom were there all together, and she reigned as peacemaker over this tribe. She understood them now and knew they had done their best. Ruthie thought she lived a futile sort of life, that she flapped round after Dick, placating him, but she knew at her age that this was important work and that by her example she had at last taught Dick the skill of accommodation. She hoped finally to pass it on to Ruth.

As she began to drift off she thought that their life now was like

some old song that you take for granted but you always find yourself whistling when you're happy. She heard Dick coming up the
stairs, the soft, familiar creak of his feet as he put away his clothes,
and then the brisk rasp of tooth-brushing. He fitted his shoes with
wooden shoe trees and drank a small dose of Andrews (as much as
would fit on a sixpence) before getting into bed.

'Are you awake, love?'

'Yes, Dick.'

'Is Connie coming tomorrow?'

'Yes, Dick.'

As soon as his arms went around her he began to fall asleep.
Old age was fine. There was a time when the habit of sex on
Saturday was as much a routine as their cinema-going. All that was
in the past, although there were rare occasions when he still felt
compelled to try. It was uncomfortable for both of them but she
understood that, like her, Dick was still layered with his earlier
selves and among them was the aggressive young man who now
and then had to assert himself. Dick still admired this younger self,
and anyway he hadn't the energy to tell him to go away so they
coped with him as best they could.

'Good girl,' Dick said in his sleep. She smiled to herself for he
always used to say that after sex. That was the bit she had liked
best.

7

Connie Herlihy had preserved her girlhood in the way other women preserve the good furniture in a locked drawing room. In a decade when women dressed in track suits and trainers, she still wore a mini dress and high heels and slept with her butter-coloured hair in rollers. Dick and Lily called Connie their glamour girl and harboured a guilty regret that Ruth was not more like her. She had arrived in Galvan's as office junior when she was sixteen and was now personal assistant to Mr Harry Galvan. She worked on a keyboard and had a car of her own but still came to see Dick and Lily several times a year, and she still called Dick 'Mr Butler'.

'Any news of the office?' Dick offered his cheek to her gleaming mouth and handed her a glass of Moscato.

'Try one of these.' Lily thrust a package at her.

'Pringles!' Connie exclaimed.

'Pringles? What are Pringles?' Dick examined the green cardboard cylinder.

'They're sort of crisps,' Connie said.

'Is that all?' Lily was disappointed. 'At that price!'

'It's the flavours,' Connie said. 'Sour cream and chives.'

'I got some of those dip things to go with them. There was a pack of three on special offer. Curry, garlic and salsa.'

'What's salsa?' Dick asked.

All day they had been getting ready for her visit, carefully rinsing and drying the good china, shopping in the supermarket. Mostly they crept past the giant coffins of Chinese noodles, Penne Arrabiata and Tiramisu, meek in the presence of food they had never heard of, but they could engage with foreign food on equal terms for Connie. Lily handed her a plate of pinwheel smoked salmon sandwiches, which had come ready-made in a container. She had prawn won-tons warming in the oven. Connie paused to admire the edible swirl of pink and white between her pink-varnished nails. 'You remember Mr Lavelle that was always sucking up to Mr Galvan?'

'Pup!' Dick said contemptuously.

'He bought one of those new town houses in Foxrock and it's been repossessed for non-payment of mortgage.'

Dick grimaced with satisfaction. 'Any word of poor Mr Janucek?'

Mr Janucek's wife had multiple sclerosis and the plump and fastidious middle-aged man had to tend her like an infant.

'I found him asleep at his desk. Doesn't get a wink of sleep any more. His sister told him she's just a heap of rubble now and should be put away somewhere before she finishes him off but he won't hear of it.'

'Of course not,' Dick said. 'She's his wife.'

The women acknowledged the steadfastness of men with a smile and Lily poured the tea.

'They were a wedding present from the girls at my office,' she said as Connie admired the pretty china cups patterned with pansies and banded with gold. 'We've kept them intact over all the years.'

In fact, several pieces were missing. What had happened to them? Some little accident, early on. An evening, just like this, but it was girls from her office who had come to visit shortly after her marriage. One of them mentioned that her old job was still open. She said nothing until the girls had gone and she and Dick were washing up and then she hinted that she might go back to work. She became excited, pointing out that he could meet her for lunch in town and they might go to the pictures afterwards. Then Dick dropped a cup. She emitted a cry of dismay, for she loved that china. But it was an accident and she didn't want Dick to feel bad. 'It doesn't matter,' she said.

'Oh, doesn't it?' he said, and he dropped a plate.

'Dick!' she cried. 'Please stop.'

'I will stop . . .' he paused to let the milk jug fall, '. . . as soon as you stop this ridiculous talk. You are my wife. I will look after you. You will look after me.'

'Honest to God, you two are a marvel.' Connie reached for one of the mysterious little pastry parcels Dick and Lily had purchased in the supermarket. 'My own parents, God be good to them, wouldn't have known a won-ton from a white pudding. You're great, so you are. Being adventurous is what keeps you young.'

Neither Dick nor Lily had even heard of won-tons before spotting them on the freezer shelf that morning, but they simultaneously reached and chewed.

'Any signs of romance?' she asked Connie.

'There is someone, but at this point I can't say anything definite.'

Lily nodded with pleasure. Miss Herlihy fitted her glamorous image of a career girl and reminded her of her own office days, which had been among the happiest of her life. She would have liked Ruth to talk like this, but she no longer asked Ruth about men for her daughter tended to respond by talking about sex.

'I'm off for an autumn break to Positano. That's in Italy. I'm told the men are very nice there, although you have to watch your bottom. I'm doing two nights a week on the sun beds so that I won't look like a Boland's sliced loaf when I get into my swimsuit.'

Before she left Dick asked her about her car and she mentioned a small problem with her windscreen washer which enabled him to go out and examine the car from all angles. The weather had turned chill and he had to hold on to his hat, but he didn't seem to notice, although he normally felt the cold. As she drove away they waved until the car was out of sight.

'Italy!' Lily was lively after several drinks. 'Imagine being able to change your climate the minute a chill sets in. Isn't it great for young girls, nowadays, trotting all over the globe? We'll have to look up Italian food next time she comes.'

8

～✹～

When Dick brought her tea in the morning Lily was suddenly struck by how frail he was. He looked gawky inside his striped pyjamas and for a moment her heart hurt with compassion.

'Let's do something nice today.' She thanked him for the tea (awful, awful, he had never learnt any domestic skills), and patted his sharp arm. 'It's such a lovely day. Maybe we could go for a drive.'

'Leave it with me.' She was surprised by his abrupt tone, but then she remembered he never liked unexpected things. She drank the tea looking out the window. She liked autumn, the soft light and clean air, the lush rhubarb and ruby varnish that tinted leaves before they withered. She watched a leaf come down, a frivolous descent, as if it was embarking, not dying. It did not simply drop off the tree but detached itself fastidiously and then glided into freefall, a flimsy scrap of gold against the wide, cold sky, like a teenager leaving home. Ruth.

They went to Mass, as they always did. In their early married days they read that husbands and wives should never let the sun set on their anger. They developed the custom of saying a prayer that required a response. They weren't angry any more, but the habit of prayer persisted. It was Lily's suggestion, after Dick retired, that they should pray together in the morning too. He did not know how to use up a day without work so he was happy to go along with anything she said. As the Mass ended they emerged from the huge church like two small cuckoos from a clock. When families were poor it had been full every day, the collection plate brimming with coins from slender wage envelopes. Now that people were rich they had found something else to fill their time.

'No need to shop today,' she said. 'There's plenty left over from Connie's visit.'

'Well, then. I'll leave you to it. I have business to see to.'

Was he still a bit put out about her asking for a drive, she wondered as she walked home alone, but by lunchtime he had about him a Christmas air. 'You're right, love. You need a break.'

Lily looked up from setting the table in surprise. 'No, I'm all right.'

He smiled broadly and then laughed at her. 'You never ask for anything. How's this for an outing?' He reached into an inside pocket and produced a harshly coloured brochure. Lily put on her glasses and leafed through the glossy pages. Men and women with roasted skin strolled hand in hand past swimming pools the size of football pitches. The women were bare-breasted and both sexes wore thongs in ice-lolly shades. There was a time when pictures like this would have been banned in Ireland. Big scrolled letters boasted different destinations: Barbados, Antigua, Seychelles. The prices, in smaller figures, were in thousands. All the places looked the same. She pretended to be interested, turning the pages until she got to the end.

'What do you say, love? A second honeymoon. We never really had a first one. No expense spared.'

She got a sudden picture of herself and Dick, dressed only in primary-coloured thongs, like shorn sheep garishly striped after dipping. She shivered slightly. She had always been a modest woman.

'You're cold,' he said eagerly. 'You need a bit of heat in your bones.'

'No, Dick.' She pushed the brochure back firmly. 'I'm fine. I just wanted to go for a drive.'

'I saw your face when Connie talked about her holiday. Matter of fact, that's what gave me the idea.'

'I was pleased for her, but I'm too old for that sort of thing.'

Dick put the brochure away carefully. 'You mean I'm too old. You couldn't be bothered going with me.'

'I'm grateful,' she added, and she was.

After lunch she rang Ruth. 'Your father's not mean. I just wanted to say that. He wants to pay out thousands of pounds to take me on a foreign holiday. Some place on the far side of the world with a name like seashells and boiling sun and swimming pools.'

Ruth whistled. 'So when are you off?'

'You know me. I don't like the sun. It gives you cancer.'

'You turned him down?'

'I thanked him, but yes.'

'As he knew you would.' Ruth laughed. 'Cunning old fox. He was just creating a distraction from the money that's gone missing.'

'Ruth, that's not fair. As a matter of fact we are going away. First class hotel, but in Ireland.'

Her heart sank as she said it, remembering the boredom of such holidays, sitting on a grey-shingled beach, walking around the pier, drinking endless cups of coffee and making small talk with fellow guests who changed their outfits three times a day. Well, she had brought it on herself. And then she had to coax Dick, who had been brooding since she turned down his offer.

'I've been thinking. It would be nice, a little holiday. Somewhere luxurious and not too far away.'

'That money is no longer available,' he huffed.

'That's all right.' She was a little taken aback. 'I have a bit put by from the housekeeping. It's easy to save with just the two of us. My treat, Dick, what do you say?'

She cashed the cheque Ruth had given her and booked a weekend from an ad in the *Irish Times*. She had her hair done and staked her blouse with a brooch Dick had given her years before, which she had never worn. The hotel was really beautiful, although it was quiet because it was the off-season. There was an awkward moment when Dick went out to the car, then Lily saw him bounding up the thickly carpeted stair with a dirty plank of wood, under the warning eye of a porter. 'I've got a bad back,' Dick called out loudly. 'Can't sleep in a strange bed.' Oh well. It was no worse than travelling with children, who could always be counted on to embarrass you.

They went for small walks in the wooded garden of the hotel, ate cream cakes in a tea shop in the town, visited the church and wandered around the few shops, buying postcards and souvenir fudge. In the evening they invited a guest in the lounge to join them for drinks. 'I come here because I can talk to my husband, away from the children,' the woman confided.

'Where is he?' Lily looked about, for the woman seemed to be on her own.

'Oh, he's dead. But we used to come here every year.'

The offer was for two nights' bed and breakfast and one dinner, so on the second night Lily said they would eat *à la carte*, anything they liked, off the menu. They had a sherry first, in the bar, by the fire. 'You do me proud,' Dick said. 'You are the finest-looking woman here.' In the restaurant they ate fillet steak with chips and mushrooms and a half-bottle of red wine. Dick wore a grey suit and a red tie. He made jokes with the waitress and then covered Lily's hand with his own. 'This is my bird,' he said, thinking he was being very modern.

The raw-faced young woman looked at him warily. 'Anything else you'd like, sir?'

'Yes, please. A lightly boiled egg,' he said, and he laughed.

'It's a joke,' Lily had to tell the girl, who was writing it down.

'I've never seen him look so happy,' she thought, and then with surprise, 'I'm happy too.' It had been a memorable weekend, a glowing time, an autumn blaze.

In bed that night his old bones clamped around her. She was briefly startled when his hands went under her nightdress. She said her prayers to pass the time, distracted by the interesting thought that her body had never given in gracefully to its functions. She mostly hadn't cared for sex, she had had problems when she got pregnant. No doubt, when her time came to die, she would go out roaring. As Dick struggled and gasped like a man running away from some demon in a nightmare, she wondered what the widow said to her husband now that he was dead. 'I must tell him,' she thought. 'I must tell him I love him.' But he was asleep, the demon left behind, herself locked up safely for the night in his arms and nothing showing in his face but the totality of a child's slumber.

9

✦

They came back to bleak winter, to flayed trees and flying roof tiles. As soon as he had checked all the rooms of his own house, Dick went to look in on their neighbour, Miss Mespil, who lived alone and was almost ninety. Lily lit the paraffin stove, waiting for the blue glow to yield something other than its paraffin smell, then she began cutting up turnips and onions for an Irish stew. They both enjoyed stew, but the long simmering also helped to warm up the kitchen and make it bearable. Even for November it was bitterly cold. Lily always took a nap in the afternoon with a hot water bottle. She tired easily because of low blood pressure, but it also filled the gaunt period between the bustle of morning housework and lighting the evening fire.

She measured rice and sugar into a bowl for pudding. She had been doing these tasks for so many years that she could have done them blindfold or blind drunk. She could hardly remember now the anguish she had experienced twenty years ago when Ruth left home and she had realised that this was her life and nothing was going to come and change it; she had felt as shoplifters must have done when they were deported to Australia, surrounded by expanses of nothing to which they must feed their strength and energy. Now she liked her life and her home. It was the kind of house that didn't look much different after cleaning so she didn't have to worry about housework and could spend her time thinking. And she could always put on another cardigan.

After the food had gone into the oven she sat close to the stove with a cup of instant coffee and a cigarette and a new book by Germaine Greer which she had got from the library. The book was very interesting, suggesting a tyranny of sexual freedom, not just over women, but over men as well. Even feminism seemed to have mellowed over two decades. She read that the principle of free love, which was supposed to bring happiness to both sexes, had turned into a sexual fundamentalism, denying people the right of disinterest and imposing on all a gruelling quest for gratification. *The sex mystics shrink from no ordeal which the sacred duty of orgasm might impose.* The result, according to the author, was that women made themselves too readily available, while men, denied their role as hunter, were losing interest in women. Imagine that! Sex really was meant to be a conquest for men. Ruth's generation thought they knew it all. She put the book down. She was cold and the heater seemed to give no more warmth than a candle. She would save her reading for later and do some hoovering to stir her circulation. As she stood up she saw that the kitchen window was open. Dick must have opened it to throw bread out for the birds. She pulled it shut and stepped into the hall. Icy draughts engulfed her. The doors to the dining and drawing rooms were open and so were the big windows. Poor Dick! He had opened the windows and then forgotten all about them. But why had he opened them in such a storm? She fastened them and went upstairs. Air, sharp as knives, gusted out from every room. She must ask him, when he got home, why he had done such a foolish thing. No, better not. It would upset him to think his memory was going. The warped old sashes squealed as she hauled them down.

Dick said Miss Mespil's roof had leaked. He had to move her to another room. He began to quake quietly with mirth. 'The whole fucking ceiling fell in!'

'Dick!' Lily was shocked. He never used bad language. 'What a thing to say! I can't see that Miss Mespil's roof is a laughing matter.'

'No, love!' He tried to recover himself. 'That is what she said. When I asked her how she had fared in the storm, she said the whole f—' He stopped under his wife's reproving eye. 'Miss Mespil, who never used a swearword in her life!'

'It's old age,' Lily said. 'That and the shock.'

He was serious again. 'If that is old age, then it is a terrible thing, that it would strip a person of their gentility.'

He brooded while she made the tea. It was a part of his personality that he laughed and cried quite easily, and after he had enjoyed a good laugh, he was sometimes depressed.

'Lil, I've made a fool of myself,' he said quietly.

She poured the tea. 'Yes, well we all do that from time to time.'

'I invested money. Some fellow conned me out of some money.'

Ah.

'We'll be all right. It wasn't that large an amount. But it's set me back. I feel my judgement is gone.'

'Investments are never predictable.' Lily chose her words with care. 'It's not a thing to go into at our age. If we have enough money then let's just be thankful for that.'

'It's nothing to do with my age. He said he was a broker and now he's skipped the country. It's my judgement of people that's gone. I liked the fellow. I thought he liked me.' His eyes were wet again. He looked straight at her, not trying to hide anything. His eyes were of the palest blue. Washed clean, they were an infant's eyes.

'Maybe it's just a hitch,' Lily said, although she didn't think so.

'Maybe he's just gone on a trip and everything will be all right when he gets back.'

'I've been trying to track him down for weeks. I've been getting the runaround. Yesterday his wife answered the door and she told me he had gone away. She said he'd left her without a penny.'

'The poor woman!' Lily said.

'The woman's lying. They are in this together. A couple who would con money off a pensioner . . .'

She waited a moment, sought for words, as though testing ice with her foot before putting her weight on it. 'Yes, well we're in this together too. We are, aren't we? Perhaps in future we should discuss matters like this before you do anything.'

'What do you mean?' His eyes sharpened. In an instant they were an old man's eyes.

'I've noticed that sums of money have gone missing, quite large sums.'

'Nothing has gone missing.' His voice was taut. 'What are you saying?'

She bent to light a cigarette to avoid his gaze. 'You were kind enough to open a joint account. I couldn't help noticing that cheques had been made out without any explanation.'

'You require an explanation for every penny I spend? I would like an explanation. Get me the cheque book and tell me what you are on about?'

She fetched the cheque book and turned the pages. The incriminating stubs were gone. They had been removed very carefully so that no scrap of paper remained, not even in the staples. She could have pointed out to him that numbers were now missing in the sequence of cheques, but she knew he would find some way to confuse her. There was, however, a new stub, freshly entered, for the sum of two hundred and fifty pounds. 'There,' she said feebly. 'What about that one?'

'Ah, yes! What do you suppose that is for?' His jaw tightened. He pushed his pudding bowl away. 'I have purchased an orthopaedic mattress so that we can have some comfort in our final years. I should have known better than to try and share a thing like money with you. Do I now have to account for every penny I spend?'

'No,' she ploughed on miserably, 'but I know how much our ordinary bills are.'

He sat in silence, drumming a dry tune on the table with his nails. He looked as if he had received a blow. Oh, say something, she thought.

'You think that is all my role in life is now?' he obliged her. 'Paying the bills. After a lifetime of earning money and investing it wisely so that we could have a secure old age, so that you could go gallivanting over the globe in a bikini . . . !' She sighed and shifted uncomfortably, but did not protest. '. . . I am to be confined to putting my signature to payment of debts, like a prisoner exercising in a yard.'

Oh, poor Dick! He was depressed and frustrated at having no role in the world. It still happened to him every so often. He felt thwarted having to spend all his time in the company of a woman. She should have known better than to take Ruth's advice and tackle him about the missing money. After all, Ruth had left home precisely because she could not understand him. She, Lily, was the one who understood him.

'Go and see Mr Reilly.' She put a hand on his arm. 'Let him deal with this broker.' Mr Reilly was their solicitor, or rather he had acted for them in the matter of paperwork, the conveyancing of their house when they were young, of their wills when they were old. He seemed like a bit of an old stick to Lily but it would give Dick an opportunity to talk to another man.

'And throw good money after bad?' Dick looked at her coldly.

She knew from that that he had already been to see Mr Reilly, and had exhausted the man's patience.

'No, I have methods of my own.' He stood up from the table and began pacing the room. 'I intend keeping watch on the man's house. I have all the time in the world. I'll sit in the car and wait. Sooner or later he will show up.'

'What if he doesn't? Dick, be sensible. You'll catch your death, crouched in a car in this weather.'

'He would come home if he feared for the safety of his wife or his property.'

'Oh, Dick!' Lily was almost angry now. 'I won't have this sort of talk.'

'Won't have? Won't have?' His face, when he turned from his pacing, seemed to have been replaced by a flat black-and-white snapshot. 'You do realise, don't you, that this is your fault?'

She shrugged. Her heart began to pound. She remembered this mood from long ago. What had she done? Why couldn't she just have said that she loved him and that she understood him and was sorry he was hurt? What was happening to her dear old Dick?

'The money I had put by for our holiday – the holiday you turned down – it was that money I handed over into the hands of a criminal. All of this is entirely your fault.'

Cold seeped through the house like a flood. Each time she closed the windows, Dick opened them. With a sigh, she secured them once again. When a knock sounded at the door, she rehearsed what she would say as she went downstairs.

To her dismay she discovered that the front door was ajar. Anyone could have walked in. 'I was just on my way out,' she told the young man. That was to explain her outfit, for she had taken to wearing a coat all the time.

'I won't keep you.' He seemed embarrassed. 'Is your husband at home?'

'No, he's out.' Her face fell into despondency as she thought of Dick, sitting in his car in the cold outside some strange woman's house. 'I don't know when he'll be back.'

'Could you just give him this?'

'What is it?' She looked at the blank envelope he handed her.

He seemed uncertain as to whether he should say anything. 'Could I come in for a moment? Can I talk to you?'

He looked a nice young man and he could have walked in without her invitation. She ushered him into the freezing drawing room.

'Please understand that I hardly know your husband. He sometimes comes to a pub where I have a drink. He always tries to buy a round. He's a nice old fellow, and, well, I've enjoyed talking to him. He asked me about my plans and I suppose I told him. Last time I saw him he told me he had faith in me and handed me this. I didn't know what was in it until I got home.'

She opened the envelope. There was a cheque for five hundred pounds, made out to cash. Lily felt as if she had won the pools. 'How did you know where he lived? He's been looking for you, I'm afraid. I hope he hasn't been bothering you or your wife.'

'No, not at all,' he said. 'I haven't actually got a wife. I only mentioned this to you because I don't think he's very well. I've noticed he doesn't drink a lot but he gets very excited and confused. Sooner or later he's going to go handing out money to someone who hasn't got a conscience. Oh, his address was on his business card. That's how I found you.'

She sat in the cold room, clutching the cheque. To think that he still carried business cards because he needed a purpose in the world. And he was lonely. He was like a lonely schoolboy handing out sweets to buy friendship. Men spent their lives striving for success in the world and then it was taken away. At the end they were left with old women and it was no use, no use at all because old women didn't care about that sort of thing. She had imagined they were into safe waters and were content just to be together, which only went to show that she didn't know as much as she thought. She felt tired, suddenly, like a swimmer who realises the shore is much further off than he imagined. She sat where she was until the angelus bell rang noon and then she got up and went to the kitchen to make a shepherd's pie.

When Dick got home Lily found it hard to claim his attention, for he was busy flinging open all the windows she had closed.

'I have good news, Dick. What are you doing? This place is like an ice-box.'

'The place stinks!' He ran about urgently, as if there were evil spirits to be given exit. 'I must have air. I cannot breathe.'

She put the cheque by his place at the table. The curtains swooped over the room on arctic gusts. Dick sat down in hat and muffler with several jerseys under an oilskin coat. In spite of the discomfort, she looked forward to the moment of appeasement. 'Your broker called round this morning. He brought your cheque.'

Dick picked up the slip of paper. His expression did not alter. 'What broker?'

'Nice young man. He was concerned about you. He sent his best regards,' she embellished. 'Oh, but Dick, he says he isn't married.'

The cheque was thrown down and Dick glared at her. 'Do you have any idea what you have done? You have interfered in my business. You have ruined a perfectly good investment. The man who swindled me out of money was on the wrong side of fifty, and that cheque was for a thousand pounds. I trusted the younger man. I would have trusted him with my life. I listened very carefully to what he had in mind and was confident he would have doubled my money. You seem determined that we should spend our final days in the poorhouse.'

'Dick, I didn't interfere. The man brought the money back himself.'

He glittered like frost. 'That is what any decent man would have done. If I had been there I would have pushed the money right back into his pocket.' There was silence but for the whistling of the wind. 'If I had been there, if I had been there,' he spoke gently now, as if reciting a poem. 'Everything in life is a matter of timing. Lily, love, did you know that?'

'I'm not sure what you mean,' she said cautiously.

He smiled at her. Old pals again. 'Us meeting. Ruth coming to us. All timing. The good and the bad. I often think of it. I often think of a particular night . . .'

'What night?' She was wooed back into the dance.

'You probably won't remember. Not long ago I woke to find an intruder under the bed. I could have seen the fellow off but at that moment you chose to wake up and turn on the light. Perfect timing.'

'Ah.' Lily's heart sank. 'Well, no real harm done.'

'I am glad you think that. I have since discovered that my cash box is missing. A number of vital documents and several thousand pounds in cash.'

'Ruth, it's Ma.'

'What's up, Ma?' Ruth recognised it at once, the tear in the silence, the cry she had been listening out for. Her mother spoke in a whisper, as if she did not want to be heard.

'Nothing's up.' Defensiveness crept into her voice. 'Everything's fine. We're fine. We had a nice little holiday. Your pa's a bit depressed.'

'What is it, Ma? Do you want me to come round?' She glanced at her watch. It was quite late, after eleven.

'Not now. He'd go mad. I've got to go.' She covered the phone with her hand and Ruth heard her call out into the house, 'I'm in the toilet, Dick. I'll be down in a minute.' There was a pause so long that Ruth thought they had been disconnected, but then she was back. 'Ruthie!' Weariness broke up her voice. 'What have I done? What have I done?'

10

Ruth woke to the sound of an alarm. She sat up abruptly, feeling stiff and unsettled, and found herself in an armchair, facing the television's test card and tuning signal. Too uneasy to go to bed after Ma's call she had fallen asleep watching an old movie. She glanced at her watch. Five in the morning. She could still get in a couple of decent hours' rest. She switched off the television but an alarm still sounded inside herself.

She swore as she struggled into her overcoat. Why in hell hadn't she gone straight over when she got the call last night? Needles of rain hit her as she ran through puddles to her car. She turned on engine, lights and wipers and put her foot down.

She slowed down on the Merrion Road as a small cat froze in the centre of the dual carriageway. As she got closer she saw that it wasn't a cat but a rabbit. It faced her like a timid boxer, then bounced off into a garden where it gnawed on a primula. As the city advanced, eating all the green and crowding the skyline, the margin of wildlife ceased to retreat. It settled into small wilderness pockets off housing estates and main traffic arteries and developed a taste for convenience foods — chicken-in-a-carton, Miracle-gro greens — ignoring its odd surroundings with the politeness of aunts at an orgy.

As she drove towards the city, new houses flickered past her like sheets of stamps. Places which had been country when she was a child were now just houses – not villages or neighbourhoods but building blocks, most of them ugly and ill-planned, all of them costing more than fifty thousand pounds and the half-decent ones up to a quarter of a million.

From the age of about fourteen she had been fascinated by houses; not the design of them, for in the Sixties there wasn't a lot of architecture, but the fact that there were so many of them, and always more being built, and that each of them contained a secret. The books she read then were a helter-skelter, 300-page scramble for some tremulous female to get a man, and the story ended when the man asked her to marry him. Nobody ever wrote about marriage itself. Once this summit of romance had been achieved, the ropes were withdrawn and the people were marooned there. She had just found out about sex, and it seemed incomprehensible, outrageous, a trick played on girls that even their mothers knew about. Even if they got to like it, which seemed unlikely, she couldn't see how doing that could use up a whole lifetime, but it did. When young women entered their houses as wives, they never came out again, except with a pram or for the shopping. Girls who made so much noise together in their teens, once married fell silent like birds in the depths of winter.

Ruth used to stop outside houses on her way home from school and listen. There wasn't a whisper. Yet she knew from the papers and from her own home that plenty went on behind closed doors. People in houses had entered some agreement to keep their troubles indoors like little house pets. The only thing that was allowed to show was respectability. Pa had always impressed on her that theirs was a good house, but to her child's-eye view, good was a light-filled concept, like angels. Ruth thought most houses gave off darkness rather than light, and a faint odour of captivity, like cages in a zoo. She stopped reading novels when she found that she was not the only one who thought about the personality of houses. She had come across a passage written at the end of the last century by the literary cousins, Somerville and Ross, concerning a part of the city close to where she had grown up.

> *An August Sunday afternoon in the north side of Dublin. Epitome of all that is hot, arid and empty. Tall brick houses, browbeating each other in gloomy respectability across the white streets, broad pavements, promenaded mainly by the odd nomadic cat; stifling squares, where the infant of unfashionable parentage is taken for the daily baking that is substitute for breezes on the Bray Esplanade or the Kingstown Pier.*

For the first time, she began to consider that domestic life might be different in the country or even in alternative settings. From then on Ruth read everything she could find about houses, their design, their spirit, the way that they could march across a landscape as an invading army or nestle into it like cushions strewn on a carpet, how they could harbour darkness or capture light. Or love. It stopped her in her tracks when she read (quite recently) of a conversation Virginia Woolf had had with a friend about life's happiest moment, and she had said, 'I think it's the moment when one is walking in one's garden, perhaps picking off a few dead flowers, and one thinks: My husband lives in that house – and he loves me.'

Her teenage diaries, which had previously sandwiched her claustrophobic outpourings, became populated with sketches of dream houses. At first they were storybook cottages with thatched roofs and roses round the door, but then she realised that such dwellings were meant to be looked at from the outside. Inside, they would be dark and bug-ridden. How to make light and space without sacrificing beauty or comfort? She began to look for architectural books from other countries. By the time she was sixteen, she knew without any doubt what she wanted to do with her life.

There was a dream quality to the early morning, the puddles steely in the dawn, the first commuter traffic scattering the gulls on O'Connell Bridge. Soon she was sliding around the back of the city into the old, solid suburbs, which were now the quietest part of Dublin. By the time she reached her parents' street a faint powdering of soot on the bricks was the only evidence of the city. She sat in the car, enjoying the warmth, reluctant to step out into the rain. It was only six o'clock. Her parents would be fast asleep. They would think she was crazy. She would have to mooch around the awful kitchen until they woke. She sighed. She had never felt at ease in that damned uncomfortable house. There were no nooks that she had made her own, no memories except of irritation and oppression.

'A man's job!' Pa had proclaimed in disdain when she told him what she wanted to do.

'No, Pa,' she said firmly, while Ma looked on nervously. 'That's what I've just found out. That's been the problem all along. It's women who make families and homes. Men just make money. Architecture is a woman's job.'

She found the front door open. This surprised her far more than the encounter with the rabbit. The house, with its short front garden and railings, its curious, arched wrought-iron gate that jammed and creaked, signalling the advent of strangers, had always been a fortress. In spite of her resolve, her heart sank as she stepped into the hall. Cold draughts fell on her like a haul of fish.

'Ma?' she called out. 'Pa?'

The doors to the main reception rooms were open, as were the windows. There was something strangely blind about the rooms. Then she saw the bleached empty squares on the wallpaper.

She found her parents huddled in the kitchen in their over-coats. The room was cold beyond cold. More windows open. It had been raining in the night and wet curtains slapped the wet walls. Their possessions were heaped up or tied in little bundles; all the things they valued, silver, china, pictures, Ma's few bits of jewellery, Pa's jigsaw puzzles.

'Did something happen here?' Then she saw the shotgun. 'Ma, are you all right?'

Her mother nodded, looked at the floor ashamed.

Ruth closed the windows and put on the kettle. She tried to act calmly but her ears were pinned back with alarm. What in God's name was going on? She needed to get Ma to herself. 'You, Pa? Are you all right?'

'Tired,' he said. 'Your mother and I are going to have to part with our few items of value. We have had a setback.'

His brooding tone infuriated her but she held back a verbal swat and placed a hand on his forehead. Cool as ice. 'You've got a temperature,' she said. 'Your forehead's on fire. I'm afraid we'll have to get you to bed.'

He loved being fussed over and allowed her to lead him up the stairs. She piled up hot water bottles, put a hot whiskey in his hand.

'Don't leave me, love,' he began to weep.

'I'm not going anywhere.' She was anxious to get back to Ma.

'Sit with me,' he begged.

'Ma will be up later,' she said. 'She'll sit with you.'

'Your mother's afraid of me. It's in her eyes. My own lovely dar-ling Lily looks at me with fear.'

'We'll talk about it later. You need to rest.'

'I'm very proud of you. You know that, don't you?' He clung

to her hand. 'I could not be more proud of you if you were my son.'

'Sure, Pa.' She made him take two sleeping pills, told him they were to bring down his fever. The old bugger wouldn't lie down. 'Don't go yet.' His grip was like iron. 'I need to talk to you. You are the only one I can trust.'

'I'll be here when you wake.'

He shook his head. 'You may be here but what is to happen to me? She wants to get rid of me.' He began to weep again. 'She hasn't any use for me. I'm not a good lover any more. She lies to me. She has money. She told me she saved it from the house-keeping, but I know that's not true.'

'Ma is the truest woman in the world.'

'No, you are, you are.' His fingers scrabbled as his grip loos-ened. 'Quick, you have to do something for me. In the top drawer of my chest of drawers, a small black box and a letter.'

Curiosity made her obey. 'Open it, open it!' He fought off sleep. Inside was his father's gold watch. It had been in the family for generations. Pa smiled at her faintly. 'It's for you. I've been keeping it for you. I'm an old curmudgeon, but you're in my heart.'

'Oh, Pa.' Ruth was so moved she had to sit down. Her old pa loved her. If she didn't clear out quickly she would be blubbing worse than him. And the letter, after years of never saying any-thing, had he written down the things that were in his heart? Impatiently she began to pull at the envelope.

'No!' It came out as a groan, for he was barely conscious, but she could see he panicked. 'That is private and confidential. Post it.'

She saw now that the letter was addressed to Mrs Roger Hayes with an address in Dublin. Who on earth was that? She knew most of her parents' acquaintances. Maybe Pa really did have a fancy woman. Ask him. Ask him. But his eyes were finally closed and his open mouth yielded nothing but snores.

Ma hadn't moved when she got downstairs. Ruth switched on the oven to its hottest and left the door open to try and warm the place. Then she took down the curtains and hung them over the open oven door to dry. Ma still gazed into space. What did she see that caused such distress? Was it the pathetic little piles of their things? Ruth gathered up the bundles and dumped them in the drawing room. She set the table with homely cups and saucers and the whiskey bottle. Ma still stared. She had never cared much about possessions. Something else? Her eye fell on the shotgun. She picked it up, held it out to Ma in query. Ma got up and scuttled behind the dresser. Ruth dropped the gun and ran to take her mother in her arms. She felt like a little bird, limp and almost boneless, but with hugely beating heart. 'What is it, Ma? What happened?' For a moment Lily burrowed, as if trying to seek refuge within her, and then finding herself still external, she broke free, gave a little flap with her hands. 'Nothing happened.' Her voice only shook slightly and she gave a small laugh as she set about making tea. 'I thought he was going to kill me.'

They sat with their tea cups like stage props. Three times Lily poured dollops of whiskey into the cup and gulped it back. Cigarettes were smoked and bashed up in the ash tray. At least the place was warm and smoky now. Lily hadn't said much. 'It's me,' she apologised. 'My nerves haven't been too good lately.'

'It's not you, Ma,' Ruth said.

'Don't criticise him, Ruth.'

'I don't want to criticise him.' Ruth showed her mother the gold watch Pa had given her.

'Yes, well, as you said, he has a bit of a fever, that's what made him excitable. You can go now, dear. I know how busy you are.

I'll look after him.' She looked at her daughter and then looked away uncomfortably.

Ruth nodded. 'I'll be back later. I'm going to get Doctor Finnucane to come and have a look at him. You've got to keep him in bed while I'm gone.' She handed her mother the bottle of sleeping pills. 'Give him one of these with a cup of tea every time he wakes. I'll bring back something nice for tea. Is there anything you want?'

'I want Dick.'

'All right, Ma. Off you go.'

But Lily made no move. 'Not him.' She was barely audible. Her lips clenched ruefully between each sentence. 'I want my old Dick.'

Ruth felt foolish as she told the doctor that her father had been volatile when young and then meek and amiable when old, and lately he had been behaving oddly, giving things away (she felt a pang of disloyalty as she wrapped her fingers around the black box in her pocket), opening all the windows, sometimes displaying threatening behaviour. No, no actual violence. What did it amount to? A bit of erratic behaviour. An old man's grand gestures and tantrums.

'Has he made a will?'

It seemed a most extraordinary question until she understood what he was getting at. He thought she was afraid her father was going to give everything away before she could benefit. Of course, he had known her parents a long time. He would have seen her father as a respectable, responsible man who paid his bills on time. She stood to leave. She began to feel that she had been had, that she had been drawn into one more of her parents' private games.

'I'll call around later,' he said. 'Say around five.'

It was on the tip of her tongue to say 'don't bother,' but she held out her hand, thanked him and got in her car. She sped out to Killiney and Schubert and the sea as if the hounds of hell were after her. 'Old frauds,' she kept saying furiously. 'Old frauds. One of these days . . .' But then her hand would drift away from the steering wheel and into her pocket, diving for the black box as though it were a talisman.

Lily had not moved since Ruth's departure. Several times Dick had called out to her weakly, but she didn't respond. It was the coming back to normal life that was the difficult part. Once or twice, when it all seemed to be over, she had felt only relief. No, not coming back. That was wrong. There were two things she knew in her bones. She would never be going back to the place she had known. She was in alien country. And she would never tell Ruth all that had happened in the night.

He had been emotional during the day. Several times he seemed on the verge of tears. She was reluctant to take her rest, but he said he had letters to write and she lay awake in bed, listening for sounds of disturbance. At four o'clock he brought her up a cup of tea. 'Sorry,' he whispered.

Something was wrong. There was a sharp, metallic edge to his conciliation, like a boy about to spring a prank. She wanted to go and ring Ruth, but she was afraid. That was what was the matter; she was afraid. She was making the evening meal when she heard drawers being pulled open and things flung about all over the place. 'What are you doing, Dick?' She left the bacon and sausages, found him emptying shelves and drawers and boxes like a burglar.

'You keep out of this,' he panted. 'It is you who have got us into this jam. I should never have given you a joint account so that you could go scattering cheques like confetti. All I can do now is sell everything we own and hope that will see us through until our miserable lives are over.'

'Dick, my dear.' She had taken his arm. 'You're not well. You'll have to see someone.'

He shook her off so roughly that she fell to the ground. She wasn't hurt, but it gave her a shock. He had never been physically rough before. 'Of all the low things,' he said in contempt. 'You get us into money trouble and then try to suggest that I am in some way incapable.'

She picked herself up and went to the kitchen to continue cooking tea. There was nothing else she could do. Her hands shook as she spooned fat over eggs in the pan. 'It's a judgement,' she thought. 'I've been too smug.' She was forced now to consider the oddness of marriage, that having been bound together, a husband and wife were marooned together. For better or worse.

Dick ate heartily. Several cups of tea and several slices of bread followed his fry. He watched the news and laughed at a comedy show on the TV. He seemed to doze for a while, then as Lily filled the hot-water bottles he fetched their things and tied them into bundles, arranging them on the table like a wedding display. Then he began to open the windows. She said goodnight and was on her way up to bed when he asked her to wait a minute. She turned around and found herself staring into the barrel of a shotgun. For some reason, she wasn't at all surprised. She backed off as he advanced and shrank into a chair. He was smiling at her, one eye squinting through the sights. 'Bang!' he said. He put down the gun and laughed.

He began walking around the room, the gun under his arm, his hand on the trigger. Whenever she tried to get up he turned and pointed it at her. The thing that upset her most was that the picture of the Sacred Heart was missing from its place over the mantelpiece. When he had stripped the pictures from the walls he had taken that too. Some people thought the Sacred Heart was morbid, with the dainty fingers touching a bleeding organ, but Lily felt that the suffering Christ with his compassionate heart was there to gather in her small troubles and make them useful. So long as He was with her, she didn't suffer alone.

The wind had risen and made a Greek chorus in the gaping panes. The gusting curtains chuckled and snaffled. Dick's polished boots creaked as he paced the floor, back and forth and back again. At each turn he would lean towards her, angling the gun, caressing the little coiled switch. 'You think that I am just an old man, an old work horse who has served his time and is no further use to anybody. Bones for glue. Ah, but I am of some use. I make sport for those who like to prey upon the feeble, who find amusement in vandalising dignity. I can be ignored, abused, swindled, mocked. Once, I was a person to be reckoned with. You know that.' A swift turn, a moment's toying with the trigger. 'A figure, if I may say so, of considerable authority. Yes, Mr Butler. No, Mr Butler. Kiss-my-arse, Mr Butler. I ruled without. I ruled within. My servants called me Lord . . .' he gave Lily a look of challenge and reproach, '. . . and master!' He aimed the gun and Lily tensed. 'Let women be subject to their husbands as to the Lord, because the husband is the head of the wife, as Christ is the head of the Church.'

The weapon slumped in his arm. 'No one expects their life to change. No man does. No man expects to be stripped and left standing naked, the rings pulled from his fingers, the gold from his teeth. I am not a child. I cannot run to my mother's apron strings for comfort when I am betrayed and humiliated. I am not an old man either. Not old, merely a prisoner inside this rotting cage, having to stand by helpless while his manliness is spat upon and kicked to the ground, and his obedient wife slopes away to be replaced by a nanny who treats him like a pet dog.'

Lily listened to the howling night. She wondered how Miss Mespil was faring with her ruined ceiling. She would be sitting patiently under the leak, imagining that Dick — nice kind Dick — would come and help her out in the morning. Poor old soul. Lily realised then that the roof of her own world had been ripped away. She thought of the nights, all the nights, she had lain in Dick's rigid embrace, when the wind and the snow were as distant as wolves in Siberia. In spite of the cold, she was falling asleep. She yawned and felt her face split like a grey rock.

'You thought I had gone,' Dick said cunningly, and she opened her eyes, surprised by the unlikely nocturnal drama to which she was still a party. 'You thought I had crept away obligingly to die, to be replaced by a pet dog. I played the dog to please you. But dogs get kicked. Dogs get kicked.' He laughed, a playful giggle, and stroked her cheek skittishly with the barrel of the gun. 'Lie down with dogs and get up with fleas, eh?'

'He's mad,' she thought. At the same time, some distant part of her applauded. It was the largest speech he had made in years and everything he said made sense, within its own terms. If his audience had been a large crowd of old men instead of one old woman at the end of a gun — or even a crowd of old men and one old woman at the end of a gun — they would have thrown their hats in the air and cheered. He was right to feel cheated and thwarted. Even if he was to blow her to pieces he would have her sympathy. In fact, it seemed unfair in a way that the only one to share this outpouring was an old woman, shivering with cold and cringing with fear.

'What is it, darling? You're not afraid are you?' Dick was peering into her face. 'Poor old blighter, wouldn't hurt a fly, wouldn't hurt a flea.'

He sat back, exhausted. His mild blue eyes stared into the distance. The gun rested on his knee. 'I'm cold,' he complained quietly. She got up to close a window but darted back to her seat when he saw her. 'Are you cold?' he asked. 'You must be cold.' He wrapped his arms around himself and began to rock. 'Get me a coat, love. Can't get up. Too cold.'

It was only when she was in the hall that her knees began to quake. She thought she was going to faint. She swam towards the hall-stand but it seemed too far away. She needed something familiar. Her hands were on the telephone and she dialled. Ruth. And then of course there was Ruth's laconic tone, ready to condemn Pa. And of course, she was compelled to defend him. Loyalty died hard. Ruth didn't understand the nature of marriage. You couldn't be half married, couldn't spit out the bits you didn't like. But Ruth sounded genuinely concerned. And Dick was always slightly afraid of their daughter; he was unlikely to try and bully her. She was still fighting with herself when she found she had left it too late. She covered the phone with her hand as Dick bellowed from the kitchen.

The gun was cocked, ready to go off, as she returned with the coats. She stood with her hands up, one coat in either hand, her lips moving in prayer. 'Let him pull the trigger. I'm too tired to go on.'

'Ha! You thought I was going to shoot you.' He took his coat from her and put it on, shifting the gun from hand to hand as he struggled with the sleeves. 'Put on your coat!' He pointed the weapon again. 'That's the spirit. Make them hop! The worm has turned. Poor old bastard's had his balls pinned back on.'

In the few minutes she had been gone he seemed to have had a transfusion of energy. 'Now we'll see who's old and helpless.' He spoke softly through gritted teeth. 'For everyone who does me down, there will be blood. This is my friend.' The gun was wielded. 'My last remaining friend. The rest of the world has deserted me but my friend does what I say.' He held the weapon to his mouth and whispered: 'Shall we tell her what we plan to do this night?' He smiled and nodded eagerly, then looked at Lily, his voice grim again. 'It might interest you to know that I have tracked down your so-called broker.'

'Who?' Lily asked.

'Don't play the fool with me. The man who cheated me out of money. Shall we just say that in due course he returned to his home, as I had predicted he would. The rat always returns to its lair.'

'What did you do?' she whispered.

'I pretended that we were still friends. I hinted that I had valuables, played the idiot to suggest that I had no idea of their worth. I told him that he could inspect the goods if he came to my house between two and four in the morning.'

'The middle of the night. Why on earth . . . ?'

'Precisely what the police will ask when his so-called wife attempts to explain his disappearance.' He began to laugh, doubled up with laughter. 'Slaughtered by a penniless old-age pensioner while inspecting his pathetic possessions at two in the morning.'

'Oh, why, Dick?'

'Because I have nothing to lose. Not even you. You have been against me from the start.'

'I want to go to bed,' she said. She hauled herself up stiffly. He ran at her with the gun and she let out a cry of fright. 'You stay,' he commanded. 'You have been the cause of all this. I will leave his brains painted on the wall as a souvenir for you, to remind you that it is your fault and this man's death must be on your conscience.'

She could feel his bitter disappointment as the night wore on. Even his enemy had forsaken him. He summoned up other adversaries whom he would butcher, any old spite or slight, like a losing gambler searching his pockets for small change. So many enemies, so many old resentments were rounded up in the cold kitchen. She had imagined that they had limped away into the fog of time, but he had hoarded them. He had always been a hoarder.

As with sirens in city streets, she ceased to hear him ranting. Then there was only the cold. She had stopped shivering because she wasn't trying to defend herself against it. She only felt its dead, cold weight which lay on top of her like an icy corpse. It was as if she was buried deep under the earth. There was even comfort in the hypothermic possession. She began to drift. Tiny bubbles floated out of her brain. The laments of the wind became the soft whisper of the sea. She was strolling under hot sunshine, wearing nothing but a lime-coloured thong. It was remarkably pleasant. Every so often a shark reared out of the sea, showing teeth like broken glass, but she did not mind for she knew he only meant to eat her. She felt thirsty and someone handed her a lime-green ice lolly.

She awoke to find something cold jostling her teeth. Her mouth was dry but she explored the metallic hardness with her tongue. Consciousness came with a jolt and she felt a painful clattering against her teeth. A ballooning swoosh of fear filled her up as she realised that the barrel of the gun was in her mouth.

'Will we end it all, Lily, dear?' Dick was crying. The gun shook and he clawed the trigger. 'Nobody cares if we live or die. I'm too cold to go on.'

She couldn't think of any reason why not but then an awful thought struck her. If he killed her first his courage would fail. He wasn't a particularly brave man. He would be left alone to cope with the mess and the blame. She couldn't speak so she joined her hands together and held them up in a supplicant pose. Dick looked disappointed. He sat down and gazed ruefully at his gun as if he was a boy with a very good toy and nobody wanted to play.

★

'He's as fit as a fiddle,' the doctor said.

'Oh, good.'

'Couple of geriatric disorders, but that's to be expected at seventy-eight.'

Lily watched him, pale and small and hopeful. Like most women of her generation, she revered doctors and believed that they wielded power over life and death.

'And there's his mind. He seems troubled.'

'It's only recent,' Lily said. 'He doesn't like the winter. He suffers from the cold.'

'It's not my field but I suspect a bit of paranoia.'

'Can you give him something?'

'I'll give you tranquillisers, but I think he should have some tests.' He scribbled on two pieces of paper, one with the prescription, the other with the name of the hospital. Lily picked up the second note. She shook her head rapidly. 'That's a psychiatric hospital. He'll go mad.'

The doctor looked at Ruth. She bit down hard. She had promised not to interfere.

'I could get someone to have a look at him here. Tell you what, if it makes it easier I'll say I'd like a specialist to look at him. Won't mention "B" for brainbox. Here's the name of a very good man. He's young, but he's a professor. Tim Walcott. Ring him and make an appointment. I'll have a chat with him first.'

Ruth could see her mother wilting. She made a mental note to shove some tranquillisers into her as well as Pa. She had a feeling that as soon as she was out of the door the two of them would be making up and conspiring afresh. She picked up the phone and handed it to the doctor. 'Could you please ring Professor Walcott now, from here?'

★

Ruth offered to sleep on the sofa. For safety's sake she thought her mother ought to spend the night in her old room. 'I'll sleep with your father, like I always do,' Lily said.

In the middle of the night Ruth woke, worried by the silence. She crept up the stairs and went to take a look at her parents. She was oddly shocked to find them wrapped around one another, stiff and secretive as silver spoons.

11

Tim Walcott looked about twelve. He wore gold-rimmed glasses and was short and slight. His large head was framed with thick, light brown waves, strangely brain-shaped, an effect that immediately caused Ruth to think of him as Tim Walnut. He had a pleasant face, but he looked too confident for a twelve-year-old. As he strode beaming into the hall, she had an urge to trip him up.

Ruth and Lily drank tea and smoked cigarettes while The Walnut was upstairs with Pa. By the time he came down they were both frazzled with nicotine and nerves. He smiled at them and sat down. Neither Ruth nor Lily smiled back. He didn't say anything but regarded the teapot with a kindly and expectant expression until Ruth was forced to get him a cup and saucer. He wondered then if he could trouble her for a biscuit.

'How is he?' Ruth was annoyed at being made to ask.

He sipped his tea and then gave her his friendly attention. When he spoke, she was surprised to hear an English accent, flat as a cloth cap. 'He's mad.'

Lily looked as if she really had been shot. Ruth had to stop her hand going to her pocket, where she kept the gold watch. 'This is ridiculous. You have only been with him for a few minutes. You are upsetting my mother.'

He nodded sympathetically. 'It's a bad word, isn't it. Worse than bloody or damn. But if I don't say it, it will be hanging in the air, lurking behind every other thing that's said. Best to clear the air.'

'Stop patronising us,' Ruth said, scarcely aware that she was patronising him. '"Mad" is an antiquated term. If my father has a nervous disorder, then we'd prefer its medical designation.'

The Walnut looked vague and regretful. 'Bi-polar disorder. But that's only a guess.' He took off his glasses and polished them on the end of his jumper. Ruth now saw that he wore those severe frames in order to look older. Without them, his wide green eyes were those of a ten-year-old. 'Your father's head has taken a wrong road. It might be a long road. Best look at the ancient signposts first.' He tore open the pack of biscuits and studied them with care before selecting a chocolate sandwich. 'Mad, senseless, deranged, mental, insane, confused, demented, crazy.' Crumbs sputtered as he expounded. 'Deranged might do. Have you a dictionary?' Neither woman made any move until Ruth received a look from Lily which suggested that the only way to get rid of this madman was to do as he said. With a glare, she got up and fetched the frayed old Webster's, friend of her home-work days. The Walnut licked his fingers, pushed his spectacles back on and thumbed with a leisurely sort of enjoyment. 'Deranged . . . Here we are!' He looked at his audience to make sure of their attention. 'Thrown into disorder. That's about right. We won't say he's mad any more.' He nodded agreeably at Ruth. 'We'll say deranged.'

He pounced on a pink wafer biscuit. 'I still like mad, though. Tell you why. It's close to "magic".' He flipped open the diction-ary again. 'Magic! The supposed influence of supernatural powers to influence events. Any mysterious or extraordinary quality of power.' The book was slapped shut. 'He has that, hasn't he, extraordinary power? Now, where did he get that from, poor old fellow like him? You see, there is a bit of magic in madness.'

Ruth was getting more and more irritated. He was just a show-off, trying to impress them with tricks of learning. 'We don't need the benefit of your entire education,' she said. 'We would just like to know what you found out about my father.'

He smiled at her, almost coyly. 'You're mad at me, aren't you?' He smiled, pleased with his joke, and was then serious. 'He's showing signs of severe paranoid delusion and he's very excitable. He's deluded, but at the same time he's mostly very lucid. And he's no fool. He's foxy, and I can't yet tell if he's foxing himself as well as the rest of us. The point is, even if he did start out by working up his own fantasies, he's no longer in control of them.'

'He was always so clever,' Lily said. 'I used to think he could have been anything if he had the chance. He plays the piano. He understands about money. He wrote a poem once that was pub-lished in the paper.'

'He's still clever.' The doctor spoke through a mouthful of ginger crunch. 'Maybe more so than the rest of us. Psychiatry's a young science. Yesterday's madman may be tomorrow's genius. Beethoven and Van Gogh were both a bit loopy. In my view, most madmen are remarkable. They're explorers, travellers beyond the rim of consciousness. Not surprising if they pick up a few bugs and get sick. That's all it is, madness. Mad just means sick. If you get fluid on the lungs it's pleurisy. If it's fluid on the brain, it's insanity.'

He had eaten nearly the whole packet of biscuits which Ruth had bought specially for Pa. She looked pointedly at the pack and The Walnut looked calmly back at her. 'If you don't mind, I'd like to have a private word with your mother.'

Ruth shot a challenging glare at Ma, but The Walnut was a doctor, even if an infant one, and Lily nodded 'all right.' Ruth was so furious she could barely trust herself to speak. 'I have to go anyway,' she told her mother. 'I'll look in in the morning. Goodbye, Dr Walcott.'

'Professor,' he corrected mildly. He waved away a non-existent apology.

'Sorry.' He offered Lily a contrite expression. 'Where I come from, we call a spade a muckshifter.'

Lily spoke in a soft and regretful way. 'I'm sure you're clever but I've lived with Dick since before you were born.'

'Cleverness doesn't come into it. It's all in books. It's common as dirt, madness, but people still feel ashamed when it hits their family.'

'That's all very well for you to say,' Lily rebuked. 'You've never been through anything like this.'

He wondered what she had been through. He thought she looked like a witness in an interrogation cell, someone being forced to give incriminating evidence. 'Would you like a cigarette?' he said. Her fingers trembled slightly as she put one in her mouth. He reached across quickly to light it. When he had blown out the match, he put his hand lightly over hers. Her fingers felt cool and waxy, surprisingly soft and delicate. She pushed the cigarettes across to him.

'I've just given them up,' he said. 'Only thing is I can't stop eating. I hope it's not too obvious.'

Lily noticed that he seemed gentler after Ruth's departure. 'What do you think of my daughter?' she asked.

He scratched the back of his neck and grinned. 'I can diagnose her for you straight off. There's a girl who's in love with her father. Well, she's not done so badly. She got you.'

She gave him a strange, sad look. 'Second prize. She's very clever. She got that from her father.'

'He's always been a bit extraordinary, your magician, hasn't he?'

Lily had to bend her head because tears had come into her eyes. She never cried. The feel of that boy's hand was very comforting. 'Ruth doesn't understand him,' she said.

'I'd say he takes a lot of understanding.'

'We were happy.'

'You've been very good for him. He knows that, underneath it all. What's happening now began, I think, a long time ago. Windows were left open inside his head and strange things blew in. Over the years, with great patience, you managed to get those windows shut, but somehow they've blown open again.'

Lily thought of the windows open all over the house, the strength and passion with which he had summoned the elements indoors. 'I think he wanted them open.'

'Maybe.' The boy nodded slowly. 'Raging against the dying of the light.'

'Will he ever be all right again?'

He stood up. His wide green eyes seemed innocent of anything except the hope for more food. Beneath the brashness he was a caring person. For the first time, she wondered what it would be like to have a son. 'Where do you come from anyway?' she asked.

'Durham, north east of England. Mining country.'

'Not a lot of psychiatric professors there, I imagine.'

'Not a lot of miners either, these days. Plenty of madmen though.' He patted the empty biscuit pack with regret.

'Prat! Bloody little prat!' Ruth drove along the coast to avoid traffic. She didn't want the main road to fall victim to her rage. She began to calm down as she passed Sandymount Strand, then Sandycove and finally her own Killiney Bay. The storms had passed, leaving a rinsed sky, a holy winter light. The sea was a flimsy silk garment, lace-edged, tousled on the sand's muscular ridges. The only sign of the turbulence was an extraordinary array of items – logs and barrels, bones of beasts, the odd shoe and supermarket trolley – vomited up from the depths of the sea.

When she got home she fetched some wine, turned on the music and perched on her window seat. Peace would not come. Ridiculous, cocky little Professor Prick, making word games out of her father. Schubert did his cajoling trick of throwing in a little gypsy music and her mind began to ease. Why was she so mad? *Mad*. She lifted back the sheet and peered at the corpse. Yes, she could identify it. For a while there, driving home, she had been something short of rational. Deranged. Thrown into disorder. She remembered Lily's hushed warnings years ago: 'Your father will go mad.' If Professor Prick had come into their lives at that time, she would not have been short of a 'told you so' to Ma. But he had come now. He had come when, for the first time in forty years, her father had told her he loved her. The undersized little psycho-shit had to tell her (smiling) that her father's love was worth nothing because he was out of his mind.

She felt a snivel coming on. Must be the booze. Or maybe the cold of that bloody house. 'Hot bath and then bed,' she told herself. She stripped off and tied up her hair, waiting for the bath to fill. The steamy mirror showed a fine-figured woman, still young, but with a kind of encompassing grimness, a heaviness of body that seemed to issue from the heart. Her looks were the sort that could be maintained with a minimum of effort. Her skin colour was good and she was tall. A bit of exercise, a tint for her hair. Why had she actually let herself go? All the talk of men and marriage didn't really wash. She was well able to pick up a mate and well able to drop him too. It was her father. She understood that now, for the first time. Having tried and failed to win his love when she was a little girl, she demonstrated her indifference to him by destroying what he might come to value. She knew he liked beauty and delicacy in women. It was what he loved in Ma.

She thought about this until the water got cold and then she climbed, dripping, on to the floor. So what if he was mad? If mad meant that he could shed his inhibitions, show some feelings, then she would prefer that to sane. Okay, he was excitable, a bit of a menace in ways, but since he had been taking the tranquillisers, he had been both rational and benign. She didn't actually care if he was daft as a brush if she could finally get through to him. 'He's seventy-eight and I have never known anything about him,' she thought. 'All I've ever had is Ma's version.' Ma had meant everything for the best but it was just possible that in shielding her from him, she had kept them from getting close.

She had an urge to fling on her coat, drive back to the house and shake him. Make him talk. Anything. He would probably be asleep. Ma had mentioned a poem. Pa, a poet! From what secret compartment of his blustery brain had verse flowered? She had never in her life seen a single written word of his. Ma always signed birthday cards. Had he always had a soft and thoughtful side that could not be spoken, only committed to paper? How would she know? She remembered the letter. Mrs Roger Something. Private and confidential. Who was this woman to whom he poured out his heart? Had he mentioned his difficult daughter, his determination to make her take his love? 'I have to know,' Ruth justified. 'It's been too long and there's too little time. I have to know what goes on in his head.'

The envelope, which had seemed clamped shut like a mollusc, began to gape promiscuously in the steam of a kettle. She poked the sticky edges with her finger and the letter was in her hand. For a moment she felt hot with shame. Reading other people's letters was an absolute taboo, like grave-robbing or incest. And if there really was another woman, then it was disloyal to Ma for her to know. Pa's romancing would probably be Victorian, unbearably sentimental. Dearest heart! Heavenly angel! Light of my life! Like the heart-shaped conversation lozenges tasting of talcum powder, which she had sucked as a child. Who was it who wrote that sentimentality was the eau de Cologne on the dung-heap? Dry-hearted smart-arse! She longed to hear the maudlin phrases, to try them on like a child dressing up in adult's clothes. Even her lovers had never talked to her like that. She hesitated for just an instant and then smoothed out the folded blue Basildon Bond. 'Sorry, Mrs Roger Hayes, but he's mine too.'

'Dear Cunt . . .' Ruth was still smiling. Her brain would not register what she had read. Cunt looked like a playful nick-name, like Puss or Little Bear. Cunt! She slammed the letter shut.

Serve her right. She had gone looking for trouble and she had found it. She fetched an ashtray and a box of matches, dropped in the letter and set light to it. And immediately put it out with her thumb. How quick she was to judge. Suppose Pa had fetched up with some racy old bird who liked a bit of earthy language. Ma had always been something of a prude. The men Ruth had gone to bed with often used words like 'cunt' to get the juices going. Y*es, but not as a form of address.* Maybe he was just trying to get his own juices going. It couldn't be all that easy at seventy-eight. And Pa loved to be modern. And he always got it wrong. She began reading again.

Dear Cunt,
It is a commonly known fact that in younger days you made money by selling your body to men. Now that your syphilis-rotted cadaver no longer attracts filth of that type you have resorted to preying on pensioners for a living. Since you are an ugly bitch who must curse every time she looks in a mirror, it might interest you to know that I could make you

uglier still. How would you like a bottle of acid thrown in your raddled mug? You would first burn as in hell, which will be your final destination. Then the flesh would slip from your bones like candle-grease. Please communicate to your so-called husband that I have the necessary and will be waiting to pay my respects if he does not forthwith return my thousand pounds.

Yours etc.,
Richard E. Butler Esq.

She sat for a long time. Maybe hours. She was stiff as a board when she dragged herself up and went to the window-seat, poured some wine, left it there. She went to the fridge, poked about until she found something with protein and put it in her mouth. She had to spit it out, knowing she would be sick if she tried to swallow. She got her diary, returned to the window-seat and sat with her pen in her hand. She tried to think of something to say about her father, but all she could think of was Ma. All those years performing her anxious dance. Bow to the right, bow to the left, see to Ruth, deal with Pa. The whispered warnings, the ritual appeasement, the inevitable consequences. When she woke in the morning, still crouched in the window-seat, she found that she had written a single line in her diary. 'He went mad anyway.'

'He just wants you to have some tests,' Lily said to Dick.

He had been in the chair by the bedroom window, dressed and ready for an hour. He had taken a great deal of care with his preparation; a fresh shirt, his best suit and tie, shoes buffed until they shone like conkers. And then the suitcase. He had packed it himself; his good brush and comb set, cologne, a large-print detective novel, small valise of writing paper and stamps. He wants to make a good impression, she thought with a pang. He looked so spruce, *dignified* was the word that came to mind, that it seemed somehow dishonourable to be sending him off to have his head looked at. She gave the name of the hospital. 'He's a psychiatrist, Dick.' She couldn't hoodwink him, no matter what the cost to herself. Not after all the years.

'I know that.' Dick smiled, tolerant of her fussing. 'He told me. Bit of trouble with the nerves. Common as indigestion. I just need winding. Ha, ha! Take the wind out of my sails.' He still loved corny jokes and puns. 'Nothing to be afraid of,' he reassured Lily. 'No more than a visit to the dentist. Not that the dentist could do much for me.'

'You don't mind, then.' She left his bedside and went to the window.

'Course I don't mind a visit to the dentist.'

'Oh, look! There's Ruth. I'll just go and let her in.'

'He's had no tranquilliser!' Lily wanted to show Dick off. The hospital had asked for him to be admitted free of medication; his head was clear as a bell and he was brave. When she saw her daughter's face she said nothing. Let Ruth see for herself.

Dick lay in bed, the sheets pulled up to his chin, his face gaunt and closed, the effigy of a dead knight. His clothes hung carefully on the end of the bed. 'He's taken his clothes off again!' Lily said in disappointment. 'Dick, Ruth's here. We're ready to go.'

'I'm too tired.' He opened a plaintive eye. 'All I need is a little peace and quiet.'

'Wait downstairs,' Ruth said to Lily. 'I'll see to him.'

'He had his suit on.' Lily peered in disbelief at her husband. She went to his side and shook him gently. 'Come on, Dick. You'll rest in hospital. The sooner we get going the sooner it will all be over and you'll be back home.'

'Whoever got a rest in hospital?' His head shot up angrily. 'Breakfast at six in the morning, bedpans, needles up your arse.'

'Leave it to me,' Ruth insisted.

'Ruth, love.' He patted the bed. 'Sit beside me. Stay and have a little chat. We hardly ever seem to chat.'

She eyed him steelily, held out the garments. 'Put them on, Pa, or I'll put them on myself.'

'They'd look funny on you!' He began to snigger, then seeing that he got no response said huffily: 'All right. Turn your back.'

He was a little bag of bones. The drawers and vest billowed. 'Hold out your feet,' she said. 'I'll put on your socks.'

His feet felt blunt and stiff, like a small child's feet. It was almost impossible to get the socks on. While she wrestled, he stretched his scraggy torso and in a leisurely gesture pulled off the vest he had just put on. Ruth rammed the socks on to the unyielding feet, grabbed the vest from his hand, stuffed it over his head.

'Put on your shirt,' she bullied as she seized his trousers and attempted to ram the long stovepipe limbs first into one leg and then the other.

'Can't,' he said. 'Too weak. Can't lift my arms.' She guided one arm through a sleeve, bent it, fed the other arm through and started on the buttons with fevered haste. He began to laugh. 'Stop it! You're tickling me.' He wriggled as he laughed. The trousers fell off, two puddles of cloth around his ankles. They entered a whirling burlesque, he giggling and flinging garments in the air. Once he reached out and gave her a sharp uppercut to her jaw. She continued buttoning and lacing and zipping. It was like trying to parcel a live cat.

'You can't!' Lily said in anguish when she saw him. 'You can't let him go out like that.' The tie looked like a schoolboy's tie, ends askew, knot too tight. Several buttons found themselves in the wrong slots. One of the socks had gone astray and above his polished shoes a bleached ankle showed.

They drove past the ancient parts of the city: Christchurch, Thomas Street, Guinness's Brewery, James's Street, past another lunatic asylum (now a psychiatric hospital), founded on the benevolence of Jonathan Swift, who had seen the swarming insane of the city when he was Dean Swift of St Patrick's Cathedral, before he himself had gone mad. They passed through Dublin's historic heart, with its warm, yeasty brewery breath, its huckster shops selling old furniture and cheap vegetables and the River Liffey running parallel. Today her own heart sank with each familiar landmark. What was it The Walnut had said? Ancient signposts to a long road.

'What's taking so long?' Ma whispered. She and Ruth sat on hard chairs in a corridor.

'Yes, well, hospitals,' Ruth said. 'We'll go for a nice drink when it's finished.'

Forty minutes passed. They heard a roar. 'Pa!' Ma jumped and her face went white. 'Stay here,' Ruth begged as she went in the direction of the noise, but Ma scurried after her.

'They are trying to commit me to an insane asylum!' Pa bawled. His parched face showed rage and terror. 'They are trying to make me commit myself.'

Lily's fingers drifted out to Ruth's arm. 'Call Professor Walcott.'

'What can he do?' Ruth asked.

'Call him.' The dainty fingers dug into her sleeve.

'Professor Walcott?' She rammed the coins into the box. 'Ruth Butler. I'm sorry to disturb you, I hope you're not too busy.'

'Yes, well, I am busy,' he said cheerfully, 'but if I wasn't busy, I'd be broke.'

'It's my father.' She spoke grudgingly, frost in her tone. 'We're at the hospital. We're having trouble admitting him. He won't sign anything.'

'Listen carefully. Calm him down. Tell him he doesn't have to do anything he doesn't want. Take him to the canteen. Get him a cup of tea and a nice sweet cake. Leave your mother with him and go to the hospital shop. Get a pile of things, anything you think he'll fancy. Let him know he only gets them if he's a patient. I'll meet you in the canteen.'

Dick greeted Tim Walcott gaily. He was eating a pink cake with coconut icing. 'I'd like one of those,' Tim said. 'Can I get one or do you have to be a patient?'

'I'm not a patient.' Dick licked coconut from his lips. 'Nor will I be.'

'Oh, right so.' Tim shook his hand. 'I'll not be seeing you again. Pity. I thought we might enjoy a game of cards, or Ludo if you prefer. But you look like a man for whist.'

'I used to like whist,' Dick admitted.

'It's not for everyone, hospital life.' Tim bit hugely into the pink cake that Ruth had reluctantly set before him. 'Regimented, bit like army life. But it's a man's life. Only place I know these days where the men can be together and get looked after by a team of pretty ladies. They even bath you. Plus of course, you save money. All this is coming out of your own insurance. And you get presents from visitors.' He inspected the sweets, the fruit, the magazines and soft drinks Ruth had assembled. 'Look at these nice goodies. They look as if they're going to someone in hospital.'

Dick went back to the office with Tim Walcott. Ruth waited tensely with her mother until word came back to them that he was in a ward.

There had obviously been no second struggle with his

garments for he appeared very neat and composed in his pyjamas. He was looking around at his new companions, five men ranging in age from about nineteen to late sixties. He was the senior member. Apart from the teenager, who stared into space with a look of horror, the men seemed agreeable and content. The man in the next bed, good-looking and in his fifties, was telling Dick that tea would be served shortly and Dick seemed pleased with this information. 'This is Mr Arthur Ferris,' he introduced Lily to his new companion. 'We have been getting to know one another. And this is my wife, Lily.' Lily turned to shake hands with the stranger when a slap across the face sent her reeling. 'This is my wife, the bitch who had me locked up, thrown into a mad-house after fifty years of marriage.' Dick began to claw his way out of the blankets and scramble towards her. Lily did not move. She seemed completely petrified. Ruth was trying to pull her out of the way when someone rang a bell and two nurses hurried into the ward, pinning her father back by the arms. It was almost with a twinge of regret that she noted they were not the pretty ladies The Walnut had promised, but two burly and expressionless males.

12

⚜

In the night, a man screamed. Dick tried to follow the cry as if it was a complicated piece of modern music. It began with a screech like an electric saw, then dipped into a hollow of desolation. The cry's ending was ragged and frail, the tearing of a moth's wing. He could feel the man's fear. It was like dipping one's fingers into blood. Then he looked at his fingers and saw the blood. He had been carving the cries into his arm with his nails.

He understood the language of those howls. It was almost reassuring to know that the terror was shared. Real terror was not when you had walked into danger and used adrenalin to save yourself as best you could; it was when you had been delivered into peril by those you loved. It had happened before. A long time ago, when he was six. It was his first day at a new school and his mother was dressing him up with shaking fingers. 'We'll show them.'

He put his fingers over his ears, not to shut out the cries that kept him company, but the different calls from that other time, ages ago, ages, ages. He had not trusted his mother ever since, had held on to the rails of life only by imagining another woman, soft and beautiful, girl and mother. Mother to him. *Lily*.

There was a strange, sour smell in the room. Was it the smell of food or old wounds or just too many men together? Men were not meant to be together, it was not natural. An abomination in the sight of the Lord. Women were clean creatures. One to every man was a better arrangement.

How did the other men sleep? All around him were snores, grunts, snuffles. To block out the racket he tried to think of music (must ask Lily to bring a radio and earphones). He summoned up Elgar's cello concerto. The music was so familiar that he was able to play the notes with his fingers on the counterpane. Odd that no one else in the family loved beauty as he did. Possibly Ruth did; he had never asked her. He thought it unlikely. Maybe it was just as well. If Lily felt the same way she might not have looked at him.

Had she looked at him? He couldn't remember. Men were such idiots, never knew what women were thinking. Never thought about it, until it was too late. One read in the papers of men accused of rape who thought they had had the all-clear. *She said no but she meant yes.* Girls in pretty dresses. Lily had not said no but she had been a docile girl. *She said yes but she meant no.* Maybe she had never loved him, just waited her chance down the years to get rid of him. He couldn't tell. Couldn't bloody well tell. 'Shut up, you bloody fool!' he shouted at the old man who screamed. The shouting stopped and there was silence.

What was he doing here? He was among mad men. Lily had nothing to do with it. He was certain of that now. It was Ruth. Women without a man grew hard. Lily was never hard. All he had to do was get out of here and go home to his wife. If any bloody fool tried to stop him, he would knock him to the ground. He wished he was wearing a suit but beggars can't be choosers and he had a cardigan and cravat to hand. He put these on over his pyjamas and stepped on to the cold floor, tracing circles with his foot until he located his slippers. He had an urge to whistle for courage but best not to give himself away.

As he groped his way between the beds the screams began again. Such an awful sound! He could be among murderers. Perhaps that poor man *was* being murdered. He felt afraid. He had always felt afraid, all his life. Put on a brave face, a suit and tie – best bib and tucker – but no one knew the cost. At last he reached the door. He whistled under his breath as he turned the handle. Nothing happened. Damned heavy door. He held it with both hands and tugged with all his might. His heart flipped like a pancake. It was locked. At the thought of this his fear was replaced by rage. Tears poured down his face. He tugged on the door and roared. At once it opened. He could see the wan slice of corridor light. He was free. As he slipped out, a fat white ghost slid in, pushing him back. No, not a ghost, it was a ward orderly. 'Back to bed now!' The man's voice was gruff but not cruel. 'There's a good fellow.' Dick hoped he was going to come with him to keep him company but he pushed him in and locked the door from the other side.

He shuffled back to bed with tears falling down his face. He heard impatient noises from the other beds. This new commotion had woken the other men. No one would respect him now. He had lost his dignity. Without that he no longer existed. Bed. That was it. Just crawl under the blankets. As he levered himself between the sheets he encountered the shape of another man's leg. He looked up sharply. There was a man glaring at him. 'Sorry,' he said. He had come to the wrong bed. Where the hell was his own bunk?

The man in the bed put out a hand. 'Hello,' he said in a young voice. 'My name's Dick Butler.'

Dick let out a gasp and jumped back. He began to tremble all over. But it could not be him that jumped back for he was already in his bed. He had never left it. He moved further away until he backed into the next bed. Another hand touched him and he jerked away. Was this Dick Butler too? Were all the beds filled with his other selves? But then a man (nicely spoken) gave another name altogether. 'It's Arthur Ferris. That's poor Donal in your bed,' he whispered, 'Donal Quinn. If he sees an empty bed he gets into it and introduces himself by the name of the proper occupant. Back to bed, Donal!' he called out in a loud, authoritative tone. The boy scrambled away into the dark.

Dick continued to cry after he had got into bed. 'Where am I?' he cried. 'Where am I?'

'You're in hospital,' the nice man in the next bed reassured him in low tones. 'We're all in this together.'

But Dick knew that his neighbour was in a different space and that he himself was alone and in hell. Yes, that was it. He had died and gone to hell. What had he gone to hell for? He had always been a good man. Never looked at another woman. Well, *looked*, yes. Men were made like that. But nothing more. He had been faithful in his heart as well as his body. But he knew. He knew in that same heart what he had done. He had lusted after his wife. That wasn't on. That wasn't what marriage was about.

13

From the window Lily watched a ragged necklace of birds squalling with jitters as they set out on their long winter flight.

'You heard what they said, Ma.' Ruth's voice was dull with patience. 'He's not allowed visitors.'

If they looked back they would have seen the coils of chimney smoke like notes of music on the steely sky, the soft mist of pollution that cradled little houses against the glare of infinity, the occasional, terrifying fat santa exploding from points of light on the roofs of hypermarkets. Do birds have memories? Homing instincts? As the first frost silvered their wings, were they warmed by pictures of sticky fledgelings, of summer banquets of fallen apples stuffed with worms and beetles, and cat-wary afternoons of napping on new-mown hay? Did the darkness extinguish their world, leaving them dangling from the stars? No food, no water, no rest, no shelter, nothing but the painful beating of their wings. No faith or hope, only an instinct for another world, of light and sunshine and rest.

'I'm not a visitor.' Lily's voice was bleak and tight. 'I'm his wife. He needs me.' When she turned from the window her daughter put a cup of tea in her hand, and she held out the vessel like Oliver Twist until Ruth tilted the whiskey bottle.

Ruth rang the hospital daily. They were guarded, as hospitals are. He was settling in nicely. Early days. Best leave him to get adjusted (it had been a fortnight). Hard to say when. These things varied from patient to patient. She felt like Lady Macbeth. She could not wash her hands of the deed, was amazed by the weight of her action. He had been such a distant presence during her time at home – a whiff of oppression – that she was over-whelmed by the heaviness of his absence. The patriarch. The pillar of the house. She reeled at the notion that she had chauf-feured her own father to a nuthouse. And they had kept him there.

'He needs to do what the doctors say.'

The teacup was held out defiantly. 'You don't understand. Married couples . . .'

It never occurred to Lily that the vast well of understanding that marriage required might get a stiff challenge from the patience needed for parents. Ruth was determined to keep an eye on her mother, to look after her as far as possible. She had imag-ined that with Pa out of the way she would be able to make great changes to the house, get it comfortable at last. She had ear-marked a neat little kitchen, inexpensive but efficient, some pretty, cheerful curtains. She planned to get in central heating. 'It'll be a nice surprise for Pa when he gets home. I'll pay for it.'

But he wasn't out of the way. He was merely absent, leaving his women in place to keep the vigil and the guilt.

'The house is fine the way it is.' Lily had been scandalised by Ruth's proposal. 'Your father would go mad. He'd think we got rid of him just so we could go tearing his house asunder.'

'All right, Ma. It's a little palace.' Ruth felt the burden of her mother's rebuke. She knew what she had done, what both her parents must believe (for they would never have done it without her). Without having touched a single stick or brick of the place, she had indeed torn their house asunder. 'Come and stay with me while Pa's in hospital.'

'I don't like the sea,' Lily shuddered. 'It makes me cold.'

'The spare room doesn't look out on the sea. I'll put the telly in your room and you can look at that all day. We'll eat frozen dinners or go out to dinner. You need taking out of yourself.'

'I don't want taking out of myself,' Lily said. 'I want to see your father.' Underneath the truculence Ruth could sense the dread in her voice. It wasn't just that she missed the old buzzard; it was that she needed to get it out of the way. She needed to face the music.

'All right,' Ruth relented, and Lily looked at her with hope and trepidation. 'I'll take you in as soon as I've had a look at the lie of the land. Just let me go and visit him first.'

When the time came, she was surprised that her mother had prepared no home comforts, no cake or note. It was Ruth who thought to pack fresh laundry. She felt like a hypocrite. She didn't want to see him. Truth to tell, having done the awful deed and got him out of the way, she wanted it to stay that way. As with the Armageddon-on-suburbia that had followed her departure from home when she was nineteen, she believed that the fallout from the blast should have blown herself and her mother clear.

But it wasn't like that. Absent or present, he was there and he ruled.

She snaffled items from the hospital shop at random: Lucozade, peppermint creams, grapes and a photographic magazine. She carried these, along with his clean socks, handkerchiefs and underpants, up to the seventh floor. When the lift opened she rang the bell and a nurse (male) admitted her.

'Why is that door never open?' she asked him. 'I'm not outside visiting hours.'

'It's a locked ward,' the orderly told her.

'A locked ward? What does that mean? My father is seventy-eight. Do you think he's going to run amok or make a break for it?'

The young man laughed warily.

Pa sat up very straight in bed and stared stonily into space. Mr Arthur Ferris in the next bed looked abashed when he saw Ruth, as if he was somehow responsible for Pa's behaviour. Pa's glance flickered briefly towards his daughter, a flinty glimmer. He looked away again.

'Hello, Pa,' she said.

He angled his head like a bird at her voice, then reached out to his bedside table and felt for his spectacles. 'Who's that? Can't see a damned thing without them.' She sat beside him on a red rexine-covered seat that looked like a commode and waited while he inspected his presents. He handed back the grapes. 'You take these. I don't like them because of the pips.'

'How are you, Pa?'

'Ruth . . .' He peered into her face. 'You've got lines on your face like a woman. Where did the years go? Remember when you were a little girl?'

'*I* remember,' she said dryly.

He reached for her hand. His jaws were sucked in with remorse. 'You think I don't?'

'I don't think you even noticed me until I was a teenager. Then all we did was row.'

'I noticed you. There was nothing I could do. Men didn't understand children then. And then . . . then . . . you were your mother's child.' He bumped her hand gently on the counterpane. 'You haven't forgiven me, have you? The things we do to children.'

'No,' she said. 'I've never forgiven you.'

He stroked her hand as if trying to iron away any creases. 'It's getting born into the world – that's the painful thing. You never recover, really. Don't know how it is that when our own children come along, we can't protect them. That reminds me of something, Ruth, something I have to tell you.' He frowned, his forehead folding in on itself as he searched his memory. 'The world's very cold when you're new to it. I'm not talking about hospital delivery, women's stuff. I mean, adjustment to the world around you, the family you grow up with, the people you're stuck with.'

Never in a million years would she have thought to hear her pa speaking like this. 'What did you want to tell me, Pa?' she asked gently. He was silent for a while and then began some rambling yarn. 'When I was six or seven my parents had a bit of bad luck. Had to sell up and move house. Don't remember the old house. I'm told it was a decent place. We moved to a roughish neighbourhood. I was sent to the local Christian Brothers' school. My mother was a snob. She hated the new house and all her neighbours, said she would never stoop to their standards. This meant that I was sent off to that rough school, where boys kicked each other's heads in to pass the time, with long ringlets, a lace collar, velvet breeches and buttoned boots.' His finger, which had been stroking her hand, now rasped in agitation, almost taking her skin away. 'They called me Violet. I stole things from my mother, tried to give away my lunch to get them to use my proper name, or even a proper boy's nick-name – Stinko, Golliers, Brownarse, Wanker. As long as I went to that school, they called me Violet. Even the Brothers called me Violet.'

'Oh, Pa.' She leaned across and gave him a light kiss on the cheek. He threw his arms around her and buried his head in her shoulder. He stayed like this until one of the domestic staff –

plump, middle-aged, female – arrived with a tray of lunch. He detached himself and gave his attention to some thick scarlet soup and slices of white bread.

'Is he behaving himself?' Ruth asked the woman.

'He's an old dote,' she said.

On her way out she stopped at the doctor's office to ask about her father. 'He seems well,' she said cautiously.

'Yes, he is under control,' said the little dry man.

She sat down. 'What does that mean?'

He looked at her with distaste, though whether a distaste for all patients' relatives, for women, or for people who made themselves at home in his office, she could not decide.

'Your father is a manic depressive,' he told her. 'Difficult to tell how long this condition has been present, but his mood swings are now extreme. We need to keep him under observation, but as long as his treatment continues I see no reason why he shouldn't remain stable.'

'What treatment?' She wanted to gather as much information as possible for Ma.

'He is being treated with lithium salts.' He noted her look of query. 'Lithium is a metal, the lightest known alkaline metal.'

'That's it? It's as simple as that? A little lead in his pencil and he's right as rain?' Ruth wanted to leap over the barricade of the desk and kiss the dour little man.

The doctor winced. 'It is not lead. It is by no means simple and it is not a cure. It is a treatment. We do not expect miracles, but we are cautiously optimistic.'

Ma walked slowly towards him. 'Come here, love.' He held out his hands but she kept her bag before her as a barrier. As she neared the bed he burst into tears. 'I've made an awful bloody fool of myself.' He looked at her with his wide blue eyes. 'Awful bloody mess, love. I don't know what to do. Awful. Worse than diarrhoea. Mind gone west.'

Ma touched his hair and took her hand away quickly as if he was a horse that might bite.

'I've been sick,' he said piteously, afraid she did not take him seriously.

'Yes, I know.' She sat down, still cradling her bag. 'That's why you're in hospital.'

'I missed you,' he said.

'I missed you.'

'Would you like a chocolate? Ruth said you were coming so I bought you chocolates.' He fetched them from his locker. 'Which sort would you like?'

'You pick one.' She opened her mouth obediently.

He leaned across with the sweet, but instead of putting it in her mouth, he seized her face in both hands and kissed her. Lily's panic-stricken eye took in the men in the ward, the gape of the boy of nineteen. 'Dick!' She struggled free. 'There are people!'

Dick watched her indulgently and then smiled at Ruth. 'Your mother's shy. Wait outside, like a good girl.'

It was half an hour before Ma emerged. She looked shell-shocked. Her lipstick was streaked. She jerked slightly as the door to the ward swung into its lock behind her.

'Are you all right?' Ruth patted the smaller woman. 'He's a bit excitable still. We'll get used to it.'

Lily gave her a long look, patient or resigned.

'Come on, Ma. You look a bit shook. Let's treat ourselves to Irish Coffees in the Shelbourne.'

They sat on huge sofas, overlooking Saint Stephen's Green. Girls in black uniform hurried past with tiered platters of crustless sandwiches and cream cakes. Americans called out for club sandwiches. An author sat, bullfrog-eyed, waiting to be recognised. Lily, sifting rather than sipping her Irish coffee, as if trying to extract the alcoholic content from the froth surmounting it, seemed in a kind of trance.

'Well, Ma,' Ruth prodded gently.

'I don't think there's any whiskey in this,' Lily said. 'They do that, you know, in hotels, try and short-change people with an Irish coffee.'

'It's in there,' Ruth promised. 'You'll know when you've drunk it.'

'Well, I don't think mine's got much whiskey in it.' Lily was polite but obdurate. 'I'd like a small whiskey in a glass.'

Ruth beckoned a waitress. Hell. She had built up Ma's hopes too high. 'We've got to make allowances,' she explained. 'They haven't got the balance right yet with his medication. Poor old devil seems to be swirling around in a time machine. Right now, it seems like he's about fourteen.'

'What do you mean?' Ma looked bewildered.

'He's fairly boisterous.' Ruth began to laugh. 'What did he do in there? Try to get you into his bed?'

'We talked.' Lily still had her dazed look. She glanced around nervously, as if she was afraid Ruth was making an exhibition of herself, but she was only on the lookout for the waitress with her proper drink. 'Ruth, married love . . .'

Ruth watched her with amusement. 'Yes?'

'It's not like ordinary affairs that come and go.'

'No, Ma.'

When the drink came, Lily drank it neat in disapproving, ladylike sips, which nonetheless seemed to deplete it in no time. As always, drink made her talkative. 'Marriage is blessed by God, which means that along with the difficulties you are given . . .'

'. . . The strength to bear them. Patience, tolerance, forgiveness,' Ruth recited the old litany.

'No, what I mean, Ruth, is that in an uncommitted relationship, romance runs its course. When you get tired of the other person, that's an end to it.'

'Sounds good to me.'

'As you know, Father and I had our difficulties early on but then we became pals. That is no longer the case.'

'I'm sorry, Ma. I shouldn't have laughed. All those wasted years.'

'Well, maybe they were.' Ma had her martyred look, jaws set, eyes brimming with nobility. 'But my generation was very inhibited. And now, you see, Pa's inhibitions have been lifted. He's a different person, Ruth. As I was saying about marriage. Along with the difficulties . . . We can talk to each other about anything.'

'And what is it that you talk about?' Ruth smiled indulgently.

Ma spoke with the stunned and superior look of one declared unto by an angel. 'About love.'

'It's as if he's on some character-enhancement drug.' Ruth sloshed out wine for her old friend, Max Feldman. 'It's not just mood-enhancement. His whole character has intensified. He's turned into a bit of an old devil – quite a lovable one, but rather racy. And the astonishing thing is that Ma loves it. Ma who was always so proper, never even cared for sex, or so she said! My own view is that she really was a sexy woman but Pa was such a dry old stick that he put out the fires. Although obviously not entirely.' She knotted the claret-coloured velvet dressing gown, her post-coital luxury and one of her few concessions to fashion. 'You know, my mother has made a diet of virtue. She looked around the table of her life and saw that there were no treats at all – no finger food, nothing lip-smacking or juicy. So she poured herself out a great big bowl of virtue, said "This is lovely", ate it up, poured some more and has been chewing away ever since.'

Max smiled at her through snake-like eyes which contained an agreeable mix of selfishness, intelligence and sex. 'Do you know . . . ' he reached for the wine bottle and gave an approving nod at the label ' . . . that after bed, you talk even more than usual about your mother?'

14

Remember in old movies, how the screen would go black leaving only a central image in a circle? That's how it was, Ruth thought. When Ma's eyes met Pa's and she tottered towards him, the whole damn, grim ward disappeared. There was only the two of them, breathless and happy. Oh, happy. Ruth didn't think Ma had ever been really happy in her early married life. It was as if some suspended action had taken place between their first romantic meeting and this final emotional connection; like an old love story where a woman is parted from her lover and waits a lifetime for him and they finally meet up again when they are old.

Ruth watched the crazy love affair in awe and even some envy, for she was a part of the vanished scene. She didn't exist for them in their rapturous sphere. Who knew where they were or what they saw?

What *did* Pa see? Lily never thought about her appearance. She had the slightly squashed look of someone who has been dodging the blows all her life. She wore slacks, stretch polos, lace-up shoes. She disliked any form of social life because it meant you had to dress up and go to the hairdresser. She had been a lovely-looking woman but hadn't minded getting old. Old age was a fine excuse to wear comfortable clothes.

Ruth did not ask the same question of Ma. Ma had never really liked men. She did not find them comfortable to be with. Bound by her age and generation to a certain level of respect for the hairy sex, she still resented their authority. She liked children, she liked innocence. Pa was now an eager puppy, wagging his tail to pieces as she shuffled towards him in her anorak and trainers. She would have been ill-at-ease with excessive exuberance in a man or woman, but everyone loved it in a child or puppy.

As to love, Ruth couldn't comment. She believed people talked an awful lot of rubbish about love, either lying through their teeth or using the word the way Victorians put frilly skirts on piano legs, as a fancy cover-up for lust. There was no doubt that Ma was like a kitten up a tree, but perhaps it wasn't only Pa. Maybe she had also fallen in love with her new life. She had at last achieved the perfect existence – a life entirely free of compromise. She did not have to live with a man and yet she wasn't alone. She was a married woman with a long and unblemished record like a senior girl scout, and yet she did not have to settle for the eked-out emotions of veterans of wedlock. Whenever she saw Pa it was at the fever pitch of courtship. And then she could go home again.

She visited him nearly every day, taking a complicated series of buses. Twice a week, Ruth drove her. She enjoyed the convenience of being collected by car and having lunch in a nice old city pub, but when the door to the ward was unlocked, her face registered the tug of loyalty, the obligation to express her gratitude to Ruth and the desire to be alone with Pa. Whatever it was that was going on between those two, Ruth knew she couldn't compete. She handed Pa his bag of sweets, kissed his cheek and then went out the imprisoning entrance and down to the canteen, where she drank tea and read a paper until Ma reeled in, looking proud and punch-drunk.

As a routine developed, boredom set in and she found herself doodling on a paper napkin while she waited. Why were all institutions so . . . *institutional?* Why were patients on the highest level separated from the canteen by seven storeys? If the aim was to bring them back to normality, surely there should be a feeling of everyday living in the place of healing. She began making sketches for coffee-shops-cum-libraries that might be set up on, say, every second floor – informal, easy-going areas such as you might see in a secondhand bookshop, with old pine furniture and user-friendly sofas, flowery curtains, a smell of coffee and some nice home-made cakes or biscuits. Books could be donated by patients who had finished with them. It would be a homely place for relatives to visit. If the hospitals could not afford to staff them, or even to organise them, volunteers would easily be found. And why not a massage and aromatherapy centre? What about a beauty shop? A soothing water garden with patio seating so that people could sit out in summer? Next time she came in she would prowl around and see if any useful space was going begging. She might make some proper sketches and submit them to the health authorities. Her tea cooled at her elbow as she idly redesigned the canteen. It was an uninspiring place, with no nooks or relaxing areas. Young patients drank coffee and stared into space, while people up from the country grimly shovelled large plates of food into themselves to prepare for the ordeal of visiting their crazy kin. The patients, she found out from scraps of conversation with table companions, were a mixed bag – alcoholics, schizophrenics, drug abusers, depressives. Not what you could really call mad, and yet each of their families must have faced whatever sort of nightmare Ma had faced to reach the end of their tether and hand their flesh and blood into this latter-day bedlam.

She was well aware that her plans were a pipe dream; hospitals were never really designed for patients. All the same, she was enjoying herself. Enjoying herself. She considered this odd notion and discovered that when she thought about her old parents, sitting up there moony-eyed together, she felt only enormous relief. For a while there, before Pa had been stabilised, she had been pitched back into childhood, into that rollercoaster scramble for a place in the family and a share of affection. It was like falling over the edge of a steep cliff, tumbling down the pebbles towards the sea. Now that she was safely returned to the top, she could go back to her own life.

She looked at her diary and saw that there was a march on that afternoon – a protest against the planned closure of the city centre hospitals. How could a city have a centre without hospitals? And she could do with a good march. When she had dropped Ma home she returned to the city. She felt a pleasant surge of adrenalin as she joined a group of nurses, doctors, volunteer workers and took up the battle cry: 'More healing, less wheeling, less dealing!' A faint but exhilarating sense of menace crept in when the march was joined by a mob of inner city residents with their numerous offspring. Two small boys appeared on horseback, their unkempt steeds harnessed with ropes. The horses skittered, the crowd contracted and Ruth found herself unavoidably trampling some lesser mortal.

'Sorry!' She turned to offer assistance and found that she had stepped on Tim Walcott. 'What are you doing here?' she demanded ungraciously.

'I am a medic,' he said.

'I thought you had a private practice,' she said.

'I have.' He was busy trying to straighten out his placard. 'Christ, I wouldn't want to get in the way of your solo mission to save the world.'

'Sorry,' she said again.

'That's all right,' he conceded affably. 'What's the word on your father?'

The police had arrived and the crowd had straightened itself into disciplined lines but the chant rose to a full-throated cry. 'He's a manic depressive,' she shouted across the city. Tim nodded and threw his voice into the chant.

'That's not too bad, is it?' Ruth cried over the crowd. 'I mean, lots of people suffer from depression.'

He didn't answer. His spectacles glinted as his eyes darted over the crowd. To her surprise, he reached out and took her hand. 'Run, Ruth,' he said quietly, as a flaming bottle flew over the heads of the protestors towards the police. She looked around quickly and saw that a group of small boys, protected by a flank of burly inner city dwellers, had armed themselves with missiles. As another weapon sailed towards the police they began to move forward and the march sagged suffocatingly in on itself.

Tim extricated them with remarkable dexterity. She saw that he had a small girl by the other hand. 'I don't know whose she is, but I couldn't leave her on her own in there,' he said. 'Wait here. I'll hand her over to the cops, give them something worthwhile to do.'

'Wait for what?' she wondered, but she had been winded by the crush and needed time to regain her breath. He was back in a minute. She allowed him to lead her into a café and accepted a cup of pale and sudsy coffee.

'How's your mother?'

'Fine, actually, although I still worry about her.'

'She worries about you.'

'About me?' Ruth sounded surprised.

He shrugged. 'No family. Not settled down. I suppose she thinks you're not one thing or another – neither a frivolous fashion plate nor a happily married woman.'

'Ha!' Ruth said. 'You've just perpetrated an oxymoron. Happily married!'

He laughed. 'I've seen happy marriages. Not often, granted. Most people try it at least once. What makes you different?'

'I remember as a teenager reading something Bertrand Russell said — that the problems in marriages arose when husbands and wives became one another's policemen. That really gave me the creeps.'

'Corny old Kahlil Gibran said much the same thing.'

'Who?' Ruth wondered.

'Haven't you ever read *The Prophet*? No, I don't suppose so.' He gazed into her eyes and recited like a child:

Give your hearts, but not into each other's keeping.
For only the band of Life can contain your hearts.
And stand together yet not too near together:
For the pillars of the temple stand apart,
And the oak tree and the cypress grow not in each other's shadow.

Ruth made a face but she felt strangely moved. 'I'm glad to see we think alike, even if our reading tastes differ.'

'No, Ruth, we don't. I've always wanted just one person of my own. I never had any ambition to be a cop, though — not even a member of the marital police — which brings me back to why I wanted to talk to you. It's about your father. Has anyone explained to you about manic depression?'

'It's all right,' she told him. 'I realise he probably is a bit dotty, but they've got him on lithium and he's high as a kite. Ma's quite high too, as a matter of fact.'

'They didn't explain, did they?' He shook his head and spooned more sugar into his coffee. 'Hospitals never do. Being high as a kite is just one of the phases of manic depression. When sufferers are in elation they are highly emotional and given to spending large sums of money, quite often on total strangers. But then they suffer a slump and go through a phase of chaos and despair and think everyone's against them. Even the people they love and trust.'

'It's not a phase,' Ruth said stubbornly. 'They've got him stabilised.'

'That's good. But it may not be the end of the story. Treatment by medication is aimed at inhibiting the manic side of the character, but when the mania gets damped down it also stamps on the creative personality. That can cause other problems.'

'He's fine. He's happy. I've never seen Ma so happy.'

'Well, I'm sure you know all about it. My own view is that manic depressives need therapy along with medication. The shifts of mood can be too radical to cope with. One moment you think you're God, the next you're nothing. And hospitals don't often look for root causes. Manic depression can be a coping strategy for something that's basically too hot for the sufferer to handle – maybe going back to early childhood. I'm just saying he's not responsible. I'm just saying, if you need help, Ruth, I'm here.'

Ruth began to be irritated by him. 'I thought doctors weren't supposed to advertise.'

Tim Walcott stood up. 'I wasn't talking about business.' He raked his pockets and flung an embarrassing quantity of small change on the table. 'In a screwed-up country like this a shrink is never short of work. I was talking about friendship, but that's the one thing you don't seem to know about.'

She felt shaken after that and had to go and telephone her snake-eyed acquaintance, whose vocation was the avoidance of domestic encumbrance, whose special skill was a nifty manipulation of the 'e' zones. 'Hi, Max? Why don't you come and see me?'

'What's on offer?'

'Mediocre moussaka or a very good fuck.'

'Most women will still run like little dogs with stones thrown at them when a man says: You are unfeminine, aggressive, you are unmanning me.' Lily was reading the introduction to *The Golden Notebook.* 'It is my belief,' Doris Lessing had written, 'that any woman who marries, or takes seriously in any way at all, a man who uses this threat, deserves everything she gets. For such a man is a bully, does not know anything at all about the world he lives in, or its history . . .'

She put her finger on the page and turned the volume carefully upside down on the table. She knew absolutely that Lessing was right, but she also knew she was not absolutely right. For one thing, she had married Dick long before anyone had thought about men's attitudes to women. And the other thing feminism had never come to terms with was that men of Dick's age were incapable of change. Their prejudices were set into them, like the rings of a tree.

Doris Lessing had been Ruth's legacy. After her daughter left home Lily had gone to her room to gather up the souvenirs of her childhood. She had not been surprised, not really, to find that there was nothing of childhood there, nothing but rows of dry and dusty books. A few of these were girls' stories, and there was a time in her early teens when she read romances, but the shelves were crammed with books relating to the structure of buildings and the rebellion of women. Ruth had never spoken to Lily about her feminist library and Lily was distressed to think of her daughter, so young, immersed in heresy before her life as a woman had even begun. She had made up her mind to shut the door on that room and forget about it. But then, with the grim fascination with which people slow down to inspect the carnage in a traffic accident, she found she had to go back into the room and sample her daughter's diet of anger.

The first books she had read were *The Female Eunuch* and *Sexual Politics* and they had set up in her a resentment that burned like a rash. But it wasn't all about anger. She had made friends with Simone de Beauvoir, Doris Lessing and Betty Friedan. So much of the minefield of life had been cleared by these brave women; minutely they examined the flaws in the structure of marriage that made a boy and girl into master and slave, that demonised female ambition and yoked clever girls to domestic service, that compelled men and women to stunt one another's lives and destroy their freedom. There were men who thought about and suffered for these things too. That had been a tremendous revelation. When she discovered this, she went at once to Dick to explain what damage had been done to them. Poor Dick had been upset. He thought she had turned against him, that she was complaining about *their* marriage. She had not mentioned feminism to him after that, and when she looked out for the new feminist books in the library, she read them when he was not around. She had no wish to provoke him. That was why she could not discuss her huge discovery with Ruth. Ruth would use it as an excuse to confront her, to try and try and make her change her life with Pa. She wasn't interested in changing her life. She only wanted to make sense of it.

She went to the oven where the delicious smell of a Denny's steak and kidney pie told her that lunch was ready. It came in a tin, and you only had to take off the top with a tin opener and pop it in the oven and the pastry lid rose, crisp and golden. And while it was baking, it heated the kitchen. Since the day Dick went into hospital, she had not peeled a potato nor taken out the frying pan. Mercifully, she had almost forgotten the sticky, cloying sensation of semolina. She had done no ironing, as all the clothes she wore were of the easy-care variety, and no bed-making, for as soon as she got used to sleeping alone she slept so soundly she barely disturbed the blankets. She ate Ryvita for breakfast in order to avoid the annoyance of bread that would go stale, and had it again with a boiled egg for tea, or sometimes with cheese and slices of onion and a dash of Yorkshire Relish.

She had got used to housework over the years, but could never really see the point of it. Men liked to see women performing small useless chores all day for it was what they had seen their mothers do. No man alive could bear to watch a woman sitting and thinking. They imagined she must be plotting. It was why there had been so few profound women thinkers throughout history, or why so few had been recorded. Some might have said that women could do their thinking while they got on with the ironing or wrung the sheets or made the bread. But they couldn't, because if they dared to think too deeply while thus engaged, they would go mad. At this last word, she shifted uncomfortably. All the same, she supposed a few women had gone mad, just from the futility of their lives, and people had put it down to menopause. Was this what had happened to Dick? Was it just the sense of futility?

She remembered with pleasure that it was a visiting day. She struck out her pale lips with two scarlet swipes of lipstick, armed herself with the black folder Dick had asked for and set out on her date.

15

The photograph shows a girl on a beach. Stretched out on a towel on the shingle, she wears a striped bathing costume with cuffs on the thighs, like cycle shorts. Her ripe breasts look provocative under the stretchy horizontal bands of colour, but her legs, very slender and shapely, are pinned together and pointing shyly. Her eyes are closed and she has a blissful look, half amused, as if she is posing or the photographer is teasing her.

Dick picks at the celluloid nooks and eases the picture out of its page in the album. He studies the back, where it has been catalogued in neat hand-writing: 'Bettystown, 1938'. 'Glorious summer. Strawberries as big as apples. We went to the beach on my motorbike. Cold for you, maybe. Lovely for me, your arms around me all the way and other men looking. Jealous. Walked along the beach to warm up. Togs and sandwiches in a bag. Then dropped down beside each other in the sun, easy as two old marrieds, just lay there letting the sun soak in. You never knew, did you, I used to pretend that's what we were, two old marrieds. Pretended I was lying beside you in a bed. I won't tell you what went through my head. I could smell your sun-warmed skin and from the corner of my eye I saw your little figure. When I jumped up and said, "Race you to the sea!" I had to do that, jump into icy water! How lovely you were. I couldn't wait. But it wasn't just John Thomas, you know. Not like nowadays. Oh, he was very eager, and he'd have been no man if he wasn't. It was the simple happiness of knowing you weren't some other man's. My chest almost burst with it.'

Lily could not remember the details of each date as he could, nor the feelings he described. She couldn't even clearly recall the girl in the picture. It was like looking at an old cigarette ad. Dick's memory was as clear as a bell. Could someone really recite the minutiae of a day more than fifty years in the past? Maybe he just made up a story for each of the pictures. For Lily the fascination lay in the way the particular pose of a photograph would strike a note of memory, one which might have nothing to do with the event depicted. She remembered, for instance, the first day she really noticed Dick. She was in someone's house at a party. Vera Daly! And Vera had broken off her conversation to watch Dick's progress upstairs, probably to the bathroom. 'Look at the walk of Dick Butler. He really fancies himself.' She had noticed the grace of his long back, and a loneliness in it too, as if it needed to be touched. For the rest of the evening she kept watching out for him. He was in the middle of telling someone a joke when he turned to look at her. She found her eyes resting on his pale features, boyish and slightly mischievous, on the dark curls that had to be pressed back from his forehead with hair tonic. She had the lovely languorous cat-like feeling that she had only to wait for him to come to her, and that he would take care of her.

When they came to a picture of him sitting on his motorbike (long scarf, goggles, leather jacket), she remembered the day the bike broke down and they had to take the bus home. Neither of them had any money, but instead of explaining this to the conductor, Dick kept repeating, '*Initzigotrova!*', pretending he was a foreigner who spoke no English. The money collector appealed to Lily but she shook her head and tried not to laugh as Dick repeated more angrily, '*Initzigotrova!*' In the end they laughed so much they had to get off the bus and walk home. 'What does it mean?' she spluttered. 'Does it mean anything?'

'It means,' he tapped the side of his nose, 'Dick's a resourceful fellow. Stick with Dick.' She had a stab of memory, almost like one of alarm: that was the day he asked her to marry him. They had arrived back at her house, sticky and weary, and she brought him to the kitchen for tea and bread and jam. 'Stick with Dick?' he had appealed, in his clownish and earnest way. And she had promised him that she would.

In his youth Dick had been a keen photographer. The catalogue of their courtship was so thorough it was as if the older, more obsessive Dick had pursued the young couple like a private detective. He had caught them dancing and cycling, out on windy walks that tossed their hair, and sun that made them squint, sprawled in deck chairs with tea on a table in someone's garden, huddled with gangly groups, feeding monkeys in the zoo.

The photographs were to be rationed, one page per visit. 'Time cheats you,' Dick explained. 'Happens to everyone. You're given this great happiness once in your lifetime when you meet the person you love, and you think you have only to tie it up, secure it, and it will be yours for ever. No one tells you. The real ecstasy is in the waiting. Wonderful days. Gone in a flash. We hardly had them at all.'

Lily remembered reading somewhere that happiness was like a bird in the hand. You set it free, or it died. She had another memory, piercing and disconcerting. A few days before their wedding she and Dick were in their new house, hanging curtains. Dick was putting in a pelmet with a screwdriver and she was holding a torch. As she stood watching him (his back again) a thought swooped in like a pirate. *I don't want to marry him.* It was such an awful thought that she couldn't bear to consider it. Was it him, or did she just not want to marry? She couldn't say anything, not with her new suit bought and the hotel room booked for cake and sherry.

'We'll go back!' Dick had announced one day and Lily looked alarmed until he explained that the trip was to be taken via memory. His idea was that Lily should bring in the old photo album. They hadn't opened it in more than forty years. 'You can't concentrate on a book or television in a place like this. Started me thinking about the old days, just you and me, no responsibilities, no family, thank God. I made up my mind. Long way, but the train still goes there. This time we won't get distracted by passing towns. Won't be in any hurry to get there. Slow train going nowhere and the blinds pulled down.'

For Lily it was a fascinating journey which involved neither packing nor boredom nor harmful sun. The surprise of seeing their young selves there, pristine under dust, was like finding some delicate flower in a neglected part of the garden. She could not tell if the past had been as Dick said. If it had not been, then it should have been. She had the feeling that Dick had been a bit callow back then. If he had loved her as much as he now said, he would not have had the words to express it. Now he was all words, nothing but words, and the pieces of the puzzle could be assembled at leisure. She didn't feel self-conscious about being old, or about him being old and talking in this heartfelt way. The girl with the big breasts and modest legs was still inside her, she had always known that. And if she had been insecure then, she was insecure now. Let her have her romance at full volume. Better late than never.

On the days when Ruth drove her home, she would ask: 'What do you talk about?' It amused Lily to be addressed by her daughter as if she, Lily, was a girl returning from a date. What did people talk about on dates? Themselves, their hopes and memories. The self-indulgence of these interludes after the long-drawn-out selflessness of marriage was an unsought balm, an enchanted holding off of heaven. Two months ago she had been quite ready for death (although perfectly prepared to wait her turn). Less than a month ago, she had prayed in that long night for her own husband to slaughter her. Now, when she read out the deaths in the newspaper to Dick (he always asked for those first, before the crimes and the goings-on of married celebrities), she felt the grace of her own survival and tagged on to her devotions a request for a stay of tenure, like a child who prays that they won't die until after Christmas.

'So what are you planning?' Ruth asked.

'Wait, dear.' Lily was watching a serial on television. She gave it her fullest attention. 'Get yourself a cup if you'd like some tea.' She brandished the whiskey bottle amiably.

Over the past few weeks Ruth had watched the change in her mother. She was growing sleek and almost assertive. She no longer felt the need to please or justify. When the programme ended, she remained intent until the credits had run, and then turned down the volume with a gentle 'don't go away' gesture. 'I like *Neighbours*. I know all the people. Now, what were you saying?'

'I asked you if you had any plans for Christmas.'

'Christmas?' Lily looked as if she had just been asked if she had any plans for paragliding. 'That's a long way off.'

'Less than three weeks.'

'Is it?'

'Oh, Ma! You've been bumping into fairy lights every time you go to the hospital. You can't say you didn't notice.'

The old Ma would have apologised and laughed unhappily. The new one said she had better things to do than look at Christmas lights. She had been looking at them for three-quarters of a century and she didn't suppose they had changed. 'You want to know what I do on all those bus journeys? I pray. I say prayers for your pa.'

'Sorry, Ma, but it won't go away, you know. Why don't you come and stay with me? You shouldn't be on your own at Christmas.'

'Why don't you stay with me?' Lily enjoyed Ruth's dismayed glance around the comfortless, paraffin-smelling kitchen.

'We could go away,' Ruth said. 'I'm sure there's still time to book one of those package things in a nice country hotel.'

'Don't be foolish, Ruth. You know perfectly well your father will be expecting me on Christmas Day. Why don't you stop worrying about me? You can see I'm quite happy as I am.'

Why didn't she? It was the niggling feeling that unless she had both parents under her control, something would happen. Ridiculous! Pa was the crazy one. Ma had never done anything wild in her life, except maybe to marry him.

16

Considering how little interest she had in it, it was odd that she found herself mentioning Christmas to Dick.

He was looking at a sunny picture of three people on a picnic, Dick, Lily and another girl. They presumed that a second man was out of sight, behind the camera.

'Look at that weather,' Dick said. 'Always sunny. I don't know what the weather's like now. I've lost track of time. Don't know what time of year it is.'

'It's almost Christmas, Dick.'

'Is it? Is it Christmas?' His face lit up at the mention of the word.

'Do you remember that girl's name?' Lily peered closely at the picture. 'Josie Searson, was it?'

Lily was wearing a summer frock which looked pale grey with darker grey blossoms, but Dick recalled it as light almond green with pink flowers, the flushed pink of forced rhubarb. And he remembered her shoes, new cream wedge heels, that she had worried about when they walked through a field. 'At one point I had to pick you up and carry you. Your neck smelled like apples. And your skin, beneath the green and the pink, so pale it seemed to glow. Christmas? Could I come home for Christmas?'

'You'll have Christmas here!' She could have kicked herself for mentioning it. 'I'll have it here with you. I don't bother with all that at home any more.'

He nodded sadly, followed her finger back to the glazed mono-chrome images smiling through dappled shadows of trees that would be graceful long after they were gone. There was a cloth spread on the grass and some items of simple food. In those days people didn't bother with bottles of wine and continental salads. Dick identified each item with the same rapture as her apple-smelling skin. 'Sardine sandwiches. Hard-boiled eggs. Some sort of small cakes with jam and coconut that Josie had brought. I've never had them since but I've never forgotten them. We could have them for Christmas.'

'He wants to come home,' Lily said.

Ruth was making a supper of scrambled eggs and smoked salmon for her mother, who endured it. She did not care for uncooked fish.

'For Christmas. Just Christmas. But I said no.'

The younger woman set down the bowl of eggs carefully, as if the foreboding percussion of her heart might curdle them. 'Ma, I want you to do something for me. Tell Pa you're spending Christmas with me – at my flat. Just in case this clever notion crops up again, that will put an end to it. He would rather spend Christmas in prison than with me.'

'That place is not much different to prison.'

'Tell me something, Lily love.'

'Yes, Dick.'

'Do you think I'm mad? Look into my eyes now and tell me if you think I'm mad. I need to know. These conversations in the past few weeks have been precious to me, more precious than anything in my life. I need to know if you think they are the ravings of a mad man.'

'I think your mind has never been more clear.'

'That is all I needed to know.'

'Look, Dick! We've come to the wedding.' She was filled with pity when she looked at the stiffly posed figures, like children dressed up as soldiers. This was the point where adult life was laid upon them. The fluid girl and dreaming boy would not return. Dick knew it too. He lost interest in the album, even though there were a few nice pictures of Ruth further on. The black cover was brought down. His speckled hand laid upon it. Lily was glad to see that he did not seem depressed by this conclusion. He smiled at her. 'I'm looking forward to it.'

'What, Dick?'

'Christmas.'

Ruth should have known something was up. Ma's devil-may-care stance had slipped. She had a furtive and wraithlike air and she had reassumed an old habit of setting down objects very gently as though any sound might set off an alarm. Ruth had brought sherry and a box of mince pies to lend a hint of festivity to the house. She put two pies under the grill to warm. 'Well, that's Christmas out of the way. I've done my shopping and booked our lunch in town. I picked up a few treats for Pa.'

She could never understand why her parents used to make such a fuss about the festival. Ruth did all her shopping in Caviston's of Sandycove. While they made up her list of pheasants and smoked salmon and cheese and a few extra treats like quails' eggs and Manx kippers, she raided the shelves for nice little boxes of continental chocolates, biscuits, exotic jams and bottles of oil or olives for her friends. Then she went to The Queen's in Dalkey, loaded up at the off-licence and rewarded herself with a glass of wine and a crab crostini by the fire in the pub next door. She was going to have her own celebration with friends on Christmas Eve, and on Christmas morning would bring Ma in to see Pa and later they would have lunch in the Shelbourne. 'I won't see you then for nearly a week,' she told Ma as she unpacked a few extra rations she had brought for her parents. 'I'm staying with friends in Kilkenny until New Year's Eve and then I have to be back in town for a party.'

She enjoyed Christmas in her raffish way. She had never liked it at home as a child. In spite of the obvious effort her parents put in, the whole event had been fraught with tension and the exhaustion that accompanies stress. And she was disconcerted to note that as soon as she left home Christmas just vanished from her parents' house. Ma and Pa bought a little lop-sided tinsel tree which they placed on top of the television. They would buy a small piece of ham or pork and a shop trifle, and that was it. Had the entire overwhelming enterprise been for her benefit alone? Had they sighed with relief when released from this fiefdom?

'I bought cooked spiced beef for Pa.' She was pleased with herself. She had thought of everything, and with scarcely any effort. 'Will I put it in the fridge?'

Ma's hands rose in a gesture of alarm and then sank in one of futility.

There was a chicken there, a trunk of unseasonal broccoli in a condom of cellophane. Mauve squares of ham glistened in their plastic pack and a pink trifle in a plastic tub looked hot under its coif of cream. A small turf-coloured cake was staked with a jagged scrap of plastic holly. A jar of pickled beetroot and a net of tangerines were also chilling.

'We're going out, Ma. What's all this for?' Ruth knew Ma never cooked for herself.

'It's only two days. He'll go back on Boxing Day.'

'Ma, no!' Ruth slammed the fridge door shut. She was so tired of being the tyrant. 'Don't even think of it. He's well and happy in hospital. You know what he was like before he went in.'

'It's all settled,' she said unhappily. 'I want him home.'

'He's manipulating you, but he doesn't even know what he's doing.'

Lily bowed her head, her old self again, squashed and stubborn. As when Dick had bullied her about the holiday arrangements, she found she was unable to utter a single word. Giving in usually seemed the easiest thing to do at the time. It looked as if it would end the fuss. Instead it usually made way for some worse complication.

'This isn't kind, you know, Ma,' Ruth lectured. 'When someone is sick you have to be responsible and not just indulgent. The kind thing is to ensure that he is kept in the state where we can love and respect him.'

Ma was no fool. Her expression as her daughter spoke was close to despair. 'It's too late,' she said.

Ruth sighed. She released the martyred mince pies from the grill and cut off the burnt bits. She could find no sherry glasses and poured the tea-coloured syrup into tumblers. She didn't like sweet drinks, but she knocked it back. 'Wait a minute!' As the sickening syrup rolled down her throat, a sweet thought came into her head. 'When Pa went into hospital he had to sign those papers. He had to commit himself. Remember?'

Ma winced and gulped her sherry.

'I don't know too much about hospital regulations, but as far as I know, someone else would have to sign him out. Just don't sign the papers, Ma.'

'I already did,' Ma said.

Ruth stormed into the hospital. She ran up the stairs to burn off some wrath before barging into the doctor's office. 'My mother says my father is coming home for Christmas.'

He asked her name and gave unhurried attention to some papers on his desk. 'That would appear to be so.'

'But you said yourself that he was far from well. Is he better?'

'Ah! There are no miracle cures.'

'Will he be all right at home? Do you think he'll be all right?'

The doctor watched her with interest, this big aggressive woman felled by a wayward will o' the wisp. Children of the damned. Offshoots of imbalance. Cause and effect. 'Only if he takes his medication.'

'In that case, do you really think it is a good idea for him to leave here?'

He made a spire of his fingers and propped his chin upon it. 'That would not be my judgement, no.'

'But you run the joint.' Her anger was a dry ball behind her breast-bone. 'Why the hell are you letting him out?'

'This is not a joint and it is not a prison. Your father came here of his own free will and your mother is claiming him, out of hers.'

When Pa saw her he gave her a hangdog look and patted her hand. 'We haven't had much time alone lately, have we?'

She kept her distance. She had to retain some fight. 'Pa, there's been a mistake. Ma says you want to come home for Christmas. It's not a good idea. I've spoken to the doctor and he says he doesn't advise it. You know you've been sick. You need to be in hospital.'

She felt like a boxer dancing, ready to field the blows. He watched her bleakly, saying nothing. Then burst into bitter, abject tears.

17

Lily found the Christmas decorations in the dining room, stored in a cabinet. She pulled out the battered tinsel tree, a crib that went back to Ruth's childhood. Little dowdy metal animals, a pink-painted Jesus with a dirty nose. Children always picked up small figures by the face, between sticky thumb and forefinger. Like a blind person, they liked to feel facial features with their fingers. She held on to the smudged Jesus in the same way – a talisman, a prayer, a nudge to the sweet evocation of her own long, long-gone infant, and the feeling then, that she had brought joy to the world.

She even unearthed a box of crackers, a bit bent, but unused. She straightened the branches of the tree and perched it on top of the telly. The crib was placed on a table in the hall. She thought the crackers would look nice in that big blue bowl in the drawing room.

She opened the door to the room and stepped into a freezer. All the windows were closed but they seemed to have siphoned cold through their leaky frames. Maybe she would find a small electric fire and plug it in for an hour. She switched on the light. 'Oh!' she said. So many strange things were happening lately. She was too old for all this oddness. Heaped around the room were the forlorn little bundles of their possessions: china, pictures, spoons, trinkets. Ruth had dumped them here after that night. She unparcelled the china and carried it in small piles back to the cabinet. The pictures were rehung, the spoons and trinkets returned to their proper places. She didn't know where to put Dick's jigsaws so she stacked them as neatly as possible in the corner.

Then she peered into all the other corners of the room. She bent down and gazed under the furniture, lifting the sofa's dusty pelmets. She ran upstairs, panting, searched in the bed, under the bed, in the wardrobe, on top of the wardrobe, in the cupboards, in the hot press. She was looking for the gun. Must be somewhere. Try the cubby hole beneath the stairs. The unaccustomed bout of housework followed by the frantic search had worn her out, but she ransacked the musty space, pulling down towers of old paint tins. She located a long cold nozzle and remembered the dreadful feel of it in her mouth, but when she pulled on it it was only the hose of a broken vacuum cleaner. The doorbell went.

'I've brought the bed,' a man said.

Lily had an image of four hospital orderlies carrying Dick, strapped to his hospital cot. He was due to arrive by ambulance. She could not see an ambulance, but her mind was so full of this picture that she said nothing, just pushed the man aside and stared out into the dark.

'Well, it's a mattress really, isn't it?'

'I don't know.' Had they parcelled him into his mattress, employing it like a strait-jacket?

The expression on her face made him unsure and he reached into his pocket to check the slip. 'The Sleepwell orthopaedic mattress. Mr Richard Butler.' She watched him with polite dismay. Soon she would remember that Dick had actually ordered such a support and that it accounted for one of the mysterious cheques he had written.

'We had none in stock and had to order it. We do our best to get all deliveries in before Christmas.'

When the Sleepwell had been placed on the bed she asked him to put the other one in Ruth's old room, for she couldn't think what else to do with it. The man remained standing where he was, the discarded sleep of half a century's marriage sagging at his side. He looked pointedly at the new one as if he expected to be invited into it. She remembered then that people sometimes became greedy at Christmas. She gave him a pound and he went away.

She smoothed sheets over the unyielding plane and replaced the blankets. She fetched a pair of Dick's fleecy pyjamas and brought them to the kitchen to warm. She wondered if he would have eaten. Hospital meals were always early. He might like a boiled egg and toast, maybe a piece of Christmas cake or the mince pies Ruth had left. She lit the oven to get a bit of extra heat into the kitchen (he would feel the cold after hospital), hung the pyjamas over the oven door to air, put two eggs into a pot of water and two slices of bread under the grill. She set the table, reluctantly moving a book and a magazine she had been reading. There seemed nowhere to put them. The house looked too small for two people. Why should she think this? It used to feel huge when Ruth first left. She remembered then that she had locked the dining room and drawing room to lessen the draughts. That was why the house seemed small. Should she set the hearth in these rooms? She sighed, without moving. She had forgotten the trouble that being married involved.

Christmas morning had a sugared air; a still life, varnished and frosted. Car wheels cut the icing with a muted scrunch. Bell chimes flexed drowsily across the glassy sphere.

Ruth watched the scene from her window with a wry smile –

a quixotic notion of a dusky Semite baby's birthday, but all the same, the world looked saved. The distant sea was a baby ribbon shot with gold, gulls skated on the sky.

Over dinner the previous night she had actually joked about her parents, the two old codgers steamed up with passion, her mother's horror that Romeo was coming home to roost. She was good at funny descriptions and her guests had choked with laughter. Then they went home to sleep it off. But the joke would not go away.

She had a great urge to dress up in scarves and jumpers, go stamping up Killiney Hill and take a lot of cold air into her lungs and afterwards gate-crash one of her friends' Christmas dinners. No one could ever say there wasn't enough food to go round at Christmas. But she was tied. Love and terror and exasperation bound her. Blood was thicker than bloody brambles.

She drank her coffee, bathed and dressed carefully in a militant-looking tweed suit. If she needed to play the nanny, she had to dress for it. This bristly livery also had vital thermal value. Why on earth had she not kidnapped her mother when she had the chance, sent in some men to do the central heating? If her parents decided to kill each other there probably wasn't much she could do about it, but at least she could have stopped them dying of hypothermia.

Before she left she back-lit her stage with little lamps, put some music and wine in place (a red this time, a ballsy Amarone, planted on a table near a radiator), cut up the choicest pieces of pheasant from last night's dinner and left them under a cover. She would have them later with a salad of olives and watercress and some bread fried in pheasant fat and dipped in salt. And then pink hothouse Muscat grapes to be eaten with a searing hunk of Parmesan.

As she drove through silent streets her sighs rasped loutishly through Emma Kirkby's high, pure soprano rendition of Fauré's *Requiem*. Parents were like children were supposed to be. You never got rid of the responsibility. She and her mother were alike in certain ways; they both enjoyed their own company and neither had any small talk. The difference was that Lily still wore the guise of a child while Ruth had cast off that rig at the age of four. She wasn't wholly unlike her father either. She had to recognise that. She had his domineering personality, his temper and – what was it The Walnut had said? – 'A bit of magic!' – yes, there was that as well. She felt the power and the magic in her own work, the sparkle of exhilaration when she stepped over the edge of design. Why couldn't she be more generous, more forgiving? Parents gave you what they had and you flicked through it, looking for the one thing you wanted – *your* life. If she had had children, what would they have been like? What would they have thought of their big, grumpy mother? At least she hadn't inflicted that on anyone. At least if she ended up deranged or drunk or biting dogs, the humiliating outcome would be between her and her broker.

And speaking of brokers, it struck Ruth as a definite indication of her own increasing oddness that she had not destroyed the letter to Mrs Roger Hayes, the wife of her father's imagined adversary. Having almost set it on fire once, she then preserved it very carefully, folding it up and putting it into a porcelain bowl with a lid. It remained there, stationed on her mantlepiece, like the ashes of the dear dead.

Her parents' street was weighted down with the self-importance of celebration. Fires were lit and flashing lights made a Christmas morse behind windows. Little children dressed in Smartie colours, and teenagers, dowdy as spiders, scrambled and clumped out of cars and were greeted by grannies with outstretched arms. Fat smells emerged from houses. There was the faint, heart-touching tinkle of Christmas music on a piano. Ruth was interested to note that in one or two of the houses coiffured bay trees stood sentinel to coyly lit porches, and reception rooms in shades of claret or Chinese yellow drew light from French windows in the dining room. Partitions between the two rooms had been removed for light and space. The street was on the way up.

She breathed in deeply. What a luxurious contrast smoke and frost made, like ice-cream and hot fudge sauce. She squared her shoulders and turned to go into her own house and face the music.

The music, she realised, was coming from her house. She peered in the drawing-room window and there was Pa at the piano, stroking and touching with that peculiar wistful gentleness he kept only for the keys. And then – weirder and weirder – she saw the bright dance of flames on the brass fire fender. A fire in the drawing room! Must have been twenty years. How the crows must have rained down.

The fire had been lit, a chicken was in the oven and Pa was peacefully playing the piano. Ma looked delighted, as if she had won a great big prize. 'Come to the kitchen, love. We can have a cup of coffee and a chat while Pa's playing.'

'How is he?'

Lily took her daughter's hands in the hall. 'You'll see.'

The kitchen table had been set with an age-spotted white table cloth and the good china released from its refugee bundles. Two red candles had been dug up from somewhere. There were even three crackers. Several slices of the shiny ham had been arranged on a small plate, with a button-front of pickled onions. Another little dish had slivers of beetroot, while yet another held cocktail biscuits. The *pièce de résistance*, which Lily pointed out with pride, was a dish on which two baby teeth rested. Ruth picked it up and peered at it with interest. Priadel, a musical-sounding name, was engraved across the pristine surface of two white tablets.

'The doctor said that on no account must he skip his medication,' Lily told her. 'So I worked it out that if I put the tablets in a dish on the table, to be taken with dinner, there couldn't be any accidents.'

'You've got the pills, then?'

'I keep them in my bag.'

'Just remember how important it is not to let them out of your sight.' Ruth added her own gifts to the festive display – a bottle of port, a box of chocolate truffles, cheroots for Pa and a new giant jigsaw, a big red poinsettia. All things considered, the kitchen didn't look too bad. 'Pretend you're in one of those fairy stories where the heroine is only protected as long as she has the magic stone.'

'A fairy story.' Lily chuckled and bit into a cheese football.

'You look happy, Ma.'

Lily drank her phoney coffee. 'Yes, well, I'm not going to make any speeches for a change. I'm fine. My bones ache, though. Your pa ordered an awful new mattress for his back. It's like sleeping in a quarry.'

'Why did he do that?' Ruth said sharply. 'He's not going to need it in hospital.'

'Oh, he did it ages back! Months ago. It only turned up yesterday.'

Ruth began to relax. The kitchen was warm. She found that she could even take off her suit jacket. Pa came down, kissed her and fetched a sherry bottle. Ma quickly dispatched the coffee cups to the sink. 'Will we pull the crackers?' he proposed. Her parents sat in funny hats and Pa read out the mottoes. 'May the wind follow your heels but not your meals. That's a good one! Ha!' He shook his head in admiration. He had always been a connoisseur of corny jokes. Ruth held out her glass for more sherry.

'When I was in hospital,' Pa announced, 'I did a bit of praying. Never was much of a one for praying but when things get bad enough you'll do anything. What was I praying for?' He carved a meticulous slice of fowl and placed it on Ruth's plate. She withdrew the plate at once. She didn't want to eat too much of their food. 'To win the Lotto, of course!' He looked at Ma and giggled. 'No, seriously, I wanted to know what to do with my life. Bit late for that, you might say, but you're stuck with your life until it's over and I felt such a bloody old spare part. I never much believed in religion. Do you Ruth? But beggars can't be choosers, so I asked, and what do you know, I got an answer. I'll say no more. But for this short, blessed time that I am reunited with your mother, I am going to look after her. She's looked after me for a long time. Poor old girl's tired. I mean to make it up to her.'

'He did the drawing-room fire,' Ma boasted as she measured out the roast potatoes and broccoli.

'And I am going to wash the dishes after lunch, put a hot-water bottle in the lady's bed for her nap, and when she feels like rising there will be a cup of tea awaiting her by the fire in the drawing room, a sweet biscuit and a few old records on the turntable for us to listen to. I swear to God, Ruth, I feel like a new man. I lost all my self-respect because I thought no one respected me. Now I see that your self-respect comes from yourself. And you have to work to make yourself worthy of it.'

Before they ate their modest meal they said grace, and Ruth felt some measure of it. She also felt a new regard for the dry little hospital doctor. Clearly he had got Pa's medication exactly right. She could feel Ma's pride in him. Maybe now she would have a relationship that didn't have to be worked at or justified all the time.

When Ma produced the trifle with a flourish, Ruth's eye was on the saucer with the tablets. Nothing had been mentioned and she wasn't going to say anything unless she had to. The viscous pudding was consumed and more instant coffee produced (in dainty little cups this time), and when Pa fetched glasses for the port, Ma tore open the box of truffles. Pa loved sweets. He picked out a truffle and was about to put it in his mouth. 'Wait a minute!' He smiled at them mischievously. 'I have my own sweets.' He pounced on the saucer with an elaborate show of delight, picked up a tablet and put it in his mouth, rolling it around with sounds of pleasure. 'Mmm. You should try these. Delicious.' He lifted the saucer again, made a play of dropping it, juggled it around and then pretended to lose the tablet on the floor. 'Oops, gone!' Ma was in fits of laughter, but Ruth kept a hawk eye on the saucer. She peered closely. The tablet really was gone. 'Must have fallen under the table!' He dived down, reappeared with his lips folded over his teeth. 'Now, I've lost my damned teeth!' Down he went again. This time he popped up with buckled lips and an eye closed. 'My blasted eye's fallen out!'

Ma was helpless, wiping her eyes. 'Pa!' Ruth warned.

He looked at her in mock innocence, lips still drawn in, eye still closed. He opened the palm of his hand. There was the pill. Ruth remembered then that he used to do conjuring tricks when she was a child. He and Ma were convulsed with mirth. Ruth realised that they were laughing at her, at her foolish anxiety. She smiled grudgingly. 'All the same, Pa, you should be careful. Suppose one of them really did get lost.'

'It's all right. They gave me a few spares in case of accidents.'

How great is the dignity of chaste wedlock.

Dick wrote this down and underlined it. He came to another pleasing phrase and sucked on it for several seconds before setting it on paper. *Not fettered but adorned by the golden bond of the Sacrament, not hampered but assisted.* He went to the window and looked out. Nothing doing. Damn place, like a morgue. Feeling quite satisfied with this, he went back to his book. He began to whistle under his breath, then stopped, thinking it might disturb Lily's rest.

She would have been surprised if she had seen his reading matter. *Casti Connubii*, the book was called. It was an encyclical letter on Christian marriage written long ago by a long-dead pope. It had been given to him by a priest visiting the hospital. It was at a point when he had been feeling low. He told the priest he felt useless. Looking back over the whole of his life, he couldn't find anything that counted. The office, where he had considered himself indispensable, forgot all about him as soon as he retired. He had never fought in a war, never killed another man nor saved a life. His only proof of manhood was that he had married and had sex with a woman. He felt bad then, saying that to a cleric, but the priest had put the book into his hands. 'Your marriage is your mission,' he told him. 'That is your purpose in life.'

> *Yet although matrimony is of its very nature of divine institution, the human will too, enters it and performs a most noble part. By matrimony, therefore the souls of the contracting parties are knit together more directly and more intimately than are their bodies, and that not by any passing affection of sense or spirit, but by a deliberate and firm act of the will; and from this union of souls by God's decree, a sacred and inviolable bond arises.*

A sacred and inviolable bond. The words on the page seemed woven like a gilded wreath. He had only to press beneath his fingers to the page and happiness leaked out. He had a role to play.

He was not futile. More than that, he had a leading role. The pope had quoted St Augustine on the 'order of love'. *Let women be subject to their husbands as to the Lord, because the husband is the head of the wife, as Christ is head of the church.*

It made sense of the whole thing. No longer galley slave on someone else's tub, but captain now of his own ship. He glanced at his watch. Three o'clock. Only an hour to go until he woke Lily for a cup of tea. Already he was missing her.

On Boxing Day Ruth phoned her parents. 'I'm just heading off to Kilkenny. Anything you need before I go?'

'No, we're fine, Ruth.' Ma sounded cheerful. 'We're going out this afternoon.'

'You don't need a lift?'

'No, thanks. Guess where we're going?'

'To the hospital. If you want to see him off, take a taxi instead of the ambulance, otherwise you'll have no way to get home. Would you like me to call one for you?'

'We're going to a pantomime. We saw a bit of it on the telly last night and your father and me, we thought, wouldn't it be fun to see a panto live again? It's just a matinée. We don't want to be out late.'

'Is he driving?'

'There's nothing wrong with his driving.'

'No, but if he goes on to the hospital from there, there'll be nowhere for him to park the car and no way for you to get home.'

'Exactly!' Ma said in triumph. 'We thought of that. So we've rung the hospital and told them not to expect him tonight.'

As if it was a hotel! 'Ma! You can't. Everything has gone so well.'

'He doesn't want to go back,' Lily said. 'It's too soon. The drive over here took a lot out of him. I don't want him to go back,' she added quickly, before Ruth could set up an argument.

Ruth couldn't compete in this game. She needed her friends. 'He'll go back on the twenty-seventh, though?'

'Yes, Ruth. I promise.'

'Write down my phone number in Kilkenny.'

'Oh, there's no need . . .'

'Just write it down – and make sure he takes his pills. Are there enough?'

'They gave him a week's supply. Don't you worry about us. Enjoy yourself.'

'You too,' Ruth said.

'We'll have ham sandwiches for tea,' Lily said. 'I think there's mustard and I bought a small sliced loaf.'

'I'd love a piece of Christmas cake.'

'You can have a mince pie too if you like. I wish I'd brought some cream to go with them. We could have brandy butter, well, whiskey butter, because there isn't any brandy.'

After the pantomime they went to the Central Hotel for a drink. They found a seat by the fire. They had enjoyed the entertainment but Lily was worn out by it, especially the noise of all the children. The drink was not so much a celebration as a pause on the mountain before continuing the ascent.

'Ham is nice. Wonder why most people wait for Christmas. It stretches well. We had plenty for the dinner yesterday.'

'Ruth had none.'

'It went well today with the cold chicken leg, and still enough left over for a sandwich. What will we have for lunch tomorrow?'

Lily briefly had her caught-in-the-headlights look. She hadn't thought to buy anything for the following day because she had assumed Dick would be back in hospital. She suddenly recalled the delicatessen treat Ruth had brought for Pa before Christmas.

'Spiced beef!' she said in triumph. 'I'll see if I can get a tin of peas. Flemings will probably be open for the papers.'

'Going to Flemings are you? Oh, good. You might give him an envelope for me.'

'Of course, Dick. Is it the newspaper bill?'

'Spiced beef!' he said. 'You know, I love that, Lil. Would we save the mince pies to go with it? Anything on telly tonight?'

'Oh, lots. There's always plenty on at Christmas. There's an old Morecambe and Wise and some film about a woman who has an affair with a married man.'

The circularities of married conversation. Little mantras of reassurance that keep the steering steady; foot just touching the clutch. They didn't watch much of the film. By the time they'd had their tea they were too tired. Anyway, it was all sex. In the old days, you only got that in continental pictures. Dick was appalled when the woman knelt down in a lift and put her face into the man's trousers, but when they went to bed Lily found that the unpleasant film had sought out a dormant partner in her husband and she sighed as silently as possible as she was butted on the iron mattress. He was a good man when in his proper senses, but he hadn't been a good lover. When young, he had been too prudish to introduce her body to the kind of feelings he had, and now that he was old and he loved her, he disliked troubling her with them, so he tried to forget that it was her by ignoring her. At least with young men it was over quickly.

'Like the new mattress, love?' he murmured sleepily. Mercifully he answered for her. 'Bloody awful, isn't it? My bones poke out too much. Need some cushioning for the old bones, eh? Maybe we're just too old for change.'

18

While Lily was picking her way to the shops over a fresh fall of snow, Dick rediscovered his camera. He went to the garden and photographed the back of the house under its white muffler. He tried a close-up of icicles on the wall. Then he needed the lav, but instead of going all the way back indoors, he decided to use the outside one. It was nice there, peaceful, with a fringe of white on the door's ragged top. He could see insects scuttling, a spider waving a leg as if conducting a slow orchestral movement. A lav was better out of doors, especially on such a beautiful day, especially for men. Ladies preferred not to think about the nether regions. Men were earthy. No harm in that; nice to feel at one with the earth.

He wasn't in a hurry, which was just as well. Everything took time these days. Through the gap in the door he could see the garden's single tree, weighted down with snow. The branches were bare but for one or two tenacious leaves. He watched the leaves moving, translucent, veined, pale as wine against the light. Even though the edges were crisp with frost he had never seen such beauty, never before thought of leaves as what they were; skin – a tree's delicate skin, the patterns of the bloodline fragile and forceful as on a woman's breast. Tears came into his eyes. He felt like a prisoner who had had a last-minute reprieve. 'Dear God, save me, save me,' he said, and then he sighed, for he had never really believed in God, not in any consoling sense. He believed in the grandeur, but never considered he had any worthwhile rank. He was only a spider, scuttling in the corner. Salvation would be on sufferance. Lily was his soul.

His own smell rose around him. He took some pleasure in that. Leave religion to the women. Men had always accepted that women were better creatures. It was upsetting, though, that a new generation of women so readily accepted that men were worse. He had finished his business. No reason to stay now but he sat on. He felt tranquil here, and sleepy.

He was woken by the cold and by the stench. Foul, utterly foul. What the hell was he doing here? What was he coming to? He had not even wiped himself. He stirred angrily but found that he could not move. He was too cold.

When Lily got back she couldn't find him. She looked all over the house (even under the bed). His car was outside, but he had gone missing. It was only when she went into the garden that she heard the sound; quite a small sound, like the noise of water dripping after ice has melted. It came from the outside toilet. She pulled open the door and found Dick in there, weeping quietly.

'Get out!' he sobbed.

She ignored this and tried to help him to his feet. 'Can't you move?'

He shook his head. 'Get help.'

'I'll go next door.'

'Don't go next door,' he said. 'It's only women. Go to the Reagans. Get me the man. Tell him I'm in a jam. Just say it's something that needs a man's help.'

She pulled off a length of lavatory paper and put it in his hand. His hand remained inert. When she tried to wrap his fingers round it they would not bend. He bowed his head and wept noisily. Lily pulled off another length of paper. She edged her hand under his bottom.

'No! Leave it! Don't look at me.' His voice gurgled like a child's.

'Take no notice,' she soothed. The smell of excrement had always made her sick but she couldn't let a stranger find him like this. She tried to hold her breath as she worked. Dick moaned with humiliation. 'Think of something else,' she urged him. 'Sing a Christmas carol.'

His voice rose, earnest and frail and full of hiccoughs. At last she was able to drop the paper and pull the chain. She patted him on the shoulder and closed the door behind her. She leaned against the wall and hauled fresh, cold air into her lungs. She could still hear the wavering *Silent Night*, punctuated with tear-laden sighs, as she ran from the yard.

She felt shy about approaching the new people. They had been living on the street for a year but were still known as the new people because of the way they kept to themselves. It was the woman who opened the door. She stood there, neither welcoming nor curious, just waiting for Lily to make some explanation of herself.

'My husband . . .' Lily stopped. Dick's way of phrasing things did not come easily to her. 'Is your husband there?'

'Yes.' The woman tightened the belt of a dressing gown. Lily noticed that she was dishevelled and not yet dressed although it was almost lunchtime.

'I live two doors down.' Lily realised her neighbour must already know this. 'We need some help.'

'Come in, won't you?' The woman sounded reluctant. 'I'll get Eric.'

Lily sat in a living room that was warm and comfortable, the book-case temptingly overcrowded. The neighbour returned with cups of tea and then her husband came in. He too looked unkempt.

'I'm sorry to bother you.' Lily saw how close together they sat on the sofa, the casual way their hands rested on one another's limbs. 'If you could come for just a moment.'

'I'll come, of course,' the man said, and she caught the quick caress he gave to his wife. She realised that they had been making love when she called. While she had been scurrying back over the ice with her heart in her mouth, they had been giving affection to one another. It was like a visit to a foreign country to learn that men and women could live together with such intimacy and ease. The woman wasn't even good-looking! She could not understand why she felt bitterness. She thought she had been happy. She looked down to avoid their sympathetic gaze and saw that the cuff of her good blouse was streaked with brown. Suddenly she felt all the strain, the apprehension that underlay the whole of her Christmas, and found that she was crying into her cup of tea. 'I'm sorry,' she said. 'My husband is ill. He's in the lavatory. Out of doors. He's very cold.'

They were kind to her then and made her stay and finish her tea while Eric Reagan went to rescue Dick.

19

'I'm starting a new album.' Dick was sitting up in bed with his breakfast next morning. He seemed quite restored, eager and rosy. Perhaps it was the visit from a man.

'I was just having a practice run with the camera when I got short-taken. What I really had in mind was some new pictures of you and me. We'll build up a fresh set of memories. Something to look back on. We're not a bad-looking pair of eggs, even now.' Dick covered a slice of toast with a thin glaze of marmalade. 'Wish I'd thought to photograph the Christmas dinner. That was a fine spread you put up. Still, plenty of other things. We could go to the zoo. Or the waxworks. I'd like that – photographs with the famous.' He smiled at her, his old, wistful, boyish smile.

Lily chewed her toast and swallowed slowly. 'Dick, you're going back to hospital today. The ambulance is coming at four.'

'Four, is it? Right-o. Pity. I was hoping to do a bit of business before going back to my padded cell. I put an ad in about the mattress.'

'How did you do that?' She was bewildered. 'The newspaper offices would have been closed yesterday.'

'Who needs newspapers? Local business. By now the ad is in the window of Flemings shop.' He hopped out of bed and began to pull on his clothes. 'You did give my message to Mr Fleming? That was the advertisement. I'd really like to get rid of the damn thing before I go back. I don't mind going back, you know. I only wish someone had been able to sort me out earlier. I've wasted my life, Lily, my whole damn life. I could have been so many things – photographer, writer, maybe even a pianist. I stayed in that bloody little pen-pushing job because I was afraid to take the risk. Fear – you think at the time it's prudence but it's just plain terror and it can drive a person mad.'

The madness and the fear had gone together. He had never felt more pure-headed. He worked on his jigsaw in the morning; not the one Ruth had given him, which was just cardboard rubbish. Ruth didn't understand him. She saw his jigsaws as childish games. His own Victorian collection were objects of beauty and mystery, carved from wood, with little secret pieces known as 'whimsies', which were cut in the shape of artists' implements; a covert gift, a Mason's handshake from artist to artisan to assembler. He had just slotted a tiny, intricate easel into the wooden door of a cathedral. The puzzle was a Paris street scene full of old buildings with complicated rooflines. There was the Notre Dame Cathedral, some horse-drawn traffic, and in the right-hand corner, a woman dressed in blue. He was well acquainted with her because she had materialised beneath his hand many times but still he eked out the blue pieces, forcing himself to concentrate on bricks and cobbles. He wanted to save the woman till last. He watched the buildings come together. He was their artist and their architect. Even small things gave him pleasure, and in spite of the setback yesterday he felt he was capable of great things.

He took his pills at lunchtime as if they were communion wafers. No jesting this time. Lily watched him swallow from a glass of water. 'How are you feeling now, dear?' she asked him.

'I feel well, Lily.'

'You seem great.' She said it sadly, almost guiltily, as if she felt the unfairness of sending him away.

He kissed her. 'I shall miss you, dear. Would you do one last thing for me? Cut short your rest. It's a lot to ask, I know, but I'd like you to myself for a final hour. Would you dress up in something nice? Remember the black taffeta with the frill down the back? And high heels. Would you put on some perfume? I have a small surprise for you.'

After she had gone upstairs, she heard him whistling on his way to the lavatory. He looked at himself in the bathroom mirror. *Seems* great? Was great. Could still be great. He might cut out alcohol. Now that his brain had cleared, it was a pity to interfere with it in any way. He ran the hot tap and put a hand to his mouth, releasing the two tablets he had imprisoned under his tongue. He watched them skip in the flow of water and run away down the drain, as they had done yesterday and the day before.

He hurried down to wash the dishes, breaking off his whistling when he remembered it might disturb his wife. While she had her nap he quickly made his preparations and then crept upstairs to change his clothes. Lily was asleep. He stayed for a moment watching her tenderly, touched by the girlish smoothness that revisited her in rest. He sneaked down again and used the phone, trying not to laugh as he lightened his voice and masked it with a handkerchief. 'Oh, yes. He seems great.'

Lily came downstairs to the strains of Jack Buchanan. That took her back! She and Dick used to like him in their dancing days. She felt a bit sleepy, having cut short her nap, and a bit foolish. The old dance dress still fitted more or less but nowadays she much preferred to cover the lot in jumpers. The perfume smelled sharp. Maybe it had been there too long. He used to buy it for her every Christmas but she only used it when he reminded her.

Dick had a good blaze going. He was in his grey suit and the red silk tie with the polka dots. She was glad to see this brave show for the ambulance men. He was smoking one of the cheroots Ruth had brought and had a glass of port in his hand. When Lily came in, he bowed stiffly. 'My dear! How well you look. May I have the pleasure of this dance?'

Lily laughed. 'Dick, I'm half asleep. I need a cup of tea.'

'No, don't wake up. I don't want either of us to wake up. Here, drink this.' He handed her a measure of port.

Lily warmed herself at the fire. The spicy wine tasted strange in her dry mouth, but once she had drunk the first glass it seemed quite agreeable to have another. Dick had a rueful look. He really must be dreading going back. He put a hand on her back, on the patch of bare skin exposed by the fancy neckline. He kissed her mouth. He had always been a nice kisser. He took the glass out of her hand and led her around the furniture in a stately dance, his mouth close to her hair, breathing in the chemical flowers. 'You have always been my darling heart,' he said. 'For years I said nothing because I was a dry old stick, but now time is running out.'

She liked his body like this, courtly, inside his good suit. She let her head rest on his shoulder. A part of her said she should have more sense, but she needed comfort after her painful envy of the Reagans yesterday morning.

He held on to her tightly. 'It's never too late, is it, Lil? We make awful mistakes, but it's all right so long as we're not too proud to have another go.'

He broke off suddenly, ran to a little table, where he fiddled with some apparatus, then came back to Lily and put his arm around her. 'Smile!' He posed her by the fire with a glass in her hand, then put on another old record and left it deep frying in its dust while he stood with his arm resting lightly around her. 'This is all we need at our age, old pal.' He gently kissed her hair. 'I would be happy like this, just to go on and on like this for ever and ever.'

She nuzzled into his cheek and nodded.

'If Ruth could see us now!' he chuckled. 'Nothing really changes. The heart's a child.' He sighed suddenly, seeming close to tears, and she patted his back. 'Nothing really changes. We have it in our hands and we throw it away. We had it once before. We have it again and we are about to be parted. I don't want to be parted from you. Do you want to be parted from me?'

'No,' she said. 'I don't.'

'Say that again?' Dick urged.

Something about his voice broke through her sleepiness. She pulled back in order to think. Through a chink in the curtains she could see the night. What time was it? It shouldn't get really dark until half past four. She looked at her watch. Five thirty! 'Oh, Dick!' she said. 'The ambulance. It should have been here more than an hour ago.'

'But we didn't really want it to be here, did we?' he said gently.

'No, Dick, but . . .'

'Well, in that case, that's all right, isn't it?'

'Yes, but it's getting late. Someone should phone them.'

'Someone did phone them. This afternoon, while you were sleeping. That is my surprise. I'm afraid I pretended to be you, since you are responsible for my release, but no one seemed to notice. That is my Christmas gift to you.' He smiled his winning, clever-Dick smile as he went to the record shelf and found another oldie. He blew on it, set it under the needle and swept her into a dance. 'We are to be together until New Year's Eve.'

'How much?' the man said.

The phone had rung all the next day about the mattress. Dick was upset by the calls because he wanted to finish his jigsaw. Lily was surprised that so many people wanted to sleep in agony. She was relieved when a man agreed to come and see it. She folded up the blankets and sheets again and left the stressful bedding exposed.

'I paid three hundred pounds for it,' Dick explained to the man.

'You said it was going cheap. How much do you want?'

'I have little choice in the matter,' Dick said. 'I waited two months for that mattress, waited and waited for one night of decent sleep. If you suffer with your back you will know what I mean. Paid three hundred pounds on the nail and now I am going to have to let it go.'

'Yes, but it didn't suit you.' The man prodded the surface, as if it was a dumb beast at a market.

'It suited me perfectly,' Dick protested. 'That mattress was paradise. It was my wife who could not be suited. She suffers from brittle bones.'

'Oh, I'm sorry to hear that. I like the mattress, but what do you want for it?'

Dick shrugged. 'Offer me what you like. Offer me anything. I am not used to business. I am an old-age pensioner. As you will see if you look around you, we are far from comfortable. I am just out of hospital and I need the money to pay bills.'

The man wrote a cheque and offered it. Dick studied the amount, nodded curtly and put it in his pocket. As he was lugging away his purchase the new owner of the Sleepwell looked back at the bare springs. 'What will you sleep on?'

Dick shook his head. 'Give it no thought. My wife asked the delivery man to remove our old mattress. We will manage until I can make some other arrangement. You will find, when you get to my age, that life is rarely easy.'

'You could have our old mattress,' the man said. 'It's quite good. I was going to sell it. If you won't be offended, I'll drop it round as soon as I get this home.'

'I am in no position to be offended,' Dick said.

'What did he pay?' Lily asked.

Dick showed her the cheque for three hundred pounds.

'Oh, Dick, that's awful. The mattress cost two hundred and fifty pounds. I remember quite clearly.'

Dick began to laugh. 'Everything else that I told him was true. I am a poor old-age pensioner, just out of hospital. I only raised the ante because I thought he would beat me down. Don't you think it's funny?'

Lily didn't think it funny, but she didn't want an argument. 'At least we've finally got a comfortable mattress.' The man had returned with a really good replacement. He had refused to take any payment because it was Christmas. 'I'll make up the bed now.'

'No, don't do that. Wait until I put this away and bring back our old mattress.'

'Our old one's a wreck, Dick. What are you going to do with this one?'

He fixed her with a playful grin. 'Sell it, of course.'

'Smile!'

She blinked as a hot light exploded in front of her eyes. Dick had crept up on her and taken a photograph.

'What are you doing, dear?'

'I'm reading.' She laid down her book and arranged her features pleasantly.

'Reading, always reading! What are you reading?'

She held up the cover of the book to let him see.

'What is it about? Talk to me, Lily.'

'Oh, it's just a fem—' She had been about to say it was a feminist book, but she knew he didn't care for that. 'Just a female type of book, Dick.'

'Female type of book! Featherhead!' He ruffled her hair and went outside. She watched him strolling past the window with his shirt sleeves rolled up. The blunt fangs of icicles still knobbed the wall. She heard him whistling as he went to the shed. He came back with the axe.

When their meal was ready she went to the yard to call him. A pretty rosewood bureau had been reduced to a surprisingly small pile of matchwood, the brass fittings laid carefully to one side. 'This will make very good firewood,' he panted as he brought down the axe on the remains of a drawer. 'Woodworm!' He responded to her shocked look. 'Riddled with it.'

'Lunch is ready.' Lily retreated nervously.

She waited in the kitchen with the plates of food. It was half an hour before he appeared, his face pulled tight with excitement. 'Bring me paraffin,' he said.

She left the untouched food and obediently fetched a can of the blue inflammable oil. She found him in the drawing room. Bits of the bureau smouldered and sparked in the grate. He was holding a sheet of paper to the hearth to trap the draught. Smoke seeped out around it. 'Paraffin!' He snapped his fingers. Lily handed it over patiently but her heart was churning.

He shook the paraffin over his whining nest of kindling. The fire roared and flames shot out. 'Don't, Dick,' Lily begged in horror. She had always been afraid of fire.

He watched her with a bright smile. He threw more of the evil-smelling oil on the fire and the flames swooshed out into the room. Lily gasped as they licked the wallpaper. 'What are you doing, Dick?' she cried. 'Are you trying to set the place on fire?' He laughed and sprinkled paraffin out into the room, over her shoes and the bottom of her skirt. Lily screamed. Dick was distracted as the flames in the hearth fell flabbily back. He frowned in disappointment on the smouldering embers and then cast a sad eye around the room. 'Wormy.' His gaze fell on an inlaid chair. He picked it up, then brought it down with a crash, loosening the leg. 'Damn place is riddled with worm.' He broke the leg off and threw it on the fire.

'What are you doing?' Lily gasped.

He frowned at her. 'I'm getting the place warmed up. I've invited Eric Reagan for a drink. I thought he was a thoroughly decent fellow.'

She took a deep breath. 'You're going back to hospital. Besides, Dick, we hardly know the man.'

'I know him,' he said. 'I mean to know him.'

He kicked the dainty chair to pieces and stacked these on the fire. He began pulling books from the shelves and threw them into the flames. More paraffin was shaken in. He gathered up the pieces of his jigsaw and sprinkled them on the blaze. Books were flung on top. Fire howled up the chimney. She stood and watched until he seized an armload of Ruth's old books and she ran to save them. Dick struggled to get the books on to the fire, but she managed to hang on to a few and placed them carefully on the table.

'He's not coming!' Dick turned abruptly from the blaze. His face and clothing were blackened and the heat was terrible.

'No, well, maybe some other time.'

'Nobody wants to visit us,' he said morosely.

'Have something to eat. You haven't had your lunch.' The banalities came out dry and flat but the habit of placation died hard. She wondered why she did not just turn and run as any child would have done. She realised then that she was quite literally rooted to the spot, not just with fear but with a numbing sense of fatalism.

'Nobody wants to come to the house of an old man who is married to a hag, a shrew.' She looked up in surprise as he snatched one of the books she had left on the table and tore it in half. 'You think I don't know what you have been up to, what kind of filth you have been reading. "Female kind of thing"!' He mimicked her voice in shrill mockery. 'What kind of female would want to crush out everything decent in society? These so-called females want to destroy marriage, they want to let their dirty dugs hang down with no underwear, they want to crush the skulls of unborn infants.'

She watched her copy of Eva Figes' *Patriarchal Attitudes* burn and wondered guiltily which crack she had failed to hop over.

'You and your women's lib rags, your bitter, bilious filth, which over the years has soured our marriage!' His face was red and hectic, his mouth colourless. Little flecks flew from his lips. 'I have always been a good husband. I have paid the bills. I have been faithful, haven't I?'

Lily nodded.

'But you had to poison the well, You prefer these crazy, unwashed lesbian bitches to your own decent husband. The few days that I am permitted to spend in my own home and you won't even talk to me. You prefer to wallow in lesbian filth. You've stopped washing, haven't you? You're not my wife any more. You're one of them. I can smell you. I could smell you when we were dancing. The whole place stinks of your unwashed body. There is nothing left for me to do but to burn the whole bloody place down.'

He flung open the window. The flames staggered and then flowered as the air came in. He stormed out of the room. Throughout the house she heard the windows shrieking, like creatures caught in traps. He came back with the axe.

Ruth hauled herself out of a big old sofa in Inistioge, throwing down her paper and disturbing the cats that had settled on the dis-carded business section. Time to head back. It had been a blissful break, riding fat horses by the river, walking hairy dogs through the woods, eating big haphazard meals and talking, talking until all hours of the night, drinking large quantities from the case of good Côtes du Rhône with which she had made herself welcome. It was astonishing how you could nuzzle into a truly happy marriage. Her friends were like a brother and sister, but sexy ones. They took each other's company for granted and were both free and enmeshed. Children grew up calm and precocious in this walled garden and Ruth, who had never been a gardener, was happy just to bask there.

By the time she got back to Dublin it would be evening, and she was going to a party. She decided to give Ma a buzz before she left, wish her a happy New Year.

The phone rang a long time. Maybe Ma was at the hospital. No, more likely she was taking her rest. Damn. She might have disturbed her. The receiver was halfway back to its resting place when she heard the tiny sound: 'Yes?'

'Hi, Ma, it's Ruth. I just wanted to wish you a happy new year.' There was silence, although she thought she could hear a laboured sort of breathing. Ma must have her nose stuck right into the phone.

'How are you, Ma?' Nothing at all, just the same breaths, a bit more jerky.

Oh shit. 'How's Pa?' she asked. 'Did he go back in all right?'

The snuffles continued, like a dog trying in vain to find some familiar scent to match to a well-known sound.

'He didn't go back,' Ruth said. 'Did he?'

On the icy tear home she phoned Tim Walcott on her mobile. As he said hello, she cut across the perky tone. 'Professor Walcott, this is Ruth Butler. I'm on my way back from Kilkenny but I'd be grateful if you'd get to my parents' house as quickly as possible.

My father came home for Christmas and something has gone wrong.'

She cursed herself as she realised she had been babbling into an answering machine. At a traffic light she phoned the hospital and asked for the doctor. 'Why isn't my father back in hospital?'

'Your mother decided to keep him at home. That is entirely within her right.'

'But he's sick. Even if he has been taking his medication, it's all gone now. Can't you just send someone to bring him back? Don't you have *any* responsibility?'

'Only while he is in our care.'

'What can I do, then? Make funeral arrangements for my mother in case he kills her?'

'You would have to get his own GP to sign a committal order.'

'If I do that, will you send someone to take him in?'

'No, I'm afraid you are responsible. But I'll send an ambulance.'

As she dialled the number of her parents' doctor, her sweating hand slipped on the wheel. The car glided across the centre of the road to touch the nose of some huge leviathan hurtling into town.

'Bitch!' the driver yelled out of the window. His face was crazy with Christmas rage, even though they had both, by the mercy of some larger power, missed damage or death.

'Fuckhead!' she shouted back, into the doctor's answering machine. With shaking hands she dialled again so that she could take down the number of the locum. No reply. He must be out on call. Domestic violence and death were always at a premium over the festive season.

'Your mother upset me,' Pa said petulantly as Ruth lifted the axe from his hands.

She looked around at the shambles of the furniture. Tables, chairs, cupboards sagged at drunken angles or lay felled by the axe. There were gashes in the wall too and she wondered if this was where Ma had ducked. Ma sat very demurely on a chair and trembled.

Ruth felt sick as she closed the windows and put the kettle on. 'There's no milk.' She tried to keep her voice light but it came out as a dry bleat. 'I'll just pop out for some.'

She zoomed out of the door, the axe still in her hands to keep it out of Pa's reach, and jumped into the car, driving round and round the small streets, looking for doctors' nameplates on house fronts. On each of the doors she knocked, barging in like a mad woman, to say that her mother was in danger, her father had to be certified. She was frowned at, pushed out of the door, told that he must wait and be seen by his own doctor. By the third house she was shaking. She almost seized the doctor by the collar. He shook her off and looked at her with outrage. 'Do you know what you are asking?' he said.

And she knew it. Oh, yes, she knew it. It must be some reserved sin to go out into the streets, to seek out strange men to commit your own father to bedlam. She couldn't leave her mother any longer. She ran back to the car. Before returning home she fled into a shop, picked up milk and scattered money on the counter.

Tim Walcott was in the kitchen. He wore a bright sweater of many horizontal stripes, obviously a Christmas present. He signalled with a glance that he had got her message. She had never been so glad to see anyone in her life.

'Ah, the milkman.' He greeted Ruth's purchase. 'Just happened to be passing. Don't suppose you bought some biscuits.'

She sat down. She didn't trust herself to speak. She patted Ma's hand but Ma looked too defeated to respond.

Dick was talking away animatedly to Tim. He seemed calm, absolutely rational. What if she had succeeded in bringing back one of those strange doctors? How would anyone believe that this mild elderly man, with his courteous ways and feeble jokes, was unhinged, a terror? Even The Walnut seemed unaware that anything might be amiss. He asked Dick if he had enjoyed his Christmas, had he had a goose or a turkey?

'We had a chicken,' Dick said. 'Funds don't run to the big birds these days. Very tasty it was too.'

'Ah, well you're dead right there too,' Tim said. 'Big birds, they're all bones, aren't they? Can't go wrong with a nice, plump little chicken.'

Ma scuttled to the fridge and brought back the box of meringue nests. She opened it and laid them before Tim, as if to silently appease some gorgon. They should have been filled with fruit and cream and they looked rock hard but he picked one up and crunched with vigour.

'You never joined me for a game of whist,' Dick said.

'No, I didn't, did I? Any chance I can make amends? Tell you what, I'm going past the hospital now. Why don't I give you a lift, and as soon as you're settled, we'll set up the cards?'

Dick watched the younger man pleasantly. 'Another time. I'm not going your way.'

Professor Walcott took a piece of paper from the pocket of his jersey. He raised his spectacles to give it scrutiny. 'You are, Dick,' he said, equally affable. 'It says so here.'

'What is that?' Pa was no longer smiling.

'It's your return ticket, Dick. You did agree that you would go back. Fair's fair.'

Pa snatched the slip. His eyes scanned it. No flies on him. 'It's a committal order. You and some accomplice have signed it.' He looked furiously at Ruth and Lily. 'You are all in collusion.'

When the ambulance arrived, Ma was as shocked as Pa. She went very white and backed up against the fridge. 'I don't know what's going on.'

'Which of you did this?' He gritted his teeth and gripped the table. 'You are all in on it.'

The paramedics were friendly and calm. They called him Dick and talked to him in a man-to-man fashion. 'Don't you worry now, Dick. We'll get this sorted out in no time.' As if the problem was with the vehicle and not the patient. Dick laughed. 'I would be very grateful if you would. My daughter is not a well woman. She is given to making troublesome phone calls.'

After half an hour they said in the same friendly tone, 'We'll have to call the police if you won't come.'

'The police!' Ma said in horror.

'That's right.' The ambulance man was still addressing Pa. 'Once a committal order has been signed, the police have the power to use force. Ah, but we don't want that, do we? What's the big fuss for? Once you're back in your nice comfy bed all this will be forgotten and you'll be just as glad.'

Dick got up from the table. He looked haunted. He paced up and down, cheeks sucked in, as if seeking escape or inspiration. 'The police!' He seemed to have found what he wanted. 'Yes, call them. Do it! Do it now!' he barked at Lily. 'Why not see how you like all the neighbours watching from their windows as your husband is dragged kicking and screaming from his own house?'

Ma looked petrified. Tim Walcott watched Ruth steadily. She saw him nod his head very faintly. 'I'll do it,' she said.

As she put the phone down she felt as though all the living, beating things in her body had been replaced by some dead-weight metal. She had asked the police to forcibly arrest her own father.

Pa looked at her anxiously. He could not believe she had done it, thought she was bluffing. He sat down in anxious vigil, hands hung down between his knees, until there was a knock upon the door. He looked at Ruth again, sharply, sadly.

The gardai were huge and pleasant. 'You won't want any trouble now, sir,' they said. 'This is just a routine thing. We're only to escort you to the ambulance.'

He smiled up at them as if they had made a joke. Ruth saw that he was afraid of them. He held up his two wrists. 'No handcuffs?' Ruth and Ma had turned to stone. He went quietly to the door, turned around as if he had forgotten something. 'A viper at the bosom!' he said to Ruth. His eyes were sane and full of pain. 'I gave you life. And you have thrown me to the dogs.'

20

In the middle of the night, Lily woke. She was thirsty and she wanted the toilet. She had eaten nothing but a couple of Ritz crackers, washed down with whiskey. Something about her present state made her crave salty things, as if she needed to cry and hadn't enough salt in her. Even an ordinary thing like an egg required a mound of salt to make the bland protein go down.

She lay in bed listening. The air seemed viscid. Things seethed in it. Quickly, she reached out and turned on the light. In that double-edged moment between light and darkness, she saw the curtain move. She sat up and stared at it, daring it to twitch again. Nothing. She must have left a bit of the window open. She darted over. It was shut tight, not a chink. She had known it would be. Around the house she heard the lap and whisper of fabrics ruffled by the night. Somewhere a window was open. She put on her dressing gown and crept downstairs, barely breathing, walking on the edges of her feet to stop the steps from creaking. A squeak ran across the air like a fork of lightning. She pressed herself against the wall. It must have come from a tree on the street. She wished Ruth hadn't taken the axe; she needed something to arm herself. She waited a long time and then ran down the stairs. As she opened the drawing-room door a blob of shadow slithered out and she gasped, unable to recognise the reflected swoop of a street light. She ran at the curtains and felt the windows as if braille. Shut. Shut. Shut.

Getting from room to room was like jumping from roof to roof. The space between each of them was an abyss and she had to avoid the frightful pane of glass in the hall door because there might be a face pressed up against it.

For the first time, she understood why old people were afraid to live alone. They weren't nervous about being on their own; they were afraid because they were not alone. Once something happened to damage their trust, fear itself became the stalker. As with children, their private terrors did not live inside the head but in hidden places on the outside − in the wardrobe, behind the curtains.

She scurried back to bed and lay stiff and cold, straining for every sound. When she finally began to settle down, she remembered that she hadn't been to the lavatory nor got herself any water. She would have to do without. She couldn't face that journey again.

'You don't go in for that free love, Donal?' Dick made conversation with the boy who got into other people's beds.

'What?' The boy reluctantly dragged his gaze from whatever horrible sight he saw.

He had got to know the men who shared his ward. Arthur Ferris in the next bed was an alcoholic, a true gentleman but he said he had done unspeakable things under the influence. There was another alcoholic called Bill Turlough. He was querulous and abusive and claimed to have murdered for the IRA. There was Archie Hartigan, a cheerful fellow who gave racing tips. It was a surprise to learn that he was the one who screamed in the night. At the far end of the room was Gerry Beresford, a sad man, meek as a mouse, who rarely spoke above a whisper and ran to help others all the time, but he had killed his mother. He was a schizophrenic, as was the boy, Donal Quinn. The boy said he heard voices. They spoke in his head and gave him instructions. Sometimes they told him to inhabit the personality of others. Dick thought he just needed taking out of himself.

'I'm not narrow-minded,' he said. 'Wish it had been like that in my day.'

'Like what?' asked Donal Quinn.

'Hand under the skirt, fingers in the fur. A quick poke against a wall, away like a redshank. You haven't got any of those magazines? I'm not a prude. I like pictures of girls.'

Donal gaped at him.

'He's a clerical student,' Arthur Ferris whispered. 'He was studying to be a priest.'

Dick frowned at the youth. 'He ought to be ashamed of himself.'

Going up to bed the following night, Lily had been horrified to see that there really was a face behind the glass pane of the front door. She had to steel herself to open it before the noise of the bell upset her neighbours. 'Professor Walcott!' She stared at him in shock. I am afraid my husband is not here. He's in hospital.'

'I know where Dick is,' he said. 'It's you I want to see. Don't suppose you've got any of those biscuits?'

Lily frowned as she let him in, thinking she would now have to make a special trip to the shops to buy another pack of biscuits for Dick.

He dipped a Bourbon sandwich into his coffee. 'So, how are you?'

'I'm all right.' Lily shuddered when he offered a biscuit.

'You don't look it.' He rummaged for a chocolate digestive. 'If

I wasn't a gentleman I'd tell you you look like what the cat dragged in.'

Lily gave a long and painful sigh and tapped her cigarette against the ashtray's rim. 'I feel dispossessed. I've lost everything.'

First she had lost her husband and then her home. Ruth had removed the worst of the wreckage but the house was still booming with the horrors that had possessed it.

'You've got your daughter,' Tim said.

'I'm not sure I ever really had Ruth. Except when she was a child. She was a lovely baby.' He noticed how her face was briefly lit. 'Dick never really wanted children but when Ruth came I felt she made sense of my life. When you have children of your own you'll know what that means.'

'I like kids. They make more sense of most things than adults.'

'Ruth was very sensible,' Lily said, and she frowned.

'You talk about her in the past tense,' he pointed out.

'She went her own way from a very early age. She and her father argued a lot, over nothing, it seems to me. Dick wasn't really an unreasonable man but Ruth always went for confrontation instead of persuasion.'

'Or honesty instead of hypocrisy.'

'She was just rebelling against her father,' Lily said.

'Maybe it was you she was rebelling against. Maybe she needed honesty from you.'

'I don't really think she needed anything from me.'

'She cares for you,' he said. 'It was she who called me – asked me to look out for you.'

'Ruth called you? I didn't even think she liked . . .' She trailed off, embarrassed.

Tim laughed. 'I don't think she does like me. But she swallowed her pride for your sake. You know something,' he peeled the marshmallow strips off a Mikado and ate them, 'you look like you could use a hug.' He regarded her sideways, as if he himself was considering administering it. 'You need a bit of minding. I think we might get you into some nice nursing home for a few days, let them feed you up and sort you out.'

Lily rose from the table. 'No!' She peered around as if seeking somewhere to hide.

He put up his hands. 'All right. It's not up to me. It would have to be your own GP, but you've got to think of yourself now. I'm serious. You've had some knocks and you'd want to take care.'

'I will,' she promised.

'Do you know how to look after yourself? It's not a thing that comes naturally to everyone.'

'I don't know.' She looked ashamed.

'It's mostly about protecting yourself. If something is making you unhappy or uncomfortable, you identify it and then you isolate it. If you can't remove it from your life completely, you find some way to distance yourself. Do you understand me, Lily?'

He felt her mind had wandered for she kept looking around when he addressed her, but when she returned her attention to him she spoke intently. 'Yes, I think so.'

'And do you think you can find some way to do that without help?'

Again she looked around. She nodded forlornly.

'You need taking out of yourself. Will we go to a movie?'

'Oh, no, I . . .' Lily looked mortified. He couldn't help smiling. As if he had propositioned her.

'An old woman like me! Don't be ridiculous, Professor. What would people think?'

'They might think you were my mother,' he said in amusement. 'They might think I was your toy boy. Which would you prefer? Will you come, anyway?'

'You're kind, Professor, but no. Anyway, I'm sure you have some nice young girl of your own.'

'I have not! And you could call me Tim.'

'Well, you will have,' she promised. 'Tim.' She coughed up the informal name with effort.

'I don't think so.' He set out two plain shortbread fingers on the table in order to get at a Kimberley. 'As my granny would say, we're all as God made us.'

'What?' Her brow furrowed and then cleared. 'Oh.' She had nothing against homosexuals. Gay, they called them now. The word actually suited Tim Walcott. But she had grown up in a time when people went to prison for that, when young girls called them 'Nancy Boys'. She had taken to Tim from the start, had even thought it a pity that Ruth hadn't found a nice young man like him, who would be a son to her. She tried to find something to say. 'Well, I like you anyway,' she managed lamely.

Tim laughed. 'I like you too. Wonderful, isn't it though, what obstacles the human heart can overcome?'

21

Lily followed the man into the flat.

'These are the keys,' he said. She was surprised that there were so many of them.

'Why would I need all those for a bedsitter?'

'Two are for the yard door from the street, and the small one is for the entrance to the flat. The outside door has to be double locked both going out and coming in.'

'Couldn't I use the front door?' she wondered, but he explained that the bedsitter had once formed part of a larger room and the partition blocked off access from the hall.

It was a basement room, shaped like a long corridor and over-looking a yard. At one end there was a sort of kitchen, and at the other a screened-off shower and toilet. The bed was along the window. Bits of furniture had been stuffed into odd corners as if to get them out of sight. There were several hard chairs and a small table. She couldn't help noticing the way the curtain slumped over its rail, like a floor cloth hung up to dry. Every item of furniture was an oddment or a remnant or something picked up in a job lot at an auction. It was soulless and impersonal without any individual imprint; not one single object suggested choice or taste. It was a ghost room – no, less than that – a fragment of a ghost room, totally devoid of history or memory. She breathed a sigh of relief. 'I'll take it.'

She sat on the bed with the grey light from the yard coming in through the floor-cloth curtain. Her suitcase was beside her – a vanity case, really – as if she was going away for the weekend. How long was she away for? She had no idea. She had done an awful thing. She had run away.

It was Tim Walcott who had given her the idea. He understood, in a way that Ruth didn't, that she could never leave Dick. She was wedded to him. But he left her with the thought that if she could distance herself she could escape the haunting. If she might get away and start again in some other place, where there would be people close at hand but no unhappy memories, she might live the kind of carefree life that single people enjoyed. So she had left home, as Ruth had done two decades before.

She experienced a pang of guilt when she thought of Ruth. What would her daughter think? She felt like a teenager giving trouble to a parent. Simply by being out in the world – even though she had never married or had children – Ruth had grown older than them. How odd that she should feel more apprehension about Ruth than about Dick, even though she had been terrified of Dick. It seemed now as if Ruth had always been a grown-up and she and Dick had always been children together, she agreeing to pretend that he was a grown-up over all those years. Almost half a century! And now he had embarked on some escapade that had gone terribly wrong, but she still had to play along and cover up for him.

She watched the sky darken. She would have to make some decisions. She ought to phone her daughter and let her know where she was. And food; she must make a list of the things she needed and go and buy them. She decided to put off the phone call. Ruth would never understand why she had left her own home to live in a place like this. She would think she had gone mad like poor Pa. But even though she had done it on the spur of the moment, she had thought it out very carefully. It had to be somewhere near home, for although she could not stay in the house she wanted to be close to shops that were familiar, and the church. It needed to be very cheap. She had no money of her own, only the housekeeping which Dick gave her when she came to visit. He had taken away the joint account book after she started looking at the cheque stubs. And she needed a place that was free of emotion, where she wouldn't feel the leftovers of other people's lives. She would explain all of this to Ruth, but later, after she was settled. First she would walk to the shops and buy the kind of things she liked to eat – frozen curry, cheese slices, Jaffa cakes, sherry, a half bottle of whiskey. Oh, tea, of course, and milk. She might get herself one of those small news-papers with stories about animals and the queen. That would do for this evening. Tomorrow she would see about renting a televi-sion. It would sit nicely on the little table and she could watch it as she ate her meal, or even when she was in bed.

She felt a kind of relief as she let herself out of the small, long room. When she was in the yard, she saw something she hadn't noticed before. There was a garage in the yard and it had been converted into a flat. Imagine living in a garage! What strange times these were. The inadequate curtains drooping on the window were the same as hers and there was a man at the sink, washing a tea cup. She felt embarrassed when he glanced up and caught her staring at him. To avoid his eye, she looked back at the house

A dozen windows with make-shift curtains showed a kaleido-scope of lives. Naked bulbs, small lamps or fluorescent strips revealed people frying or smoking or soaping themselves in the shower. Oddments of cheap furniture, plywood wardrobes or foam-filled sofas were crammed in too-small spaces. A fire-trap, Dick would have said. She was astonished to think of all those lives stacked up on top of her. She had always thought of people living in whole houses, as she had done. When she was young, she would have been excited by the prospect of so many unknown individuals; girls to pal up with, eccentric people to laugh at, maybe some half-decent-looking man who would come and borrow sugar. Now she felt only alarm, as if they might all burst into song at once.

She went out the yard door, into the dark street, turning the first key in a small hole as she had been instructed, then reaching up to aim the larger key at its lock. It was quite high up. It had been made for a much taller person. She had to stand on her toes and concentrate hard, closing her eyes and setting her jaw, before grinding the key twice.

In the familiar shops she bought milk, some neat and slender cartons of frozen food. When she passed the pub, it looked warm and friendly and she thought of going in for a drink but was immediately shocked at herself – as if she had something to celebrate. Instead she visited the off-licence where she added a packet of cheese straws to her purchases. When she came to pay for them she was surprised by how little money there was in her bag. She still had to buy a newspaper and tomorrow she was to arrange for a television. She needed money to go on the bus to see Dick and she liked to bring him something. Each transaction broke over her like a wave and it was always borne on the same tide. What have I done with my life? Why have I no money, no courage, no life of my own? She was like a child being sent to the shops for the messages, not quite understanding the money that had been put into her fist.

On the way back she was nibbled by homesickness, for her

own bed, with the picture of Our Lady over it, and her own television. Then she remembered the spooks that were in
occupation. It wasn't her home any longer.

She was tired when she reached the flat. She wanted a drink.
She stood on tiptoe, found the keyhole, stabbed the key home,
closed her eyes and twisted. Nothing happened. This was such
a surprise that she took the key right out again and waited in the
dark, holding it in her hand. She rose again on her toes and
jabbed at the hole. This time she couldn't reach it at all. Maybe
she was aiming at the wrong place. She couldn't really see. To
reassure herself she tried the small key in the lower lock. It
curled around smoothly. She said a prayer and set her bags on
the ground, then reached up and felt for the high lock. Still on
her toes and with her hand on the lock, she pushed in the
key.

A figure rushed past her in the dark. She sensed his weight and
the black hulk of his coat, like the figure of death, she thought,
although more likely it was a student in a duffle coat. But why had
he swooped at her like that, nudging her as if he had something
to impart, although the path was wide? She felt a blow to her
chest then, not from the running figure, for he was long past, his
dark coat bled seamlessly into the night. It was the realisation that
she had set down her handbag along with her shopping when she
reached up to the lock. That was why he had swooped. He was a
bag-snatcher. Although it was only shock, the blow to her chest
had a painful force. Guilt and surprise and fear. What would she
do without her handbag? No bus fare for a visit to Dick; no
money for a phone call to Ruth. Ruth would think she wasn't
capable of looking after herself, getting robbed on her first day
out. And Dick? Dick would say she was mad as a hatter, always
had been. He would put on his quiet, confiding air and explain he
had done his best to have her placed where she would be taken

proper care of, but some fool of a doctor had put him away instead.

It was a while before she could put her hand down to feel the pavement. And there was her bag, along with the shopping. Oh, what a fool she was. Her imaginary assailant was probably just running for a bus, probably hadn't even noticed her. And now she had to find the keyhole again. She repeated the whole rigmarole but she knew before she started that upset and humiliation had diminished her and however hard she tried she would not get the key in again. Tears fell down her face. She never cried. She wasn't crying now; they were just tears. What now? Call Ruth? Ruth would take over her life, destroy this little, bitter scrap of independence she had found for herself. Go home, back to her own house? The shifting shadows, like breathing corpses under grey sheets, came into her mind, and she knew she would rather stand there in the street until she died. And so she stood, waiting for death, feeling the tears go cold on her face, sliding into the warm curve of her mouth (where she had only recently felt her husband's warm kiss), until her mouth too went cold and she felt nothing at all. A kind of peace came over her, a blanket of numbness. She thought she was probably saying prayers, although she wasn't sure, so that she did not notice when a man came up quietly beside her and turned a key in the high lock.

'Oh!' She let out a little muffled note of surprise.

He glanced down at her but said nothing. He moved briskly inside and she realised that he was about to shut her out.

'I left my key,' she said, so as not to have to explain everything. She put a hand out to push open the gate, because even as she spoke, he was trying to close it. He relented slightly and she squeezed past with her bags.

'Goodnight,' she said. He said nothing, but veered off into the accommodation that had been converted from a garage. With relief, she saw the light in her window. It wasn't too bad; her own space, her own bed. As she let herself in, she saw that there was a note pinned to the door. Her spirits rose when she thought that it might be some woman in another bedsit, welcoming her to the long room and inviting her for a cup of tea or a drink. If she had someone to talk to, the whole foolish episode on the pavement would turn into a joke and they would laugh it away to nothing. There was probably some knack to the high lock and once it was explained she would not have to fear it.

She had always liked women. She would have liked a woman friend but Dick just wanted her for himself. She let herself into the flat, set down her shopping and put on her glasses to read the note.

'Please do not leave lights on when you go out – the landlord.'

She unpacked the bright cartons of frozen food and glanced at them idly, as if they were someone else's items. The notion of eating them had passed out of her mind completely. She put them in the fridge and searched the cupboards for a glass. She poured beer into a cloudy tumbler and drank it down quickly. Then she poured whiskey into the same glass and sat on the bed. When she was more relaxed, she ate a few cheese straws. What next? What next? She kept having to prod herself, like a broken-down donkey at the bottom of a hill. She would get into bed and read her newspaper. She rummaged in the case for a nightie, undressed quickly, and packaged herself into the damp and thinly covered single bed. As she scanned the paper, she became aware of some beam coming in at her, which was not from the dirty-skirted overhead light. It came from the make-shift garage room. She glanced up and saw that the man was at the window, staring in at her. She tugged at her curtain, but it was crooked on its rail and would not pull across properly. As she turned out the light, she felt as if earth was being shovelled on top of her, as if every last chink of light had been excluded, even though the garage light still shone in. Then she remembered: tomorrow she would be going to see Dick. That made her feel better.

22

⌀

'I'm worried about your mother.' Pa didn't even check the parcels Ruth had brought. 'She's done an awful thing. Walked out, just walked out of the house and left it.' He said it with the suggestion of doors left swinging behind her. 'I bought that house for her.'

Ruth could feel his panic. First his daughter had left home, then his wife. Never mind that the house was a pit of discomfort, an exploitation of female dependence and labour, it was his testimonial – a monument to his role as provider.

'Try not to worry about it.' She put away the sweets and the TV guide. 'All the recent events have been a big shock to Ma. She's just hiding out for a while.'

Dick sank back on the bed. 'I frightened her. I terrified her out of her wits. I am Frankenstein's monster. I have the heart of a man and the head of a monster. I want to be loved, but who can love me? We all have nightmares, Ruth, and some of them are living ones, but can you even imagine what it is like to live inside a nightmare – to be a decent ordinary man who every so often is taken over by a freak? This . . . this . . . *thing* overtakes me. It does and says terrible things and all the time I am shut inside. There could be no worse hell for any man. No one recognises me any longer for who I am and I am mocked and humiliated.'

'I know, Pa.'

'No you don't. You don't know what it's like to be me. Even now, when I am recognisably myself, I am locked away, helpless, while my home falls to pieces. Lily isn't like you, love. She's a child, always had every decision made for her. She's not able to look after herself. I'm a dead man that can see, stuck in here, knowing everything that goes on and not able to do a damn thing about it.'

Pa seemed very low. She supposed it was natural under the circumstances, but all the same she made a mental note to have a word with the doctor. 'If it makes you feel any better,' she said, 'I've asked Professor Walcott to keep an eye on her.'

'What do you mean?' He was sharp as a razor. 'Do you agree with me, then, that your mother is not quite herself? I think she has been drinking. Did you know that – that your mother was always a secret drinker? I have never told anyone that before. It is a private cross I have had to bear.'

She resisted an urge to stuff a pillow over his face. A moment ago she had been filled with a desperate pity for him. It was true that Ma was probably drinking more than was good for her at the moment. Who wouldn't under the circumstances? But up to that, all her life, she had never taken more than a guilty nip in her coffee.

'Ma's all right,' she said. 'Tim Walcott is just keeping an eye on her as a friend.'

'Get on all right, do they?'

'They do in a funny kind of way. She actually keeps a pack of biscuits in the house for him now.'

Arthur Ferris came into the ward. He had been to the kiosk to buy a paper. He looked distinguished in his camel dressing gown.

'This is my daughter, Ruth,' Dick said to him. 'She's an architect.'

'You must be proud of her.' He smiled at Ruth. 'Would I know your work? Where can it be seen?'

'Don't bother your head,' Dick tipped him. 'Piffling ladies' stuff!'

23

The girl in the chemist was chatty. Lily was glad of it, for she had still spoken to no one at her new address. All she had for company was the cry of a baby somewhere over her head. The assistant had blonde fluffy hair and a pink fluffy jumper. Her eyes rolled as she talked about the weather. She liked January, though, because the new holiday brochures came out. Best part of the holiday – that first sighting of the early-booking offers. Made you think about a bikini and a leg wax. You could nearly convince yourself winter was over. 'Like a lip gloss, do you?'

'No, not a lip gloss. It gets eaten off when I have a meal.'

She produced an exotic array of boxed sets and gilded containers. 'This is the Christmas range. I could let you have a bit off any of these. There's no demand at this time of year and by next Christmas they'll want the new collections.'

Lily inspected the interesting items – fluted silver batons with little mirrors that flicked up from the outer casing; paintboxes with multi-coloured fondant squares like wine-soaked liquorice allsorts. There was a vaguely rude-looking lipstick in glossy purple with a little pearlised eye at its centre, to give an iridescent sheen.

She was learning to cope with the double lock. The trick was to twist it a little to the left before turning it to the right. Now and then she got stuck but it didn't seem too bad in daylight.

'I really just wanted an ordinary lipstick. One that will stay on and won't cost too much.'

'This one's new. It's called Kiss–Proof. Won't leave a smudge when you kiss your boyfriend.' She laughed with a sound like wind chimes. 'Do you like a nice bright colour? Well, we all need a bit of colour this time of year.'

'You look pale.'

'I'm fine. I'm always pale.' Lily searched the newspaper for items that would interest him. 'It's been the wettest January in forty years. February looks even worse. A man in Tramore was killed when his car was swept into the river by a storm.'

'Are you still in that flat?'

'Listen to this, Dick. There's a new bill to ban smoking in public places! Do you think people will stand for that? We wouldn't be able to have a smoke in the cinema.'

'You should be in your own home.'

She set down the paper. 'I just need somewhere I can think.'

He shook his head several times. He was totally mystified, as if he had found a farewell note in an empty bird cage. 'Why do you want to think?'

'Dick, dear . . .' Lily sighed. She scanned the headlines again, trying to find something else that would divert him. 'Gay Byrne is being tipped to replace Eamonn Andrews on *This Is Your Life*.'

'Startling!' he said. 'You look startling.'

'Oh, it's my new lipstick,' she smiled as she remembered. 'It's a bit brighter than usual but the girl in the chemist said we need a bit of colour this time of year.'

'I liked the old one. Why did you change?'

She shrugged. 'I felt the need of a change. It's a new brand,' she told him. 'It's called Kiss-Proof. I told the girl in the chemist I wanted one that would stay on. She said, "This one won't smudge even if you kiss your boyfriend."' She laughed, remembering the girl's blithe merriment. Dick gazed at her bleakly.

'I have no visitors.'

'You have me,' she said. 'You have Ruth. I'll drop a note to Connie Herlihy. I'm sure she'd love to see you.'

'Professor Walcott never came. He never gave me a game of whist.'

'He's a very busy man, Dick.'

'Not too busy to go and see you.'

It was ridiculous, but she felt embarrassed. 'He was just passing.'

'I should think he passes by this hospital quite a lot.'

'He always asks after you.'

'Always? I was not aware that his visits to you were continuous.'

'No, of course not, Dick.' She was doubly embarrassed now, for his voice had risen and the other men in the ward were looking.

She was getting used to the flat. It wasn't a friendly place, but she slept better knowing there were people around. She was learning to manage her money, to avoid impulse buys, and she was starting to recognise other tenants. There was an elderly married couple who occupied the downstairs front rooms and she had seen them several times in the shops. 'I'm in the basement flat.' She finally worked up the courage to speak.

'I hope you're settling in.' Their tone did not invite familiarity.

'Oh, yes, but there's a baby,' Lily blurted out. 'It seems to fret a lot. I wondered if it's all right.'

'I doubt that very much,' the man said. 'The mother is not even married.'

'Someone should do something,' the woman added. 'She leaves that child alone at night.'

'You ought to complain,' the man told Lily. Lily had a better idea. Just thinking about it cheered her. She would offer to baby-sit. The girl could stay out as long as she wanted. Of course she would not accept payment. She liked the idea of a child for company.

'What's her name?' she called out as the couple turned to select a barbecued chicken.

'Emerald,' said the man with distaste.

'Miss Emerald,' Lily memorised.

'That is the child's name,' the woman said sharply. 'The mother is Hanley. Kathleen Hanley.'

As she pressed the bell marked 'Hanley' she rehearsed what she would say, that she was not offering charity. She would look on it as a favour.

The door was answered by a stocky, dark-haired teenager who unleashed a torrent of abuse before Lily could speak. 'You're one of them, aren't you?' She held the door as a barrier. 'Bloody cow! You're going to report me. I could lose my rent allowance. Emerald will be taken away. She'll be put into care. Is that what you want?'

'No, I . . .'

'How would you like to be stuck with a bloody kid all day long? I look after her all right. I'm entitled to a life of my own.'

Lily waited patiently for the outpouring to end. 'I have no life of my own,' she said. 'I wouldn't mind being stuck with a child. I'll look after Emerald. I'll look after her for nothing.'

The girl eyed her warily. Then she grew angry. 'What are you? Some kind of bloody nutter? You just leave us alone.'

'My wife is having an affair with another man,' Dick called across the ward to Bill Turlough.

He had misjudged Turlough. So what if he was in the IRA?

Half of Ireland had been in the IRA. In point of fact, he was a decent skin, though not much to say for himself. He had given Dick some of his books to read – men's books, life in the raw. Not dirty, filthy stuff, but rough in parts, spies and so forth.

He didn't see Ruth coming into the ward, because he was talking to Turlough. 'Medical man!' he called out. 'They get to see too many woman. Get in the way of putting their hands all over their private parts. Can't get enough of it.'

'Hello, Pa,' Ruth said.

'Oh, Ruth.' He addressed her urgently. 'I've been reading a terrifically good book. A bit raw, but not blue. You wouldn't give it to a woman. This group of men has to undertake a dangerous mission and in order to demonstrate that they are up to it, they must undergo a series of tests. One of the things they have to do is to masturbate with sandpaper.'

'Is that why you called me away from work? To tell me that?'

'What do you think of Walcott?' he said sharply.

Ruth sat down. 'I didn't care for him at first, but I think he's a good man – and a good doctor.'

'I'm not so sure,' Pa said. 'I think he's a bit of a philanderer.'

'Oh, rubbish,' Ruth said. 'Anyway, his private life is none of our business.'

'Unhappily it is mine. He is having an affair with your mother.'

Ruth laughed.

'You may laugh.' He gazed at her bleakly. 'But tell me this, then. Why is your mother wearing Kiss-Proof lipstick?'

She shook her head. 'I'm going home. I interrupted a day's work to get here.'

'A day's work!' he scoffed. 'I don't suppose you have ever done a real day's work in your life.'

She stood to leave. He held up his hand to halt her like a traffic policeman. 'Hear me out. I know what I am talking about.'

'I'm sorry to say this, Pa, but you're nuts.'

'Kiss-Proof lipstick! Kiss-Proof lipstick. It's as plain as the nose on your face. And that is a bloody plain nose. This is some new kind of lipstick that won't leave its mark on a man. There is only one reason on God's earth why a woman would use it, and that is to conceal the evidence.'

'Evidence of what, Pa?' She stood over him. She decided to menace him. 'My mother has never looked at another man in fifty years of married life. She could have done. She was very pretty once. And if she had done, no one would have blamed her. You want to know what I would have done? I would have cheered. But she didn't, and what's more she never even thought of such a thing. Ma's a good woman, a decent woman, and her reward for that has been to be nagged at and picked on all through her adult life. And now she's old and tired, you want to drag her name through the mud as well. It's time you stopped indulging your self-pitying fantasies and gave a thought to her.'

Nice Mr Ferris in the next bed made a screen of the business section of his *Irish Times*. Pa cringed on his pillows. All the air went out of Ruth in a gust of hopelessness. What on earth was she doing, arguing with a daft old boy?

'I do think of your mother.' His voice came out from underneath the blankets. 'I think of her all the time.'

'Sure, Pa.'

'What else is a man to do when his best girl is taken in adultery?'

She sat in the car with her head on the steering wheel. Increasingly, her visits to her parents sapped her. What was happening to Pa? He had been like a lamb before he came home for Christmas, a rather frisky little lamb, but manageable. Obviously the trip home and all the subsequent fuss had been bad for him, but he should be getting better now, after several weeks back in hospital. Instead he seemed to be on some sort of dangerous spiral, rising up and up towards what? She beat her hand on the wheel. Paranoia. She got out of the car and ran back into the hospital, up in the lift.

'I am going to get a lock installed on my door.' The doctor looked up as Ruth entered. 'And it will be there especially for you.'

'What is happening to my father?'

'He is ill.'

'I know all that, but what has been happening to him since Christmas? He seems to be in some new phase or else the miracle pills aren't working any more.'

'I'm afraid there has been a development. I've been meaning to talk to your mother.' He put on his spectacles, took out some notes and read them to her as if issuing a report on the weather.

24

Lily found a mouse. At first it was only a spoor, a fecklessly strewn trail. She had her hand in the back of the cupboard reaching for the whiskey bottle when her fingers encountered the evidence. She fetched a cloth and wiped the shelf scrupulously, catching the contents on a sheet of newspaper. Scraps of paper made a shingle with biscuit crumbs and a few mouse droppings. She studied these tokens with a kind of excitement. Imagine! A mouse in her living room.

She located a Ryvita pack with a hole chewed out of the side. There was just half a stale wafer of rye left in the box. She used to like these dusty-tasting crackers but then she preferred salty Ritz crackers or crunchy Pringles, eaten with pickles straight from the jar. Lately she wasn't all that keen on food of any kind, and anyway there was nothing in the flat. She needed something to lure the mouse. Cheese. Mice liked cheese. She might even eat a piece of Cheddar herself. It was nine o'clock and very dark but the need to attract the mouse and the thought of a nice sharp piece of red cheese to go with a beer for her supper suddenly seemed agreeable. She put on her coat and picked up her bag and keys.

On the way through the yard she could feel the eyes of the man in the garage. She ignored him, for he never said hello. He never did anything but stare. At first she had felt sorry for him, living out his life in quarters intended for a car (she imagined his accommodation still had the oppressive lead odour and that oily rags hung in his room instead of tea towels), but now she had grown accustomed to bedsit life she perceived that he had the choicest location. Although he lived alone and never had a visitor, he had the whole panorama of flat life spread out for his entertainment. There must never be a dull moment in his day. He would know the secrets of each of the residents and would even be acquainted with day-to-day changes of habit; if one had broken her diet or another beaten his wife, even if any were constipated. Up to now, she would have been horrified by the notion of spying on strangers. She had always kept to herself and her family. Reminded of her past life, she felt a sudden hankering for its comforting monotony, for the absorbing cycle of service; her arms were shaped for small labours imbued with warmth, as if those limbs sprang straight from the heart. The smoothing of sheets, the buttering of bread, the cutting up of meat and vegetables into neat pieces for a slow-cooked meal. The chores that wasted women's lives were also the breakers on the great windswept plain of time. Never mind who you married or what they were like. Marriage peopled your life and made sense of time. The repetitive female tasks that were taken for granted by men and children (and which she had frequently resented), she now saw as a prayerful litany. For every phrase there was a response. You made a bed, someone slept in it. You buttered a loaf, someone was nourished by it. You washed a shirt, someone was sent into the world bearing the shield of another's care.

Before letting herself out on to the street she looked back at the house. Young girls and men, middle-aged women, old men, old women, went about their cramped and solitary lives unaware that she saw them or even that she existed. Since coming to live in the flat she had encountered only the man in the garage, the elderly couple and the cross young woman with the baby. One day, when she passed the front door it was open and the pram was in the hallway. She had looked around before going in. There was no-one about and she was at last able to enter the hall. It was a disappointing place. The neglected paint and closed-off rooms made it look abandoned. She was glad of the baby, though, for she felt acquainted with it already. It was a little girl, about a year and a half. She gazed at Lily with that age-old look that chimpanzees have in the zoo. Lily said 'hello', and the child formed her mouth into an 'o' as if to try for speech, but then she frowned and rummaged at her blankets with her fingers.

'I'd like a piece of red cheese, please.'

'Processed or mature Cheddar?' the girl in the late-night shop wanted to know.

Lily said she didn't mind.

'What's it for? Is it for cooking or the cheese board?'

'It's for a mouse.'

The girl cut a wedge from a damp-looking orange brick. 'You'll be wanting a nice mouse trap to go with that.'

Lily looked at her in bewilderment and then shook her head and moved away with the single plastic bag in her wire basket. She chose a can of beer at the off-licence section. The whiskey bottle had been empty in the bare cupboard. She couldn't believe how quickly it had vanished. Maybe there was a whiskey-drinking mouse in the cupboard as well. She ought not to buy more. It was a luxury. But it was company; it took the edge off her loneliness. Company couldn't be viewed as a luxury.

Back in the dark lane she did battle with the high lock in the outer door. She knew it was nerves, that it was because of the dark. She set down her shopping, took a deep breath and said a prayer to St Jude, the patron saint of hopeless cases. She was surely a hopeless case. The key swam in its prescribed circle like a gold-fish. The door swung open. With relief she noted that the garage light was off. She hated having to pass that stare. Her light was off too, of course, for the landlord had warned her about wasting electricity. This made it difficult to lock the gate and open her own door, but she achieved the first task with a further petition to St Jude and then tried to find her way across the yard to her entrance. Something made the hairs on the back of her neck stand on end. She got the feeling she was being followed. It was awful how nerves got to you, but she had left the ghosts behind in her home, she must not allow them to find her at her new address. Determinedly, she turned around and reached out into the dark to assure herself of empty space. Her hands encountered bulky wool over some other bulk, a man's hard ample belly. Not a sound came out of her. She stayed there with hands outstretched but her shopping fell from her grasp and she heard the whiskey bottle break on the concrete. She put out her hand again. There was nothing there. She concentrated on the key and the lock. ('St Jude, help me, help me, help me.')

As she switched on her light, the light in the garage went on and the man looked out at her. Before she went to bed she crumbled up a small bit of the cheese and left a trail from the back of the cupboard out on to the floor. She listened as she lay in the dark. After about an hour she heard a small sound – scratch, scratch, scratch – and then a sort of hasty shuffle or scuffle. It almost made her smile to think of the mouse doing a celebratory hornpipe.

Ruth picked up the long shards of glass, the jagged ashtray from the bottle's bottom, the playful half circles from the neck, like pieces from a wicked teething ring. The rain had washed away the whiskey but left the yard with the stale morning breath of a public house. 'Some drunk!' she clucked. Ma, living in a place like this!

Ma seemed all right. She was ready in her coat and hat, waiting to go to the hospital.

'We'll have a cup of tea first,' Ruth said.

'Pa will be waiting for me.'

'I want to talk to you.' Ruth filled a kettle and put milk in the cold white emptiness of the fridge.

Ma sat down, still in coat and hat. 'I've got a mouse,' she said.

'I'll bring a trap,' Ruth promised.

'No,' Ma said crossly, and Ruth remembered that she had always impartially liked all creatures, regardless of classification or plague potential. 'I've been to see Pa,' Ruth said. 'I don't think you should visit him for a while. Something's happened. He's not quite right.'

'I know that.'

'The doctor says there's a problem with his treatment. They've had to cut back on his lithium. They've found out that he's got some physical problem; it's a geriatric disorder called scleroderma that affects his circulation.'

'He's had that for years,' Ma said. 'It's not serious. It gives him cold hands and feet.'

'Apparently it is serious. It affects the supply of blood to the extremities. Lithium is making the condition worse. In extreme cases, it can cause gangrene.'

'Pa's not going to get gangrene.' She said this as if she was as intimately acquainted with the blood that ran in the fierce blue scribble of his veins, as with the quirks of his personality. 'Anyway, I'd still go and see him if he had gangrene.' She looked closely at her daughter. 'It's worse than gangrene, isn't it?'

'He's paranoid. He's got severe paranoiac delusions again.'

Ma looked miserably at her shoes. 'Well, at least he hasn't got a gun. There's not much mischief he can do in there. I still have to see him, Ruth.'

'Then promise me you won't see him on your own. I'll take you whenever you want to go. And don't back him up if he asks me to leave. No matter what he says, I'm staying.'

Ma's eye strayed to the cupboard, to where the mouse was and where the whiskey bottle usually lived. 'The damn broker again, is it?'

'No, Ma, not the broker. This time it's you.'

25

⚜

Ma looked at the lift and then at Ruth. As they got in, Ruth was reminded of a dog she had once taken to the pound. Just before she handed it over, the dog had looked back at her, not hoping for anything, just confirming its fate.

'How are you, Pa?' Ruth tried to intimidate her father before he could get to Ma.

'I am as well as can be expected under the circumstances. I suppose I must be grateful for small mercies. My wife and I have had few mutual interests in our lifetime. She had her drink and her women's lib. I preferred art and music. Now, at least we have a common concern. Tell me dear,' he turned his attention to Ma, 'does our dearly beloved friend have any unusual passions? I am told that the young these days are entirely without inhibition. There are certain practices at which I drew the line, even within matrimony. Does he kiss you underneath your skirt?'

'I don't know what Professor Walcott does,' Ma said. 'He's gay. I don't know what gays do.' She inhaled very slowly and opened a plastic supermarket bag. 'I brought fresh pyjamas for you. Connie Herlihy's coming to see you. I gave her a call and told her you'd like to see her. You'll want to look nice when she comes.'

'Gay!' Pa scoffed. 'A gay blade you mean. That's a good one. I suppose that is the excuse he used in order to perpetrate unnatural practices.'

'Behave yourself, Pa!' Ruth said.

He looked bleakly and calmly at his wife and daughter. He even emitted a creaking laugh. 'She doesn't believe me.' He pointed to Ruth. 'I declare to God, I think she thinks it is all a hoax. You and I know the truth, Lily, love, don't we? Look me in the eye.' He laughed again and turned to Ruth. 'She cannot even look me in the eye.'

'I have done nothing, Dick. You have to stop saying these things.'

'I know what you have done. I know only too bitterly well. I know because I paid a private detective to follow you. He has rented lodgings directly opposite where you live and has taken photographs from the window of you and your paramour in every unspeakable position.'

Ma actually emitted a gasp, for she thought at once of the man in the garage.

Pa leaked his despairing laugh again. 'Look at her, Ruth! Look at your mother! Look at the guilty party. I don't even need the bloody awful evidence when she is drowning in her own shame.'

Dick had put on a cravat over his pyjamas. He wore a camel cardigan with leather buttons. His hair had been pressed and polished with comb and brushes and a faint aroma of lime and cedar came from his jaws. His eyes were full of a light brighter than intelligence – maybe something spiritual, Connie Herlihy thought.

When Lily had told her Dick was in hospital, she had imagined an ordinary old gentleman's ailment – prostate or arthritis; her own dad had had both. Lily was careless with details. She always had been. She mentioned a bit of trouble with his nerves but did not say that this place was where regular head-cases went. Imagine, nice Mr Butler shut up with axe murderers. Connie pulled down her skirt in case there might be rapists in the room. She got the feeling Lily hadn't really bothered to find out what kind of hospital her husband was in.

She had brought him a swiss roll wrapped in foil and a knife to go with it so that he could cut slices as needed for his tea, and she had saved up a very nice mixed bag of office gossip. She told him that young Miss Morrissey was leaving her job as she had taken a fancy to become a fashion model, and Mr Dempsey had been ticked off for using the office photocopier to run off his thesis and poor Mr Janucek's wife had finally passed away. 'Merciful release really. Mr Janucek's got the good sense to see it that way and has actually been seeing another lady. You'll never guess who.'

The exciting titbit had the whole office in a ferment. Miss Herlihy had imagined the news would be a tonic to her poor old friend. Instead, his eyes filled with tears and he seized her hand. 'You have no idea how I am suffering in here. I am surrounded by madmen and poor Lily, my poor wife . . .' He had to break off to blow his nose. Connie thought she would like to give a piece of her mind to poor Lily. She took out her compact and powdered her nose so that Mr Butler wouldn't be embarrassed. By the time she had distempered her complexion he had recovered his composure and he sat so straight she thought her heart would break.

'Do you still take shorthand, Miss Herlihy?' he asked.

'I never go to the office without a notebook in my handbag. The young girls that come in now, they don't even have a handbag, just a sort of bicycle tube called a bum bag. I don't know what they think they're for.'

'Quite so, quite so. You are true blue, Miss Herlihy. I wonder if I could ask you a very great favour? I want to write to the health board. I would be very grateful if you would type the letter up later and post it. I would not ask you, but it is a matter of the utmost urgency. My wife does not type and anyway, under the circumstances, I can scarcely ask her.'

'I'm on your side,' she promised him.

'Dear Sirs . . .' Dick began.

'Oh, I am sorry, Mr Butler. I don't go into the office on Saturday. I'll bring my notebook after work on Monday.'

He looked crestfallen. 'Oh, right-o. You don't think I'm being unreasonable?'

Poor nice old gentleman, shut up with loonies. She felt certain that as soon as the health board saw just how reasonable he was they would release him at once. 'It's none of my business, Mr Butler, but personally speaking, I think you should sue.'

'And how is our beloved friend?' Pa had a small, bitter smile. His eyes were very bright.

'I have no beloved friend.' Ma sighed as Ruth helped her into a chair.

'Well, give me your news. I have no news in here.'

She fed him bits and pieces saved up over the week. 'Scientists are saying that aspirin can prevent heart attacks. The gales have turned into a hurricane. Hurricane Charlie, they call it. A sixth man has died in the storms. A tree fell on his car.'

'That is not news. I can get your so-called news any day of the week.' He gestured towards the TV set in the ward. 'I want news of things that matter. Actually, I have some tidings. Next time you see your friend, ask him how he is enjoying the dole queue.'

'Tim?' Ma looked startled.

'Tim,' he said. 'The name sits in your mouth like a sweet. You cannot resist the opportunity to use it. *Tim* is now unemployed. I have written to the health board to inform them of *Tim*'s lewd and unprofessional conduct and they have struck *Tim* from the medical register.'

'Dick, you didn't!'

'No, of course I didn't.' He smiled at her mildly. 'I am ill-equipped for business here. Connie Herlihy is doing it for me. She told me she was on my side. She said I should sue.'

Ruth gripped Ma's arm to stop her saying anything more. She asked Pa what meals he had eaten during the week and if he needed any messages on his next visit.

'I have no appetite,' he said to Ruth. 'I think of my wife in bed with that smirking lothario and the food turns to sawdust in my mouth.'

26

Lily celebrated her seventy-sixth birthday alone. 'If only some-thing nice would happen,' she thought. 'Just one small nice thing would make it bearable.' And then she had a visitor.

'Connie!' she exclaimed in pleasure.

She had always thought of Connie as her friend more than Dick's. She was never able to talk to her properly with Dick around. As she ushered her inside she realised that a woman friend was what the flat had needed all along. She sat on the bed, giving Connie the only chair. Already the place looked cosier. 'Well, tell me all! Any news of the office?' She had cheese nachos in and a bottle of sherry.

Connie looked uncomfortable. Lily suddenly felt embar-rassed by the junk-shop furniture and the dirty lamp-shade which gave off pallor rather than light. She realised that the faint constant scratching of the mouse might irritate a visitor. If only Connie had phoned first. She would have tried to make the flat look nice, shopped for some proper food. She might even have eaten something herself. But then Connie would not have had her phone number. 'How did you find me?' she wondered.

'Lily, it's none of my business.' Connie came straight to the point. 'I don't mean to pry, but I don't think Mr Butler should be in that place.'

'I'm so glad you've come.' Lily took her hand and held it tightly. 'Dick is ill, mentally ill. It's a relief to have someone to talk to. I suppose I should have told you sooner, but it's hard to speak about such a thing.'

'If I were you,' Connie took her hand back to light a cigarette, 'I would find it difficult not to speak.'

'How did you know where I was?' Lily asked again.

'Mr Butler gave me your address. That's what I'm saying. He doesn't belong in there. He's as sound as a bell.'

'No, he's not.' Lily spoke patiently. 'Bits of his brain are sound but he suffers from paranoid delusion. He thinks I'm . . .' She stopped herself, seeing an indignant gleam in the younger woman's eye. Then, with alarm, she remembered something Dick had said. 'He asked you to send a letter.'

Connie nodded, tight-lipped.

'You're not to send that letter.' Lily gripped her wrist.

The younger woman retrieved her hand and rubbed it as if an injury had been done. 'I will send it, of course I will.'

'Do you know what is in the letter?'

'He wants to write to the health board.'

'Connie, he doesn't know what he's doing or saying.' Lily was amazed to see herself as an adversary in the younger woman's eyes. She wondered what she had done, that she was to be deprived of everything she valued.

'Mr Butler was very clear in his mind,' Connie said. 'He even sent me a lovely bunch of flowers.'

'My husband sent you flowers?'

'Yes, well it was the anniversary of my mother's death. He remembered that too. All I'm saying, Lily, is there's nothing wrong with his head.'

'Has he sent you flowers before?' He had forgotten her birthday, but he had remembered the anniversary of Connie Herlihy's mother's death.

'From time to time, but we've always had that sort of relationship. I would do him a favour and he would send me flowers. When I went to see him he had tears in his eyes. He told me I was more than a daughter to him.'

'He's my husband,' Lily said. 'I'm the one who knows him.'

'Yes, well maybe I'm the one who cares.'

The mouse came out into the room to eat the cheese. It stood on its hind legs and dipped its face to its paws like a worshipper. Perhaps eating was prayer to animals, the obedience to a natural order. Its paws were tiny tortoiseshell combs. It nibbled jauntily as if the cheese were a instrument on which to blow out a tune. It watched her as it entertained her, out of the side of its modest eye.

As long as the mouse was in the room she stayed perfectly still, not moving a muscle, so as not to startle it. Yet she knew that the mouse knew she was there. At the moment it only tolerated her. Soon it would trust her. She could break off pieces of bread and let it take them from her hand.

She felt calmer now she had a companion. The mouse suited her. She thought it was like herself, small and grey and constantly on the scuttle. She had been wrong to imagine a woman friend would bring cheer. She belonged in a different world now. She had no connection with ordinary life. She didn't even want a normal pet – one that would need to be walked or that would make a noise. Anyway, animals weren't permitted in the flats. She liked the mouse's dusty silence, its busy dining, its velvet glide beneath the floorboards.

The arrival of Tim Walcott on his bicycle was a disturbance to this odd domestic harmony.

'I'm afraid you can't come in.' She guarded the door politely but firmly.

'Why not? Got a gentleman caller?'

She looked so utterly miserable when he said it that he could have kicked himself. 'Dick doesn't like it.' She kept her eyes on the ground.

'Thinks I'm your boyfriend, does he?' He laughed.

'Yes,' she whispered guiltily.

'Oh, Lily.' He put his hands on her shoulders. 'The way his head is now, he could decide he didn't like the way the light bulb was looking at him.'

'He said awful things about you.' She glanced around in a kind of desperation.

'You just have to tell yourself he doesn't mean anything he says because he doesn't know what he's saying.'

'He sometimes does,' she protested.

'His memory's still good, but keep an eye on the whole picture and you'll see that none of what he says really makes any sense. And after you've done that, just shut your ears and don't listen to anything.'

'I've always listened to him, even when he didn't make any sense. That's what wives of my generation did. We were brought up to respect men.'

'You wouldn't have a bit of respect for me, by any chance? Let me in, Lily. I'm turning into an ice lolly. Give us a cup of tea and a biscuit.'

She looked towards the garage. 'I can't.'

'Why do you keep looking away? What are you afraid of?'

'He said he hired a private detective. He said he was watching us from that flat over there. He said he had pictures of us.'

Tim wanted to laugh, but he saw her anxious face. 'Do *you* think there are pictures of us? Pictures of what?'

She dropped her gaze. She actually seemed to be considering this. 'I'll tell you what I think. I think that for years he's been having an affair with his boss's secretary. I should have seen it. He used to say she was like a daughter to him. I think he feels I've been keeping them apart ever since he retired and his resentment is coming out on me.'

The doctor shook his head in awe. 'Pensioners' passion. Whole bloody lot of senior citizens crawling with lust. You going loopy on me too? Daftness must be catching. Tell you what. I'll deal with my affair and you deal with his. Why don't I go in and confront him? We'll have this thing out man to man. Pistols at dawn.' He patted her shoulder when he saw how she flinched.

'Just a little chat,' he promised. 'I'll come back and report afterwards. Then maybe you'll give me a cup of tea.'

On his way out he glanced into the converted garage. A man was at the sink, staring out at him.

'Tim?' Lily was still at the door.

He was about to go back but she waved him away as if she had the plague. 'Do you still have a job?'

This time he did laugh at her.

27

'Dear Sirs,' Dick began again.

Connie wriggled her bottom, as she always did when she was about to take dictation. She knew from experience that almost nothing made a man (even an old man) feel as good as giving dictation.

'I wish to inform you of an appalling practice that has been taking place underneath your noses. I speak of a certain Professor Tim Walcott, who has taken my wife in adultery.'

Miss Herlihy's pen paused like a question mark in the air. 'Is this a joke letter, Mr Butler? Is it one of those competitions in the paper?'

Dick merely made an expression of contempt and went on with his dictation. It was more of an oration, really, as if he was an actor on the stage. All the madmen could hear.

'He took advantage of my present situation, i.e. infirm and in hospital, to seduce my dearly beloved wife and introduce her to a range of unnatural practices. If you have need of evidence I can supply photographs of said couple in compromising, and if I may say so, entirely disgusting situations. I require this man to be struck off the medical register, after which I shall take further legal steps privately. With all good wishes, Yours, Richard Butler, Esquire.'

★

For some reason it hadn't occurred to Tim Walcott that the small amount of kindness he had shown Lily Butler would stir up nightmares in Dick's brain. Now, why hadn't he thought of that? The couple of visits had seemed such a minor thing to him that he hadn't even supposed she would mention them. Stupid bugger! That was the disadvantage of not being married. One forgot the way in which women had to tell their husbands everything. Even if they sometimes got killed for it.

Tim watched the orderly whisper into Dick's ear and the way Dick's neck craned in indignation. He caught Tim's eye and looked away.

'Hello, Dick.' Tim came up to the bed.

Dick pushed his chin out and gave a small, bitter smile.

'Do you want to talk or would you like to play whist?'

'Was there something you wished to talk about?' Dick said.

'I wanted to know how you are.' Tim sat down cautiously.

'About time you thought of it.'

'You've got your own doctor here. Doctors hate other medics interfering. I've been keeping an eye on Lily, though. I thought you'd want that.'

'So you've got your eye on Lily, have you?'

Tim took a deep breath. 'That's right. You're in good hands here. You're safe and sound. You've got to think of Lily now. She suffered a hell of a blow. She's strong, but I think she could be in danger of a collapse. I hope you don't think I'm interfering.'

'It would have been nice if you had asked me. I suppose I count for nothing now that I am locked away in a madhouse. It would be natural for a young man such as yourself to presume he could do anything he liked with a lone woman.'

'I'm sorry about that, Dick. We could try and get another doctor if you prefer. But I don't think she'd see one, and I think she needs one. She doesn't even think of me as a doctor.

I'm just a young twerp she feels sorry for and she gives me a cup of tea.'

'You think my wife's a little off her head, do you?'

'Oddly enough, no, given the circumstances. It's her physical health I worry about. Your wife's what's called an internaliser. She takes stress inside. When people have no way to express their fears and anxieties, it's the body that ends up crying for help. I don't think Lily is eating. Frankly, Dick, I think her heart is broken. I'm only there as someone she can talk to, so she doesn't bottle everything up. But I don't want to cause trouble. What I'm going to do is leave it up to you. You're the one who has to decide. If you say the word, I'll never have anything to do with her again. If you ask me to, I'll try and persuade her to see another doctor. But now that we've finally had this chat, I want you to take full responsibility. The choice is yours.'

Dick smiled down at the counterpane. 'I think that is what is known as a Hobson's choice.'

'No it's not. There's nothing for me in this. If you want me to make sure your wife stays well then all you have to do is ask me to look out for her and we'll shake on it.'

Dick sat still and silent a long time. At last his rigid arm came out. Tim offered his hand and Dick's hand went into it. There was so little left of that hand – no flesh or muscle, no elastic, no strength, just bones wrapped in wrinkled paper – that Tim Walcott tried to pump some reassurance or comfort into it, but the hand merely lay there, stiff and cold as a garden fork.

'Our dearly beloved friend has been to see me,' Dick said.

'I know, I'm glad. It's best to get things out in the open. He came around afterwards and said you asked him to keep an eye on me.'

'He did not waste much time.'

'No, you see, the last time he came to visit I wouldn't let him in. I told him you didn't like it. So he promised to go and ask your permission.' Even as these words came tumbling out Lily knew she was saying too much and the wrong thing. She could see resentment growing like a hedge of brambles around him.

'Do you think I wanted to give that permission? How do you think I felt with that stinking Romeo standing over my bed, reeking of the pleasures he had taken with my wife? It is not fair for a man to have to face another man when he is ill and in his pyjamas. He took advantage of me as he has taken advantage of you.'

'Why did you shake hands with him?'

'Because he threatened your life.'

Lily unwrapped the parcels she had brought – a lemon madeira cake, a half-bottle of sherry and three glasses. 'Dick, it was my birthday last week. It must have slipped our minds. I thought we'd have a little celebration. I'm seventy-six.'

'He said your life would be in danger if I did not beg him to visit you. In spite of all you have done to me, I have no wish for you to die.'

She filled the glasses and gave one to him and one to Ruth. 'I'll tell him not to visit,' she said.

'No need, no need.' He made a face and knocked back the brown fluid. 'I have seen to everything.'

'But you gave him permission . . .'

'Yes. As I said, I would do almost anything rather than see your life in danger. The same does not apply to our dearly beloved friend. In fact, nothing would make me happier than to see him wiped off the face of the earth. I am, at this moment, anticipating that happiness.'

'He's a young man. He'll outlive us by decades.'

'Not when my friends have been to see him,' Dick smiled. 'I've done a bad thing, Lily. I have paid men to deal with that toe-rag. They are from the IRA and are experts in the matter of torture and death. First of all they will slice his spine. That will render him helpless to resist the rest of his punishment. Sad to say, death will not be instantaneous.'

'Pa, this is rubbish,' Ruth said.

Lily had brought a knife to cut the cake but she lost heart and put it back in her shopping bag.

Dick's smile grew wider. 'I've damaged your appetite. I'm sorry about that. I myself have had little appetite for weeks. I wish you a happy birthday.'

'You don't know anyone in the IRA,' Lily said.

'Had you not noticed that we have lost one of our little company? Bill Turlough has left us. As you know, he has already killed for the IRA. He likes to keep in practice and he was very grateful for the few bob I put his way.'

'What will I do?' Lily asked the mouse. 'Do you think I should tell the police? They probably wouldn't lock him up. Criminally insane is much the same as mentally ill, isn't it? I suppose I'll do nothing. That's not honest is it? It doesn't matter. I've never been honest.'

She had broken a slice of the birthday cake into crumbs and sprinkled these in a fine line along the floor, starting at the cupboard. When she got to the table, she assembled an assortment of different-sized containers, her suitcase, some boxes, a few books, a stool, and made a sort of stairs. These were also scattered with crumbs. The last of the crumbs were on the table, where the mouse accepted her invitation to dine.

'I've lied to Ruth. All the talk about marriage! In fact, I used to envy single women. I used to think it must be lovely for a woman to have her own income and no one to tell her what to do. I always imagined single women hadn't any worries. I'd see them at the bus stop with their smart suits and neat little bags – no message bags – and I pictured them spending their money on clothes and holidays and going to the pictures and always having a good time. I never imagined them short of money or growing old alone in a room like this, day after day, year upon year, with no human touch and no one to talk to.'

The mouse had progressed from the crumbs to a larger lump of cake which she had left at the end of the trail as its reward. Its teeth worked at a diligent erosion all around the edges, effecting a sort of topiary, but it paused every so often to regard Lily with a bright, intelligent eye.

'I used to want to see Ruth settled. I wanted to see her with a husband and children. Maybe I resented her independence. If she was tied she'd have to be closer to me, and I wanted her in my sights. I wonder now if I might not just have been a little bit jealous. Why am I telling you this?' She held a piece of cake between her thumb and forefinger and the mouse's nose twitched. 'Why don't I tell Ruth? Why do I never say anything that means anything to my own daughter?'

The mouse put its paws together like a Japanese lady, enquiring with the utmost politeness if she would please put the cake down.

'Because I've learnt nothing.' She put the piece of cake in her own mouth and ate it without noticing. 'I thought I was perfectly resigned, to life and to God's will, but I'm not. I've learnt nothing. I've done nothing with my life and I've learnt nothing.'

She broke another piece of cake on to the table. 'Maybe I have learnt something. Maybe I've learnt patience. It was nothing to me to wait four hours for you to poke your head out and then decide whether or not you were going to trust me.'

When the small grey creature had finished its cake it did a strange thing. It crept up, took her finger in its paws and turned it over. Then it butted her finger with its nose and took a large leap back, amazed at its own audacity.

Lily was enchanted. She dealt a reward. 'It takes a long time to learn patience. More than three-quarters of a century. You're a quicker learner. It only took you a month to decide to trust me. Well, I suppose you have no choice when you're hungry. Maybe you've got babies to feed. I'll leave a nice big chunk of cake in the cupboard just in case. But you can trust me. That I can promise.'

28

Dick wanted to get rid of Ruth. He felt she undermined his authority, just the damn size of her. She flattened him, as surely as if an elephant had sat on him.

'Ruth, dear, would you go to the post office and buy me a Lotto ticket? I feel lucky today.'

'I'll bring you one next time we come,' she promised.

'Oh, all right.' He looked crestfallen. 'It's just that I feel lucky.'

'Go on, Ruth,' Ma urged.

Ruth didn't want him to get mopey. 'I'll be back in ten minutes.'

As soon as she was out of the door Dick began to laugh. 'That got rid of her. She watches us like a hawk. I can't get my wife to myself for a minute.'

'Well, now we've got ten,' Lily said.

'I needed a private word with you,' Dick confided. 'That matter we discussed last week – I don't think Ruth took me seriously. On reflection, I'm glad. Ruth is a single woman and she doesn't understand the rights of married people. She might take it into her head to tell the police. You wouldn't do that to me.'

'Dick, I don't know what you're talking about.'

'I am talking about our late, lamented friend. I wanted to let you know that the deed has been done. It wasn't quick and it wasn't pretty but it is all over now. He is no more.'

'Tim?' Lily's eyes looked huge and panic-stricken.

'Under the circumstances it is best not to mention his name.'

'I don't believe you. I know it's not true.'

'Why don't you try telephoning him if you don't believe me?'

'I haven't got his phone number.'

'I shall get you a telephone directory. Do you know the strangest thing? I feel no guilt. I go over in my mind the things Bill Turlough said would be done to him and I feel nothing except the kind of satisfaction one gets from remembering a fine meal. I paid Turlough two thousand pounds. At the time I thought that was a lot of money, although I suppose it is the going rate. Now, all I can think is that for the first time in years I have spent money wisely and well.'

'You gave a madman two thousand pounds? Why would you believe anything he said?'

Dick chuckled once more. 'Call it honour among madmen. Anyway, as is customary in such cases, he sent me a piece of evidence. A souvenir of sorts, of the pathological variety – a bit messy but hospitals are full of swabs and bandages and I managed to get it packed up nicely. Would you like a peek?' He reached into his locker and took out a small tin which had earlier contained barley-sugar sweets.

'No!' Lily almost knocked over her chair as she backed away.

He laughed out loud at her. 'It is nothing! A piece of dead meat from a butcher's slab. I don't mean to upset you. I only wanted to protect you.' He put the box away carefully. 'There. It's gone. Now there is only you and me.' She gave a little whimper as he put out his hands to her. 'Oh, damn,' he said in irritation. 'We're not alone. There's the hawk.'

He smiled pleasantly as Ruth looked in anxious query at her

mother. Lily's body was twisted away from Dick in a way that made her look warped. Ruth gave Pa his ticket. 'I think we should go now. Ma looks tired. We'll see you on Sunday.'

'I don't want to see him,' Lily said.

Pa looked at Ruth in accusation. 'What have you been saying to your mother to upset her?'

Ma was shaking. In the pub afterwards she had to use both hands to keep her glass steady. She wouldn't say anything. Shame and loyalty bound her like chains.

Ruth sighed. She had hoped to relieve her mother of her sense of responsibility for Pa by lighter means, but she knew that as soon as her back was turned Ma would go back to gobbling her share of duty, and it was poisoning her. She took a folded square of paper from her bag. 'Read this. Pa wrote this letter to some woman. He asked me to post it.'

Ma's delicate hand stroked the paper.

'You've got to accept that he's not in his right mind. He wanted to throw acid in some strange woman's face.'

Ma looked at the note dejectedly, no shock in her face, but a settling in, an acceptance of insult. She folded up the paper to its original small square and nodded slowly. 'When your Pa says terrible things to me, I feel them like acid thrown in my face.'

When Lily got back to the flat she went to work at once, cutting the rinds from several rashers. She no longer had to lay a trail, she just left the food on the table. It was there that she saw the note. Someone had been in her flat. Her heart began to thump. How would anyone get in?

Of course, it was the landlord. Landlords can get in anywhere. 'Your neighbours have been complaining of sounds of rodents scratching.' She laughed. 'You have been encouraging vermin.'

'I'll have to get you gloves,' she called out towards the cupboard.

There was more. She let out a cry and ran to the unit, dropping down on hands and knees. The note said that the nuisance had been dealt with in her absence.

She groped around inside the unit. There was the trap. She cautiously felt for the wire, hoping it had not been sprung. She didn't much mind if her own fingers got broken. Her touch was met by a small, soft and portly corpse.

She sat on her haunches, the trap in her hand, idly stroking the scrap of grey warmth. She mustn't give way to grief. There was too much of it. She must think. She didn't have to see Pa again until Sunday. With luck Ruth wouldn't ring. She had half a bottle of whiskey and a quarter bottle of sleeping pills. That should see her through. She filled a hot water bottle, got into bed, and had her supper, slurp, gulp, slurp, gulp. Darkness, as it came, was as luxurious as chocolate.

She woke, feeling like hell. She had slept for twenty hours. She was cold and hungry. Worse, she was alive. There was nothing to eat in the house and nothing to drink. It was a long time before she could drag herself out of bed and by then it was getting dark, but she would have to go to the off-licence. She left the light on to spite the landlord and pulled the curtain as best she could, trying to make it look comfortable for her return.

On her way to the off-licence she passed a pub. It looked foggy and merry so she went in and had a drink. She was pleased to see someone she knew sitting in a corner. It was the young woman with the crying baby. She wanted to wave to her but the woman didn't recognise her. A drunk man sat beside Lily and sprayed spit in her face as he told her how he had once killed for his country and now it was killing him. Sometimes she wondered if men everywhere were crazy. Even Tim was quite eccentric. All the same she was glad of the company and she gave him a cigarette and let him pay for her drink.

Coming back down the street with her carrier bag containing whiskey, beer and crisps, she felt a bit better. She had been worrying about the key in the high lock, but then she was cheered by a warm colour in the sky. Bright orange flicked the black February night. It took a few seconds for her to realise that there must be a house on fire. As she rounded the corner she saw the crowd and the fire brigade and knew it was the house where she lived that was ablaze. For a moment she was frozen with dismay, but then she understood what it meant. She need never go in there again, never struggle with the lock or see the man in the garage. 'Oh, thank God,' she thought. Sparks flew into the air like gold dust and the sky was rosy. A swirling bilge of smoke was playful as dragon's breath at a pantomime. The house itself gave out deep groans and every so often there was a pop and tinkle as windows shattered and people murmured and moved back.

For the first time, Lily could see the residents of the house properly. There were about twenty of them. If all those people had lived in one house as a family, it would have seemed extraordinary, but because they were packaged away in separate units, no one ever thought to count them. Bits of their lives were scattered around the pavement – bundles of blankets and armloads of clothes, china, electrical goods. The younger tenants looked excited. A burning house meant nothing to them except a fresh start. The older people were staring up in shocked disbelief. How could they care about the place? It wasn't a nice house. Good riddance to it.

A woman darted forward and had to be pulled back by the crowd. 'My telly!' she cried. 'I have to get my telly.'

Lily felt guilty then, realising that for some of them, it was their only home. All their possessions were in there and they had nowhere else to go. The elderly woman she had spoken to in the shop was crying and her husband had his arm around her.

'It might not be too bad.' Lily tried to offer comfort. 'The firemen will soon have it out.'

'The firemen have finished,' the woman sobbed. 'They have done all they could.'

'At least they got everyone out,' the man said.

Lily looked around at pale young faces, animated and beautiful in the glow, and at old ones into which the orange light thrust deep, scouring shadows. 'No they haven't!' she said in fright.

'The firemen searched every flat,' the man told her. 'There's no one in there.'

'The baby!' she said. 'The baby's in there.'

'They got everyone. It must be out with its mother.'

'No,' Lily said. 'I saw the mother in the pub.'

A girl came running along the pavement. She was roaring but her words didn't seem to have any distinct shape. They sounded like the guttural refrain from a pop song. As she reached the house she did not stop running but continued into the burning doorway until several people pulled her back. 'My baby!' she cried out. 'I left my baby.'

'That's the unmarried mother,' one of the women said in disapproval. 'She goes out to the pub with her pals and leaves that poor little thing all alone.'

'There's no one left.' A fat man tried to console her. 'The firemen got everyone out. They would have heard her.' Lily saw with surprise that it was the man in the garage. It was the first time she had had a proper view of him. He looked a shy and lonely man.

'I gave her Calpol,' the girl sobbed. 'I wanted to make sure she'd sleep until I got back.'

'She says there's a child in there!' someone called out to the firemen.

'Which room?' The voices sounded stagey. It all seemed like an amateur drama.

'First floor. The little room beside the bathroom, overlooking the yard,' the girl shouted back.

'You're mistaken, love.' A helmeted man ran over. 'I was in there myself. There isn't a cot.'

'I haven't got a fucking cot!' She kicked and swore at those who tried to hold her. From within the house came a huge retching sound. The crowd moved back respectfully. 'She's coming down,' one of the firemen murmured.

Lily drifted towards the house. Fear swamped her but her feet kept going forward. It was like a nightmare, advancing towards the thing she most dreaded. Even as a child, she had been terrified of fire. She couldn't help going on yet she felt sure someone must try and stop her. But one of the remarkable features of getting old was that people ceased to notice you. You could walk into a room and no one looked up. You could make a comment and nobody would answer. You could walk straight into a burning house and so long as you did it quietly, not a soul would see.

As she entered the door a blanket of heat was flung at her. She had to fend this off in order to get through. The house was full of fussy sounds, little crackles, creaks and drips. Black water sluiced through the hall bearing a tide of small domestic objects – dolls and hair rollers and table lamps. Blackened blankets, panes of broken glass and lumps of smouldering wood made a lurching silt.

The smoke slammed into her nose and throat, raking out her lungs. She experienced a moment of pure panic. She couldn't go on and she couldn't go back. As she stood gasping, a thought came to her. Men in the trenches must have felt like this. Her cousin had been gassed in the war. He had been in love with her and she had been fond of him. Odd how people could be united by separate experience. Just the thought of him gave her some strength. She tried to close her throat. She knew she mustn't start coughing. She shrugged off her coat and cardigan and wrapped the cardigan tightly round her face. Then she put the coat back on to try and keep away the heat.

As she started up the stairs she heard someone in the street shout out: 'My God! That old woman! She's gone back into the house.'

'Someone should go after her.'

'It's too late. Christ, she must be off her head!'

Was she off her head? Herself and Dick, two old crazies? She probably was. For some strange reason, she no longer even feared the fire. What could it do but kill her, and she had already attempted that herself. If she died, she might meet her mouse.

The firemen had closed the interior doors and you couldn't see any flames inside the house, just the black water and the oozing fog and the horror film sound effects. It was the heat that made the going hard. She had an urge to sit down on the stairs, to just let the heat do its worst the way you did in a sauna. Once, in a hotel, she had ventured into a sauna. There was a naked man reclining on a bench and a girl sat at the foot of the bench, tending his upright penis. She had just meant to take a peek, to see what a sauna was like. The girl was stroking the man's penis as if she was moulding it, and he looked down at it through half-closed eyes, breathing shallowly. As the girl bowed her face in homage, the man threw back his head and saw Lily, or rather, he turned his gaze on her, for his hooded glance showed no intelligence. 'Ah, ah, ah,' he sighed, and he looked at her with dying eyes as the girl sucked away his spirit. Lily had closed the door respectfully and then waited to be appalled, but no, it was very interesting to discover that the rude-looking starting mechanism for the next generation had a determination of its own and could subjugate both men and women to its will.

There was a sound like a sob catching in someone's throat and then an immense tearing as the top of the stairs came away. She was startled, for she had actually sat down on the stairs and she was beginning to drift. The flames had leaked out under a door and crept along an old runner of carpet on the landing. They parcelled the stairs like Christmas ribbon. She watched without animosity as her death danced towards her. Then she remembered the child. She had forgotten that this was why she had come back into the house, to get the child. She darted to the door, opened it cautiously, then shut it behind her. She could see nothing but black smoke. She felt around the room and located a bed, a sink, a wardrobe. She thrust her hands into the wardrobe. Old shoes, plastic bags. She groped her way around the other side of the bed. There was nothing except a plastic laundry basket, full of old blankets. As her hand went over the blankets, another hand came up to meet it. Very small fingers gripped hers. The laundry basket was where the baby slept. Lily hauled the little girl out. Sticky arms went around her neck. She felt overcome with tiredness and relief. How nice it would be to end it all like this, with a child in her arms. It was just like holding Ruth when she was small. No, no, it wasn't Ruth. It wasn't her child. There was something she had to do. She didn't want to do anything else. She just wanted to hold the child. She remembered a character in an incomprehensible play Ruth had taken her to, who kept saying, 'I'll go on.'

'That's it,' she muttered into her cardigan. 'I'll go on.' She opened the door and found that most of the floor was ablaze. She was surprised when the flames actually touched her and scorched her. She was about to make a dash for it when the child started to scream; terrible piercing wails: 'Teddy! Teddy!' Lily tried to calm her but the child struggled and bellowed. She began to cough, great hacking noises. She must have survived the smoke by burying her head in the blankets. Lily battled her way back to the room. Teddy was probably the girl's only companion when she was alone in the house. She couldn't say he wasn't important. A quick prayer to St Christopher and the bear was located at the bottom of the laundry basket. The child was choking badly now. No time to think. She felt the baby's bottom and it was damp. She whisked off the nappy and wrapped it tightly around her face. Now that she had her bear, the little girl didn't seem to mind. There was a staggering sound as the house began to shift on its axis. The noise horrified her and the heat hit her like a mallet. She ran and fell down the remainder of the stairs, shot out into the street as if launched from a cannon.

'She's got the child!' someone shouted.

She wondered why the firemen shouted 'Get back!' as people rushed to help her. Another murmur ran through the crowd and people dispersed wildly as if they had been hosed. Two firemen caught and pulled her away as she felt a sputtering of hot rubbish around her and the house started to come down.

Chapter 29

Dick fretted at a window. The sky was frail as china, a bowl of cherub clouds. Where was Lily? He held on to a rosary and slipped the beads through his fingers. 'Hail Mary, where's Lily?' He had not seen her in more than a week. He had a vague memory of her saying she didn't want to see him. That made him anxious. Something else was making him anxious; something the doctor had said. What had the doctor said? He must have written it down? He was careful, lately, not to rely on his memory.

He went to his locker to look for his diary. Like Ruth, he had always kept a diary. What month was it? March. Came in like a lion, went out like a lamb. As he was meant to do. Yes, that was it. One of the nurses had mentioned St Patrick's Day.

March seventeen: 'Lily made a queen of puddings. V. nice. Went to a picture called *ET* about a creature from outer space who gets lost on earth. Stupid picture, but it made me cry. The notion of goodness winning through! Had a drink with dear Lily to celebrate the banishing of snakes from Ireland!'

He stared at this with a frown. He had had oxtail soup for lunch and jelly for afters. There was no queen of puddings. He hadn't been to a picture. He traced the writing with a finger and then tapped it. How could he have gone to the pictures and not even known it?

He stared angrily at the lines, wanting to shake the truth out of them. 'God almighty,' he said in shock. He had just noticed the full date. It was an entry for the previous year. He had had no diary this year.

He began to cry. A year ago he and Lily had gone to the pictures and had a drink together. She had made him a queen of puddings and he had taken her to bed. How had this richness slipped from his grasp? He was like ET, unable to get home. He wept harder, remembering how the creature had finally been taken to hospital and had then died. Just like Lily. She must be dead or else she would have come to see him. He got an awful jolt then, thinking he had paid money to someone to have her killed. He remembered they had had some kind of disagreement. Oh, no, that wasn't Lily. That was poor Walcott.

What would become of him now? He sat on the edge of the bed, his elbows on his knees, his head in his hands, weeping steadily.

'Shut up!' the man in the next bed shouted.

He was a new man, very bad-tempered. Ferris was gone. He was probably dead too. No, no, Ferris had gone home. His wife had come to collect him and they were very gay. Dick asked if he could go with them, but Ferris fobbed him off by promising to come and see him. Bloody hypocrite!

'Where will I go?' In spite of complaints from the next bed he rocked back and forth and cried louder and louder. 'When they throw me out of here, where will I go?'

'Am I dead?' Lily asked.

'About half,' Tim Walcott said.

She accepted this solemnly and then looked startled. 'Are *you* dead?'

'We're a bit short of corpses all round at the moment,' he apologised.

'You're not dead.' She nodded but did not smile. 'I'm glad about that. I thought you were.'

'Nobody's dead, Lily. Not even that little girl, thanks to you.'

'My mouse is dead. Where am I anyway?'

'You're in hospital. You got a bit knocked about in the fire. Look, are you really a hero, or were you hoping the fire might finish you off?'

She sat up and put her hands around her knees. 'I'd almost forgotten that. Have you got a fag?'

He shook his head. 'Not allowed in the ward, but next time I come I'll bring some and you can smoke them in the jacks.'

She almost smiled. 'Bring a hip flask. Tim, I hate hospitals. Get me out of here.'

'Not so fast, lady,' he drawled out of the side of his mouth. 'You haven't answered my question.'

'Oh, yes, your question. I couldn't bear to think of a child alone and afraid, but as soon as I reached her, she wasn't alone any more. I didn't really want the bother of going back down the stairs. That was a difficult moment.'

'Well, you're a heroine now, and a celebrity. I've brought the newspapers.'

'Pa will go mad.' She glanced at the papers without much interest.

Her hair and eyebrows had got frazzled in the fire and there were burns on her hands and temples. She was anybody's fancy, really, but he liked her. Maybe mad old Dick was right to be jealous. She was nearly half a century older than him and he had never got to grips with women anyway, but it was a rare thing to find a person of any age or sex with whom you could be honest and at ease.

'Get me out of here, Tim,' she said. 'I want to go home.'

He watched her in his cocky, birdlike way. 'I could, but I won't. You've been half-starved and half-pissed for months. I've known and you've known I've known but there was nothing I could do – or Ruth either. You're a tough old bird, but now you're going to stay here until you're fat and sober.'

'Gay, indeed!' she said crossly. 'You're just a killjoy, like all the rest of your sex.'

Chapter 30

The nurse told Dick he had a visitor. Since he had thrown a vase of flowers at Connie Herlihy, his callers had to be announced in advance.

'Oh, it's you,' he said when he saw that it was Ruth. 'Get my suitcase. I want to show you something. Under the bed.'

She hauled out his case and was surprised to find it neatly packed with his clothes, ready to go home at a moment's notice. Earlier he had complained that they had taken his clothes away.

'Open the zip compartment. There's a magazine.'

Her hand slid in and withdrew a copy of *Penthouse*.

'Put that back!' He was furious. 'Stop playing the monkey. That's dirty, filthy rubbish. No decent woman would look at it.'

She fished around and came out with a dull black-and-white photographic magazine with an old-fashioned picture of a girl on the cover. It was the magazine she had brought him on the day he was admitted to hospital.

'What do you think?' he said excitedly. 'That girl on the cover. Don't you see the likeness?'

'For me?' Ruth raised an eyebrow as she inspected the shadowy study of a girl, about eighteen and very pretty. She had wavy blonde hair and wore a string of pearls over a twin-set.

He laughed at this piece of humour. 'Good God, no, not you. Your mother.'

'Ma?' Ruth knew she must not smile, but he read something in her eyes.

'You know nothing about your mother. She is extremely attractive to the opposite sex. I would not expect you to know about that.'

'Pa, she's seventy-six. She just wants to be left alone.'

'They wouldn't leave her alone.' He began to cry.

'Pa, Ma is . . .'

'I know what Ma is. She's dead.'

'No, she's not dead, Pa.'

The tears disappeared at once. 'Lily? She's alive? Oh, thank God. I'll have a Mass said in thanksgiving.' His mood changed and he grew sullen. 'Where is she? Why didn't she come to see me?'

'She's not well. She's in hospital.'

'Oh, poor Lil.' He grew contrite and was silent for a while. 'Drink, was it?'

'She saved a child in a fire.' Ruth fought against impatience. 'The house she was living in burned down. When she comes out of hospital she'll be going home. Didn't you read the papers? It was in all the papers.'

'I can't read any more, love. Old eyesight is going. I think I'm going blind. Oh, but Lily is well and she's going home!' He clasped his hands together and jiggled them in silent celebration. 'That's wonderful news. Oh, Ruth, you have no idea how happy that makes me. Did you know, I am going home too?'

'Yes, Pa.' She felt too weary to argue with him.

'Now Ruth, I've just had a great idea. There's something I want you to do. I want you to buy pearls for your mother. She would look just like that beautiful young girl in the photograph with a string of pearls. You know, I've been a fool, fighting with her. I've driven her away. Now I'm going to fight back instead. I took desperate measures to see off the Late Lamented. I had no choice in that matter. But I was wrong to take it out on Lil. Lily's a good girl. I got her nothing for her birthday. The pearls will be a late birthday gift.'

She watched the ferocious, crab-like scrawl as he pressed his pen to the cheque book. What was he going to put down?

'About thirty pounds,' she suggested. 'I'll get a nice necklace from Brown Thomas.'

'You think me cheap,' he glowered. 'I am not cheap. I know how to do things in the right way.' He laboured with his pen for several minutes, then handed her a cheque for three thousand pounds.

After two weeks, Lily had a visit from a nun attached to the order that ran the hospital. 'I am told you are not eating,' she rebuked. 'Do you not think you are being ungrateful to those who are making you well and to God who has provided for you?'

'Don't lecture me,' Lily said crossly. 'I don't see anybody show-ing me much gratitude. I saved a child's life. I didn't get many chances in my life but I've always done what I could. Nothing came of it. I did my best for everyone and got no thanks.'

'What thanks do you require?' The sister was aged beyond gender. She still wore the old-fashioned habit and resembled an ancient monk with her pale whiskery face and shrewd, innocent eyes that were like the eyes of Lily's mouse.

Lily couldn't very well tell a nun she was furious because no one would let her have a drink. 'My husband is mentally ill and he has turned against me,' she said instead.

'Alzheimers?'

'No, he knows who I am, but he suffers from delusions.'

'That sounds unhappy for him too,' said the old lady. 'Perhaps it would be a natural thing for a married couple to get a cross they could carry together.'

'But we're not together,' Lily protested.

'No, of course not. You got one end and he got the other.'

'If you ask me, we're more like two ends of a pantomime horse,' Lily's fingers twitched for a cigarette. Talk was always accompanied by smoke. 'It's a useless sort of way to end our days.'

'Useless to you, perhaps,' the nun said. 'Try to remember that your present life is part of God's plan. Your task is a kind of sacrament. If we wish to do God's will, we must simply receive this sacrament by a ready acceptance of whatever He sends us.'

'You're talking about faith,' Lily said. 'I used to get comfort from religion but now I think you can't have faith unless you have hope.'

'I believe the reverse is also true,' said her ancient visitor.

She was thinking about this when a blonde woman in a satin negligée came and perched on her bed. 'I'm Frieda – a gallbladder,' she divulged. 'And what is the cause of your woes, flower?'

'I made a mess of my life.' Lily gave her a discouraging look.

The woman responded with a laugh that was like boots sinking into stones. 'Didn't we all?'

'I don't know anything about other people's lives,' Lily said. 'My own has taken up all of mine.'

'Well, I shall tell you then.' Frieda leaned close to confide. 'I have brought five sons into the world. They conspire with my husband in depressing me.'

'You mean, oppressing.'

'*Au contraire*! I mean they depress me. They keep telling me to be my age. I have been donating my organs towards the cause of my liberation. A thyroid here, an ovary there. I get periods of leave from family life. It is the only time I can be myself.'

'There's a lot to be said for normal family life,' Lily said.

Frieda shook her head. 'Family life outlives its charm when children grow big and brutish, and husbands small and silent. I count my remaining gizzards like money. As each one shows signs of wear, it earns me a term of freedom. I shall miss them, but I send them off with my blessing.'

'You are paying a high price for your time off,' Lily worried.

'You are quite wrong!' Frieda struck her a friendly blow. 'The worst thing — the very worst thing — is to be buried as a healthy corpse. By the time I bow out there shall be nothing left but the squeak. What remains of my life is dedicated to liberating that invisible slave army of giblets that lives inside every woman. And do you know what? I have never felt so well in my life.' She peered at Lily closely and with concern. 'You don't look well, though?'

'I'm all right, really,' Lily said. 'I hate hospital. I'm not like you. I can't be myself in here.'

'Oh, but maybe this is the real you. I'll bet you're really *nice* most of the time. No matter! I have the cure.' She took a small brown bottle from her handbag. 'It is blessed water from the holy well of St Patrick.'

She took off the cap and Lily covered the top of the bottle with a finger to receive a drop. Frieda was helpless with laughter. 'No, not like that.' She held it to Lily's mouth and Lily sniffed.

'It's whiskey,' she realised. 'Paddy whiskey.'

'Just as I said.' The woman gave a conspiratorial wink. 'From the holy well of St Patrick.'

Lily glugged like a baby. To her surprise, it tasted horrible. Without realising, she was getting used to being on the dry. Her next caller was Connie Herlihy. She looked so smart in her bright green suit with a floral scarf at the throat. Lily would have liked to tell her how well the colour suited her but she was wary of her glamour girl now.

'Sorry,' Connie whispered.

Lily looked up in surprise.

'I'm ashamed of myself. I wanted to tell you before but I was embarrassed. I had to see you anyway. There's something I have to tell you. I've got a gentleman friend.'

'A gentleman!' Lily's face was suddenly eager.

'An older man, but a real gentleman! Course we've known each other a very long time. Do you know who I mean, Lily?'

She was at a loss for words and even for feelings. Her first reaction was an unexpected shaft of hope. Maybe this strong young woman would take over her burden. Imagine never having to worry about Dick again, never to tense in apprehension of his moods. 'I think we should go and talk somewhere else, Connie. Do you have a cigarette?'

When they reached the windowed area that was reserved for smokers, Lily saw how the other woman's face was lit up. It wasn't just the green suit. 'It's Mr Janucek!' Connie said, and Lily had to rummage around for some suitable expression.

'You guessed, didn't you? Well, it wouldn't be hard, I know. I used to try not to talk about him too much, but I couldn't help it. We've always been close, ever since I went to work at Galvan's. Then, when his poor wife got sick, he would sometimes take me for a cup of coffee and pour his heart out. She passed away, poor Mrs Janucek. We haven't had a courtship as such. Well, it wouldn't be right with Mrs Janucek just buried, but he said to me, "Connie, you've been my mainstay. Let me make you my wife." '

'You could have a child.' Lily smiled with genuine pleasure. 'That would be a fine thing for Mr Janucek – a fresh start.'

'Nothing was said when his wife was alive. We both knew, but we never thought he'd be free.'

'You'll make a very good wife. Marriage isn't easy, though. You can know your partner but you can't know what life has in store. Look at poor Mrs Janucek – and Dick.'

Connie bit her lip. 'He seemed so normal.'

'Yes, I know that,' Lily said.

'That letter I told you about. I couldn't take it down. I couldn't even tell you what was in it.'

'It's all right. I know what was in it. He doesn't know what he's doing.'

'He threw a vase of flowers at me. Oh, Lily, I'm sorry. I swear to God I'd no idea.'

Lily patted her hand. 'No one knows what happens inside a marriage. It's better that way.'

The old nun brought lives of the saints for her to read. She liked the two Teresas – Teresa of Ávila, whose relationship to God was like that of Jane Eyre to Mr Rochester, alternatively sniping and swooning; and little St Thérèse of Lisieux, with her flirtatious face and her child's stoicism. These books made her think and thinking made her hungry. Hospital food was not appetising, but she enjoyed the small enamel pots of tea and plates of sandwiches. She no longer felt an urge to climb out the window and run through the streets in her nightie, looking for a drink. She had grown unused to alcohol and even found it difficult to get through Frieda's friendly offerings. Instead she would ramble down to the hospital chapel. She was sitting there, breathing in the cool, waxy air which seemed to her like oxygen, when Ruth arrived to take her home.

'Already?' She looked at her daughter in dismay.

'I thought you hated it here,' Ruth said. 'If you don't feel able for things I could book you into a convalescent home.'

'Oh, I'm able for things. I feel fine, but . . .'

But she felt she didn't want any of it any more, the house or her marriage or the life she had carried all those years. The hospital

had been warm and safe and people were friendly. While she had
been there she scarcely thought about Dick, although she prayed
for him all the time. As they drove home, she had that same look
she used to get before stepping into the hospital lift.

'All right, Ma?' Ruth said.

She experienced a suffocating sense of panic as the car veered
off the city highway and slowed down to negotiate the narrow
streets of the suburbs.

'I'm all right.' I'll go on.

And there was her house. Her house where she had held a torch
while Dick screwed in a fitting a week before they were put
together for life, and she knew that she should not marry him; her
house which they had excitedly filled with cheap oddments from
the back rooms of auction houses; where they had proudly
presided over little tea parties, like dolls-house parties. And when
she had walked through her door with the blanket-wrapped scrap
of Ruth, the mismatched ingredients of marriage seemed to come
together, risen and golden, like a cake. Her house, where the old
oddments of furniture had claimed squatters' rights and the face of
marriage became her own face, feeding off her life and energy
until she was old and used up and calmed down, and then whatever remained of the people she and Dick had been or might have
been were content just to prop one another up, until . . .

Ever since the old nun had come to see her, there had been a
question in Lily's mind. Had Dick felt the same way she did, that
he had done his best with the chances he was given, and nothing
had come of it? Were they shouldering the same burden? She
sighed, missing him, for like it or not, they had grown to be the
halves of one another.

'Let's go in, Ma,' Ruth said. 'We'll have some tea.'

'Yes, tea,' Lily smiled. She thought of how her curtains

whispered in the night and shadows slithered round the walls. It must be great to be Ruth, to whom a house was just a house.

'It's warm in here.' Lily sniffed the unaccustomed air.

'Yes, I dropped by the house and turned the heat on before I came to collect you.' Ruth hung up their coats and went through to the kitchen. The table had been set and there were flowers in a vase. 'A new table cloth!' Lily fingered the pretty floral print. 'That's nice. About time too.'

'I left some sandwiches under a cover and the kettle's on a simmer, so all you have to do is sit down and light a cigarette,' Ruth said.

Lily did as she was told. She hadn't had a cigarette in days and the first intake of smoke made her eyes water. She blinked and looked up, and there was the Sacred Heart, hanging on the wall, just as He used to. No, something was different. The walls were always a dirty beige. Now they looked fresh and clean. She began to feel sleepy. It must be the heat. She struggled to stay awake for there was something nagging at the back of her mind, some remark Ruth had made. 'You said you turned on the heat,' she remembered.

Ruth smiled. 'Haven't you noticed? No, you wouldn't. I've had the kitchen redecorated – new paint, new curtains, new flooring. And that strange sensation called warmth is because I've had central heating put in.'

She had been careful not to do anything too fancy, knowing Ma would feel ill-at-ease in ornate surroundings.

'Central heating!' Lily repeated this as if Ruth had said she had had a nuclear power plant installed. 'But the cost! Oh, Ruth! Your father . . . !'

Ruth sat down and took her mother's hands. 'If you want to know, Pa paid for it, although he doesn't know it yet. He gave me a lot of money to buy you a present. He'll never know, Ma. He's never coming home again.'

'Pa paid for it,' Lily beamed, and Ruth felt absurdly slighted. 'It does feel lovely. The place is really lovely. How is Pa?' she said then, with a frown.

Ruth bit into a sandwich. 'I'm almost afraid to say it, but I think the worst is over. You know the real trouble is that you've never known how to handle him. You gave in to him, which increased his sense of power, when you should have just walked out.'

'I did once,' Ma said quietly. 'I did walk out.'

'You did?' Ruth was astonished.

'It was shortly after you left home. I had just found your feminist books.'

'You read *The Female Eunuch* and *Sexual Politics*? I don't believe what I'm hearing. My ma, a closet feminist?'

Lily choked slightly as she sampled a cigarette. 'I liked those women. They were real thinkers. But those books were meant to change the lives of a new generation of women. Older women were only case histories. When I first read them I just felt angry and cheated of my life. I blamed Pa. Men were supposed to be to blame for everything back then. I just walked out without a word.'

'Where did you go?' Ruth shook her head, unable to take in this secret in her mother's life.

'A boarding house. I was going to go to England and see if I could get a job doing housekeeping or something. I was quite excited.'

'But you came back.'

'Pa said that if anyone had to leave home it should be him. You see, he was always a gentleman. He promised that if I returned to the house he would leave. And he did leave. But I found him in tears outside the door one day so I let him in.'

'You gave in,' Ruth said.

'Yes, but it did make a difference. He was more respectful after that. For a long time we got along very well.'

Ruth nodded in admiration of her mother's stand. 'The short, sharp shock usually works. As a matter of fact, you may have inadvertently done it again. He got a hell of a fright when you didn't turn up to see him in the past few weeks. At the moment he's very contrite and wants to make it up to you. He's stopped going on about you and Tim Walcott. In fact, he seems to have some daft notion that Tim is dead.'

'Poor Pa.' Lily looked crestfallen. She was probably remembering the time she had found him outside the door in tears. 'I'll have to go and see him.'

'I didn't tell him you were coming out of hospital. I think it's best to leave things for a while. You need to get your strength back.'

For once Lily didn't argue. She was too damn tired. She tried to eat a sandwich and concentrate on what Ruth was saying but a foghorn yawn blared up from her boots.

'Bed!' Ruth said.

She went to her room; her own room, just for sleeping in, with its wide bed, heavy curtains and the picture of Our Lady on the wall. And now, beneath the window, there was a big white radiator, which occasionally gave small contented groans, like a dog in its sleep. She put her hand on the hot pipes and looked out the window at the blank faces of other houses. How glad she was to be back on her peaceful street, which contained its assorted lives as companionably as a row of books upon a shelf. She would never again be stared at by the man in the garage. She would never again envy the lives of single women.

'Hail, Holy Queen, Mother of Mercy,' she prayed as she got

into bed. The bed was hot too, baked dry by the electric blanket. 'Hail our life, our sweetness and our hope. To thee do we cry, poor banished children of Eve.' That is how she had felt in the long room. Banished! Yet she had had a place to sleep and food to eat. She thought of refugees, women forced to flee their homes with no food or money and nowhere to go, families getting scattered, the waking up in a hostile night to wonder where your children were. And family life, she thought, in spite of its wars and waste, was all there was. What would she do without Ruth to take her home from hospital and turn on her electric blanket? What if there was no Dick to act as a mirror for her vanished life?

31

'I've had my marching orders.' Ruth found her father dressed and ready. He looked very thin and anxious.

'Go back to bed!' she said in a panic.

'I'm all set.' He smiled at her mildly.

'You're confused. I'm not taking you home. Not yet,' she added, to soften the impact.

'Then I will bloody well get a taxi.' His eyes grew baleful and he moved shakily across the ward. To her immense dismay, an orderly unlocked the door for him.

'No, wait, Pa. Come back! Just for a minute.'

'I have business to attend to.' He was pulling on his gloves, fussily shunting his fingers into their casings. 'What do you want?'

'I just want to get a box of chocolates to leave for the staff,' she improvised.

'If you say so.' He returned reluctantly and sat by his bed. 'I like to do things in the proper way.'

Ruth fled to the doctor's office. 'My father's got some mad notion that he's going home. I can't seem to persuade him otherwise.'

The doctor looked up from his papers. 'I am never quite sure who in this family is sane and who is not. Your father is quite correct. He is to leave this institution. I would prefer if he were to transfer to another one, but whether he goes to a nursing home or to his own family is entirely up to you.'

'What are you talking about?' Ruth suddenly felt that the whole world had gone mad. 'How can he possibly leave? Why weren't we notified?'

'Your mother was informed by post several weeks ago.'

'My mother has been in hospital. Why did no one tell me?'

'Did your father not mention it to you? He said he did.'

She had a vague notion that Pa had rambled on about a home-coming, but of course she had taken no notice. 'Why are you sending him home? Are you saying he is better?'

'He is not better and there is little hope of him ever getting better. The truth is that his health is deteriorating. He has a number of age-related complaints and his eyesight is failing. At this point we feel he would be better off in a geriatric institution.'

'You mean an old folks' home? But they're not equipped to deal with mental illness.'

'He cannot remain here. His health insurance has run out. He is no longer covered for treatment in this hospital.'

'If he goes to a nursing home, he's going to have to pay. Why can't he pay to stay here? He's not short of money.'

The little man made a spire of his hands. 'The simple fact is that we can do no more for him here. There are many patients in need of beds whom we *can* help – younger men with family responsibilities. The treatment we have prescribed for your father can be administered by any competent nursing home.'

'But any nursing home isn't going to accept him,' Ruth protested. 'Who's going to take a crazy old guy who is quite capable of wrecking the joint if things go against him?'

'Ah. You will have to see the registrar about that. There are, I understand, a number of rest homes which will accept patients in any condition.'

'Oh, I daresay there are.' She was yelling, but it was only for the small satisfaction of raising her voice. 'In any condition mostly means incontinent. Filthy, money-grubbing kips with urine-soaked mattresses. My father is a very fastidious man.'

'Miss Butler.' He spoke very softly to emphasise her uncouthness. 'I would suggest that you restrain your imagination and devote yourself to a thorough research of the nursing homes with beds available. You are not the only woman in the world whose elderly parent has become a liability. Beds are scarce at all times, even in such establishments.'

'And what is to happen while I am doing this . . . *research*? I can't believe you left my poor father to break this news to me! My mother is just out of hospital and is in no condition to take care of a physically and mentally ill old man.'

'In that case, I shall come with you and say as much to your father. He can be a surprisingly reasonable man if he is approached with consideration. We will keep him here for two more weeks.'

Eventide, Naomh Muire, St Jude's. Ruth read down the registrar's list. She almost laughed when she came to St Jude's. It took a particular sense of humour (or lack of it) to name a joint that took care of impossible cases after the patron saint of impossible cases. She wondered why the owners of the homes did not even try to give them happy names. There was nothing cosy or cheerful, only the suggestion of marginal maintenance and entombment. Perhaps it was because Ireland was a young country. All the provisions and care facilities were for the young. If Pa had been a homeless boy instead of a sick old man, he probably would have been given a luxury flat and someone to look after him, his own computer and foreign holidays, no matter how delinquent his behaviour. Old folks were just put out to die, and if they didn't that was their hard luck.

There were twelve homes on the list. Two of them were at the sea; bleak boarding houses, probably, on their last legs in no-longer-fashionable resorts. Most were in giant terraced houses that no one wanted any longer, except rich speculators who would rebuild them. They would have no lifts and patients unable to use the stairs would be exiled to their rooms with a tray and commode. Only four were within commuting distance. It had to be one where Ma could visit.

And what of Pa? She still held in her mind an image of him sitting beside his suitcase, like an orphan waiting for someone to claim him. When the doctor had told him they needed to detain him another two weeks he merely nodded curtly, but Ruth had seen the tears in his eyes. If he was going to go mad, why only mad in patches, like Don Quixote, so that you could still see the pain in his shrewd, anxious eyes that understood and were afraid?

How on earth could she tell Ma that Pa was being sent home? How could she break the news to Pa that he was not? She needed someone to talk to. She should, at least, have had a sister or brother. None of her friends was in this sort of pickle. Anyway, she couldn't discuss it with her friends. She was too used to making light of her parents, to making an entertainment of them. But the joke now seemed long over.

'It's me.'

There was a pause. 'Actually, *I* am me. Who are you?'

'It's Ruth, Ruth Butler.'

'Oh, that me. How are you?'

She sighed. Why on earth had she picked on Tim Walcott? The trick-acting little twerp always got her back up. And why had she expected him to recognise her voice?

'Look, I need to talk to you,' she said briskly. 'It's about my parents. Are you very busy?'

'I definitely am if you don't withdraw that icicle you've got up your arse. If you can manage that, Ruth, I could use a drink. Say about seven. Maguires?'

He listened carefully to what she had to say. Odd that such an opinionated chatterbox could also be a good listener. 'The first thing is,' she said, 'can you can stop the hospital from throwing him out? It just doesn't seem possible that they can behave like that.'

'The first thing is . . .' He took her two arms and held them. 'Calm down. No, I can't do anything about the hospital. It's not my hospital and I can't interfere. Anyway, I have to say, I can see their point of view. There's not all that much they can do for your dad and there are an awful lot of young people with psychiatric disorders.'

'Young people! Everything is for young people.'

'Yes, well that's the way of the world. And the second thing is, don't alarm your mother. Lily is going to take her cue from you. Try to make out that this is a positive development. Say he really must be much better or they'd never let him go. Tell her he'll be nearer to where she lives and it will be easier for her to visit.'

She tried not to be irritated as he called for a packet of crisps to go with his beer. 'It's a lie.'

'Yes, and maybe she'll know it's a lie, but it will get you both through to the next stage. One step at a time, Ruth.' He tore open the pack and began to munch voraciously.

'And what's the next step?'

'Go and see the nursing homes. Maybe they're not as bad as you think.'

'I think they probably are.' She handed him her list. 'Do you happen to know any of these?'

He scanned the list with a faint smile. 'No, but . . . Wait a minute. Boswell House, I know that one. It's actually very good. It's quite expensive and rather grand. I'm afraid there's always a two-year waiting list, though.'

'So it's the Eventide or St Jude's?'

'Pretend you're sending a child off to school. Make a list of any particular requirements you have and then you'll know what questions to ask. Find out where the bathroom is and the television, ask to see a menu, check how often the sheets are changed. If you like the look of a place, ask the name of the visiting GP and then go and see him or her. Process of elimination. You'll get there.'

'I hope I get to be as good a liar as you are,' she smiled. 'It's not a bit like sending a child to school. That might be nice in a way, breaking the bond and then getting your child back with new skills.'

'Oh aye, and a few bruises. Have you thought about having children? I mean, other than your two geriatric ones.'

'Not really. I had other things on my mind. I'm too old now, or I feel it at any rate.'

'You're not too old,' he said. 'You should think about it.'

'Don't lecture me.' She drained her gin and glared at him.

'I'm not lecturing you.' He brooded into the bottom of his crisp bag, but there were only crumbs left. 'I'm lecturing myself.'

'The trouble is . . .' She fished out her lemon slice to extract its stimulating sourness. 'I never liked family life. All I ever really wanted was to make a nice independent life for myself, but now, precisely because I have no other responsibilities, I have to take over my parents' lives.'

'The trouble is,' he said, 'you want a map before you take a step. Maybe you should take a leaf out of your father's book.'

'Now there's a brilliant notion!'

'Just one leaf, not the full log pile. Did you know that the word "mania" has a female root? It's after the Maenads, those groupies of Dionysus, the Greek god of wine.'

'Didn't they go a bit over the driving limit and run around in a frenzy doing all sorts of unspeakable things?' Ruth frowned into her glass.

'See, being brought up as girls in ancient Greece, they were probably very repressed, so the minute the lid was off they went berserk. But everyone should do just one crazy thing in their life. Oh, you've done very nicely for yourself, just as I have – years of study and a good job with decent money, but there's one thing holding you back from discovering the real you.'

'What's that, you unconscionable little know-all shit?'

He beamed at her. He looked quite fetching when you weren't sober. 'Fear of fecklessness.'

Ruth made her mind up that she would take the next home, no matter what it was like. They had seen five; gaunt and cold or gaunt and overheated, with big, badly furnished common rooms and tiny, claustrophobic bedrooms. The old people looked yellow, forlorn, forgotten. She knew that elsewhere there were comfortable retirement homes that were more like hotels, where the elderly were pampered and indulged. But not on her list, not on the list for impossible cases. Bed-wetters couldn't be choosers.

'This one will be better,' Ruth lied to Ma. 'I can feel it.' There was no driveway so she hoisted the car on to the pavement in front of a big, red-brick terraced house on a busy road with trucks rumbling past.

The room was just a chip of a room, a fraction the size of the claustrophobic space Lily had rented. It seemed to be all plumbing pipes and partitions. An electric heater had been turned on and it hummed busily, but a huge window sucked out the heat again. There was no wardrobe, only a curtained-off corner for hanging clothes and a tiny lamp too feeble for reading. The woman who called herself a matron seemed more like a boarding-house landlady.

'How much?' Ruth said.

She whistled when the woman told her. If the house was fully occupied, she must be making a fortune.

'We'll take it,' she said.

'I'm sure he'll be very comfortable here.' The coarse-looking woman lovingly patted a lumpy duvet patterned with purple cubes. 'I'll want a deposit.'

Ruth wrote out a cheque for fifty pounds and handed it over without asking any questions. 'We usually request a week in advance,' the matron said, but Ruth ignored this and quickly bundled her mother out before she could see the desolate old faces staring from the common room.

Halfway home, Ma began to cry. 'I can't.' Ruth looked around in alarm. Her mother's whole body was contorted with anguish. 'I can't put him into a place like that.'

Ruth patted her. 'I'll keep looking. I'll find somewhere better,' she hollowly promised.

She tried everywhere, even places by the sea which Ma would hate, even ones that were too far to get to by bus. She had a sneaky notion of booking him into some remote rural residence where he could just endure like a gnarled old tree. Although he was frail, his will was so strong that she had a feeling he would live for ever. The homes weren't all terrible but they all had an inerad-icable sense of doom. Old, abandoned faces looked at her with naked woe. There was rarely any gentle lighting to soften the blow of those faces. Couldn't they do something to cheer the places up? Free cannabis, fresh flowers, music, a cat or dog, even the smell of fresh coffee would help. As usual, she found herself redesigning the institutions into a living place instead of a dying one.

'We've still got a week left. We'll find somewhere.' She was exhausted, but tried to keep cheerful for Ma. Ma seemed to have been made narrow and wary again by disillusionment. She stood in the doorway, holding it open a crack. She appeared to have forgotten to ask Ruth in. 'Ruth, your pa's got a lot of nightmares in his head.' She spoke patiently but with determination. 'He has to be in surroundings that are reassuring. You do understand that, don't you?'

'I'm not going to let him come home and kill you.' Ruth was equally obdurate. 'The hospital won't give any guarantees about his behaviour. Look, we can't discuss this on the doorstep, aren't you going to let me in?'

Lily gave a deep sigh before pulling back the door. And there was Pa, bent but brittle in his good suit and tie. He was so much the rightful tenant of this gloomy old house, so much the falling-down lord of his falling-down castle, that Ruth felt poleaxed.

'Hello, Ruth.' He eyed her shrewdly. 'Didn't want to put you out so I took a taxi. They said I might stay a few days more, but I was worried about your mother. Come in, won't you?'

Ruth shook her head. She had no idea what to do.

'Have you tried every single place?' Ma whispered.

'Yes. Every one except Boswell House, which is meant to be good, but it's got a two-year waiting list.'

Ruth had been admiring neat borders of hyacinth and narcissus when a young and pretty woman answered the door.

'I'd like to see the matron,' she said.

'I am the matron. Susan Sweetman.' She was in her thirties, smartly dressed, with glossy brown hair.

'It's about my father.' One step at a time. As she followed Mrs

Sweetman, she felt the warmth of the house. A couple of old ladies actually smiled. A girl handed round tea in china cups to people gathered in a pleasant drawing room. After what she had seen before she felt she had entered some Mary Poppins zone of geriatric care.

'Look, I realise you have a waiting list and you probably wouldn't take my father anyway, but . . .'

The woman smiled and patted a chair.

'My father has a depressive disorder.' She sat down cautiously. 'He has been in a psychiatric hospital but they now feel he is well enough to move to a nursing home.'

'Does he have a name?' Susan Sweetman said. 'Do you have a name?'

'He's Dick Butler. I'm Ruth.'

'Well, it's nice to meet you, Ruth. I look forward to meeting Dick.'

Ruth felt like someone hugely in debt who has just learnt that they have inherited a fortune. Her head went blank and Mrs Sweetman's words drifted out to the air. She would have been happy just to sit on this comfortable sofa and watch them float about like party balloons. 'But . . .' She forced herself to be alert and in command. 'You have a waiting list.'

'We've just completed a new annexe with twenty extra beds. Eighteen of them went to people on the waiting list but I have two to fill.'

'Private rooms?'

'All our residents have private rooms. Is there anything else you want to ask me?'

'No.' She still felt dazed. 'The place is lovely. I can feel that it is. But there are things I have to let you know.'

Susan Sweetman listened while Ruth told how her father had threatened to throw acid in a strange woman's face and to kill her mother with a gun.

'Your poor father! Why are you saying these terrible things about him?' She looked shocked.

'I'm afraid you won't keep him if you find out later what he can be like. The one thing I don't want is for Pa to get settled in and then to be thrown out.'

'Come on, Ruth,' Susan Sweetman said. 'We'll give it a go.'

'Where is this place?' Dick whispered to Lily. 'The girls are very pretty.'

'Are you all right?' Lily kept her voice down, not wanting Ruth to hear.

He had been there a week. His room was pleasant, with a view of the garden. He had his own television set and the furniture was comfortable. He seemed all right but Lily couldn't leave it alone.

'Where am I?' he said again.

'It's a rest home, Dick. Is it nice?'

'Well, it's not home. Naturally I would prefer to be at home.'

Her face fell. Her mouth struggled for something to say and he looked at her sharply.

'We are one person, dear. We are meant to be together.'

'Yes, I know,' she said sadly.

'How is he settling in?' she asked Mrs Sweetman. 'Does he say much about going home?'

'They all talk about going home,' the matron said, 'much in the way children talk about heaven. If it came to it, they might not be all that eager to go.'

Lily went to see him every day. The home was only a mile from where she lived so she was able to walk there and back. She enjoyed the visits, for although the nursing home was efficiently run, the regime was relaxed and she could have a cup of tea with Dick, or even a drink if she liked. It was like meeting him in a hotel. One resident kept her pet poodle in her bed. Another had a nephew who came once a week with a bottle of vodka which they consumed together in her room. Mrs Sweetman said that she liked people to do whatever made them happy, within reason. She believed it kept them young. Dick didn't mix much with the other elderly people but he got on well with the nurses. The change of venue seemed to have wiped from his mind his furious preoccupation with Tim Walcott. One day when there was nothing much on the television, he said, 'Would we say a prayer, Lily? My faith is in lousy shape and I'd like to spruce up a bit before I meet The Boss.'

Lily was enormously grateful for this. He had at last entered a phase of acceptance. They developed a routine where she would go and have tea with him and then they said the rosary. Later on they had a drink and watched some television. Then she could go home, back to her own house. It was lovely to walk into a house that was already warm rather than having to keep your coat on while the paraffin stove did battle with the cold. She often said a quick prayer as she shut the door behind her. Faith and hope had come back together.

She bought Dick a bunch of flowers. He looked at the egg-yolk bursts of colour worriedly. 'Is it time I went home, Lil?'

She hung her head in guilt and submission. 'Yes, Dick.'

He continued to frown at the flowers. 'Could we leave it a bit longer, dear,' he said. 'Got to get my sea legs.'

32

'I'm thinking of having a party.' Dick crept up behind Mrs Sweetman as she was arranging roses in a bowl.

'You're a terrible joker, Dick.' She had brought an assortment of greenery to go with the flowers. She tried a spray of dogwood in her display and then took it out again. 'Well, it's nice to see you cheerful.'

'I have every reason to be cheerful.' The toes of his shoes creaked as he moved around to face her. She noted with approval that he no longer spent his time in bed but dressed very sprucely every day. She liked her old gentlemen neat, but they were sometimes less disposed to it than women. 'In two weeks' time my dear wife and I will have been married for fifty years.'

'That's a great achievement.' She poked a sprig of purple lilac in and pushed it about. 'Your wife seems a lovely woman.'

'Yes, she is a lovely woman. Of course, in her day she was a very lovely woman.' As he talked Dick paced in front of her like a dog eager for its walk. 'She is getting on now. Anno Domini! I can't say I'm sorry, really. Between ourselves, when she was young I could never rest easy, knowing other men were after her.' The matron gathered up leaves and trimmings on a newspaper. 'In point of fact, there was an incident with another man,' Dick confided. 'All the fellow's fault of course. He was a doctor, meant to be treating her. Should have been struck off! In the end, it was God who struck him off. I can't say I shed any tears. Ah well. All a long while ago. It took a toll on my health, though. I was very ill for a time.'

'Yes, well . . .' Mrs Sweetman wiped her hands on her apron. She did not care for confidences from patients. She had not seen Dick Butler so chatty since his arrival.

'I'd like a cake with our names on it,' he said.

Good God! He was in earnest. He had made very good progress since his arrival three months ago, but a party! She abandoned the roses and gave him her full attention. 'Let me think about it. We'll have to see what Mrs Butler says.'

'Not a word!' Dick cautioned. 'The party is to be a surprise. Perhaps we could have a small spread – sandwiches, say, and bottles of sparkling wine. I was wondering if we might take over the drawing room? I'll pay, of course.'

She did not like to discourage her old folks from independent activities so long as they had the money for it. 'I suppose it would make a nice change for the other residents,' she considered. 'We might even get a pianist.'

'This is not to be a free-for-all,' he warned.

Mrs Sweetman pursed her lips. She had noticed that he did not mix with others in the home. "Have you thought this out? There's a lot of work in a party. Two weeks isn't much notice.'

'What work?'

'You have to send out invitations for one thing. That's a big chore, looking up everyone's addresses and writing out all the envelopes.'

He laughed at her in that way he had. She could never quite make out if it was good humour or derision. 'You think I am capable of nothing. Dear lady, you will have to forgive me, but I got carried away in my eagerness to please my wife. The invitations have already been dispatched.'

'Oh, Dick!' She shook her head in exasperation. 'That's very bad. Without asking me first! You haven't even said what date it's to be. Suppose it doesn't suit?'

'One can hardly alter the date of a golden wedding anniversary to suit.' He spoke with the shrewdness with which she had become familiar. She sighed. Nothing to be done about it now, but she didn't care for the loss of authority. 'Maybe I could let you have the dining room – after the other residents have finished their tea.'

'Would you like to see the invitations?' he offered. 'They are proper cards engraved in silver. I sent away for them myself.'

'I've a lot to do now, Dick, but I suppose I'll be getting my own invitation in due course.'

'I thought I made myself clear on that point. It is to be a private celebration.'

She didn't respond. She was used to old men. 'You just have to promise me one thing. You are to let your daughter in on this big surprise. And if I were her I'd pass the word on to your wife. Not everyone likes a surprise, you know.'

'Allow me, after fifty years of marriage, to know better than you what pleases my wife,' he said.

'You're not watching the television?' Lily noticed. 'Will I turn it on? There's a Ruth Rendell mystery.'

'No,' he said. 'No telly tonight. I thought we might take a little stroll.'

Lily let him take her hand, feeling the tension in his bony grasp, and her own face fell into lines of sadness as she sensed the eggshell delicacy of his hope.

'Darling.' He squeezed her fingers. 'Do you know what day it is?'

'Of course I know.' She presented him with a small box of chocolates, and her cheek to kiss. 'It's our anniversary.'

'We'll go to the dining room. We'll have it to ourselves now the tea is over.'

She wanted to protest that they had his room to themselves, but she knew by now the labyrinthine plot-lines that lay behind Dick's most casual suggestion and that to argue was an act of sabotage.

It was a fine room and how elegant Mrs Sweetman had made it! There were ornaments on the mantel and a lovely gilt carriage clock was reflected in a gilt-framed mirror. It was like a room in a real home, with flowers and crystal on the sideboard and pictures on the wall. A table set with good china and a tempting display of sandwiches and savouries showed great respect for the residents. There were even bottles of wine and a cake. 'They certainly look after people very well here,' Lily said, 'but I thought you said the residents had had their tea.'

Dick only smiled. 'Have a look at the cake, dear. I think you'll find it's rather special.' It was large and square and white, like a wedding cake. There were letters in blue icing: 'Dick and Lily – 50 years.'

'Oh, Dick,' she smiled. 'Mrs Sweetman got us a cake. Isn't that nice?'

He shook his head. 'I did it. All of this is my doing.'

'You've invited the residents to come and have a drink with us,' she approved. 'That's very nice of you. I couldn't be more pleased.'

He shook his head. She could feel him beginning to grow impatient. 'Can't you get it through your head? This is a proper party. Not for doddering old imbeciles.'

'Who are the guests, dear?'

'I sent out fifty invitations – one for every year of our marriage.'

Lily began counting up their acquaintances. She couldn't think of ten, never mind fifty.

'Hail wedded love!' Dick quoted Milton. 'Mysterious law, true source of human offspring!'

'Where's Ruth?' she asked.

'Ruth has had her invitation.'

'Why isn't she here to help?'

He sat down and patted his knee in summons, but Lily chose another chair. 'You didn't tell her!'

'She has been sent her invitation, like everyone else. You have to understand, dear, I needed to do this on my own. A final gesture, if you like. I wanted to make it all up to you, but even more, I had to prove myself capable. I know I've been an awful bother but I don't suppose it will be for much longer. I wanted us to have one really grand evening – blot out all the other rubbish.'

'We've had lots of grand evenings.' Lily hankered after their normal quiet hour at the television. 'Every marriage has its troubles.'

'That's the spirit. That's my girl. The only good thing I ever did, the only wise, was to marry thee.'

'Dick, that sounds like something out of a book.'

He smiled and put up his hands. 'Guilty! I have been looking up some apt quotations. Thought I might say a few words.'

She noticed the neatly folded square of paper protruding from his pocket. Poor Dick! What trouble he had gone to. He had written a speech. Compassion and anxiety brewed in her chest, like the mother of an awkward child at a school concert.

'Fifty years! Do you realise you and I have been together since before the nuclear bomb was invented?' He patted his knee again. 'Come here, dear. There is something I want to tell you.'

'What time are they coming?' she asked.

'Seven,' he said, and he sighed. She clawed at her cuff discreetly to consult her watch. It was almost half past. Where was

Ruth? She could see that his hands shook as they rested on his knee and wondered if it was nerves or old age. She got up and went to him. His legs felt hollow and she was afraid to put her weight down. His hands touched her, insect frail, and he whispered in her ear. 'Tonight, you are to stay here with me. When the guests have gone, you and I will remain.'

'Oh, I couldn't. Mrs Sweetman . . .'

'I have already asked Mrs Sweetman and she has given her full blessing.'

Lily wondered if he was telling the truth. For some reason, the idea made her feel ashamed, as if she was to stay in a hotel room with someone who was not her husband. 'I've no nightie,' she protested feebly.

'Yes, you have.' He handed her a box tied with ribbon. Inside was a baby doll nightie in chiffon nylon, such as might be seen in films of the Sixties. Dick startled her with a squeeze. 'I am determined to make this a night to remember.'

How had he got hold of such an odd item? Lily examined the garment. Did he send one of the nurses to buy it?

'Don't you like it?' he said in alarm. 'I should have got you something else.'

She could sense the strain of her weight on his knees so she moved back to her chair. Although everything was so nice she had a feeling something was missing. 'Are you sure they put seven on the invitations?' It was getting on for eight.

'Don't be ridiculous, Lily.' He hated to be challenged. 'I wrote the invitations myself. Wrote them and sent them out myself.'

'Weren't you great, Dick?' she said to calm him.

'I even picked them out myself and sent away for them – rather a nice little card with silver letters.'

Cards! That was it. Why were there no cards? She knew Dick had got on the wrong side of a few people over the years, but surely they would have sent a greeting even if they didn't want to come to his party.

'That wine looks inviting.' She picked up a bottle and began to grapple with the wire cage over the cork. 'Would we have a glass?'

Dick held up a hand. 'Not until the guests appear!' He gazed forlornly around the empty spaces. Surely someone must come.

'Did anyone ring to refuse?' she wondered, and Dick shook his head. 'Fifty years! I don't know where they went. Can't remember 'em.' He was uneasy, waiting for his party. He had taken from his pocket the piece of paper with large scribbles on it, and every so often he glanced at it. 'I remember when I was a boy. That, I remember perfectly. Do you know, Lily, I sometimes wake up with my heart pounding and think my mother has found out something I've done and I'm about to be punished. And then other times, I think it must be summer, it must be time for the holidays and I'll be free. I hated school, and yet after I left, the rest's all a blur. Can't recall a damned thing. Except you. You are all I have of all those years.'

'And Ruth,' Lily said. Her heart had begun a light, fast patter, like a child running from a room. Where was Ruth?

'When it comes down to it,' Dick said, 'my marriage is the one event in my whole damn life that means a thing, and yes, let's drink a toast to that. To hell with guests who haven't the common decency to turn up on time.'

He wrestled with the cork which eventually came out with the right sort of pop. 'In the end, it proves exactly what I said. There is only you and me. That is all that counts.'

'Who did you ask?' Lily felt tense, and the champagne was cold and sour in her mouth. She would have liked a proper drink.

'Scum,' he spoke softly. 'Just scum.' She said nothing and after a while he named people who lived on their street, including poor Miss Mespil who had recently passed away. With great clarity he recited the names of distant relations they had not seen in years, cousins of Ruth whom she had played with once or twice a year as a child and who were now middle-aged; shop-keepers, a bank manager, a priest, old colleagues from his office, including Connie Herlihy at whom he had thrown a vase of flowers. 'A toast!' He raised his glass. 'To you and I.' He drank the wine in several swallows, then hurled the glass at the wall.

Lily watched the vessel fly apart. A damp, frothy trail like spit ran down the wallpaper. She glanced at Dick and his eyes seemed full of the same sharp, shiny splinters as those that sprang from the glass. She tried to swallow some champagne but the festive bub-bles met a cold fizz of panic rising inside her. Dick caught her eye and she saw the faint beam of exultation there. He might have no power elsewhere, but he could still control her. 'I must do some-thing,' she thought, and with an effort managed to get to her feet. 'Toilet,' she smiled faintly as she goaded herself to flight.

Susan Sweetman felt sorry for the little woman who blundered into her office. Panic made her enter without knocking, but she still had an old-fashioned woman's trepidation in regard to authority.

'Mrs Butler! Sit down. How are you enjoying your party?'

The old lady moved towards a chair but did not make use of it. 'No one came.' She looked at the floor.

'Not even your daughter?' Mrs Sweetman said sharply.

'Oh, please! Do something. He shouldn't be having a party. It's not good for him to get excited.'

'I'll round up the other residents.' The matron didn't have to ask. She knew something had gone badly wrong. 'I did offer before, but he said no.'

Lily nodded. 'Quickly. He's more likely to behave if there are others there.'

Mrs Sweetman put an arm around her shoulders. 'I'll get the

nurses and as many residents as I can muster. I'll bring a camera. We'll make it into a party yet. Now, you go back there and tell him I'm on my way. That should keep him quiet.'

He was on the floor when she came in. She crept around him cautiously and saw with relief that he had stooped to pick up the pieces of broken glass. 'Isn't this what the rich do?' He showed her the fragments with a bashful laugh. 'They throw the glass in the fireplace when they have drunk champagne. Maybe I got it wrong.' He put the pieces in an ashtray and sat down quietly.

'I ran into Mrs Sweetman in the corridor,' Lily said. 'She's coming to take a photograph.'

Dick made no response to this information. 'We, of course, are not rich or important. Nobody cares if we live or die. But we can still make our mark.' He leaned forward to select a fresh glass for himself. The glasses were all the same, but his fingers hovered as if trying to choose the right one, and then, with a careless gesture, he swept them all to the floor. 'Please come,' she prayed. 'Someone, please come.'

'They were only rubbish anyway,' he said softly. 'Catering stock. At least the drink and the cake have survived.' He picked up a bottle and examined it. 'Not a bad wine, quite good enough for our bloody fifty years. Shall I cut the cake?'

'Don't do anything, Dick,' she said.

'Don't do anything, Dick,' he echoed. 'That's my theme song. *Don't do anything, Dick.*' He put a tune to it and sang in a comic baritone. He raised the bottle, then brought it down in the centre of their anniversary cake. '*Don't do anything, Dick.* I know what I'd like to do. I'd like to smash the whole bloody lot of them, smash their faces.' He began to club the cake, his face intent as if he saw a particular set of features instead of blue icing on white. He clouted it over and over, laughing as it spread in an oozing white and yellow mash over the table.

'Mind, Dick,' Lily begged. 'The good china!'

'In the way, is it?'

'Oh!' she sighed as he swept the pretty cups, saucers and plates off the table.

Lily edged towards the door. Dick ran and caught her by the wrist. 'So you'd run out on me too, would you? Well, this one's for you.' He took a picture from the wall and put it in her hands. He led her to the fireplace, lifted her arm, then brought it down so that the frame smashed on the corner of the marble mantel-piece. 'One for you, and one for me.' He let her arm go and picked up Mrs Sweetman's carriage clock. Lily only made a small whimper as it broke. One by one the pictures came down. They shattered on the corner of the marble ledge with a ladylike, tinkling sneeze.

'There is no air in here. I need some air.' He tried to open the window but it had tricky security catches. 'Fuck the bastards!' He raised a battle cry before lifting up a chair and hurling it through the window, where it shattered the pane with a spray of glass like a tidal wave.

It seemed to Lily that this was followed by another wave – a chorus of awe – and that it came from behind her. She looked around and saw that fourteen elderly residents had just come in, followed by Mrs Sweetman with her camera.

33

She ran all the way home. When she saw the look in their eyes she just pushed past them and bolted into the street. It was *her* they had been staring at. She was the wife. She must be responsible.

When her breath gave out she clung to a railing. The thing she couldn't get over was that the sun was still shining. All of that had gone on while it was daylight. Boys and girls loitered outside a pub. Flowers blowsy after a day of heat turned up their faces for the final rays. An elderly couple strolled along at their snail's pace, out to take the evening air, inclining considerately to one another, smiling mildly as they tossed back and forth familiar opinions.

'Ruth, Ruth!' she moaned into the telephone, and Ruth, who had been sharing a pleasant dinner with Max, felt a tearing at her centre, root-splitting as the yanking of a tooth. She spent the night watching over her mother, looking with love at the small lump in the bed, wondering wearily why love was always such a bloody mess while sexual pleasure was so clean and simple. At a certain point she lay down beside Ma and took childish comfort in this. She slept for a while and woke with a surprising feeling of happiness. She had been revisited by some memory of childhood, some cherished moment connected with this room. She found that she was studying her hand in the bruised light. The happiness resided in her palm – not that big capable hand, but a tiny, canapé-sized limb, receiving a current of love, like a dinky wall plug. She was amused by the notion of her small self already a sensualist. She reached out for her mother's sleeping hand. The cool and waxy fingers somehow failed to fall into focus with the memory.

All the following day they talked. Ruth thought they were like Victorian servants, trying to scrub out some ineradicable stain left by a feckless master. 'Where can he go now?' Ma said. Ruth looked out the window to where summer was trapped between high walls. As a girl she remembered the hot, lonely sensation of the garden, the way the heat pressed down on you like a sneaky old uncle. Ma had built up a little pyramid of butts in her ash tray. It looked like a Skid Row culinary presentation. A *croquenbouche* of coffin nails. She knew her mother didn't really expect an answer. There was nowhere else for him to go. This was the grand slam, for which he had been rehearsing all his life, falling out with those around him so that he was pushed ever closer to the edge of the cliff until there was no one but Ma left to hang on to him, and the only choices were for her to let go or for him to pull her over the cliff.

'Suppose we paid someone to come and live in the house and look after him here.' Ma was busy hacking away at a fresh clump of jungle.

Ruth pulled her attention back from the garden. 'Within a week he would have found fault with the person and fired them, or else he would say they were having an affair with you.'

Ma gave a small shudder. 'Sorry, Ruth.' She kept her head down as she began to gather up the tea cups and put them in the sink. 'It's my fault. I should have gone for help the minute he mentioned a party. I ought to have phoned you.'

'No, it's my fault,' Ruth said.

'Now, that's ridiculous. How could it be your fault?'

'I should have been there. I'm really sorry. I'm a lousy daughter. I had a date. I forgot all about your anniversary.'

'But you had your invitation?'

'I got no invitation. Of course, if I had, I would have put a stop to the whole thing at once. He's no fool. He probably realised that and forgot to send mine on purpose.'

'A date!' Ma realised what her daughter had said and smiled in pleasure. She put down the Fairy Liquid and came back to the table.

Ruth grinned at her mother's surprise.

Ma took her daughter's hand. 'Are you in love?'

Ruth laughed outright. 'No, Ma.'

'Oh.' Ma looked despondent. 'Just sex, then.'

'Something like that.'

She picked up her handbag and peered into it forlornly. Out came the pink powder and red lipstick. She batted her nose disaffectedly with the old powder puff. 'Well.' The puff went back into the compact which was returned to the bag. 'We'd better go and see how Pa is.'

Neither of them made any move, then Ruth said, 'Let's not. Not today. He'll be up to his ears in sedatives. I'm taking you out to lunch. We'll think about Pa this evening.'

Ma stayed crouched in the car like a captive. She did not begin to relax until they were in a seafood restaurant in Howth and had sherries before them and a nice bottle of wine in a bucket. Ruth ordered the kind of food she knew her mother liked – prawns with pink mayonnaise, then poached salmon and new potatoes. They had a table by the window, and even if Ma didn't care for the sea, you couldn't fail to be melted by its charms on a day like this, when it seemed to have been scattered with cheap diamanté.

'Maybe Mrs Sweetman could recommend somewhere.' Ma dipped into her sherry.

'We're not going to think about him until this evening. Remember? And that means we're not going to talk about him either.'

She finished her drink. 'What about your date? Was he nice?'

'He's nice. He's intelligent and he's good in bed.'

'If he's nice, the rest doesn't matter all that much.'

'I think it does.'

Their starters appeared and Ma's fingers flexed with pleasure at the totally pink arrangement on her plate. 'You know,' she speared a prawn, 'I used to think that you had to put out specific signals to attract the opposite sex – that no man would look at you unless you had on your high heels and war paint. All the girls of my generation believed that. I used to worry about you. I thought you'd never get a man with your naked face.'

Ruth rinsed her mouth with the delicious wine. 'There are different sorts of signals,' she said. 'I don't really care for the kind of man who goes for blatant sex symbolism. I prefer a more subtle type, who just looks into your eyes and reads the dirty writing.'

'I can see that.' Ma avoided her daughter's eye. 'But sex is one thing. What about courtship – flirtation, dancing, dinners, presents? For most women that's the best part, and men like to be seen out with a pretty companion.'

'They do when they've paid for her,' Ruth agreed. 'They like showing off their purchase. But don't you see, Ma, all that belongs to an era of impoverished women? You sold the only thing you had, which was your looks. I've got my own money. I'm not waiting for a man to take me out to dinner.'

'Of course women should have their own money, but they should spend it on themselves,' Ma argued. 'What your generation doesn't realise is, a man doesn't value something unless he has to pay a price. And we girls did have a very good time when we were young. I don't think I'd have bothered much about men if it wasn't for the amusement they provided. Apart from that, men and women have nothing much in common, except of course . . .'

'Sex.'

'Well, I know I'm old-fashioned, but most of the time I couldn't see that sex was worth it – not for a woman.'

'You know something, Ma?' Ruth glugged down her wine and looked out at the sparkling view with satisfaction. 'You're right and you're wrong. I do believe I'd rather have a date with you than with most men. But good sex is definitely worth it.'

Ma shook her head, disapproving or disbelieving. 'I think you've all been brainwashed. Do you know . . .' her eye was on the waiter as he brought their plates of poached salmon, ornamented with little spears of asparagus '. . . There are women nowadays who actually take a man's . . . that *thing*! . . . in their mouth.'

Ruth almost choked, for Ma never bothered to lower her voice and the waiter looked haunted.

'I mean, Ruth, it's not a pretty sight,' Ma said as her main course was set before her. 'You know, I actually saw it once.'

'Most married women do.' Ruth tried to give the waiter an apologetic smile.

'No, no, it was in a sauna,' Ma said proudly. 'I'd never been in a sauna so I just thought I'd take a peek. And there was this man and woman. A lovely girl – wearing lipstick – and she went right down and . . .' She took a piece of asparagus on her fork and ate it with caution. 'I wouldn't do that if you paid me a thousand pounds. And even *normal* sex.' Her voice crept down on the word, as if she suspected none of it was quite normal.

'Well, it might be all right for a big woman like you, but I can tell you it's no picnic for someone my size, lying under the weight of a man.'

'But men lean on their elbows.'

'Your pa never leaned on his elbows.'

'A private word, Mrs Butler . . .'

Lily hung her head like a guilty schoolgirl summoned by the head mistress.

'You know, he's been a very bad boy.' Susan Sweetman put on her glasses to go through some papers. 'He did a great deal of damage and caused a lot of disruption.'

'I know.'

'I'm very sorry, Mrs Butler, but I've no option but to give you this.' She folded up a slip of paper and handed it across.

Lily sat with the paper on her lap. She stroked it nervously but made no move to unfold it.

'The sooner we get this business out of the way, the sooner we can decide on the next step.'

'I understand,' Lily said. 'I really do understand.' She took the dismissal note but did not look at it. 'It's just that . . . I don't know what I'm going to do.'

'Is money a problem?' Susan Sweetman said.

She shook her head. 'Where will he go, Susan? Who'll have him now?'

'Merciful hour, woman, we're not going to sling him out. This is just a bill for the damage. Check it, won't you? I had a proper valuation done.'

The bill was for almost two thousand pounds. Lily read down the long and meticulous list: window, chair, pictures, china, clock, carpet, glasses. In spite of the enormous sum, she could only feel a great rush of relief.

'He's our responsibility now,' the matron said. 'You can rest assured we'll take care of him to the end.' She saw how the elderly woman still sat taut and unconvinced, awaiting retribution. 'Your daughter did try to warn me. He's a handful and I can only guess what you've been through, but we get all sorts in here and I've the staff and the resources to deal with it.'

'I'm so grateful to you,' Lily said humbly. 'You can give the bill to Dick. He still writes the cheques. I think he'll be very glad to pay for what he's done.' Her whole body gradually eased. Mrs Sweetman had often noticed how women of her generation hated financial responsibility. Absolved of this and of her worst worries she relaxed. 'If you're not going to throw him out, what did you mean about the next step?'

'That was what I really wanted to talk to you about. We thought maybe we should step up his medication. I have to warn you, though, it could have secondary consequences.'

'What sort?' Lily wondered.

'It'll quieten him down a bit.'

Lily noticed that after each of Dick's episodes, he seemed beaten down and shattered like a village after a hurricane. He slept a lot now. Maybe it was the extra medication. When he woke he appeared vague, even unsure as to who Lily was, although he knew that he loved her. His frantic hand would come from the blankets to find hers. Sometimes he woke in terror. 'I've gone blind,' he cried. 'I can't see any more.' When he was properly alert he was able to sit up and watch television, but Lily noticed how he felt for things as well as looking for them. On one occasion when he awoke and was afraid, he started up in the bed and began a frantic clawing through his blankets. 'I've lost it,' he cried in panic. 'I've gone and lost it!'

'What have you lost?' Lily asked patiently.

His face grew blank as he searched for his thoughts. 'My faith,' he said.

'Then we'll pray together,' she said. 'We'll just keep praying together.'

'What if there's nothing?' Words came out in a tangle of anguish. 'All our lives we've been paying in, stumbling along like blinkered horses. Suppose we've been embezzled, tethered to a bunch of tricksters. What if, at the end, it turns out to be just another stunt to keep us apart?'

'Our Father, who art in heaven . . .' she began.

'I wonder if there's art in heaven? When I was young I used to go to galleries to look at pictures. I could stand before a painting for half an hour. That made me feel close to some greater force. Why did we never go to look at paintings?'

'Hallow'd be Thy name.'

'Bloody mumbo jumbo. I can't say those words any more.'

'Just run the beads through your fingers, Dick. I'll say the prayers.'

In spite of the comfort of Mrs Sweetman's promise to take care of him, she felt sad. She had watched Dick growing old and vague and she had assumed that she would be the one to look after him. She felt that his life was running out and that she was only clutching at strands of it instead of holding the flow and ebb of it. It was how one of today's working mothers might feel, and increasingly, he was like a child. His face lit up when she brought him sweets and he liked to look at cartoons on television.

They were watching television one evening when he fell silent, and she turned to find him in the grip of panic. 'What's wrong, Dick?' She took his hand and shook it, quite hard, for he was in some private torture chamber.

'Lily!' he cried in surprise when he saw her. 'Lily, I've used it all up.'

'Don't fret,' she soothed. 'Whatever it is, we'll get more. What have you used up?'

He cast around for words and then he pointed at her, his face distraught. 'Your life. I've used it up along with my own. Look at you! You're an old woman. I've used up your youth.' He began to cry, covering his face with his hands, then opening his fingers to peek, giving a little moan of pain before hiding his eyes again.

'No, look at me, Dick,' she said. 'It's all right. I'm an old woman. We're both old. It doesn't matter.'

'Am I old?' he said.

'Yes, you are.'

'Older than you?'

'Yes, Dick.'

'My God!' His voice sank to a murmur. He seemed appalled. 'Then it's all over. The game's up. Thought I didn't feel too chipper and I can't see a blasted thing. You get old and then you die – that's it, isn't it? They dig a hole and throw you in, cover you with clay.' He sat with clenched jaw, grimly hugging this information. 'You run along home, love. It could be a long wait and it's bloody cold under the earth.'

'Cheer up, old pal,' Lily said. 'I'm going nowhere. As long as you're here, I'm here. It's not over yet, you know. There's plenty of time. Maybe even some good times.'

He sank back on the bed and began to relax. Before he drifted into sleep, he frowned and mumbled, 'You can't have a good time with an old woman.'

The summer was washed away by a tepid deluge. Roses were punched into pulp and the prim napery of gladioli drooped into tea-stained rags. People scurried past in squelching sandals and black umbrellas swooped over her head, bearing on their backs the weather's thumping morse. Back and forth Lily walked. She knew every dog and doorway on the route to the nursing home. It was like going to school as a child. She had become acquainted with people along the way – a woman who was always out scrubbing her step; a girl who had to negotiate a go-car down a long flight of stone steps and who had a bruised look. There was an elderly gentleman who seemed to pop out to prune his hedge whenever she passed and tried to detain her in conversation. She didn't mind talking, but she preferred to think as she walked.

She thought that a lifetime was just like a day of watching television. In the early hours there was a sequence – nursery programmes followed by school serials. After that it became a jumble – a comedy half-hour and then a drama full of sex or murder; a boring stretch that seemed to go on for ever in which people did nothing but talk nonsense; an interlude of romance; more mayhem, more boredom, then nothing. Like life itself, it had very little to do with what one perceived as one's own existence. When celebrities were interviewed they always said they had a wonderful life, but she doubted that there was anyone whose dreams and reality fell into line – people who married their ideal partner and fulfilled all their ambitions, who lived in the kind of house they liked and had wonderful friends and whose children turned out the way they wanted. Lily wondered if people's ill-fitting lives were a warning that they were only on hire, that in the end they would only be cast-offs, but the soul would go on.

On to what? If Dick died, she would have no idea where he'd gone. Heaven was meant to be perfect happiness. She didn't know what would make Dick happy. Would he be tamed in heaven or would he have to go on probation until he learned to behave? Purgatory. A place of purification. That would make him furious. He never believed that he was in the wrong. Maybe he was in purgatory now.

'Lovely evening missus,' sang out the woman who scrubbed her step. Lily hadn't even noticed that the sun had returned. The wet flowers looked radiantly bedraggled, like children coming out of the sea. The woman was jubilant at the change of weather. No more mud to sully her work! Would she in due course earn an eternal reward of scrubbing a step that would never get dirty? But then she'd have nothing to scrub. Odd, though, the things that made people happy. She said a quick prayer, that Dick would have some happiness, either here or in the next life.

'I've made a friend!' Dick was flushed and smiling, his pale eyes tinged with youth again.

Lily was delighted. It was one of her small disappointments that he had set himself against acquaintance with any of the pleasant residents at Boswell House.

'You don't mind, dear? She's very nice. I knew she had some regard for me. She used to stop by for a chat.'

'Oh, a lady!' Lily smiled.

His fingers tapped against the counterpane. 'There's a bit of an age difference.'

'So long as she's not after your pension,' Lily laughed. 'Do I know her? I've said hello to a few of the lady residents in passing.'

'Those old biddies!' Dick said in contempt.

One of the young nurses came in to take his temperature. As she leaned forward with the thermometer, Dick whispered in the girl's ear. She nodded and left the room.

'What was that about?' Lily asked. Dick was smiling quietly to himself.

'I asked her to bring us a nice cup of tea. I thought you looked tired. I thought you'd like a cup of tea.'

'Oh, I wouldn't want to put her to trouble,' Lily said, and Dick almost smirked.

'Nothing is too much trouble where I am concerned.'

'Tell me about your friend,' she said. 'Is she a widow?'

'Hardly.' He laughed out loud.

The young nurse returned with cups of tea and biscuits on a tray.

'Bring it here!' Dick patted his knee.

'I hear he's made a friend,' Lily said to the girl.

She took a cup from the tray and set it beside Lily. She gave a wry sort of smile for a young person.

'Fix my pillows,' Dick commanded. She made the tray secure and then leaned over him to arrange his support. He watched her approvingly, then placed his two hands on her breasts.

'Dick!' Lily cried.

'Now, Mr Butler,' the nurse warned indifferently.

'It's all right,' he said. He was looking at the girl, who had taken his hands firmly in hers and returned them to the covers. 'My wife understands. Luckily she is a very broad-minded woman.' He took a meticulous sip of his tea and then slowly selected a biscuit. 'This is she!' He spoke casually to Lily. 'This is my lady friend. Her name's Tracy.'

Lily's mouth dropped open like a fish, but she managed to retrieve it. 'Thank you for being so kind to my husband,' she said to the girl.

'She's not being kind!' Dick protested. 'I'm not so far gone that I need a woman to be kind to me.' As Tracy attempted to settle the tray he patted her bottom. 'She's got a smashing little figure, hasn't she?' he said eagerly to Lily. 'You might as well know it. Our relationship is of the usual type between a man and a woman.'

34

'I have to tell you something.' Pa's voice was faint and Ruth had to lean close to hear him.

'What, Pa?'

He frowned as if he needed to gather his thoughts and then he began to laugh, a faint monotonous scrape like furniture being cleared from a distant room. 'Thing I read in the paper. This man had a dog and they lived near a wood and the dog kept bringing back contraceptives that had been left by couples cavorting. His wife found them and she gave her husband bloody hell.' His face grew long again. 'Serve him right. Dirty filthy things.' He brooded as if some great wrong had been done him. 'I'm tired,' he said. 'Will you put me to bed?'

She raised a combative eyebrow. 'Okay,' she surrendered. 'Get into bed and I'll tuck you in.'

'Put me to bed. Carry me.'

She continued to brood until he held out his arms. She tried to hoist him but his arms went up without raising his body and she had the alarming feeling that if she tugged they might come away, leaving the rest of him behind. This wasn't something she could do half-heartedly. She put an arm under his legs and one under his arms and cradled him. As she lifted him her heart fell sideways for there was nothing left of him, nothing that suggested a man or even an adult, only thin, thin bones wrapped in cloth. It was like carrying a bundle of sticks. His eyes stayed on her, wistful and piercing as she put him on the bed, straightened out his legs and pulled the blanket over him. She hoped she was brave enough to tuck him in and kiss him. As she patted the blankets around him his melancholy look faded and his eyebrows were smoothed with contentment. When she bent to kiss him he opened his eyes. 'Do something for me.'

'Sure, Pa.'

He broke free of his parcel of wool and sat up quite energetically, shuffling through some papers on his locker. 'Post this.' He held out an envelope. 'Send it registered post.'

Oh, Lord. What was he up to now?

He watched her challengingly before removing a small box from under his pillow, which he placed in her hands. A bribe? There was a brooch inside, decorated with pearls and aquamarine – quite pretty in a sentimental way. 'I just wanted you to see it.' He took the box back.

'Ma will love it.'

'It isn't for her.' He was frustrated by her stupidity and spat as he spoke.

'Who, then?' She wanted to calm him but she was also curious.

'For Tracy.'

'Who's Tracy?'

He shook his head impatiently and rang the bell by his bed. A young nurse came in and asked what he wanted. 'Not you!' he said. 'I want Tracy.'

The girl giggled and withdrew. A few minutes later Tracy appeared.

'Tracy, darling, I have something for you.' With trembling hands he offered her the brooch.

The girl was embarrassed. 'I couldn't, Mr Butler.'

Tears came to his eyes. 'All my efforts come to nothing. I have a loving heart, but no one is pleased by me.'

Ruth nodded at the nurse. 'Take it.'

She looked uncomfortable. 'It's lovely. Thanks very much.'

His face was wreathed in a sweet smile. 'You're lovely.' He stretched out his two hands and lightly touched her breasts. The girl backed away. 'Now, Mr Butler.'

'Did you know?' he queried Ruth affably. 'I have always favoured big-breasted girls.'

Bright-faced, Tracy ran from the room.

'She's mad about me,' Dick confided. 'Frequently returns after lights out. I don't have to spell it out.'

On her way out Ruth was stopped by the matron. 'I think you should know. He's failing quite rapidly. He eats almost nothing and he's very weak.'

'Is he dying?' Ruth asked abruptly.

Mrs Sweetman was made uncomfortable by this direct question. 'He hasn't got any terminal condition but I've seen so many old folk go this way. I wanted to tell you first so you could prepare your mother.'

Before posting his letter Ruth prudently peeked at the contents, but it was only a renewal of his driving licence. She checked over the form. The spidery writing was hard to decipher but he had meticulously filled in the details. There was a section requesting details of physical disabilities in which he had volunteered, 'Temporarily blind.'

She needed a holiday. The old blighter was going to go on for ever. She decided not to pass on the matron's warning to Ma. He had hoodwinked Mrs Sweetman, and he had nearly got her for a minute too, but she wasn't going to have Ma upset for nothing. It was impossible to know how consciously he strove to provoke, and impossible not to be provoked, impossible not to forgive him. He was in for the long haul and she needed her strength. Venice, she decided. Churches, paintings, palaces, food and booze. If the weather held, she might trek off to Elba. There was a marvellous hotel at Biodola where the rooms were pretty bungalows on flower-covered hills and the sheltered beach had sea warm as bath water. She bought an expensive pair of sandals and a bronze-coloured swimsuit. Other than that she just packed a raincoat for Venice and some slacks and shirts. As the plane lifted off the ground she felt life flowing back into her, youth, hormones, even. She waited with relish for flight service to begin and automatically looked around to see if the passengers included any sexy-looking men.

The call came on Saturday. 'Mrs Butler, dear, I've sent for a priest.' Mrs Sweetman's voice was calm but Lily understood at once what she was saying. She beat against a wall of panic as she looked for Ruth's postcard from Venice with a hotel number on it. Her fingers had grown too big for the dial holes and she kept getting the number wrong. As she waited, her eye fell on the picture of old and grimy water. The buildings were faded and their elasticated reflections dangled in the water like dirty laundry. She thought it looked an awful place. When she asked for Ruth there was a foreign gentleman who kept saying, '*Buon giorno*,' and '*Pronto*.' 'Ruth Butler,' she shouted down the line. 'Ruth Butler.' A girl came on the phone. It wasn't Ruth, but she had some English and she said that Signora Butler had gone away.

No Ruth. What would she do? She burrowed into her overcoat and shut herself out of the house, experiencing once more that wave of homesickness that had become her shade, her persistent haunting.

Mrs Sweetman was waiting at the door. 'Stay as long as you want. Ring the bell if you'd like a cup of tea.'

She sat by his bed. His face was long, as if composed in thought, but it was probably just the effort of breathing. The counterpane was covered in papers. She did not look at them but took his hand under the blankets and rubbed his fingers. 'Dick,' she whispered.

He woke with an effort. He looked startled, as if he couldn't remember where he was, and then at once started trying to get up. 'Now, see here, Lily . . .' He began scrabbling at the papers, pulling them together, shuffling them into a lump. 'These are important documents, bills and bank statements and so forth.'

'They're not important, love.' She tried to take them out of his hands, to cover his hands with her own. 'They don't matter at all.'

'I can't make head nor tail of them,' he said. 'I don't even bloody well know if I paid those bills. I assume you can tell me.'

She looked into the jumble of print. Most of it referred to things she did not know about, had never seen before, and her eyes kept blurring so that she could not even see the figures. She made a half-hearted attempt to study them and then shook her head.

'You don't know?'

'No, Dick.'

He stared at her as if trying to make sense of her. 'Don't you know anything?' he said in contempt.

'No, love,' she whispered.

He fell back on the bed. 'Get out of here and leave me in peace.'

She was on her way out when she heard Mrs Sweetman calling her. Something swooped past her, an angry rush of nothing. Her knees bent and she held on to the doorpost. 'Mrs Butler . . .' She heard the matron's voice, soft and regretful.

'You'd better come back.' She didn't have to go anywhere. She didn't have to see.

In the night she had a dream. She was in a church. As the ceremony ended, the congregation vanished and there was just herself and the priest. He turned towards her with a kindly expression and he blessed her. 'The marriage is ended,' he said. 'Go in peace.' When she went out the sun was shining. She walked away on high-heeled shoes and she realised that she was young again; she was a young girl and she was free. Her body and her spirits were buoyant and her whole life was ahead of her.

When she woke, the feeling of elation remained and she stretched out in the bed feeling light and euphoric. She remembered then that Dick was dead, poor Dick, a corpse in the bed, his spirit departed. 'I'm free,' she thought. The notion swam into her, seductive and profane. The marriage is ended.

The realisation of this brought a rush of pain. Well, she would have to cope with that too. But deep inside she would be sustained by the seed of her own life, reaching up for the light. There wasn't much left of her life, but it was money unspent.

'At least poor Dick is safe,' she told herself. 'He is in the hands of God.'

As she said this she felt impatient to get back to sleep again. She wanted her solitary sleep. Rather than emptiness, she had the feeling of a hectic but fulfilling schedule ahead. As she began to drift, she remembered how Dick's faith had deserted him, his mystified look as she recited prayers at his bedside. He hadn't believed in anything, except her. How could she go in peace, when he would not?

She kept her eye on the coffin as they lowered it into the earth. Little splashes of mud hit the wood and her hands went out in dismay. An awful thing to do to someone. It was like throwing stones at them, or stuffing earth into their mouth. Her own throat clogged at the thought of him helpless in the dark. When he did not rise up to wreak havoc on those who had offended him she suffered the kind of blind fright a beast might feel at an abattoir. He had abandoned her. Or she had abandoned him. Often she had been to funerals of old acquaintances and had tried to reassure the shocked survivor that their grief would in due course be followed by release. But it wasn't so. Married couples placed their lives in one another's hands. When the Bible spoke of 'flesh of my flesh', it wasn't to do with sex, although it seemed to be. It was the ingrowing toenails, the bowels, the arteries. Married people became interested in each other's frailties, when no one else was. When one went down, they took the file and case history of the other. This was what death was; not what happened when the heart gave out, for if one believed, then that was the start of life. Death was what happened to those who were left behind.

Afterwards she sat in an awful black hat in a room where people were laughing and kissing one another. Who had organised a get-together? She herself would never have thought to celebrate Dick's death. She kept looking around for Ruth. All the people there seemed to know one another better than she knew them. At first she had difficulty in placing them, and then she realised they were the people who had failed to come to Dick's party. Why had they bothered to turn up to his funeral?

'You must try to remember him as he was.' Connie Herlihy bent down to talk to her and Lily noticed the soft pleating of her hips. She would be one of those women who grew fat once married. 'Poor Dick, he was not himself towards the end. We all remember him as a very fine man.'

How did she know he was not himself? Had the fine man merely been an outfit he wore, like his spruce suits? Could the fury have come out of nowhere? She tried not to duck as some female bulk descended and lips with red wax in the cracks aimed at her face. It annoyed her that people kept disturbing her, for she had to think. She had to think fast. Dick had been carried off. Nothing had intervened to save him. Now that she had lost him, she was compelled to find him. She tried to claw her way back over the rubble of the recent past, trawling through the wasteland of her middle years. She wanted to return to when she first saw him, when the very sight of him suggested safety. But her effort to go back went wrong. She was sliding down a tunnel. Her early years flew past and still she skidded until she came to a point in her youth and stopped. But she wasn't a young woman. She was a little girl. She stared in confusion at the furred and pow-dered grown-ups who pressed around her.

That night she was given a sedative. Heavy blankets of drowsi-ness pressed in on her alarm. Nothing could quench that worm of fretfulness, the knowledge that they had done that thing to him and she had let them. She got up, stumbled to the window and stared out, shivering. Parents of abducted children must feel as she did now, knowing the child trusted them to come and save them. When she accepted that sleep had finally slunk off she went down to the kitchen to make tea. Afterwards, she had to clean the ash-tray, empty the teapot, put away the milk, rinse the cup in the stone sink. The effort exhausted her but it had to be done, oth-erwise it would be waiting for her tomorrow. For years and years she had railed against the description of herself as housewife. She was a wife, yes, but neither house-proud nor house-married. Even though it upset Dick, she had to make these distinctions. She had been wrong all along. Her relationship to Dick was over. Her relationship to the house was what endured. Ruth would try and persuade her to sell up and move to somewhere smaller and more convenient, but she knew she would stay. Day after day, for the rest of her life, she would serve the ungrateful house, without any particular skill or devotion, but faithfully. Then one day she would drop dead, and after a decent interval the house would get another wife.

35

Grief and guilt hit Ruth in two separate chunks. She had gone to get away from her pa, had avoided phoning home because she did not want to be reminded of him, had returned, tanned and ready for anything, to discover that she was too late.

'Your father is buried.' Ma was tight-lipped. 'You were in Italy and your father is under the earth.' She did not mention death.

She took her mother in her arms. 'I'm so sorry. This has been awful for you. Things will get better.' She didn't know she was crying until she felt the cool dampness of her hair where tears had run off her face.

Ma detached herself politely. 'I'm all alone now.'

'No, I'm here,' Ruth said, 'I'll stay here with you.' But she knew that too late was too late. Her mother wouldn't look at her.

'Your pa was all sorts of things, but he was steadfast. All my life he was there, rock solid. A wall that I could lean against.'

'The Berlin Wall,' Ruth muttered under her breath.

But she missed him too. The triangle that had been her family went lopsided with a spoke missing. Her own life, which had always presented a retreat from her family, lost definition with nothing for comparison. She felt angry that her wily old pa had given her the slip. She wanted to drag him back and make him tidy up the mess he had left behind, to shake him until he confessed that he loved her, that at some point in time he had loved her.

She fell asleep in her old bed, cold from unuse, and dreamed that her father held her hand. She felt gilded by the pride and fondness in his touch. Waking, the dream only left a sour taste. As far as she could remember, her father had never touched her. She got up and made some breakfast for Ma.

She had imagined that with Pa gone there would be an automatic closeness between her and her mother, but the offers of meals, drinks or drives were met with a bleak look of reproach. Ma seemed intent on a sort of spiritual suttee. She was glad to have Ruth around, though, for the practical things. 'You go,' she said when Mrs Sweetman phoned and asked for someone to collect his possessions.

No one ever thinks about the refuse of the dead, the unpaid debts and dirty washing, the tattered scraps of secrets. She peeked into the wardrobe. He had always looked neat and she was surprised to see that his clothes were shabby. She pulled open a drawer in a chest and a great pile of papers sprang at her. Gingerly she emptied the drawers – a jumble of bills and statements, some socks and hankies, half-written letters trailing off to nowhere, a photograph album, a little book of Victorian verse. To her surprise, there was a brown envelope with RUTH scrawled in his outsized hand-writing. Then she came upon a pile of small white envelopes, stamped and addressed, also in his wayward script. There were about fifty of them, made out to relatives and acquaintances of her parents. She even found one addressed to her. Each contained the same thing – a printed card, edged in silver and ornamented with bells: *You are invited to a party to celebrate the 50th wedding anniversary of Dick and Lily Butler.*

★

Lily tested the cliff face carefully, seeking a safe foothold. Far below, something dark and fathomless foamed. She clung on with her fingertips and inched down, heart in mouth. No, that was wrong. Her heart was in her slippers. It was her guts that were in her mouth. She found a purchase, green and mossy, a little foothold in memory. She had located a time, shortly after they were married, when they discovered that Nuala and Will Cusack had taken a flat nearby. At once, the blank-faced street became a neighbourhood. Lily and Nuala walked to the shops together. They would stop off for a cup of Irel in one another's houses, the plumes of cigarette smoke exclamatory as they binged on female conversation. The relief of talking to a woman after the stiff circularities of male conversation! The talk that single men made with single women was all based, in the long or the short term, on getting them into bed. After marriage there was nothing left to say. After that, it boiled down to meals and rules – oh, and getting them into bed. Nuala called her Lils, which no one else did, and there was a special personality that went with the name. They got drunk on coffee essence, they laughed until they reeled.

Ruth came in, loaded down with bundles. 'A few of Pa's bits and pieces. Would you like me to help you sort them out?'

Lily shook her head. 'Later.'

'You look tired, Ma. Why don't you go for a rest? I'll bring you up some lunch.'

'I'm all right,' Lily said. 'I'd like a cup of tea.'

But when the tea was made Ruth hovered over her, a large, solicitous shadow getting in her light, and Lily had to ask her sadly, politely, to go away. She felt a stab of conscience as Ruth removed herself. She was lucky to have her. She would sort all this out later, but right now there wasn't time. She had to get in her harvest while the daylight lasted. She had a feeling that Dick's personality would fade in due course, but for the moment it was strong and she must make use of this time. She had to find the happy memories and gather them in.

Nuala and Bill. On Saturday nights they met in one another's houses to play cards. They made egg-nog with cheap sherry, put cheese and pickles on sticks, played records and flirted mildly. Happy days. Lily smiled. She lit a cigarette, trying to recapture the atmosphere, but the tea was all gone and it made her choke. And then she realised that she hadn't been remembering Dick at all. She had no picture of him in the foursome. It was buxom and intrepid Nuala she saw so vividly, languid Bill with his slick of yellow hair and his horses' teeth. What had become of them? They must have moved to another neighbourhood.

Nuala and Lils, eyeing one another's waistlines, as eager to plough into fertile fields as boys are to jump into deep canals. Then one night as Nuala was pouring out the egg-nog Lily had to rush from the room to be sick. Nuala, hurrying to help her, found Lily in the bathroom, green and ecstatic.

'Lils, you're not . . . ?'

Lily wiped her mouth, burped and nodded. 'I think so.'

Lily began taking long walks. She walked at a fast pace, stopping now and then to find herself frowning at a view of the city she had never seen before. Sometimes she would arrive at a church or a public house and go in and rest. Or she would wander into a run-down café and sit at a plastic table with tea and a pink bun, filling herself with smoke. All the time she trembled on the brink of anger. She could have left him at any time. She knew that when young she had been good-looking and attractive. She had stuck by him and he had run out on her. 'Till death do us part' meant nothing when she made her vows because you didn't believe in death when you were young. She could be glad, even, that his old self had been put to rest, but he had slipped away whole. Her only memories were of the cruelty and chaos of his recent behaviour, not of his real self. Once, she wandered into the open entrance to a sausage factory and walked through the works where people were mincing pig meat and aiding the pink mix into edible tubes, and as she looked for an exit at the other end, a man in a red-blotched overall stopped her and asked her was she looking for something. The question was so direct that she could only stare a him, mouth opening and closing like a fish, and she knew by the gentle way he led her back on to the street that he thought she was nuts.

She had been pregnant. Nuala Cusack was right. She had been dizzy with sickness and delight. When they got home Dick put his arms around her and she blurted it out at once. 'I'm going to have a baby.'

'We can't afford it,' he said. 'We don't want anyone else.' As if it was another man instead of a child. When she lost the baby, he was jubilant. He tried to be sympathetic but she could see it in his toes, the spring in them as he walked, the tinge of relief at the edges of his mouth. After that he had made absolutely certain there would be no more babies. He didn't care what he did. He was like someone defending his castle against marauders, bolting the doors and then bricking up the windows. He even locked himself away so that there was no contact between them, no sex and no affection since the two went together where he was concerned. He didn't even care about sex so long as intruders could be kept at bay. It went on like that for years, until she put her foot down and they got Ruth.

Ruth sat on the bed where she had played and plotted as a lonely child. On her lap was the brown envelope with her name penned in jagged script. She began picking at an edge of the envelope and then stopped herself, remembering his last letter. It was infuriating to think that his obstinate hand still stuck out of the coffin. He was gone. If there was anything he wanted to say, he had had every opportunity to say it. It was just herself and her mother now. But that was the problem. Ma had run out on her. She had neglected her work and stayed in the dismal house to take care of her, but Ma, she believed, was actually walking the streets in order to avoid her. It wasn't fair. She had been hurt by Pa's death too. What was the matter with her? Self-pity wasn't really her style. To her surprise, she heard a familiarly cocky and irksome voice in her head. 'It's boredom, Ruth.' She swore loudly, flung down the envelope and phoned.

'Tim?' She had never called him that before.

'Ruth Butler!' he said.

'How did you know it was me?' She was at once suspicious.

'I haven't got a lot of girls in my little black book,' he laughed. 'Fewer still who ring up offering to take me for a drink, which I take it you are?'

'Correct,' she conceded dourly, 'in all but syntax.'

'The thing I can't understand is why she's so determinedly bloody miserable.' Ruth had drained two gins and emptied several bags of emotional rubbish over Tim Walcott's head. She felt eerily disconcerted by the ease with which she unburdened herself. Maybe it was the drink or maybe she had been alone too long. 'I hate to say this, but she doesn't seem to be quite right in the head. When she's not wandering round the streets in bag-lady mode, she just sits in the kitchen staring into space like a zombie.'

'What do you think she's looking for?' Tim said.

'She's looking for him, I'm sure of it. It gives me the creeps, Tim. I know it's been a shock, but it's got to be a relief as well.'

'He's been her life's work.' Tim hailed the barman for a cup of hot nuts.

'And she has performed her part with extreme valour.' For once Ruth failed to be irritated by his munching. 'Nobody else I can think of would have put up with him. Now she's done her job and she's earned a break. I'm there for her but she hardly seems to notice me.'

'You're there, Ruth, but is she there?'

'Oh, not psychobabble,' Ruth pleaded. 'And no, she's not there since you ask. She's trying to claw her way down into the earth after him. Why can't she just let him go with her blessing? Pa was never an easy man to live with and the past years have been pretty close to hell.'

'That's the point, really, and I wasn't talking psychobabble. You've never been married.'

'As she never fails to remind me.'

'Marriage is all about compromise, or "rubbing along together" as people put it. That rubbing involves more than a certain amount of friction and wear. What happens is, people sacrifice whole chunks of their personality in order to get along with someone else. And it's usually the woman who does most of the adjusting. The more difficult the marriage, the more of their personality they lose. I am talking textbook here, but it's relevant. When a partner dies, the survivor can't simply pick up that spare part of their personality and slap it back on. It's missing, worn away. So someone like your mother hasn't just lost a husband. She's lost about two-thirds of herself. Personality grows back but it takes a long time. What your mother's really looking for – although she probably doesn't know it – is herself.'

'Help her, Tim,' Ruth begged. 'Please.'

'I'll come and see her but there isn't a short cut and there isn't an easy route. At the moment the best thing you can do is go back home and get on with your life.' He finished the nuts and pleated the paper cup into a complicated origami. 'How are you, by the way?'

'Oh, I'm all right.' She drained her drink and stood up to pay.

'Really? Well, I'm not. I'm bloody starving. Why don't you buy me some dinner?'

'Ma'll be expecting me.'

'Got a roast in the oven and the candles lit, has she?' He grinned.

'No,' Ruth grudgingly smiled. 'More likely a ghost in the oven and a fag lit. Let's go.'

Around midnight she dropped him off at his house, a neat little terraced dwelling on the canal. To her great surprise, he leaned across and hugged her. His body was extraordinarily light, and not just physically. He felt like a man who carried his own baggage. 'What's that for?' she said.

'I'm always free with my favours when I get my dinner paid for.'

'Look, I know I'm pretty difficult to resist, but you're gay. Ma told me.'

'Didn't you know?' He patted her back, tap, tap, as if trying to wind her. 'Every girl should have a gay friend. It's the in accessory.'

'Didn't you notice?' She tried to detach herself. 'I'm not absolutely famous for "in" accessories.' But his arms stayed locked around her back and she felt the joints of her shoulders coming uncrunched. Only by an effort of will did she keep her head from his shoulder.

'Have you cried, Ruth?' His mouth touched her neck but in a detached and dreaming way, like a baby.

'Not much. I'm good at keeping up a brave face.' She had grown relaxed against him. She didn't feel at all aroused but he felt wholesome and good.

'You and me both. Go on, have a blub. I don't mind. Give me an alibi.'

'I don't want a blub. Anyway, what's your excuse?'

'I had someone die on me too. A friend. I was looking after him. That's why I haven't seen much of your mother. Do you know, Ruth, your body feels very different from your personality. You feel little. You feel like a child that needs to be hugged.'

The minute he said it, tears came to her eyes. 'I lost the knack,' she mumbled. 'I'm not little. I got too big too soon.'

'No, Ruth, you're never too big. There's nothing to it. Just do what I'm doing. Do it to me. Please.'

The minute she put her arms around him, he began to cry. He did it easily and not clumsily. It seemed like the right and proper thing to do and she did it too, although it came out differently for her. She bawled strenuously. She didn't give a damn. It was the most comfortable thing she had done in years.

Lily wasn't all that pleased to see Tim Walcott. His fresh face, which she used to find quite touching, seemed annoyingly healthy at a time when she was navigating the underworld. And she had a feeling he wasn't here of his own accord. She would have been willing to bet that Ruth had put him up to it.

'Have you talked to anyone since it happened?' Tim sat down although she hadn't asked him. 'I mean, really talked?'

'I don't feel like talking.' She tried to discourage him. 'You've got to give me time. I'll talk when I feel like it.'

He had brought a box of chocolates, but she declined them with a disapproving shake of her head. He sat down and began eating them himself. 'Have you grieved for him, Lily?'

Lily rounded on him furiously. 'Have you come around here to tell me my business? I looked after my husband for fifty years. I have responded to his every need. And now you are going to tell me how to respond to his death.'

'No, I'm not,' he protested. He took off his spectacles to enhance his innocence. 'I wish I could, but I can't do that. I can help, though. You see, we're all taught how to love, one way and another. Our mothers usually do that if no one else does. But no-one ever teaches us how to grieve. You're not supposed to show your negative feelings. It embarrasses people and it makes your nose run. Have you cried, Lily?'

She realised with surprise that she had not.

'That would be a start. Use an onion if it would help. No, I'm being a smartarse, don't do that. But if you had some old letters he wrote you, or some photographs. What about all this stuff on the table? Letters, photographs, it looks like. Must be something in there.'

'I don't think so.' Lily shook her head.

'You don't think what? That there's anything there that would make you cry, or that it would do any good if you did?'

Her lip shook as she glanced at the jumble on the table. 'He played tricks on me. He could be cruel. I'm afraid to look in case he's left something to hoax me. I prefer to trust my own memory to find what I need.'

Tim pursed his mouth and expelled a long sigh. 'I know he played tricks on you. What we'll never know is if he knew it too. Don't be leaning too hard on your poor old memory. The memory also gets injured in a bereavement. Well, now I've seen you I know you can't be rushed, but there are a few things you can do. One is to defuse this minefield here.' He picked up the papers on the table and began to put them into piles. 'Bill, state-ment, mmm . . . letter to private detective.' He settled to the task, throwing out what he felt she was best off not seeing and folding the business matters together. 'Now that lot's for Ruth or for a solicitor if she can't figure it out. This one is for you.' He handed her the black photograph album and a little book of verse.

'Was there anything else?'

'Let your daughter help you. She needs you now as much as you need her.'

'Ruth's not here. She went home this morning.'

'Good. At least one of you is getting on with life.'

'Ruth never let anything interfere with her life.'

Tim sighed, a joint bid for patience and composure. 'Lily, have you ever wondered why you put up with so much from Dick, but with Ruth, nothing ever seems enough?'

He was relieved that she did not answer at once but actually paused to give this some thought. 'She had a lot to repay. I went through so much to get her. I had a miscarriage early on. Dick didn't care. He never wanted children. Then years went by and I was desperate for a baby. In the end I told him I'd leave if we didn't have a child.'

He selected a sweet and then dropped it back in the box. 'How did Dick react to his role as dad-under-duress?'

'Oh, Dick didn't have much to do with her. Once, when she was little, I left him to look after her while I was in hospital. That was a mistake. Child rearing isn't a man's business.'

'It was his business, Lily. He was her father just as much as he was your husband.'

'If you want to know . . .' Lily suddenly seemed compacted with ire, a small, injured animal squaring up for battle. 'When I came back from hospital I found that he had moved her cot into our room, right beside his bed.'

'So?'

'I don't suppose I have to spell it out. You might not think so now, but Ruth was an exceptionally pretty child. My husband was always a very sexual man.'

Tim sank his head in his hands. 'Good God. I don't believe this. You're not suggesting that Dick . . . ?'

'I'm not suggesting anything. I wish this subject had never come up. I never thought it was a good idea for men to get too close to children. Well, I was right, wasn't I? Look at all the publicity nowadays, about men abusing children.'

'So after that you kept Dick and Ruth apart?'

'We had an awful row and Dick went into a sulk. After that he just ignored her.'

Tim groaned. It was a long, harsh lament that seemed to sandpaper his soul. 'Dick Butler was never a child abuser. You were suffering from simple jealousy. You thought he'd stolen away your heart's desire.'

'Have you finished lecturing me?'

'No. There's one more thing.'

'What thing?'

'You have to let the poor old bugger rest in peace. It's too late to be demanding happiness from him now. The scores have all been squared in some other court. He can't make it up to you and he can never play tricks on you again. He's gone, Lily.'

36

My dear friends,

We are here for an unfashionable celebration — that of an enduring marriage. We live in an age when marriage is out of date, when people move from partner to partner as if at a dance. There is no longer any shame in trading your old partner for a hothouse bloom, purchased when in first flower. But marriage is not a hothouse flower. It is a tree that grows over a lifetime and offers shelter and stretches out its roots to nourish future generations. And life is not a dance. It is a journey — a long and painful journey in which the highest and most glorious point is to know and be known by another human being, intimately, compassionately, as one can only do in long and happy wedlock.

Dr Johnson once said: 'A man who does not marry is only half a man.' When I married Lily I thought I was a man and a half. I saw myself as her superior, her protector. Over the years I have come to know that she is the strong one, the wise one, the one who would not bend in the wind. With patience, with goodness, she taught me to love. Because I was not worthy of her I know I have not always given her the happiness she deserves. But I have loved her with all of my poor heart. I saw myself as the conquering hero, but yet my only brave deed was to cast my life at the feet of one beloved stranger. I have pursued many goals but I can say, Lily, in the words of the writer Philip James Bailey, 'I remember the only good thing I ever did, the only wise, was to marry thee.'

The helper in the Oxfam shop found the note in the pocket of a man's grey suit in a bag of clothing left by a woman. She stared a long time at the injured-looking letters before folding the paper and putting it into her handbag. She had not enjoyed the blessing of an enduring marriage. She wondered if the tall, bad-tempered-looking woman who had left the bag of clothes was Lily. She wondered did the woman know her luck.

37

~~~~

After she had aired the flat and bought food, Ruth put on some music. She closed her eyes to let Mendelssohn's violins wash over her brain and woke four hours later to find violet light seeping in her windows from the sea. Oh, home sweet home. She cooked up some food which was just a binding agent for garlic and olive oil, and allowed her rooms to absorb a Mediterranean reek. While she ate she listened to her answering machine, beaming as she came to an invitation with lecherous intent. She had escaped from her parents again. She could wave her legs in the air. There were interesting business proposals too; someone was trying to raise money for a giant leisure centre in Tallaght for the millennium and wanted her to submit a design. These messages were a chorus of approval for her adult self. At home, she was only recognised for her role as daughter. She supposed it was the same for everyone. That was how humans inadvertently kicked their young out of the nest, by disavowing their engagement with the larger world.

She phoned her enticer and told him she would be ready as soon as she had had a bath. When she sank into the hot water, inertia claimed her limbs again. She would lie on the bed for five minutes. Her friend could wait while she dressed. She felt

comfortably randy as she snuggled under the blankets in her tow-
elling robe. Maybe they wouldn't go out at all. Pleasantly obscene
images bobbed and blurred in her mind, disturbed only by some
shrill and distant bird. What sort of bird was that? Doorbell bird,
she thought in her sleep.

The leisure centre would be modelled on the plan of a Moroccan
casbah. She preferred to think of it as a village rather than a
centre. In her mind she named it Ocean Village. The outer section would have flats, small shops, a covered food market, ethnic
restaurants and craft centres. Concealed in the middle would be
the recreation area with pool, exercise rooms, racquet courts.
There would be a Turkish bath for women only, based on one she
had seen in Glasgow which was limpid as a harem, lit only by star-
shaped coloured skylights in the ceiling. Also in the centre would
be a courtyard with a children's play area, outdoor seating and a
juice and coffee bar. People living in low-amenity developments
were sometimes referred to as the underprivileged. She wanted to
design a place where they would feel privileged.

Her initial exhaustion was replaced by a rush of energy. She had
filled her flat with plans for the village and frequently got up in
the middle of the night to eat an apple, listen to music, wrestle
with some problem of access or lighting. She walked on the beach
every day, pacing through the waves in gumboots, wondering
how to curtail her enormously ambitious plan to the amount of
valuable land that might be allowed to the project. It was vital to
the intimacy of the scheme that the buildings should look low and
organic, that there would be lawned areas with rose and palm trees
and cactus, but she knew everyone else would say that the same
facilities could be incorporated into a multi-storey at half the
cost.

She cleared the furniture to one side of her living room and began to make a plan – not a proper architectural model, for her design was far from final, but a hotch-potch composed of suitably shaped food cartons and a pile of little gift boxes which she had purchased. She bought a cat-litter tray and filled it with water, adding a squirt of blue bath oil to represent the swimming pool. How would she stop the courtyard from becoming a noisy football ground? Children needed somewhere to play, but she wanted the village to be an oasis of peace. She would need more ground – a parkland with swings and sandpits. She spread a green scarf on the ground and dotted little pots of parsley and basil around. No, this was ridiculous. She knocked over the pots in frustration. The plan was turning into a pipe dream. Her site was now almost big enough for an airport. She began to crumple up the boxes. The phone rang and she took it off the hook. Oh, Lord, maybe it was Ma. Full of remorse she phoned her mother. Ma sounded tired and indifferent. She responded guardedly to Ruth's offer to come and visit: 'Not at the moment. I'm all right.'

Energy became restlessness. Ruth couldn't sleep. She stayed in a dressing gown so that she could be up or down at any hour of day or night. Begin again. Suppose she divided the plan into two phases. Start with the leisure centre and when that was successfully running, try to get a commitment for the second stage, which would have the food market, restaurants and craft centres. But if she retained the parkland without the casbah development, the village could not be secured at night; there would be a security hazard and the play area might be used for drugs and vandalism. Cut out the parkland? Let the little shits play soccer in her courtyard and kick balls through her Turkish windows? Not on your life!

On her way to the kitchen she stood on the swimming pool, where it mingled with the fallen plant pots to make viscous muck.

She thought about cleaning it up, but what the hell? In a few weeks her whole leisure village would probably look like that anyway. She sat on the floor, dispiritedly munching a stale bread sandwich. The doorbell rang. 'Go away,' she muttered. It rang and rang. She strode across her rubbish heap and picked up the phone to the intercom. 'Kindly fuck off,' she said.

'I will if you'll join me,' said her friend, Max.

She leaned her head on the phone and pressed the buzzer.

'Ruth, Ruth,' he said. He carried flowers and wine. They trailed in a helpless way, as if he had brought them to the wrong address.

'What, what?' She was almost amused.

'Your lovely flat! Your lovely self! You both look like shit.'

'Well, thank you, Max. I haven't looked in a mirror for a while, so it's useful to have your appraisal. As to the rest, you are looking at twenty million quid's worth of millenniumspend.'

'Oh, don't let it go so cheap.' He kissed her gingerly on the cheek and dangled his handsome overcoat from a finger, casting about for a safe place to rest it. 'Put it in for the Turner Prize first.'

'Don't mock!' She took his coat and aimed it at a chair. It missed and he watched it sliding into the mire. She was more careful with the flowers and the wine, which she placed on a table. When his hands were free she moved into his arms. 'What you are looking at is creative angst. It is a vital part of any worthwhile artistic process.'

'Yes, well, there's angst and angst, darling.' He began to kiss her properly. 'You look as if you're undergoing the less productive variety. What the hell is up with you?'

'Oh, nothing.' She broke away and made a futile attempt to brush back her hair with her hands. 'My father died.'

'Let me get you a drink,' he said. 'I'm very sorry, though by all accounts that should have come as something of a relief.'

'I know.' She sat down. 'But it's not tidy. There isn't any sense of resolution.'

He poured her wine, sat beside her, rubbed her hands as if they were cold. 'Not much resolution in life or in death. I thought that was a thing we were agreed on, Ruth. I thought it very grown-up of us.'

She picked up the flowers, which had been thoughtfully chosen, as if for a daintier woman. 'I just felt a need to make some point. I thought if I could produce something absolutely wonderful and life-enhancing there would be some meaning to the whole damn thing.'

He put an arm around her and watched her with compassion. 'I have to tell you, darling, that what you're talking about has nothing to do with architecture. What you are attempting to do is replace life with life. The desire is to recreate your family.'

'Bollocks!' Ruth took an angry gulp of her wine. 'I've been trying to get rid of them all my life. Anyway, I seem to have almost succeeded.'

'Perhaps I should have chosen my words more carefully. What you need is to create your own family. I think you should consider having a baby.'

She considered throwing his own flowers at him, but then remembered Pa aiming a vase of flowers at Connie Herlihy. She smiled as she imagined Max plucking damp anemones from his suit. 'Do you really think so?'

'As an indirect descendant of Freud, that is my considered opinion.'

She sat frowning at her dirty fingernails for a time, and then pointed one of them at him in query.

Max looked appalled and reflexively crossed his legs. 'Don't even think of it. I'm sorry, love, but I got over my father's death a long time ago. The thing about me is, I really like my life.

Everything I've said I actually mean, but I've known for a long time that a lot of what you said was a reaction against your parents.'

'Why bring it up, then?' she said querulously. 'What business is it of yours if you don't want to get involved? I don't even know if it's damn well true. I've never thought about it.'

He took her hands and held them tightly. 'It's only my business because I'm your friend and you know and have always known that I'm only your friend, even though our bodies are very, very good friends. And it is not absolutely true that you haven't thought about it. The truth is, darling, that you have consciously not thought about it.'

'What now?' she mused. She looked utterly wrecked and done in.

'We could move to your bedroom, if it is any less untidy than this.'

She sighed and sloped off to bed, leaving him to follow or not as he chose. As usual, they had a very good time, although he was perturbed when she clung to his neck and burst into tears.

Max stayed a few days. He made her rest and brought her newspapers to read and interesting sandwiches with fresh basil and vine tomatoes or smoked salmon and cream cheese and pickle. While she unravelled, he cleaned the flat. She heard him tipping Ocean Village into the bin and then there was scrubbing and intensive vacuuming. He was so calming and kind that she tried to work up some domestic hankerings but it didn't work. Max was Max. The pleasure of his company came from his self-containment. It was what she admired and enjoyed and it would be absurd to try and change him. She read the papers with interest. It seemed odd to her that there was a whole universe out there with things going on – murders and lotto wins and miracle babies – while she and Ma had been locked into poor Pa's peculiar world. A name caught her eye, which for some reason looked familiar. Mr Roger Hayes. He was an accountant convicted of fraud. He had swindled several pensioners out of their savings. His wife, Elaine, was now being asked for detailed accounts of her own investments. Roger Hayes. She knew no man with that name, yet it rang a bell – quite a rusty one. Roger Hayes. Not Mr but Mrs. She got out of bed and fetched her handbag, emptying a seemingly endless amount of detritus on her bed. Her heart felt hollow and painful when Pa's gold watch fell on to the cover. She went through the papers and there it was – a rather mangled missive, but instantly recognisable as Pa's sprawling hand. Mrs Roger Hayes. Pa said her husband had done him out of money. He had camped outside her house in his car. He had threatened awful things in the letter. But he had been right. Perhaps he had not been quite so crazy after all. The bastard had tried to swindle him and by all accounts the wife was in on it too.

Max looked alarmed when he came in with a delicious little tray and found Ruth covered in litter and with a furious expression on her face.

'Are you all right, darling? Is there anything I can do?'

'Get me a stamp and an envelope,' she said. 'I want you to post a letter.'

She copied out the address, added a stamp and handed it to Max. And nice, amiable Max obligingly went out and posted Pa's old letter, threatening to throw acid in a woman's face.

In the middle of the night Lily was woken by a soft thump. She lay still, hoping for some ordinary explanation. Perhaps she had left a book on the other pillow and it had fallen. There was silence and then a gentle exploratory rustle. She had often wondered how she would react if an intruder came now that she was alone in the world. She frequently met other widows who had been robbed or burgled, and they lived with dread, double locking their houses, never going out after dark, never answering the door. She hated the thought that she might end up like that. She hauled herself up on her pillows. Let him kill her and get it over with. To her astonishment, the trespasser was getting into her bed. He was climbing between the blankets very carefully, as if anxious not to disturb her. Not a young man either – quite an old man, face set in granite folds of loneliness. She peered at him closely, not wanting to turn on the light, and then her heart almost gave out. 'Dick!'

He did not look at her. He was wholly intent on his chore. He slid down in the bed and pulled the blankets up to his chin. Nothing else happened. Her heart began to slow down although alarm still fizzed in her system. 'Dick,' she said after a while, 'where did you go?'

He gave no answer but turned towards her and took her in his arms. He was cold. His grasp was hard as if no flesh remained, only will and bone. She gasped as the chill bit through her nightwear. Foolish to ask where he had gone. He hadn't gone anywhere. He was like a child at boarding school who pretends, through fear, to accept his fate, but then climbs out the window in the night and doggedly heads for home. She sensed that he had not quite forgiven her for letting him be taken. His hand withdrew from her back and with the same silent concentration with which he had got into bed, began to pull up her nightdress.

Ruth was feeling so much improved after her friend's visit that she somehow expected her mother to have been ironed out too. Ma looked wretched, far worse than when she had last seen her.

'Oh, my poor little parent.' She put her arms around her. 'I shouldn't have left you on your own.'

'I haven't been alone.' Ma's breath came in gasps.

'Who's been here?' Ruth put her hands on her mother's shoulders to steady her and Ma clung to her in fright.

'Your father.'

Hell's bells! She'd spent enough time searching for him.

'He came to me last night. He's not at rest. He's trying to get back at me. I'm too scared to sleep at night.'

'Are you absolutely sure you're not sleeping?' Ruth sat her down and put on the kettle. 'Maybe it was a dream. It's natural to have vivid dreams when your mind is upset.'

Ma shook her head. 'I saw him, Ruth. I felt him. He was as real as you are.'

'I know you think that, but it's just not possible. Pa's dead.'

'Yes, of course I know that. That's what's so awful about it.'

'But if you accept that, then you must realise it was only a dream.'

'It wasn't a dream.'

'A ghost? Do you believe in ghosts?'

'It was a supernatural experience.'

'Just one?'

'No, he's been to see me three times.'

And what about Tim Walcott? How often had he been to see her after his promise?

'I wouldn't let him in,' Ma answered, when pressed. 'He wanted to make me cry.'

'Why didn't he call me?' Ruth muttered, but she realised it had been tact that made him leave her alone.

'What will I do, Ruth?' Her mother was desolate. 'I've no one left to tell me what to do.'

'That makes two of us,' Ruth wanted to say. Instead she patted the older woman's arm. She would have to become the parent now. 'Pa loved you. It's natural that he should worry about you. He just wanted to let you know that wherever he is, he still loves you.'

'It wasn't love,' Ma said. 'He wanted sex.' She hung her head. 'I had to grit my teeth.'

Ruth was startled to see that her mother was as shamed as a woman who had been raped. To cover her own inadequacy, she looked over the post. 'What's this?' She had come upon an envelope addressed to Pa and containing a cheque.

'It's a thousand pounds,' Ma said. 'I don't know anything about it. There's nothing else.'

Ruth felt inside the envelope in case Ma had missed something. No, nothing explanatory. She studied the signature on the cheque. It was the usual resentful scrawl with which people part with money. She couldn't make out the surname. It was just a gate with a snake attached. The first name began with 'E'. 'E' and a loop. El . . . Elaine! She knew at once what the surname was. It was Hayes. The money was from Mrs Roger Hayes.

'What is it?' Ma worried.

'It's just a little investment Pa made.' Ruth couldn't help smiling. She felt flushed with triumph. She had avenged her father. 'Here!' She handed Ma the cheque. 'It's yours.'

Ma made no move to take it. 'I can't go spending your father's money.'

'Yes, you can,' Ruth said. 'It's all yours now.'

'Put it in the bank, Ruth. Pa was very careful with his money. He would have hated to see it wasted.'

Really it was hard not to argue with Ma, but Ruth had a sudden brainwave. 'You know what this money was for? It was for that foreign holiday he wanted you to take. When you wouldn't go, he invested the money.'

'I should have gone,' Ma said sadly. 'He was very disappointed. That was the start of all his troubles.'

'No, Ma! The troubles were there anyway. They'd have come out sooner or later. The thing is, if Pa was still around, he would want you to have that holiday – as a present from him.'

'A holiday?' Ma looked more stricken than ever. 'On my own?'

'Of course not. You and me! We'll go right away – as soon as we've got you a passport and a few summer clothes.'

'No, Ruth, no!' Ma seemed unutterably startled. She almost clung to the kitchen table. 'I can't possibly go at a time like this. I don't feel like it. Just give me one good reason why I should.'

Ruth put her arms around her and felt her shivering – a little, scared, run-over creature. 'Because ghosts don't go on holidays.'

38

'So this is abroad.' They were at an outdoor table by a picture-book harbour where bright little boats clinked like ice in cocktails. Ma had adapted with surprising ease. She wore a peaked white hat and a red polo tee shirt, blue slacks and white lace-ups. Although she did her best to dodge the sun, her bleached face had gone the healthy brown of an egg.

Ruth had picked their destination with care. Her mother had never flown before and wasn't interested in beautiful scenery, but she liked nice hotels, bustling villages, churches and cafés. They flew to Nice where she had booked two nights at the Negresco. That ate up most of Pa's cheque but she was betting that Ma wouldn't dare to entertain ghosts anywhere so grand. She was pleased to hear snoring beside her in the next bed at night. As soon as her mother seemed well enough, she rented a car and drove along the coast. Ruth would have liked to go into the hills but Ma wasn't interested in scenery. Mostly, she liked staring at other people.

'Look at that!' She leaned forward, stabbing her finger in a very direct aim and speaking loudly.

'What, Ma?' Ruth lowered her voice to set an example but Ma was too excited to listen.

'The old woman at that table over there. Look at her, she's old, but she's wearing leather shorts and a stetson. Doesn't she look frightful?' she said eagerly.

The woman turned and glared at Ruth in fury. She wasn't actually old, no more than sixty. Ruth hoped she spoke no English. Ma continued to stare. 'She would have been pretty when she was young.'

'What would you like for lunch?' Ruth said hopefully. 'There's fish and chicken or you could just have a salad.'

Ma took the menu from Ruth, but did not look at it. 'I often wondered about the rest of the world. I used to think the biggest difference between single girls and married women was that single ones got to see the world.'

Ruth smiled, noting that in Ma's vocabulary, single females were always girls and married ones always women. 'This is definitely abroad, but I don't think it qualifies as the world. The world is what's on the news, so really, you've seen as much as anyone.'

'It doesn't seem real on the television. Even the terrible things – war and famine – you think they've gone when they're no longer on the screen. This is the real thing. Do you think if I hadn't married Pa I'd have got to see the world?'

Ruth tipped back her chair to let the sun at her nose. 'Probably not. It has more to do with the age we live in than marital status. When you were young only the very rich went abroad. Now everyone goes.'

'Well, I'm lucky to have you,' Ma said. 'I'd never have done this without you.'

'But Pa wanted to take you abroad.' Ruth felt surprised and grateful for her mother's small concession.

'It was an awful place, Ruth. People walking around half naked, no shops, no churches. You understand the kind of things I like.'

'You know, I used to feel excluded when you said that you understood Pa and he understood you.'

Ma was silent for a while. 'Yes, I did say that, didn't I? I thought it was true. The truth is, we accommodated each other. Maybe I just accommodated him. We understood each other's weaknesses. We never understood each other's dreams.'

'Tread softly, for you tread on my dreams.' Ruth remembered Yeats.

Ma's mind was miles away. 'But as you get older your dreams fade. It's your frailties that become absorbing. That's the thing you can share in a marriage. You marry a stranger, Ruth, but when you get old your husband is the only person in the world who understands that old self. No matter who he is. We looked after each other.' She looked at her daughter. Her face was suddenly flattened by loss. 'Then all that changed. Do you know what the worst thing was? I'd already done all the adapting. There weren't any more concessions left to make.'

Ruth wished she could think of the right thing to say. Her mother's mouth was compressed. She couldn't read her expression for her eyes were hidden by sunglasses.

'Ruth.' Ma leaned forward confidentially.

'Yes, Ma.' Ruth spilled over with pity.

'Look at that!' This time her tone was low and conspiratorial, although she was aiming with her finger. Ruth winced inwardly. Ma was insatiably curious about foreigners and their habits. 'What is it?' She refused to look.

'Those people over there. They're having cocktails.'

'Good idea!' Ruth waved to a waiter. 'Let's do the same.'

'But it's only lunchtime.'

'Yes, but this is abroad.'

Ruth began making new sketches for Ocean Village. Watching

people at play, she saw her scheme afresh. She would abolish the playground, but have a crèche adjoining the courtyard and a small section where toddlers could play. The food hall would have to wait. The small exterior units would only house little shops. Now that her mind was at peace it seemed remarkably simple. When she went back home she would have to make a proper presentation. For the moment, she was content.

From time to time she found herself wondering where her father was, if he was bone and dust or angel or a recyclable spirit as in the Buddhist faith. In the mornings after breakfast she and Ma went to Mass. Ma spent about an hour in church. She was praying, she told Ruth, for the repose of Pa's soul. 'We're always told to pray for the repose of a person's soul, but I never thought of what it meant before. You see, Pa can't be the only one. There must be lots of restless souls or it wouldn't crop up.'

Although she had shed her faith long ago, Ruth didn't mind diving out of the sunshine into the cool gloom. Churches in France were not the gaunt prayer stadiums of home. Smelling of wax and incense and old stone, they pandered to a hedonism of the spirit with their exquisite art and architecture, their long, tapering candles and banks of country flowers. One could imagine angels nesting in the eaves. After Mass they went for coffee and then strolled along the promenade looking for an interesting restaurant for lunch. In the afternoons Ruth swam or sketched and Ma rested, then they would have tea and go for a drive, stopping at small villages to browse in shops or a market. If they found a nice-looking place, they stayed there for dinner. Ruth marvelled at Ma's healing powers, her childish curiosity and willingness to be pleased.

'Do you think the prayers are working?'

Ma nodded. 'I think he's gone.' She looked almost regretful.

'You've got your memories,' Ruth said gently.

Ma said nothing until they were seated for lunch at a spectacular hotel with a bottle of champagne before them and then she said; 'About the memories. I've only got bad ones. I don't know where the good ones went.'

39

When Lily got back she thought the house felt lonely. Her home had missed her. She switched on a few lamps to take away the bare look, and then the television. While the kettle was boiling she nipped upstairs to put on the electric blanket for later. Walking back down, her feet conversed with the familiar creaks. 'This house knows me better than anyone,' she thought. 'It won't ever tell or criticise.' She was glad to be home.

Odd, though, to come back to the start of winter. That was the sort of thing young people took for granted, that you could step on a plane one day and it would be summer and the following day you might fly back to snow. She did not think the casual attitude of the younger generation made them sophisticated. She believed the entertainment culture had blinkered them. For centuries now it had been accepted that the world was round, when it was clear to her that it was a layered universe, pages flying open like a book in the wind, prophecies and visions, nightmares and dreams revealed; that babies could be born to geriatrics; that war could be a television programme – you could eat your supper while watching a holocaust; you could sail through the air like a bird to orchestrate a change of seasons.

If Dick had been there they would have talked about the

weather all week. It surprised her how much she missed the small talk of marriage. She had never been much of a one for small talk, but she realised now it was how older people adjusted to the dizzying shifts of the world. You tossed the marvel back and forth until it became familiar and shared and then you could put it on the mantelpiece like some peculiar present that you would never use.

Lily remembered when her mother first read about the washing machine. They had spent the day scrubbing sheets in a metal tub in the kitchen. Her mother said that if they finished the wash by four they could go to the pictures. She mangled and her mother hung, both of them red-faced and raw-fingered. There was a good breeze that would get them dry and they watched this while they ate a meal of bread and cheese. But then came a big wind which toppled the pole and the whole wash fell down in the mud. Neither of them said anything. They took in the washing, fixed up the line again, rewashed all the clothes. When they were finished it was too late for the pictures. Mama put another few kettles of water into the tub and then she eased herself in to relieve her sore back. Lily built up the fire and made her mother cocoa and brought it to her with the paper and Mama read in the bath, calling out interesting items to Lily. Suddenly she had begun to laugh. 'Look at this, Lily! There's a machine for washing clothes. It's been invented in America. You just throw them in and press a button. It gets most of the water out too. You will have one when you are married. You can keep your hands nice and soft and wear a white blouse just one morning and then throw it in this washing machine. How men will hate that! No more wash day!' She laughed, threw down the paper and then she put her hand to her face. Drawing up both her elbows she leaned back in the grey water and she wailed.

Lily had never had a washing machine. Dick thought it wasted hot water. 'We are into a generation that has never known want and all it does is waste,' he said. And the issue of the washing machine was forgotten because she agreed with the principle of his argument, even though she knew he exploited it to suit his purpose. Right to the end, in spite of Dick's oddness, his madness, they had been able to make small talk. The saddest thing was that they could not have talked in this ordinary way about his illness.

'Imagine, Dick — last week you thought I was a girl again, pursued by other men.'

'Yes, I remember that, Lily. Youth isn't all it's cracked up to be. Jealousy is the very devil for men. Literally drives them off their heads. I'm glad we're old.'

There hadn't been anyone else she could talk to in that familiar, clichéd way. And because she had no one to talk to, she had no acceptance of what had happened. No one had been able to explain it to her — not Tim, not Ruth, not the doctor in the hospital. Both she and Dick had had to stand by helpless and frightened while he was sucked into the vortex. He did not die like an ordinary person. In the end the fury overtook him and burnt him out. In the end. The end.

Ruth was right. She must just get on with her life. People who lose a limb do. ('Imagine, Dick, waking up and finding a leg missing — that long stretch of yourself. Would you miss the ingrowing toenail?')

She realised she was frightened of time. Dick's illness had been an occupation in itself. Going in and out to the hospital on buses or walking to Boswell House had used a lot of hours. Ruth was kind, but she did not want to move into her daughter's life. It wouldn't be good for either of them. Lily preferred to let that friendship develop slowly and tactfully. She had been surprised to discover that there wasn't any shortage of money. All she had to do was find a way to use up the days. She would start slowly, giving herself little tasks to do.

Ruth brought the holiday photographs. She took them from their paper folder and fanned them on the table. They both looked well in the pictures and the settings were beautiful. She would start by putting them in an album. Dick's old album still had plenty of free space.

The holiday seemed more real when it was in the pages of a book. Pressed on to the smooth grey cardboard, it belonged in memory. Looking at them now, herself and Ruth in bright colour, she could feel the hot, herb-scented breeze, taste the delicious food and feel the warm female protection of Ruth's company. She saw for the first time that there were similarities between herself and her daughter. They had the same frank gaze, an ironic edge to their smile. Had that developed over the years, through common understanding? She was surprised by how comfortable she had been with Ruth. She had felt more like a woman friend than a daughter. If she stopped trying to turn her into a daughter, she might find a woman friend. That would be a great thing. She realised that an hour had passed, a pleasant and absorbing hour in which self-pity and anxiety played no part. That is what photographs did, they put a freeze on time so you could explore it at leisure.

Like a diver coming on sunken treasure, she plunged, turning back to the early pages. The grainy images were warmed by a different sun, a gentler sun made for picnics and play before the canopy of the ozone had grown ragged and dangerous. Warmed too by unfamiliar, untried desire, the boy and girl were shiny and unfinished, still stuck with feathers from the nest. She traced her own features – unconsciously beautiful, selfish, hopeful. She had never lived. She had seized the first good thing that came her way, Dick Butler's unconditional worship. She had been seeking her-

self in Dick – an acceptable, lovable version of herself. She felt a
rush of forgiveness for her young self. She had only been a child,
and all children wanted to be loved. And Dick? Had he tried to
find himself in her, his better half? She saw him as a boy setting
out on a voyage, seeing only calm seas and paradise islands. Had
the quest of his lifetime led to a ceaseless battering and then ship-
wreck?

Going through the pictures she was surprised by how right they
looked together, the boy and girl, Lily and Dick. They were both
diffident and modest and good. She felt very strongly now that
they had been put together for some purpose. That notion had
not struck her before. It had all seemed random and blurred. It
came to her that the extremes of old age might be thrust upon
people to bring them back to the original point of their meeting.

A tear fell on a page of the album and she wiped it away,
stroking, as she did so, the smooth jaw of the boy who looked so
proud and pleased. She felt tired suddenly, and shut the album
carefully. She went up to bed and slept off several months' exhaustion, disturbed only when Dick appeared, apparently out of the
wardrobe.

'Have you come back?' she asked him. She wasn't frightened
this time.

He shook his head as he sat on the edge of the bed to remove
his shoes. 'I was passing by and I recognised the house.'

She nodded. His voice was so gentle she was afraid to speak in
case he might vanish.

'I don't suppose I could stay a moment?' he said. 'I'd like a last
look.'

How valuable this small exchange seemed to her now. 'What
do you want to see?'

'Earthly love. It's really beautiful, you know. We just can't get
the hang of it.'

'Why can't we?' She wanted to touch him.

'Because we don't know how to love ourselves.'

'Could you put your arms around me, Dick?'

His hands were warm. He was still old but he had the freshness of a boy. Warmth and light enfolded her. 'Don't go yet,' she appealed. The stiff, sour feeling of grief dissolved as she clung to him. She felt light as summer.

In the morning she couldn't be sure if it had happened or if it was a dream. It seemed absolutely real, she could still remember every sensation, yet she woke feeling refreshed as from a really sound sleep. She went at once to phone Ruth. 'Your father came to see me last night.'

Ruth groaned. 'Not again!'

'No, Ruth,' she said excitedly. 'It's all right.'

'I suppose he wanted sex.' World-weary Ruth offended her. She had forgotten everything. 'Yes, well it made him happy,' she said.

'You've spent a lifetime trying to make him happy. Can't you understand that you don't have to do that any more?'

'Well it made me happy too,' Ma defiantly declared.

40

⌒⌒⌒

The crisis was over. Ma was on the road to recovery. Ruth sighed. She ought to be delighted but she had wanted to lead her mother onward, not let her scuttle back to the twilight zone. She wanted to be a part of the circle. She had always assumed that being grown-up meant being free of your family. Now she understood that there was a sequel, that getting older brought a need to redis-cover your source. First Pa had run out on her and then Ma. They had finally done it. They had closed the circle and shut her out.

But not quite.

She had in her hand the brown envelope which Pa's crazy handwriting designated as her legacy. If she opened it, she was giving him the last word. She didn't have to look. But the need to feel his hand on her forehead made her break the seal. Three sheets of foolscap paper fell into her lap. Aptly named. They were hand-written and undated.

Dear Ruth,
Yesterday was the first day of summer. Let's hope it contin-ues. You, no doubt, are enjoying the fine weather but I have not been really warm all year. I have the electric blanket on all night at a low temperature but despite this, in the last few

weeks I have been awakened every night by the cold, absolutely freezing, and the odd thing is, the cold is coming from inside myself. Like the man said, I feel that the cold of the clay is upon me. To tell the truth, if Mr Thomas Cook were to offer me a one-way ticket (free, of course) to the Promised Land, I would gladly accept.

I am sure you will realise I am not writing this letter just for the hell of it, as writing of any kind is an awful chore. The fact of the matter is, I wanted to take you into my confidence. Lily is tip-top as far as everyday expenses are concerned, but when it comes to bank matters, she is all at sea. It might surprise you to learn . . .

The page ended and Ruth eagerly turned it over. The next sheet was the start of a fresh letter, the writing rambling even further, so that a paragraph took up a page.

Ruth, darling,
I am in a sorry state. There have been various indications over the past six to nine months that all has not been well with my beloved Lily. I haven't the strength to write much now. You may have some understanding of the way things are when I tell you that last Tuesday . . .

That was it. End of message. She took a deep breath before picking up the final slip.

Dear Ruth,
I think I am near the end of the road but it's a strange thing, I have no idea where I'm going. I suppose that's in order since none of us has any idea where we come from. All I really know is the places where I went wrong. There is

something I have wanted to tell you for a long time and I have decided that before I meet my maker . . .

The writing trailed off the end of the sheet. Nothing else. She turned over the pages carefully and stared at the blank paper for a long time before putting them back in the envelope and picking up the phone.

Tim Walcott was amused by Ruth's summons. If he said he was busy she would have thought he was being difficult. She had an air of *droit de seigneur* where he was concerned, as if he only came into being as soon as he came into her head. It probably made her attractive to most men. Actually, he quite liked it. She was intelligent and confident and there wasn't any foreplay to her conversation.

'How's Lily?' He spread plum sauce on a pancake, thistled it with shreds of spring onion and dropped on morsels of duck. She had asked him to meet her for dinner this time. Must be a major debate.

'Ma's all right.' Ruth sipped a whiskey and picked at the duck without bothering with any assembly. 'She's fine, I suppose. Actually, I should be pleased. Last time I saw her she talked about Pa with tears in her eyes. I have a feeling she might be going to try and canonise him. Tough work, but Ma was never a shirker where he's concerned.'

'Why aren't you pleased, then?'

'I thought we'd be the best of pals if Pa was out of the way, but it's him she wants.'

He put down his chopsticks, which she thought kind, considering how hungry he always was. He touched her arm lightly and cautiously. 'Give it time.'

'Anyway, I didn't ask you here to talk about her. I need a

favour.' She scowled and tweaked a shred of cucumber with her chopsticks, as if it was a stray hair on her chin. 'Remember a conversation we had some time back. You said I should think of having a child. Well, I'm thinking.'

'And you want my approval. I approve – absolutely. You'd be much more approachable with a bit of sick on your shoulder.'

'No, I want more than that.'

'Sick all down the front of your dress, then. Better still! Very fetching.' He had eaten three pancakes and assembled the fourth with care, like a work of art.

Ruth didn't smile. 'Be serious. This isn't easy. I can't do this alone.'

'Knowing you, I wouldn't be surprised. But I don't see where I come in. You want me to be the godfather?'

'I want you to be the father.'

Tim laughed. She looked in disapproval at the even spread of his teeth, and how his face went pink. She had a startling vision of his pink-faced miniature.

'Ruth, this is a joke, isn't it? Bloody hell, it's not, is it? What are you up to? You want to find the world's least likely father and then forget he ever existed. I don't really think you've thought this out.'

'Yes, I have,' she said. 'I've thought it out very carefully. I definitely don't want to get married but I don't want an anonymous sperm donor and I don't wish to spring this on someone who doesn't want a child. I quite like you in my own peculiar way and I know you'd make a good father, and since we haven't got passion in the way we're much less likely to fall out than most couples.'

He sighed and set down his chopsticks, looking at his perfect pancake with regret. 'What's all this really about, Ruth?'

'You're the shrink.' She paused briefly, took a large gulp of whiskey. 'I've had some letters from my father.'

'So that's what they mean by post mortem!' He laughed and she eyed him stonily.

'Daft scribbles, as you'd expect, but they almost knocked me off my perch.'

'What did they say, these letters?'

She took the envelope out of her bag and handed it across. 'What do you think, Tim? Was he really trying to tell me something or is it just the ravings of a nutty old guy?'

For an instant, after he had read them, he thought of telling on Lily about the old man's long-ago effort to connect with his daughter. Raise the anchors and let her sail away. Of course he didn't. It was none of his business. Maybe that wasn't what Dick was trying to tell her anyway. And maybe the moon was made of Dolcelatte. Maybe there was another way to set her on the right track. He was silent just a moment too long.

'Tim, what are you thinking?'

'I think . . .' he took his spectacles off and polished them on a sleeve '. . . you should let me regress you.'

'What?' Now it was her turn to look gobsmacked. 'You mean roll around the floor and yell while you stand by looking understanding and superior?'

'Sounds like the normal run of things where you and I are concerned.'

'No thanks. I'm not prepared to be your guinea pig and I'm not prepared to make a spectacle of myself.'

'Bloody hell!' Tim thumped the table. She was rather pleased that she had finally managed to irk him. 'What were you asking me to do if not to make a spectacle of myself? Ruth, I'm trying to help.'

She nodded, which was the nearest she could get to apologising. 'I don't know. I'm not sure I could do a thing like that.'

'It's not a big deal, Ruth. It's just a way to access hidden memories.'

'I couldn't do it if there was anyone else around.'

'No one but me. Promise.'

'Isn't that a bit . . . intimate?.'

He gave a sharp bark of mirth. 'You're a pain in the ass, Ruth Butler, but you're very good value.'

'Imagine your life as the pages of a book. The book is open and the pages are flying past. They're going backwards. Back, back to the beginning. You can stop them whenever you like. I'm with you but I want you to forget all about me. Just close your eyes and let your mind slip away.'

'It's still here.' Minutes had passed when she opened one baleful eye to remind him. She didn't really know if she believed in regression but she didn't feel comfortable about it. The truth was, she was bloody terrified. She had come a long way. She hadn't ever meant to go back. Tim went on talking until she began to think the word 'relax' had a slippery, jellylike sound in his flat English accent. This distraction yanked her off guard. Her good hard concentration and her familiar, reassuring surroundings were whipped away from her and she was alone and in the dark. She wrapped her hands around her knees. She sank her head in her lap and moaned. She began to wail, a piercing, desolate lament.

'That's all right. You're all right, pet,' Tim said.

'Don't leave me,' she whimpered.

'I won't. I'm here,' he promised, but his voice didn't find her. She was talking to someone else.

Tim reached for her hand and she took his eagerly, seeking out his index finger. Her fingers curled around it. All the tension gradually left her body. Her other thumb went into her mouth. She smiled. She stayed like this for some time. Then she began to shriek.

'Where were you?' he asked as she emerged, back to the

daylight and her living room. 'What age were you? Can you remember anything?'

She looked at him in surprise. 'I was about two. I was scared because I was in the dark and Ma should have come to me but she didn't. It was Pa who came. I was crying and after a while Pa put out a hand – no, just a finger. I took his finger and held on. I was very interested because his skin was much rougher than Ma's but it smelled nice. You know, that memory almost surfaced recently but I thought it must have been Ma. I couldn't let myself believe it was my father. That's all, really. No, Ma appeared then and I think there was a row. That's when I started to yell. But the thing is, my father and I made contact. I loved him, Tim, and he loved me. I don't know how I know that, but I do.' Tears poured down her face and she rubbed at her cheeks with her hands. 'Of course, it never happened again. Anyway, I probably imagined it.'

'No, Ruth. It's a memory. You can't imagine a memory. Would you like to go back again? You said there was a row. Maybe you should have another look at that. We didn't really retrieve a whole lot there, except that you were a very noisy baby.'

She shook her head slowly. 'No. I think I found what I was looking for.'

'Can you remember anything else?' he pressed her.

She frowned, concentrating. 'Yes, actually. If I'm not mistaken, you called me pet.'

'Certainly not!' he put his hands in his pockets. 'I was talking to a little girl of two.'

'Well, thanks anyway,' she said. 'You'd make a nice father.'

'Are we back on that subject?'

'No. No. Never mind.' She poured two very large glasses of wine and drank hers down thirstily. 'Would you like some supper? I made a pasta thing that can be heated in the microwave.'

She assembled a garlicky salad. She felt fine, as if she had been to a really superior health farm. 'Now it's your turn for some regressing.' She put a great big bowl of pasta on the table. 'Fair's fair. You know all about me. I know nothing about you.'

Tim made a gesture that combined a shrug and a grimace. She realised he never talked about himself. He sighed and looked with yearning at the food. 'If we skip teething and wanking, I got hooked on heads after reading Laing.' He came to a full stop and devoted himself to the meal. He remained silent until he had drained a second glass of wine and only a few leaves and crumbs remained of the meal. 'And yes, since you're looking at me like that, I did think I could escape my own problems by focusing on other people's.'

'So you put on your serious specs and said "Give me your muddled masses".'

'Anything for afters?' He played for time.

Ruth frowned. 'I've got some Amaretti biscuits. You can have them with your coffee.'

He sighed. 'After college I hit the hippy trail. Went to California to find myself.'

'And you found Kahlil Gibran.'

'Oh, aye, and an Australian backpacker called Chris.'

'Did your parents mind?'

'My dad went completely flaming berserk, told me I was a waste of space, a waste of money, a bloody ponce – and that was only when I told him I wanted to study psychiatry. He thought real men earned their living by their hands, by the sweat of their brow. Shrinks were all charlatans, scoundrels who hypnotised women in order to get their knickers off.'

'How does he feel about gays?'

Tim's cry of laughter was without mirth. 'He doesn't believe in them. They're a joke down the pub. Fairies! Bloody pansies! If my father thought he had a son who fancied other men, he'd have had to do away with one of us.'

'So you cleared out. Very diplomatic, if a little cowardly. Well, it sounds like you're as well off.'

Tim finished a fourth glass and reached for the bottle. 'I was crazy about my old man when I was a little lad.' His hair and skin were getting a hectic look. She realised with amusement that he was getting drunk. 'Still miss the old bugger,' he slurred wistfully. 'But he's happy any road, thinking I'm here with some nice Irish colleen.'

'And so you are,' Ruth said. 'At this moment in time.'

He offered her a winning smile. 'And so I am.' His eyes were beginning to close. She must be a dab hand at regressing.

'I'm off to make some strong coffee,' she said. 'Otherwise you're going to end up sleeping here on the sofa.'

By the time she came back he was fast asleep. She sat beside him to drink her coffee. She felt grateful for his dogged friendship. Dogged. The word suited him. He sprawled on her sofa with the deep insouciance and presumption of a dog. She let her hand rest on his hair and felt perfectly at ease. Next to Max he was the lightest male company she had ever known.

When she got up the following morning she was relieved to find that he had already left. Bibulous heart-to-hearts are always a hard act to follow. She had a busy and demanding day. Having completed her plans for Ocean Village she was now trying to persuade two developers to incorporate a row of retirement cottages into a smart new townhouse scheme. She realised that this was more than an ordinary professional interest, but was assuring the Kilmangan brothers that the innovative path for city development was to establish new communities. 'All these townhouses will be occupied by wealthy career couples with one or two children. It's neither safe nor natural for children to grow up with no elderly people around. And the young people feel it too. They know their children are in a social desert.'

'So it's rent-a-granny?' said Kevin, the hefty one.

'If you like, except the grannies come free. And I'd like a small square with flowers and benches where children can play and the old people can sit and watch them – supervise them too.'

'Suppose the retirement cottages become the most sought-after accommodation in the development and the young people try to grab them for themselves,' said Finn, the foxy one.

'It simply makes the whole development more desirable.'

She was winning. When the phone rang she seized it impatiently. 'Yes?'

'I've never done it with a woman,' Tim said.

She was so surprised she felt winded. She turned away from her visitors and took a deep breath to steady herself. 'We'd better arrange a meeting,' she said. She hoped Tim's laugh couldn't be heard in the room. 'If you're busy we could try it on the Internet.'

They met in the Unicorn Minor – small, busy, impersonal and close to town. Bloody hell, she looked daunting, Tim thought when she entered the restaurant. He should never have teased her. She shrugged off her overcoat and sat in silence until he handed her a glass of wine. 'I'm almost a man.' She touched her glass to his. 'Pa used to think so.'

Tim laughed delightedly. Then he grew serious. 'Ruth, I would like a child. Actually, I've been thinking about it ever since you said it. Maybe it's not so daft as it sounds. Apart from your offer, my parental prospects don't look so bright. Do you think we could share a kid? I mean, I wouldn't settle for a birthdays-and-Christmas arrangement. I'd want to borrow it for decent stretches.'

'That's certainly a point in favour,' she said. 'I've always been nervous about the notion of being totally tied down, but I reckoned you'd take it off my hands from time to time.'

'And kindly don't call it "it",' he said.

'It might be nothing,' she said. 'I'm forty-one. I've had some tests and everything's in working order, but it's very likely on a go-slow.'

'Oh, I fancy I've got a way with diffident ovaries,' he grinned. 'What are we supposed to do then? One screw and a novena or keep at it until your hens stop laying?'

He had finished his chicken and began eating her risotto. 'Will you hate it?' she said. 'Will you hate having sex with me?'

'I've had no one to hug for a while now. I need a lot of hugging. I got a good squeeze off you a while back. In my experience, a fuck goes well after a good hug. How about you? Will you worry about sex with a gay man?'

Ruth stopped in mid sip. 'Should I?'

'No, you don't have to worry. I haven't always been good but I've always been careful. Fear of fecklessness, remember?'

'Not any more, it seems.'

'That makes two of us, Ruth. You've just taken a dive into very deep waters. How do you feel about it? I'm not talking about sex.'

She thought about it. 'I feel sort of weak, but that's probably just shock. I feel . . . free. Now, isn't that odd?. I should feel trapped, but I feel as if I've just made an escape. I feel . . . bloody starving. Sod! You've eaten all the food.'

He leaned forward solemnly. 'Ruth. Never say "sod" to a queer. It's not polite.'

'Oh, my God!' she groaned. 'I might have known. He's coming over all masterful.'

'And Ruth!'

'What now?'

'I'll expect you to put on some lipstick and some black lace at the very least. If I'm going to break a lifetime's rule and shag a woman, I want to *know* it's a woman.'

41

ᐁᒍᒌᒋᐧᐤ

'You're wearing lipstick!' They were driving to the cemetery on a cold winter day and Ma had been staring at Ruth in a sidelong way. Her voice was startled and accusatory. It made Ruth smile.

'It's no big deal, Ma. It's only lipstick.' They both went silent then, remembering Pa and the Kiss-Proof lipstick.

Actually she had been surprised by the complications this single cosmetic introduced to her life. Her lips were dry and the colour stuck in the cracks. She had to use salve for a week before it sat right. That was fine but it showed the roughness of her neglected skin. She succumbed to a moisturiser. She was quite pleased by the way the lipstick emphasised the colour of her eyes. It made her look striking. It also showed her wild, hairy eyebrows and she was forced to have them professionally plucked and shaped. She even went so far as to get her hair done – a swept-back style with a bit of colour and a short, choppy fringe. She was quite pleased with the end result. If it wasn't exactly a transformation, it was a truce. She had given up her battle. She was no longer at war with the world.

When all this was done, she had to keep her appointment with Tim. A spot of discreet thermometer work (almost unnecessary, she had always been prompt), and then the usual curt summons.

Tim was affable and unreadable. 'My place or yours?' he said.
Now there was a poser. She had never been to his house but she
could bet it would be haphazard and a bit cute. Crumbs in the
bed, of course. On the other hand, he had agreed to her flat for
the regression. She didn't want to claim all the power. She had
asked him for a favour and he had been nice about it. 'Yours,' she
said.

It was the damndest thing she had ever done in her life. Images
of his irritating habits filled her mind as she hauled on her black
lace underwear (she didn't have to buy that; people would have
been surprised by Ruth's lingerie drawer). Would he keep something to munch beside the bed while he made love to her? Could
it be called making love? At the back of her mind was the aggra-
vating feeling that Tim Walcott had set out to conquer her whole
family with his charm, and he had succeeded, pretty well except
for Pa. Good for Pa. She paused, stocking top in hand, as she suddenly thought of how Pa would have felt about his middle-aged
daughter going to bed with a homosexual in order to get knocked
up. He'd have gone mad. Poor Pa. He'd have had her sympathy. It
was weird.

Tim proved oddly courtly and old-fashioned. She gave him
marks for a tidy house, nice jazz playing, sheets that were obviously brand new. He had got in candles and wine. They drank
some wine and chatted for a bit, then he took her by the hand
and brought her to bed. She was glad he had requested the underwear because it meant she didn't have to take all her clothes off.
She felt too big for nudity.

They regarded each other across the white, white sheets, and
then he stroked her face. For once he did not laugh. He treated
her with the utmost care and tenderness. She would have liked to
make a joke of it all but his slightness and his earnestness made her
think of a child attempting to cook, and she was moved. He was

nice, Tim was. He was really nice. She held him affectionately and became aware that they could end up just hugging each other, possibly weeping buckets for good measure. She was prepared for this. At least there was one thing straight and gay men's sex had in commmon; she moved down his body, giving his skin the benefit of her black silk. 'No!' he said. It was a gasp and a command at once. He took her face in his hands. 'No, Ruth, no,' he said more gently. He pulled her level with him. 'I know this is bloody peculiar, but it's special. I want it to be special. For you. I've had all kinds of sex, but never procreative sex.'

'Me neither,' she said.

'Never sex as miracle. Never put my genes into anybody, and thought I might win a prize. Don't think me too much of a prat, but if there is a child I'd like it conceived in something close to love.'

It wasn't like any sex Ruth had ever known. It wasn't like sex at all. More an alchemy without much hope of an outcome but with awe at the potential. And there was a heart-thumping tenderness. Must be like this with a brother and sister when they find each other's bodies and try to express love. Afterwards they were shy with each other, moved and shaken. They made silly jokes then, camped it up and got drunk. 'Same time next month.' Tim kissed her hand and bowed as she tottered off. She knew he was hoping, as she was, that there would not be too many months. They both had touched some deep chord – mutual need or sympathy – that was only a hair's breadth away from love. They also both felt that they had broken the rules.

The minute Ruth stepped out of the car at the cemetery, she knew she was pregnant. It was snowing. The little crumbs of ice dazzled on the distressed steel sky like an arty minimalist decor. She went round to Ma's side of the car to let her out and then forgot what she was meant to do as she stood gazing at the swirling dots of white, some lifted by the wind so that they seemed to be flying, others meandering down in a languid descent. She put out a finger and trapped a flake, flattening it on her bright mouth so that she could feel the cold. Snow was meant to be cold. It was meant to nip at the skin like an insect bite. She could feel nothing. The weather had become a visual effect. She was wrapped in an invisible field, warmed and distanced. She wasn't herself any more. Her period was only slightly late but she had no doubt at all. She had turned into a placental outer layer to some other life, some unknown future generation.

Ma had to clamber out of the car on her own. Her reproachful struggle brought Ruth back to earth, and she reached into the car for the holly wreath and the pot of Christmas roses they had brought to put on the grave. It was an old graveyard and the greening slabs were like the balding velvet backs of stately dining chairs. Pa's grave still looked new and unfinished – a rookie in a veteran regiment. Ruth placed the wreath on the mound of clay and then inserted the pot of flowers in the centre so that the greenish blossom spread over the shiny holly. It looked like a table decoration in a fashionable magazine. Ruth was rather pleased with it but Ma was disappointed. 'We should have got chrysanthemums – something with a bit of colour.'

They paused to read the inscription. 'Richard Butler, beloved husband and father.'

'Look!' Ma pointed with pleasure. 'There's a space left on the stone for me.'

'Don't be in a rush,' Ruth murmured.

'It's nice, though,' Ma said, 'the notion that we'll be united in death. Marriage vows are only supposed to take you as far as death, but I'm still married to him. I'm not rushing. I'm glad to be alive and I'm grateful to you, Ruth, I really am, but I miss him.'

'That's because you devoted your whole life to him and there doesn't seem to be anything else, but that will change, I promise you.'

'How can you promise me?' Ma stuck her hands in her pockets and faced her daughter.

'Because I know. Tell me, what was the happiest time in your life, absolutely the happiest?'

'When you arrived,' Ma said without hesitation. 'That was real joy.'

'Short-lived.'

Her mother did not contradict her. 'That's the nature of joy.'

'And what now?' Ruth wanted to know how her mother felt about her now, but the weather was wrong for flesh and blood confrontation. They were just two more spectres in the swirl of snow.

'Now I have to pray for your father,' Ma said.

Ruth sat on a nearby headstone and smoked a cigarette. She noted that she was sitting on Eleanor Carter who died in 1942, aged thirty. Probably from childbirth, she thought wryly. Ma stood over Pa's grave in an abject posture, one hand on her breast, her head bent and snow drifting on to her hair. She was there a long time. When she had finished she came to join Ruth, accepting a cigarette.

'Aren't you cold?' Ruth felt guilty. She no longer felt the weather but poor Ma must be frozen.

'No. I like being here with Pa.' Ma shuddered, but she seemed more relaxed, as if she had drawn serenity from her husband's bones. 'You know, Ruth, I finally figured out why your father and I were put together. I'm an old soul on this earth. I know my way around. But your father, I think he was a new soul. The world must be a terrifying place if you've never been here before. It seems only right that you should be given an experienced guide to take you by the hand. We all thought he was being difficult. He wasn't difficult. He was just scared. Do you think that's crazy?'

'I don't know, Ma. But you're definitely an old soul. Anyway, you were never the crazy one.'

'Nor you.' Ma took her hand. 'You were always sensible.'

'I'm not so sure about that. Ma, I've something to tell you.' Ma's face shot around, hooked by the whiff of apocalypse.

'I'm pregnant,' Ruth said.

Ma made no response. She seemed quite calm. She put the cigarette to her mouth and blew out smoke. But her grip tightened on Ruth's hand and she could sense the current of astonishment that ran through her body.

'How long?' she said.

'About five minutes.'

Ma put up no argument to this. 'I knew there was something different about you. Are you planning to get married?'

'Hadn't you heard? Sensible girls don't go all the way.'

'Do you know who the father is?'

'I do, and you know him too. It's Tim Walcott.'

Now Ma positively glowed, not just with satisfaction but with personal triumph. 'I knew he wasn't really gay. It was just a matter of meeting the right girl. I wouldn't mind you marrying him.'

Ruth laughed and Ma laughed too. She didn't quite get the joke, but she was pleased. She rose on tiptoe to give her daughter a kiss. 'It's nice here, isn't it, Ruth? Next time we come we'll bring a flask.'

As they retraced their steps past stone markers made anonymous by night, it came to Ruth that they were walking through a silent city, a dignified community that had laid to rest all the ordinary madnesses: jealousy, love, grief, aggression, ambition.

Generations were here, basking under the snow and the stars; a democratic mulch of rich and poor. It pleased her to think that she had chosen the perfect venue for her tidings. If any news were to matter to the dead, it must be that life goes on.

Ma linked her arm, limping slightly because of her toenail. 'Of course, you realise who this child will be?' It was such a startling question that Ruth turned to gaze at her mother, but it had grown dark and she couldn't see her expression, couldn't tell if she still smiled.

'It'll be your father, coming back.'